THE
BEAST
PLAYER

THE
BEAST
PLAYER

NAHOKO UEHASHI

Translated by CATHY HIRANO

SQUARE
FISH

GODWINBOOKS

HENRY HOLT AND COMPANY

NEW YORK

JEH

SHEEMIYA

HUSBAND

MEEMIYA

WIFE

YOUNGER
BROTHER

DAMIYA

THE DIVINE KINGDOM OF LYOZA

HUSBAND

HALUMIYA   HUSBAND

DAUGHTER   HUSBAND

SEIMIYA

THE YOJEH FAMILY TREE

SQUARE
FISH

An imprint of Macmillan Publishing Group, LLC
120 Broadway, New York, NY 10271
fiercereads.com

Square Fish and the Square Fish logo are trademarks of Macmillan and
are used by Henry Holt and Company under license from Macmillan.

Our books may be purchased in bulk for promotional, educational, or business use. Please
contact your local bookseller or the Macmillan Corporate and Premium Sales Department
at (800) 221-7945 ext. 5442 or by email at MacmillanSpecialMarkets@macmillan.com

Library of Congress Control Number: 2018945008
ISBN 978-1-250-23326-4 (paperback)   ISBN 978-1-250-30747-7 (ebook)

Originally published in the United States by Laura Godwin Books/Henry Holt and Company
First Square Fish edition, 2020
Book designed by Trisha Previte
Square Fish logo designed by Filomena Tuosto

5   7   9   10   8   6

LEXILE: 840L

For my mother

PART ONE

THE TODA

SOHYON'S FINGER FLUTE

I

THE TODA'S LAMENT

Elin woke to the sound of the door opening. It was not yet dawn. In the blackness outside, the rain drummed incessantly on the shingled roof. Elin could vaguely make out the shape of her mother as she washed her hands in the dirt-floored kitchen, then turned and trod softly to the sleeping area. As she slid under the covers, she brought with her the scent of rain and of Toda, the huge water serpents that bore men to battle. Toda Warriors were easily identified by the distinctive musk-like odor of the membrane coating the Toda's scales. It clung to them wherever they went, and to Elin's mother, too; it was a sweet, familiar scent that had surrounded Elin from the moment she was born.

"Mother, was that thunder?"

"It's a long way off. Don't worry. The storm's over the mountains, not here. Now go to sleep."

With a deep sigh, Elin closed her eyes. The image of her mother's white hand slowly, cautiously caressing the Toda hovered in her mind. She loved the stillness of her mother's face as she gazed at the enormous beasts. Her mother was in charge of not just any Toda, but the strongest—the Kiba or "fangs." These formed the vanguard of the Toda forces. Not even the fathers of her best friends, Saju and Chok, were entrusted with the care of the Stone Chambers reserved for the Kiba. Elin's heart filled with pride when she thought of how highly the Toda Stewards regarded her mother's skill as a beast doctor.

She followed her mother to the Chambers whenever she could, even if it meant she had to sew, haul water, or do other chores later. But although she longed to stroke the serpents' hides, her mother had warned her never to try. "The Toda are fearsome creatures," she had said calmly, her eyes following their gliding forms where they churned the surface of the deep, dark pool. "If you got too near, they would sense you instantly and snap you in two, then swallow you in a single bite. You've seen me touch them so often you think it must be easy, but don't let that fool you. The Toda will never be tamed . . . They aren't meant to be tamed. Toda Stewards like me, and even the Riders, wouldn't dare touch them without a Silent Whistle to immobilize them." She opened her palm to reveal a small whistle.

Elin had often seen her raise it to her mouth. She had also seen the Warriors blow such whistles in unison so that they could swiftly saddle and mount the Toda while they lay as stiff as logs. Once perched on a Toda's back and grasping the two long horns protruding from its head, a Warrior could prevent it from thrusting its head underwater and move it as he willed. On land, the Toda resembled dragons and could outrun a horse on their sharp-clawed feet. But in their true element, water, they slithered like snakes, with their legs tucked close to their bodies. Ferocious beasts, with hides impervious to arrows, they could rend a horse and rider asunder with a snap of their jaws, decimating enemy troops.

During the spawning season, the Stewards crept into wild Toda nests and stole one or two eggs from the many that had been laid. As soon as the eggs hatched, a flap-like scale over the hatchlings' ears was partially removed. Elin had watched her mother do this once. "It's to keep them from shutting out the Silent Whistle," she had explained. Once astride their mounts, the

Warriors placed covers fashioned from Toda scales over the ear holes to block out enemy whistles.

Elin's mother's eyes had grown dark and sad as she gazed at the Toda swimming around the pond. Rolling the whistle absently in her palm, she had said, "If you still want to touch them when you become a woman at fifteen, then we'll see." Disturbed by the hollowness of her voice, Elin had pressed her no further. But how, she wondered, was she to wait five whole years until she reached fifteen? How, when all she could think about was what it would feel like to touch those shimmering, iridescent scales?

Her friends, Saju and Chok, told her she was strange to even want to. Girls, it seemed, were afraid to go anywhere near the Toda. Elin could understand to some extent; she, too, found them frightening. When they plunged to the bottom of the deep pool and slithered back up to the surface, cloaked in black water, it made her skin crawl, and yet she could not take her eyes off them. For some reason, they made her forget everything else. She could have spent all day just watching.

Often she wondered if they slept at night, but she had never managed to join her mother on the midnight patrol. Every time she heard her mother preparing to leave, she tried to force herself awake and get out of bed. But her eyes remained glued shut.

Tonight, yet again, Elin sank back into slumber before her mother began breathing peacefully beside her.

An earsplitting noise rent the air, startling Elin awake. It sounded like wind whistling full force through a cracked pipe.

How long had she slept?

Her mother flung aside the covers. It must be dawn already because Elin could see her more clearly now. The keening sound went on and on, setting her teeth on edge. She covered her ears.

"Mother! What is that?"

Without responding, her mother threw on some clothes and slipped her feet into straw sandals rather than her boots, which would take too long to pull on. "Stay here," she said as she raced outside. But Elin could not possibly stay behind with that noise echoing all around her. She had to know what was going on. Flinging a coat on over her pajamas, she hurried after her mother.

The rain had stopped but the ground was sodden and her sandals slipped in the mud, slowing her down. The doors of the neighbors' homes flew open and other Toda Stewards rushed out into the street. Their families followed and soon a crowd was surging toward the eastern bluff, deep inside of which were carved the Toda Chambers. It was from this direction that the shrill wailing came.

A huge fissure ran up the gray rock face, almost as if the cliff had been wrenched open by giant hands. At the bottom where it met the ground, it was wide enough for several adults to walk abreast. The guards posted at this entrance to forestall enemy raids were peering anxiously inside, unsettled by the eerie sound, but they stepped aside with relief when they saw the Toda Stewards approaching with Elin's mother at their head.

Torches burned in the walls every thirty paces, illuminating the tunnel and making the damp rock glisten. The tunnel opened into a large cavern known as the Hall, beyond which branched many smaller tunnels. These led to the Stone Chambers, a series of huge individual caverns built three centuries before by the Stewards' ancestors. Each was equipped with its own pool, or Pond. How they had been dug so deep, no one knew, but there were countless underground Ponds, each separate from the others to prevent the fiercely territorial Toda from killing each other. No more than ten could occupy a single Pond without fighting. Channels known as Toda Ways connected the Ponds but were kept sealed by gates of thick oak, raised only when the Warriors rode the Toda out for training or to battle.

Now the caverns shook with a cacophony that rose from every Pond, bouncing off the walls and reverberating through the Chambers. People clapped their hands against their ears and gritted their teeth as they entered the cliff. Though the walkways that ran alongside the channels were only dimly lit, Elin's mother raced unerringly down the one that led to the Kiba Chambers, without even bothering to cover her ears.

By the time Elin caught up with her, most of the Toda Stewards were already there, standing like frozen statues in one of the Chambers. Pushing her way through, she was greeted by a strange sight. Giant logs glowed dimly on the surface of the Pond. Her mother, chest deep in water, reached out to touch them. Elin gasped as she realized what they were. The Kiba! She started toward her mother but someone grabbed her shoulder. Looking up, she saw that it was her grandfather. He was staring at her mother, his face rigid.

"Are they dead?" he asked.

Her mother nodded.

"All five of them?"

Again her mother nodded.

Elin suddenly realized that the eerie whistling had ceased. The ensuing silence was broken by the sound of running footsteps. Three men burst into the cave.

"The Kiba in the next Chamber are dead, too!" one of them shouted.

A gasp rose from those assembled and Elin felt her grandfather's hand tighten painfully on her shoulder. "What about the others?" he asked.

"The Trunk and Tail units are all fine . . . They've stopped whistling in mourning. They're still agitated and swimming in circles, but they seem all right."

Elin's grandfather looked around at the Stewards. "Go to the Chambers under your charge," he said sternly. "I don't want any Toda injuring themselves against the rock walls of the Ponds. We must not lose any more!"

The Stewards nodded and hurried from the cave. After watching them leave, Elin's grandfather walked toward the pool. "Why did this happen?"

Elin's mother kept her eyes on the rigid Toda, lifting their scales to peer underneath. "I don't know yet," she responded.

"Did they suffocate on these washu?" He gestured at a thick swarm of glowing insects.

"No. Their gills are clean. These glow bugs must have gathered after they died."

"Did you administer tokujisui, the herbal potion reserved for the Kiba? Surely you must have noticed something wrong during your midnight rounds." But Elin's mother just shook her head wordlessly. He glared at her for a moment, then said grimly, "That you could let all the Kiba die . . . It's unforgivable. When the inspector comes, you will be interrogated and punished for this crime."

Elin's mother turned her head slowly and looked up at him. "I know. I am ready."

He clenched his fists. "Really? You're ready, are you? Sohyon. You know that I, too, must be ready. As chief of the Toda Stewards, as your father-in-law, I, too, will be questioned. They will want to know why I let you, an Ahlyo, take care of the Kiba, the priceless gems of the Aluhan." His voice shook with anger, then dropped to a murmur. "Were it not for Asson . . . If you had not been heavy with his child . . ." He shook his head. "No, that's not the only reason. Your skill as a beast doctor is outstanding. That's why I defied everyone's protests and obeyed my son's wishes. But if I had known it would come to this . . ." He almost spat out the last words and, wheeling away from her, left the cave.

Elin's knees were shaking so hard she had to drop to a crouch. "Mother . . ." she whispered. "Mother . . ." She looked up into her face, but Sohyon just stared at her blankly. Gradually, however, a glint of life returned to her eyes, and she smiled faintly.

"It'll be all right," she said.

"But he said it's unforgivable, a crime."

Her mother caressed the flank of a dead Toda. "That's what your grandfather says, but you know, the Kiba have been wiped out like this before, in his father's time. They're bigger and stronger than any other Toda, but they're also more susceptible to disease. Everyone knows that." She stood looking at the Toda, apparently oblivious to everything else, even the frigid water. Her eyes held more than sorrow, as if she was concealing a deep anguish inside.

For a long time, Elin stood with her mother looking at the dead Toda and listening to the indistinct voices of the Stewards reverberating along the rocks from other Chambers. Glowing insects swarmed around the torches that had been thrust into holes drilled in the rock. Many more hovered around the corpses in the water. Watching them, Elin suddenly said, "Mother, do Toda smell differently when they die? Or did their smell change because they were sick?"

Her mother's head jerked up as if she had been lashed with a whip, startling Elin. "Why do you say that?" she asked, her eyes boring into her daughter.

Elin blinked. "It's just . . . their smell seems different than usual. So I thought that might be what drew all these bugs . . ." Her voice dwindled away. Her mother stood rooted to the spot, staring at Elin with a stunned expression.

"Go on," she urged.

Elin blinked again and said, "I know that washu live near water, but I've never seen them in the Toda Pond before. You know how you told me that different types of flowers attract different insects because of their distinctive fragrances? Well, I thought that the washu might have been attracted to the Pond because the Toda's scent had changed."

"You . . ." her mother began and then stopped. There was admiration in her voice but her expression remained unreadable. She shook her head. "Elin," she said quietly. "You must not tell anyone what you think."

"Why?"

Her mother smiled. "Some people are naturally suspicious. If they thought you had made that story up to help me, you might get into trouble."

Elin frowned. She felt like she was missing something. Her mother seemed to have evaded her question, yet she could not figure out why she would do so.

Sohyon waded wearily to the edge of the Pond, placed her hands on the stone floor of the cave, and hauled herself up. Elin ran over and grabbed her robe, pulling on it to help her out. Her skin was as cold as ice. "Thank you," she whispered, stroking Elin's hair tenderly. Then, turning toward the Pond where the dead Toda floated, she knelt on the stone and bowed her forehead to the ground. She remained that way for a long time. Water from her sodden garments spread slowly around her in a dark pool.

9

2

THE AHLYO, PEOPLE OF THE MIST

By the time Elin and her mother left the communal bathhouse, the setting sun was gilding the mountain slopes.

It had been a very long day. After seeing that the Toda corpses were borne to the great stone hall and laid out on straw mats for easy inspection the following day, Elin's mother had spent hours closeted with the other Stewards in the gathering hall. Elin felt sick with worry. When her mother did not return for lunch, Saju's mother, who lived next door, fed her. Sohyon and the others finally exited the hall very late in the afternoon, looking exhausted. Elin was waiting outside the door, and her mother took her by the hand without a word and led her home to get a change of clothes. Then they had headed to the bathhouse.

Because the Stewards spent much of the day immersed in the icy waters of the Ponds, a communal bathhouse was a necessity for Toda villages. Copious amounts of wood were burned to heat the large pool of water, and the bathhouse was located on the western edge of the village to reduce the risk of fire. Elin and her mother always entered the baths last, after the Stewards and the women, and used the leftover hot water. It had been this way ever since Elin could remember, and she had never given it a second thought. Today, however, as the two of them soaked in the empty bathhouse, she began to wonder why her mother always chose to come when no one was there.

Although nobody said so, Elin had always sensed that there was a gap between them and the other villagers. Now things she had noticed from time to time suddenly began to fall into place, taking on new meaning. She thought of her friend Saju and the way Saju's grandparents always treated their granddaughter with affectionate kindness. They even lived together under the same roof, and Saju's cousins often dropped by to visit. Elin, on the other hand, had never lived with her grandparents. Her grandfather, the

Chief Steward, had always intimidated her, and her grandmother never smiled at Elin or her mother, even though she shared rice cakes with them when they visited on New Year's Day or other special occasions. Nor was Elin close to any of her uncles, aunts, or cousins. She often wondered why her grandparents chatted comfortably with the rest of her kin but not with her, yet she had never voiced this question, not even to her mother. Something warned her not to.

Sohyon was different. She was taller than any of the village women. Walking beside her now, Elin wondered when she had first realized that the shape of her face and the color of her eyes were different. It was probably the day Saju had said, "Elin, your eyes are green, like your mother's. Do all Ahlyo have green eyes?" Then, lowering her voice, she had asked, "Can you do magic, too, Elin? Were you bitten by a devil? Everyone says it's wrong to make children with an Ahlyo. They call them Akun Meh Chai, 'devil-bitten child.'" Elin had smiled blankly without answering. Somehow she had known that it was safer to dull her mind and let such comments pass over her. Instinct told her that if she played dumb and didn't ask questions, she and her mother would suffer less grief.

As they stood watching the sunset clouds skirting the mountain ridges, Elin snuck a peek at her mother. Do you belong to the Ahlyo, the People of the Mist, Mother? What was Father like? Am I Akun Meh Chai? She burned to ask these questions, but no words came to her. Turning, her mother looked down at her, perhaps sensing her gaze. "You must be tired," she murmured. Then she smiled. "How about some wild boar for supper tonight?"

"Really?" Elin exclaimed. Wild boar cured in miso was a special treat reserved for celebrations or festivals. "We're really going to have boar for supper?"

"We sure are. A delicious meal is just what we need to chase away fatigue and make us strong for tomorrow."

When they reached home, her mother told her to light the fire and went into the back room. She returned with a small package.

"What's that?" Elin asked.

Ignoring her question, her mother said, "The rice has been washed already. Could you put it on to cook? I'll be back by the time it's ready." Then she went next door to Saju's house. She was gone for such a long time that Elin wondered what on earth they could be talking about. Just as the fragrance of steamed rice began to fill the room, her mother finally returned. She knelt before the stove and checked the fire.

"That smells great, Elin . . . You must be hungry. I'll start cooking the meat." But she showed no sign of moving. After staring at the flames for a long moment, she drew the whistle from her robe and cast it into the fire.

"Mother!" Elin exclaimed.

Sohyon stood up and drew her close. "I'm sorry," she said hoarsely. "What I've done will make life so much harder for you . . . Yet to be honest, I'm glad that I'll never have to use that thing again."

Elin looked at her in surprise. "Why? Don't you like taking care of the Toda?"

Her mother shook her head. "It's not taking care of the Toda that I mind . . . It's that whistle. I've always hated using it." Stroking Elin's hair, she spoke in a low murmur, as if she were talking to herself. "I hate watching the Toda freeze whenever I blow it . . . To see beasts controlled by humans is a miserable thing. In the wild, they would be masters of their own destiny. I can't bear watching them grow steadily weaker when they live among men . . ."

"Is it bad for the Toda to be raised by humans?" Elin asked. "I thought that special potion, the tokujisui, was supposed to make them stronger."

"It makes their fangs harder and their bones larger than Toda in the wild. But at the expense of other parts."

"What parts?"

Sohyon rested her hand on Elin's head and thought for a while. There was regret in her voice when she finally spoke. "I've told you much more than I should have. Forget what I said. None of the other Stewards have noticed, and if you told them, it would only cause trouble. Promise me you won't tell anyone."

Elin frowned. This was not the first time her mother had made her vow to keep silent. "All right. I promise. But in return, tell me the answer. Please. What gets weaker?"

Her mother smiled. "Think about it. What can Toda in the wild do naturally that Toda raised in the Ponds can't? I'm sure you'll find the answer for yourself one day. But when you do, don't tell anyone. Not until you understand why you shouldn't tell them what you know." She ruffled Elin's hair and then gently drew her hand away. "Go on, now," she said. "Get some meat out of that jar."

While Elin took out the meat and scraped off the miso, her mother made a hollow in the ashes inside the oven and spread a large lacos leaf on top. Elin's eyes grew round as she watched. "What're you doing?"

Her mother laughed. "Watch and see." Taking the lump of meat from Elin, she placed it on top of the leaf and spread the sweet, shredded flesh of the lacos fruit on top. Over this she sprinkled a little spicy miso called toi. Quickly tucking the leaf around the meat and fruit, she covered the entire parcel in hot ashes. After that, they waited for what seemed like forever. Just when Elin thought she could bear her hunger no longer, her mother removed the parcel from the ashes and placed it on a large unglazed plate. As she unwrapped the leaf, a cloud of steam rose, giving off a delicious aroma.

The sweetness of the fruit and the spiciness of the toi had permeated the tender steamed boar, filling Elin's mouth with a deliciously complex flavor. She began devouring the meal, oblivious of all else. "It's good, isn't it?" her mother asked. When Elin nodded, she laughed. "Try pouring the juice over the rice." Elin obediently poured the liquid remaining in the leaf over her rice and took a large mouthful. This, too, was delicious. "Lacos trees keep their leaves year-round, even in winter. You can find them easily if you look along mountain slopes exposed to the sun. I used to cook with them just like this when I wandered through the mountains. They're a good substitute for a pot and they also take away the odor of meat and give it a very pleasant aroma."

Elin put down her chopsticks to listen. Her mother's face looked so peaceful. Elin had never heard her talk about the past like this before. Now, she sensed, was the time to ask her questions. Her heart beat a little faster. "You mean, you didn't grow up in the village? Where did you live?"

Her mother searched her face, as if noting the tension in it. "We traveled from one place to another. I never told you about myself, did I? You never asked either . . . Did you think you shouldn't?"

Elin nodded and her mother nodded back. "You're old enough to understand much more now," she said. "Tonight let me tell you about myself and about your father." She rested her plate on her knees. "You heard your grandfather call me an Ahlyo today, right? What do you think of when you hear that word? The villagers call us Ahlyo, 'People of the Mist,' because they see us as tall and mysterious, appearing out of the mist and vanishing back into it. They see us as peddlers of effective remedies who excel at the healing arts. But they also see the Ahlyo as outlandish strangers, followers of unfamiliar gods. Is that how you see them?"

Elin gave a small nod. A smile touched her mother's eyes. "To outsiders, that's probably what we would look like . . . After all, we don't settle in one place or live with other people, and we have protected our own way of life. But Ahlyo is not our real name. The first people who met us heard it wrong, and the sound of it, 'Ah' meaning 'mist' and 'Lyo' meaning 'people,' probably fit the image of what they saw. But our true name is Ao-Loh, 'Ao' meaning 'oath' and 'Loh' meaning 'guardian' or 'protector.'"

"Oath?"

"We swore an oath to protect ourselves from repeating a terrible, terrible mistake made long ago. My mother taught me that the Oath was more important than my own life or the lives of my family. Because we dedicated our lives to obeying the Oath, we called ourselves the Ao-Loh."

"What mistake?"

Her mother remained silent for some time, as if searching for words. "It was disastrous—a gross violation that brought men and beasts to the brink of extinction. My ancestors vowed that they would never allow that to happen again and they became wanderers who lived in the wild and served neither the Yojeh, the True Ruler, nor the Aluhan, the Grand Duke. Since that time, every Ao-Loh, from the moment of birth, is strictly raised to adhere to the Law . . . They are forbidden to marry outside their people and they must never settle down in one place." A sad smile touched her lips. "Elin, I broke the Oath. The moment I met your father and chose to live in this village, I ceased to be an Ao-Loh."

Elin blinked. "But . . . what about your parents? Where are they now?"

"My father died young . . . And I suppose my mother must be living the life of a wanderer still."

Not knowing what to say, Elin could only stare at her. She could not grasp the idea of this Oath or the Law. Why was it wrong for her mother to love her father and live in this village? Why would anyone forbid her to see her family just for that? She frowned as she mulled over these questions in her mind.

"Was my story hard to understand?" her mother asked.

"Mmm."

"I suppose it would be . . . Wait until you grow up then, Elin. When you've become a woman, remember what I just told you and think it over carefully. By then, I'm sure you'll understand it much better." She beckoned Elin to her. Setting down her plate, Elin walked over and sat on her mother's lap. Sohyon wrapped her arms around her, just as she had done when Elin was small. "I met your father on the rocks of Samock. I was looking for chachimo, the purple flower that helps digestion, but instead I found a man lying halfway down the cliff."

"That was Father?"

"Yes . . . He had lost his footing while out hunting deer."

"Was he hurt?"

"He'd hit his head, and his leg was broken."

"So you helped him, didn't you?"

Her mother smiled and gently rocked her. "That's right. That was how I met your father. Asson . . . He was a kind and gentle man, not at all like your grandmother or your grandfather. He didn't talk a lot, but when he laughed, it was like a ray of sunshine bursting through the clouds. It brightened up everything. You're just like him, you know . . . You warm my heart just by being here." She hugged Elin close.

3

SOHYON'S FINGER FLUTE

Elin stood among the women, taut with anxiety as she watched the approaching horsemen. They rode in single file, flanked by grim-faced foot soldiers bearing spears. Most of the villagers, their faces somber, had gathered in front of the meeting hall to greet the Chief Inspector and his troop. Elin's mother was there, too, standing with the Toda Stewards, one pace in front of the crowd.

The inspector, robed in red with an ornate sash and black coronet, did not deign to dismount. He glared down at the assembled Stewards. "Is it true that you let all ten of the Aluhan's precious Kiba die?"

Elin's grandfather stepped forward and bowed deeply. "It is true. We beg your pardon."

The skin around the inspector's temple twitched violently. "Who was in charge of the Kiba?" he shouted. "Step forward!"

Elin started. She saw her mother step toward him and bow respectfully, her palms pressed together before her chest. "I cared for the Kiba."

The inspector's eyes widened. "What? . . . You can't be . . . An Ahlyo?" Eyes flashing, he turned to Elin's grandfather, the Chief Steward, and roared in a dreadful voice, "You! What were you thinking? How could you let an Ahlyo wench care for the priceless gems of the Aluhan!"

The Chief Steward's face was rigid. "Forgive me, your honor, but this woman has outstanding skill as a healer—"

Raising his whip, the inspector lashed out. Blood spurted from the Chief Steward's brow. He pressed a hand against the wound but did not retreat. He continued to bow low before the inspector.

"'Outstanding skill!' Of course she has outstanding skill, you fool! She's an Ahlyo. It's in their blood. But listen carefully! Being skilled in medicine is not enough. The most important qualification for the care of the Toda is unwavering loyalty to the Aluhan! How can you call yourself Chief Steward and be ignorant of that!"

Elin's grandfather raised his head. "I beg your forgiveness. This woman was cast out of the Ahlyo more than ten years ago. She married my son and became one of us. She no longer obeys the Law of the Ahlyo and has sworn fealty to the Aluhan."

The inspector snorted. "So you say, but for the Ahlyo, the Law supersedes all else. They will kill even their own children for breaking it." He glared at Elin's mother. "Tell me. Why did all the Kiba in your care die? If you are so skilled in medicine, then surely you know what caused their deaths. Answer me!"

"Please allow me to explain," Elin's mother said. Her voice was hard. "The cause of death was poisoning."

A hush fell over the assemblage. The inspector frowned. "What? Poison! What do you mean by that? Are you saying that you fed them poison?"

Elin's mother shook her head. "No . . . The tokujisui that we give the Toda has some very powerful ingredients. All the Stewards know this. But the mucous film that covers the Toda's scales has protective properties. If the tokujisui mingles with this as it is being consumed, no adverse effects occur and only the beneficial properties remain. Yesterday morning, however, I noticed thin patches in the mucous film. As I had seen no evidence of this the previous night before when I made my midnight rounds, I administered the tokujisui as usual."

The inspector's eyes narrowed. "You mean this change occurred within the space of just a few hours? Why?"

Elin's mother looked up at him and shook her head. "I don't know."

A heavy silence fell over the square. The inspector turned abruptly to the soldiers behind him. "Seize her!" he barked. "She will be questioned and then punished."

Elin began to shake. Pain stabbed her heart. "Mother!" she cried, but before she could run to her, Saju's mother grabbed her from behind and held her.

17

"You must stay here!" she whispered, clamping a beefy hand over Elin's mouth to smother her wails. She was a large woman and strong. Though she fought wildly, Elin could not escape the arms that held her. She watched through tear-blurred eyes as her mother was bound with ropes and marched away.

Of the next three days, Elin remembered almost nothir.g. Apparently, her mother had asked Saju's parents to care for her and had given them a large sum of money saved from her earnings. They took Elin home and treated her with kindness. Although the logical people to care for her should have been her grandparents, her mother and Saju's parents knew all too well how they would feel about that. Saju and her parents tried to comfort her, but Elin's mind was consumed with grief and fear, and she only registered their voices as sounds far off in the distance.

On the night of the third day after her mother was arrested, Elin woke from her slumber and went to the outhouse at the far end of the garden. As she was returning to the house, Saju's mother's voice rose shrilly inside, and Elin froze in her tracks.

"You mean they sentenced her to the Judgment of the Toda? Tomorrow at dawn?"

"Shh! Not so loud! What if you wake the children?"

Saju's mother dropped her voice, but as she was a naturally boisterous person, Elin could still hear her from the garden. "But how could they? Regardless of the crime, how could they do that to her? It's far too cruel a punishment . . ." Her husband said something so quietly Elin could not hear, but then Saju's mother spoke again. "Ah . . . So that's it. The Aluhan will hold the inspector responsible if he can't explain their deaths. So he's going to blame it all on Sohyon. But to let the wild Toda devour her, that's terrible . . ."

Elin did not stay to hear more. Taking care to tread quietly, she set off at a run. Guided by the light of the moon, she slipped behind Saju's house and through the trees to her own home. Cold hands seemed to grip her throat, strangling the breath from her. She must help her mother. She must, or her mother would be killed at dawn—by the Toda.

The Judgment of the Toda: a punishment reserved for informers and traitors of the Aluhan. Elin had heard the villagers speak of it with dread. Bound hand and foot and weighted with stones, the accused were thrown into Lagoh Marsh, where the wild Toda swarmed. She stood trembling on the cold earthen floor of her house. She must leave quickly, before Saju's parents realized she was gone. If they found her, they would bring her back and keep her inside until the execution was over.

Elin knew where Lagoh Marsh was. It was a long way from the village, but there was still time before dawn. If she traveled as fast as she could, she should make it before the execution started. She grabbed her mother's dagger from where it hung on the wall. Surprised by the weight of it, she almost dropped it. The blade was keen and sharp. If it could cut through tough Toda scales, it should be able to cut the ropes that bound her mother. She would hide along the banks of the marsh until they threw her mother in, then swim out and cut her bonds with this dagger.

Slipping it inside her shirt, she pulled a lantern off the shelf. The hearth had long since grown cold. Even the embers buried in the ashes had ceased to glow. Elin hastily struck a spark from a flint and lit the lantern. Then she exchanged her straw sandals for leather boots and ran outside. The spring moon glowed hazily against the indigo sky, and the trees and grasses slept peacefully, dark shadows in the night.

Pressing her lips firmly together, Elin set off for the marsh.

It was a long night. Though she walked and walked, the mountain road went on endlessly. Occasionally she heard unidentifiable creatures darting through the underbrush, rustling the leaves. "Mother, Mother," she whispered over and over again, forcing herself to go on. She focused all her thoughts on the future. Once I've saved her, we'll leave the village and wander the mountains together, just like Mother used to do when she was young. She pictured the two of them walking through the wilderness, taking shelter in towns along the way. She recalled the taste of roasted boar and her mother's warmth. And as she did so, the dark mountain road grew less frightening.

By the time the trees thinned to reveal a field of reeds stretching out before her, the dark sky had paled to blue and then to a red-tinged gray as night turned to dawn. She had just begun pushing through the reeds when the thunder of drums filled the air. She could feel them reverberating in her stomach. *Boom. Boom.* A startled flock of birds rose from the marsh. The drums rolled on.

The thick reeds were far too tall for her to see the drums, but she was certain that wherever they were, that was where her mother must be. A terrible thought seized her. What if the drumming was the signal for the execution to begin? Maybe they were going to throw her mother into the marsh as soon as it stopped. Her heart began to race and her chest tightened. She tried to run toward the sound but the mud sucked at her feet so that she could barely walk. Stumbling, she grabbed the reeds for balance and the sharp stalks sliced her hand. Still she kept on, doggedly heading toward the drums. She must reach her mother before they stopped!

The sun rose, and the world around her brightened. The reeds ended abruptly, giving way to steel-gray water that spread far into the distance. Elin's mother had once told her that the marsh was a series of swamps and lakes connected by rivers that led as far as the Yojeh's territory to the west. Along the bank Elin saw a temporary camp. Huge drums had been erected on stands, and Warriors beat upon them with large sticks. Others carried a boat down to the shore, watched by a small crowd. Elin could make out the inspector astride his horse. There were more than just Warriors gathered on the shore. All the higher-ranked Stewards were there, too, including her grandfather.

Just then, her mother was dragged from a tent. Elin gasped, and a chill spread through her body. Her mother was drenched in blood, and her hands were bound behind her. Two Warriors gripped her under the arms and half lifted, half dragged her toward the boat. Clenching her teeth, Elin desperately choked back her sobs. But it was rage, not grief, that churned inside her. Thick ropes bound her mother's legs, and to these was tied a heavy stone. When they loaded her into the boat, Elin drew the dagger and discarded the sheath. The boat bearing her mother was pushed into the water.

Can I make it? Elin wondered. It looked very far, but she was sure she could swim that distance. Crouching down among the reeds, she yanked off her boots. She was just about to wade into the water when she realized that she couldn't swim with the dagger in her hand. She thought of stuffing it back inside her top, but what if it fell out? With every moment of indecision, the boat moved farther out into the marsh. There was no choice. Clamping the dagger between her teeth, she slid into the water and felt its frigid grip envelop her. The dagger in her mouth forced her to keep her head up, and she struggled desperately to suck air through her nose and mouth. Her jaw was soon numb from the weight.

Boom! With a thunderous drumroll, her mother was tossed from the boat. The rowers watched her plunge into the water and then turned the boat back toward the shore. Sohyon disappeared for a moment but then her head broke the surface. Elin swam doggedly toward her, defying the weight of the dagger, which threatened to drag her underwater.

"What's that?" one of the Warriors said. "Is it a pup?"

"No. It looks more like a child." This caused a stir among those assembled.

"It's a girl. And she's got something in her mouth."

"A dagger? Is she trying to rescue that criminal?"

One of the Warriors notched an arrow to his bow and looked up at the inspector. "Shall I shoot?"

Still astride his horse, the inspector shielded his eyes with one hand and stared at the small figure struggling to stay afloat. He snorted. "That won't be necessary . . . Look."

Ripples disturbed the water's surface, circling in a wide ring around the condemned prisoner. Large shadows twisted and turned sinuously beneath the water. "The drums have woken the Toda. They've found the live bait we threw in."

Elin's grandfather watched the scene unfold, his lips parted. The girl was his granddaughter, just ten years old, trying to save her mother. What a pitiful sight. No, he chided himself. It's better this way. After all, she's Akun Meh Chai. She'll be better off dying with her mother. The child was unclean, the product of a union with an outsider. She should never have been born; she was a mistake that must be corrected, erased. Like this. It was fate. So he told himself, but when he saw the black forms of the Toda slowly break the surface behind her, his flesh crawled.

Sohyon struggled to keep her face out of the water. Although the marsh was not very deep, her feet did not reach the ground. The stone tied to her legs, however, appeared to be resting on the bottom, and she was no longer weighed down. Blood gushed from a deep wound in her midriff, made purposely to attract the Toda. With it, she felt her life slowly ebbing away. She opened her eyes with great effort, prying open lids swollen from repeated beatings. The sight that greeted her left her stunned. Elin. Elin swimming. Toward her . . . What's that in her mouth? My dagger! A hot lump rose in her throat as she grasped what the child intended to do. Tears blurred her vision.

"Elin!" She kicked frantically with her bound legs, trying to reach her daughter. Elin looked like she would drown any minute. The dagger was too heavy. Sohyon could hear her throat rattle as she struggled to breathe through the saliva pooling in her mouth. Finally she grabbed the dagger with her right hand and swam with her left.

"Elin, here! Grab my shoulder!" It was only when she felt Elin's small hand fasten onto her shoulder that she saw the wave of water behind her. The Toda! Countless Toda, swimming in an ever-tightening circle. As they circled, the beasts eyed each other. Sohyon had seen them do this before when stalking large prey. They were testing each other to see who was the strongest. Once this had been decided, the most powerful Toda would attack first.

"Mo-mother," Elin spluttered. "The . . . rope . . ."

Sohyon twisted her body and shoved her hands toward Elin. Still gasping, Elin took a deep breath, puffed out her cheeks, and dived under the water. The ropes were thick and saturated but Sohyon pulled them taut, making them easier to cut. The dagger was sharp enough that after repeated attempts, Elin was able to make a large rent in the ropes. Feeling them begin to fray, Sohyon gritted her teeth and pulled her hands apart with all her strength, tearing the bonds. Then she grabbed Elin and dragged her up, raising her head from the water. Elin coughed and gasped for air.

Sohyon hugged her in a fierce embrace and pressed her face against her daughter's cheek. "Thank you! Thank you!"

"Mother, the ropes, on your feet . . ."

"It's all right. I can do it myself. Give me the dagger." But as Elin passed her the knife, Sohyon felt a subtle change in the Toda's movements. The test of strength was over. There would be no time to cut the ropes. In moments, the first Toda would begin the attack. She knew that with the deep wound in her belly she had never had any chance of escape. But for Elin, there was a way . . . There was a way, but she had been taught that she must never, ever use it, not even to save the life of her daughter. This Oath had been ingrained within her marrow from the time she was born. If she broke it now, in front of all these people, she could precipitate a disaster for which she could never atone, not even by laying down her life.

Sohyon looked at the little child before her, her face wet with tears and marsh water. The turmoil gripping her heart burst and vanished. Hugging her daughter close, she whispered, "Elin, you must never do what I am going to do now. To do so is to commit a mortal sin."

Elin stared back at her, uncomprehending. Sohyon smiled and held her head with one hand. "I want you to survive. And to find happiness." She threw the dagger aside, put her fingers to her mouth and blew. A high, modulated whistle split the air. The Toda stopped immediately and the churning water grew still. But they were not frozen. Rather, they waited quietly, heads poised as they stared at Sohyon.

The inspector narrowed his eyes. "What's going on? What's that woman up to?" he demanded.

Elin's grandfather shook his head. "I don't know. She appears to be whistling . . ."

"But the Toda have stopped moving. How can a finger whistle have that much power?"

Elin's grandfather paled. "But that's impossible," he said. "Not even the Silent Whistle can immobilize wild Toda."

Sohyon's whistle traversed the scale from high to low, ending with a strange and powerful modulation. The Toda had been listening intently, like hounds to a hunting whistle, but at this they instantly swept en masse toward her. Elin screamed. Enormous Toda heads converged on her in a spray of water. The seaweed-like mane of one touched her cheek, and she was overwhelmed by the fishy smell of their breath and the cloying musk of their membranes.

Suddenly, she felt herself thrust into the air. Her mother was hoisting her up beneath her armpits. "Elin, grab onto the horns. Climb onto the Toda's back!" Elin stretched out her arms and, grasping its horns, dragged herself up onto its back, which was sticky with mucous. "Grip hard with both legs," her mother yelled. "And don't let go of the horns!" Then she put her fingers to her mouth and whistled again. Instantly, the Toda began to swim, moving with incredible speed. Clinging to the horns and pressing her knees tight against its hide, Elin turned to look back.

"Mother!"

"Go!" her mother shouted. "Don't look back! Go!" Then the Toda surged toward her, and she vanished in their midst.

"Mother! Mother!" The spray snatched Elin's cries away. She tried to slide off the Toda's back, but the mucous clung to her clothes like glue and she could not move. The Toda snaked through the marsh water in a cloud of spray. West it traveled, always west, at great speed.

Behind her, everything Elin knew—her mother, her home—vanished, while before her stretched an endless expanse of slate-gray water.

4

THE SPIRIT BEAST

The stars were beginning to twinkle in the evening sky, framed by the silhouettes of slender branches. A young woman walked quickly along the forest path, her arms filled with brushwood for the cooking fire. Garbed in a cloak of greenish gray that hooded her face, she was almost invisible, blending into the forest shadows like a wild creature.

Suddenly, she heard a tinkling sound and halted abruptly. Tiny green lights, like flickering fireflies, gathered in the air above her and took shape.

A Spirit Bird!

The apparition of light drifted down between the trees and came to rest on a dark shoulder. What had until that moment appeared to be nothing more than the shadow of a tree was now faintly revealed as human in form. The luminescent Spirit Bird burst into myriad green lights that flitted like shining leafhoppers about the figure, then reassembled once again, alighting between two branch-like horns on its head, and finally dissolved inside it. As it did so, the figure began to glow firefly-green. Although it resembled a human, its legs were most definitely nonhuman. Opening its golden eyes, the beast stared unblinkingly at the girl.

Shaking, she lowered her bundle of kindling and knelt on the ground. She closed her eyes, calmed her ragged breathing, and listened.

The beast opened its mouth and the air vibrated with high tinkling sounds, like little bells jingling. The vibrations merged into a single resonance, similar to the sound of human speech. Holding her breath, the girl strained to hear. Finally, the humming sound ceased, and countless lights scattered from the beast's head. In the blink of an eye, it had melted back into the darkness. Sweat beaded the girl's brow. Forgetting her bundle of brushwood, she sped through the trees, repeating the words she had just heard, over and over.

Deep in the forest, where not even hunters came, a cave had been carved midway down a cliff overhanging a gorge. The entrance was small and so well hidden by a profusion of vines and shrubs that it was invisible even from close at hand. Inside, however, lay a surprisingly large cavern. Except that it was completely dry, it resembled a Toda Chamber. There were seventeen openings in the walls, each covered with a thick curtain. Behind each of these was another cave as spacious as a house, their floors covered by thick carpets so finely woven that they even repelled water. Lit by candles, the caves formed comfortable living spaces.

The girl, gasping for breath, burst through the entrance and stood in the center of the hall. She placed her fingers to her mouth and blew, making a sound like a bird warbling. As it echoed through the stone caves, seventeen curtains were flung aside, and people of all ages spilled out into the cavern. All were slender and green-eyed.

The chief elder, a white-haired woman, stepped forward, accompanied by a man. "What happened?" she asked in a quiet voice.

"I—I met a Spirit Beast . . . I think . . . It took the form of a horned beast and spoke."

At this, the crowd gasped. "It can't be," someone exclaimed. "Could there really be Spirit Beasts left in this forest? I thought they had all died out . . ."

Silencing the speaker with a glance, the chief elder urged the girl to continue. "What did it tell you?"

Her face pale and tense, the girl clenched her fists as if to keep herself from trembling. "I have no experience. Perhaps I didn't understand properly . . . but I will tell you what I heard. It said, 'The Handler's Art has been used. Someone has whistled to the Toda.'"

The chief elder's face froze. She turned to the man beside her, and he beckoned the other elders to come forward.

"Was that all it said?"

"Yes, that was all."

The chief elder nodded. "You listened well . . . You may leave now." Then she turned to face the crowd. "The elders will consult. When we have finished, we will let you know what we have discussed. Please return to your homes until then." Bowing, the people left the hall.

The elders sat in a circle on the carpet. "It was the Toda Whistle that was used. That means it could only have been Sohyon," the chief elder said. At these words, a woman of about sixty tensed and bowed her forehead to the floor.

"I beg your forgiveness for raising such a daughter. This is all my fault." She remained motionless under their gaze, her head bowed to the ground.

Finally, the chief elder said gently, "She was a clever girl, with a kind heart . . . And a strong will, too. I would never have thought she would use the Art."

Another elder spoke up. "We should send a scout to find out what happened. We must know the circumstances in which the Toda Whistle was used." The others nodded.

"And we must hurry," another said, his expression dark. "If it was used in front of others, if anyone saw that we can control the Toda, the news will surely reach the Aluhan's ears. And if that should happen, he will seek us out and try to force us to share our secret." Once again, everyone nodded.

"We must tell our people, all of them, and warn them to hide," the chief elder said. "Until we find out what happened, we must exercise extreme caution. No one is to visit the villages below."

The young scout sent to investigate Sohyon's village returned four days after the appearance of the Spirit Beast. After hearing his report, the elders sat frowning in silence for some time. Finally, the chief elder spoke. "So, Sohyon has already been executed."

His head bowed, the scout forced the words out between clenched teeth. "Yes . . . It was . . . horrible. The way she died . . . The inspector feared he would be punished for his carelessness. He accused Sohyon of killing the Toda in an act of deliberate treachery and ordered her execution. But . . ." He raised his head. "Ironically, Sohyon was directly involved in their deaths. I managed to view the carcasses, and a change in the mucous membrane was clearly evident. They had reached the breeding season."

The elders frowned. They all knew what that meant. Nodding sadly, one of them said, "Sohyon would surely have noticed that change. She gave them the tokujisui fully aware of what was happening, knowing that, because of the alteration in the membrane, the tokujisui would be lethal."

"So, in her own way, Sohyon kept the Oath," the chief elder whispered. She looked over at Sohyon's mother, who was weeping silently. "Your daughter did not renounce her allegiance to the Clan. She chose to let the Toda die rather than reveal the meaning of the change that had come over them, even though she knew she might be killed."

Sohyon's mother said nothing, swallowing her sobs.

"But she could not bear to see her child torn to pieces by the Toda," the chief elder continued. "At the very end, she gave in to her emotions . . ."

The elders, their expressions grim, remained silent for some time. Finally the chief elder broke the silence. "What happened to Sohyon's daughter?"

The young scout shook his head. "Nahson is following her trail now, but the channels there crisscross in many places. It will be difficult to find which route the Toda she was riding took. And she's only ten years old. She could not have held on to the Toda forever . . ." He closed his eyes and bowed his head, as did the elders. From somewhere far in the distance, they heard the long, lonely cry of a night bird. When the echo had faded into the stillness of night, the youth spoke again. "I grieve for Sohyon and her daughter. But there is some solace in the knowledge that the inspector is a coward."

With their eyes, the elders urged him to continue. In a firm voice, he said, "He must have been terrified of being held responsible, of having any blemish on his record of service. He commanded the Toda Stewards to remain silent about the fact that Sohyon was an Ahlyo. I overheard the villagers discussing this among themselves."

At this, the faces of the elders relaxed considerably. "Really? That's very good news indeed," the chief elder murmured. "Then no rumors will spread about Sohyon using the Handler's Art."

The youth nodded. "Yes, I believe we don't have to worry about that."

"Thank you for your work," the chief elder said. "Keep scouting carefully. Regardless of why she did it, Sohyon used the Toda whistle, and that could still potentially bring disaster. We must never allow the Art to cause another catastrophe. The souls of our ancestors formed the Spirit Beast to warn us so that the rent we made in the Oath should not unravel the threads that hold its fabric together." Then she added in a soft voice, "Even if no word of this reaches the ears of the Aluhan, the sight of us could spark rumors, and we must avoid that at all costs. Let us leave this land for a while and conceal ourselves in the mountains . . . until the flame of rumor has died out."

The elders nodded in assent.

ONE

THE BEEKEEPER

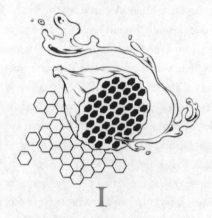

I

WASHED ASHORE

A huge saloh tree stood on the lakeshore, its blossom-laden branches stretching over the water. The soft white petals shimmered like cotton down in the morning light and honeybees flitted back and forth among them. Gazing up, Joeun smiled and rubbed his graying beard. It's going to be a good year. Those bees will make plenty of good-quality honey.

A breeze crossed the lake, rippling the surface and carrying the scent of blossoms. Joeun began walking along the shore to check the other trees but then stopped abruptly, his eyes caught by an odd sight. Little yellow-beaked birds were flocking on the bank, chirping excitedly and pecking at something on the ground. It looked like a mound of mud.

What's that?

He froze as he realized what it must be. A body . . . The unlucky soul must have drowned and been washed ashore. It was small, probably a child. What a lousy way to start the morning. What am I going to do now?

He was too far from any village to get help with a burial. But he could not bear to leave it lying there, especially if it was a child. Making up his mind, he strode toward it. As he drew near, he noticed a peculiar musk-like odor, strong and sweet. He stopped and glanced apprehensively at the lake. Could there be Toda nearby? But the surface was calm, and there was no sign that anything was about to lunge at him from the water. The odor appeared to be coming from the body. Kneeling down, he examined it closely. The limp form, coated from neck to toe in glue-like mud, looked like a clay doll. The pale face, however, was relatively clean. Joeun grimaced at the sight . . . The poor girl. She's such a little thing . . .

Her face was turned toward him, eyes closed, lips slightly parted. Suddenly, a blade of grass near her mouth fluttered. He bent close and felt her breath brush his cheek. "She's alive!" he exclaimed. He slapped her face and shook her by the shoulder. "Hey! Hey! Wake up! Can you hear me? Wake up!" She groaned weakly and opened her eyes a crack, only to shut them again instantly. "This is serious," Joeun muttered. He slipped an arm beneath her and gently lifted her off the ground. Although completely limp, she was very light.

Elin came to her senses at the sensation of warm water enveloping her body. Her hands and feet stung, as if her skin had been scraped or cut. Someone held her head and washed her hair. Wet cloth clung to her limbs. Had she been put in the bath with her clothes on? Something hard jabbed her in the back. It was a very strange bath.

She opened her eyes and saw a stranger's face looming over her. "Ah, you've come to, have you?" he said. She blinked and tried to feel what was digging into her. It seemed to be a board.

The man laughed. "Sorry if it hurts. Just hang on a little longer. I don't have a bathtub big enough for you so I filled my little punt with hot water. I can't tell if you're injured or not with all this mud on you."

Her body felt like lead, and she could not speak. She closed her eyes and fell back into a deep sleep.

The next time she opened her eyes it was evening. She was lying alone in a silent room. She gazed blankly up at the ceiling. It was a very odd ceiling. It looked like a piece of cloth made from woven twigs. The westering sun cast an orange glow on the wall, and dust motes danced slowly in the light. Her body was burning. She closed her eyes and was sucked back down into oblivion.

Terrifying dreams, snatches of nightmares, followed her. Spray wet her face. The Toda's sinuous, undulating body moved beneath her. She burned with pain, and her body felt so heavy. Again and again, she heard her mother's voice, her last words. Again and again, she saw her swallowed by the swarm of Toda. Each time she relived that scene, a sharp pain raced from her gut to her chest, as if she were being slashed in two. She could not even weep. Something gnawed away at her insides, causing her such agony that she could barely breathe.

She felt something cold against her forehead. A large hand weighed on the quilt, and another slowly and gently rubbed her back. "It's all right. It's just a dream. You're dreaming. There's nothing to fear." As she listened to that deep, calm voice, the nightmares slowly loosened their grip.

Joeun watched the girl's face as he wiped away the beads of sweat with a damp cloth. Her cheeks were as red as apples, and she was breathing shallowly. She had been crying out, disturbed by dreams, but now she was quiet. A day and a night had already passed, but she had regained consciousness for only a few moments at a time before slipping away again. He had tried to administer a medicinal brew of laoo to bring down her temperature, which was far too high, but she had not been able to swallow it. Perhaps it was too bitter. The only thing he had succeeded in making her drink was the juice of a citrus fruit named kalimu, thinned with cold water and mixed with honey and some very precious tabu chimu, queen bee milk. Considering how much she was sweating, he had better keep administering the juice.

The child could only be about ten, and she was so slight that he feared she might not survive such a high fever. Tabu chimu, however, was potent enough to transform an ordinary larva into a queen bee. He could only pray that it, along with the honey, would be enough to sustain this child's life. It was the sound of her weeping that he found the hardest to bear. She must have been through something horrific. Her cries were those of a child longing for its mother. They were wrung from her body in wracking sobs that made his throat catch.

What on earth happened to her?

Her clothes were different, resembling those worn by the Wajak, the "mixed blood" people of Aluhan territory far to the east. But it was three days' journey on horseback to the nearest Aluhan border. How could a little girl like this have traveled so far alone? Where were her parents? And why had she been covered in mud and Toda slime? Her arms, her palms, her legs from the knees down—every inch of skin that had not been protected by clothing had been lacerated.

There was another thing that puzzled him: the color of her eyes. She had only opened them briefly, but he had been startled to see that they were green . . . Could she have Ahlyo blood in her veins? What a troublesome find. This might turn out to be more than he could handle. He sighed. "But now that I've taken her in," he murmured to himself, "I hope she makes it through."

His greatest fear was tetanus. Wherever the mud had been ground into the gashes, her skin had begun to fester. If her wounds were just infected, he could treat them. But if she had tetanus, there was nothing he could do. Worrying, however, would get him nowhere. It was better to treat the swollen cuts than not. He rested his chin in his hand and thought.

Should I try it or not? It's an effective cure for inflammations, but it's also a strong toxin. Even some adults react to it so strongly that they stop breathing. Is it safe to use on a child?

The girl opened her eyes. Her lips moved. She must be thirsty. Joeun slipped a hand under her head and raised her gently. With his other hand, he grasped a bowl and brought it to her lips, pouring a little of the juice into her mouth. She drank it with small gulping noises.

"Is it good?" he asked. She seemed to be lucid. Maybe now she would be able to answer. "Have you ever been stung by a bee?" he asked. She looked up at him with fever-blurred eyes, but then shook her head ever so slightly. "So you've never been stung by a bee. You're sure of that?" She nodded and then closed her eyes. Laying her down again, Joeun made up his mind.

He stood up and walked over to a shelf, from which he took a bamboo tube and a beeswax candle. He lit the candle and walked outside into the chill night air. Bundles of dried hasaku, an oil-rich plant, hung under the eaves. He grabbed a bundle and lit it. Thick smoke curled up from the stalks. Going round the house, he walked over to a grove of trees where a row of beehives stood. He went up to one, knocked on the lid, and opened it. Slowly, he waved the smoldering torch near the opening, wafting smoke over the exposed surface. Once he was sure that the bees swarming around the edges of the nest had grown quiet, he picked up first one and then another and slid them into the bamboo tube.

"Sorry to bother you," he murmured and, closing the lid, returned to the house with the tube. Inside, he held each bee up to the light and removed its stinger with a pair of bamboo tweezers. He laid the stingers out on a cloth and returned the bees to the tube. Then he clasped his hands in prayer for a moment. Without their stingers, these bees would die. They were only tiny little insects, yet to Joeun each one was a precious treasure. He was sorry, but he could only ask for their forgiveness.

"And now . . ." he whispered. He pulled back the covers and examined the girl's arms and legs. The worst wounds were on the inside of each knee. He frowned. The saddle on a horse could rub a rider's legs raw in this very spot, but the wounds on her legs looked more like they had been sliced by something sharp. Joeun gingerly stuck the stinger into the swollen skin next to the open sore and pulled it out again immediately. She jerked slightly and frowned, but then closed her eyes again. He repeated this process for her other wounds, taking care not to insert the needle very far, so as to limit the amount of toxin he injected.

"Well, that's done . . . I just hope it works." He wiped the sweat from his brow and, placing a bowl of falan, an antidote for bee poisoning, close at hand, prepared to stay up all night to watch over her. If her fever dropped by morning, she was sure to recover.

Elin woke to the sound of birds warbling. A breeze wafted in from somewhere, bringing with it the scent of morning dew on grass. Her nightmares had vanished without a trace, and she could see the world around her clearly now.

She turned over slowly and saw a large man sitting cross-legged on the floor beside her bed. He was sound asleep, with his arms folded and his head hanging. The weight of his head pulled his body forward, but when it reached a certain point, he jerked himself upright, eyes still closed. Then, once more, he began to tilt.

Elin watched him lazily. He must be very tired. He drooped further and further forward, then suddenly pitched onto the ground, smacking his head loudly on the floor. He groaned and opened his eyes, then stared around him with a startled look as if wondering what had happened. Elin covered her mouth with her hand. She shouldn't laugh, but she couldn't help it.

The man rose and blinked. "So you can laugh, can you?" he said, then burst out laughing himself. He was a complete stranger, as huge as a bear, with a bushy beard, yet, perhaps because of that laugh, Elin did not feel afraid. He stopped and looked at her again. "Seems like your fever's gone. You look refreshed . . . Do you feel all right?"

Elin nodded.

"Good, then. Let me see those cuts on your knees." He pulled back the covers, and she realized that she was wearing a very large shirt tied at the waist. Although the sleeves had been folded over multiple times, her hands were barely visible. She must be wearing the man's pajama top, but for her it served perfectly as a nightgown.

He examined her knees and looked relieved. "The swelling has gone down a lot since yesterday. You'll be better in no time." He pulled up the covers. "You've got strong luck, you know. You went to the brink of the netherworld but came back again."

At his words, memory flooded her mind. The sight of her mother overrun by a swarm of Toda filled her eyes, and a searing lump of pain rose from her stomach into her throat. She burst into tears. Mother . . . How she longed to see her. Mother, Mother, Mother . . . Curling up into a ball, she began to weep as if the sobs were being wrenched from her chest. The man reached out and patted her through the covers. She recognized his touch. It was the same hand that had comforted her while she lay dreaming.

"It's all right. Cry as much as you need to," he said. "Tears are the soup of sorrow. The more tears you shed, the more they will wash away your grief. Eventually you'll be able to forget what caused you so much pain."

His words rippled through her mind. Could that be true? If she cried and cried until she had no more tears left, would her sorrow lessen . . . would she gradually forget her mother? She closed her eyes. She did not want to forget her mother. Definitely not.

But the tears kept flowing and would not stop. Hiccupping, she took a deep breath and clenched her teeth, trying to hold back her sobs. Her breath came out in a groan, and she coughed violently.

The man tapped the quilt sharply. "Hey now, don't try to stop. It's better to cry."

Elin shook her head and buried her face in the pillow, squeezing it tightly as she tried to stem the flood of tears.

"What's wrong?" He rested his hand on her back, his voice full of concern.

In a muffled voice, she forced out the words. "I . . . don't . . . want . . . to cry."

"Why?"

But she did not answer, nor did she raise her face from the pillow. Frowning, he stared at her for a few moments, but then rose with a grunt, as if he had decided that it was better to let her be. She listened to him puttering in the dirt-floored kitchen, and her sobs gradually subsided. Lifting her head, she tried to sit up but was overcome by a wave of dizziness and hastily lay back down. She thought that the dizziness would never pass, but gradually it eased. She still felt shaky, however, like an empty shell. Her head ached, and her fingers trembled. Wiping her tearstained face with her hands, she turned her head on the pillow to look toward the kitchen. The man was squatting in front of a clay oven and holding a pair of tongs over the coals. He seemed to be toasting something. White morning light poured through the open doorway, and a pleasant aroma wafted her way, making her stomach growl. Hunger suddenly gripped her, and her mouth watered.

How long had it been since she had last eaten? . . . She realized with surprise that she had had nothing to eat since supper at Saju's house many days ago. No wonder she was so ravenous.

After working in the kitchen for some time, the man finally brought a steaming bowl to the sleeping room. "Here. Breakfast." He put a hand under her head and slowly raised her up. "Do you think you can sit?" Elin nodded. There was no dizziness now, perhaps because he had moved her so gently. "Good. In that case it's probably better if you feed yourself. Here."

Elin blinked at the contents of the warm, wooden bowl he handed her. Instead of a steaming bowl of rice such as she was used to, she saw what looked like toasted rice cakes covered in milk and thick golden honey. She bit cautiously into one of the toasted cakes, and a deliciously sweet and savory flavor filled her mouth.

"Do you like it?" the man asked. She nodded, her eyes round, and he grinned. "You can't beat my honey! It's the best in the land! My precious little bees worked hard to make it."

As honey was expensive, Elin had never been allowed so much before. It was far richer and more fragrant than any she had ever tasted. She ate greedily and as the food filled her stomach, warmth spread through her. Now that the sharp edge had been taken off her hunger, she was curious. "What's this?" she asked, holding up one of the dried cakes.

At first, the man looked puzzled, but then he said, "That's fahko, unleavened bread made with mixed grains. That's what we always eat. We grind the grain, mix it with water, and bake it. It's good, right? What do you usually eat for breakfast?"

"Rice and soup," Elin said in a small voice.

"Really? You are a Wajak then. The Aluhan's land is far larger than the Yojeh's, where we live. You've got enough land and water to grow plenty of rice."

Elin looked startled. "You mean this isn't Aluhan territory?"

"This is Sanolu County on the eastern edge of the territory ruled by the

Yojeh. It's pretty mountainous, so cereal grains like wheat and barley grow better than rice. That's why we eat fahko." He smiled at her. "You didn't even know where you were, then? Where are your parents?"

Her face clouded. Feeling the tears rising in her throat again, she bit her lip, held her breath, and shook her head. If she opened her mouth to speak, she was afraid only sobs would escape her lips.

"You mean you have no parents, no family at all?" he asked gently. Elin only nodded, keeping her head down. The man frowned. "What happened? How did you wind up lying on the lakeshore covered in mud?"

She did not look up, nor did she answer. For some reason, she was afraid to voice what had happened—her mother's execution, the endless ride on the Toda's back as it plowed through the water, the fact that she had finally fallen off into the lake.

Watching the girl sit in silence with her head bowed, the man sighed. "Never mind then. If you don't want to talk about it, I won't force you. But at least tell me your name. Mine's Joeun. What shall I call you?"

Elin flushed. She hastily returned a piece of fahko to her bowl and knelt formally in front of him. The scrapes on her knees hurt, but she ignored them. How could she have been so rude as to sit gobbling his food without a word of thanks and without even introducing herself? Even though he had saved her life, brought her here, and nursed her. Her face burned with shame. She placed both palms against her chest and lowered her forehead to the floor in the posture of highest deference.

"My name is Elin. Thank you so much for saving me."

Joeun smiled. "Elin, the wild apple that grows in the mountains. What a nice name." As he watched the little girl before him, so prim and proper, questions clamored in his mind. She was obviously not the daughter of some drifter or traveling performer. She must belong to the artisan class, or perhaps an even higher rank. Although the clothes she wore were not the most expensive and were somewhat the worse for wear, they were cut of good cloth. It was true that the Aluhan's territory was richer than that of the Yojeh, but still, only those of middle rank or higher could eat rice for breakfast every day. And her bearing, her manners, her language—they all indicated that she had been strictly brought up. All artisans, whether Wajak ruled by the Aluhan or Holon ruled by the Yojeh, took great pride in their skill, and although their lifestyle was simple, they had a steady income. If she had been raised among such people, then why had she ended up here?

Even more troubling were her eyes. In the morning light, he could see them clearly. Although almond-shaped like a Wajak's, they were green. Artisans hated drifters. Would one really marry an Ahlyo? No. In the first place, the Ahlyo would never allow it. Marital unions outside their people were forbidden. So what on earth was she? The more he thought about it, the more puzzled he became. *I guess I'll just have to wait. It'll become clear in time.*

"Lift your head," he said to the girl. "I'm sorry I interrupted your breakfast with questions. You're just recovering from a fever, so you'd better eat up."

Elin raised her face, bowed once again, and then reached for some fahko. The weakness she had felt earlier seemed to have vanished. Joeun picked up his bowl and began wolfing down his breakfast. It was very quiet. She could hear no sounds of people working outside. There was only the sound of two mouths chewing and the warbling of the birds.

When they had both finished eating, Joeun swiftly cleared away the dishes and spread out a thin blanket on the sleeping platform next to Elin. "I was up most of the night, so I'm going to sleep now. You should rest today, too. If you need to use the outhouse, it's to the right when you go out the door." So saying, he rolled himself up in the blanket. In no time at all, Elin heard the sound of muffled snoring.

Lying on her side, she gazed around the house. From somewhere out back, she could hear the lazy bleating of a goat and the squawking of hens. There was no tolling of a bell to summon the Stewards to a gathering, no sound of Saju's younger sister crying, no dogs barking. The sounds and smells of this morning were not at all like home.

Mother . . . she whispered in her mind. *What should I do now?* But her mother was gone. There was no one to guide her. Even if she went home, her mother would not be there . . .

Fear washed through her at that thought, making it hard to breathe.

Should she ask this man to lend her money and find her way home? Saju's mother was there in the village. Maybe she could live on her own if Saju's mother helped her.

She frowned. She tried to imagine what life would be like, and something sour and bitter rose like bile into her throat. She saw her grandfather's face, the expressions of the Stewards, as they watched her blood-soaked mother being tossed into the swamp. Even though she was one of them, they didn't try to help her. Just the thought of meeting her grandfather made her want to vomit. She could not stand to see his hard, unfriendly face or to listen to his unkind words. Those who had stood by and let her mother die lived in that village . . . not her mother.

Elin threw an arm over her face.

2

THE FLIGHT OF THE QUEEN

"You're looking much better today," Joeun said as he came in from his morning chores. "Yesterday your face looked like a shriveled apple plucked from the pond, but today you've got a rosy glow in your cheeks." He smiled. "Just goes to show, kids get sick quick, but get well even quicker . . . Would you like to try going outside today?"

Elin nodded. She was tired of staying in bed.

"Your clothes are dry. Go ahead and put them on. If you go out in my pajama top, Totchi and Noro will laugh at you."

Elin looked at him in surprise. She had not been aware that anyone else lived in this tiny house. "Totchi and Noro?"

"My horse and goat." He held out her clothes, which had been hanging on the wall. Elin blushed. Those weren't her clothes—they were her pajamas! She had been running about in pajamas ever since she had overheard Saju's parents talking. She was mortified by the thought.

"What's the matter?" Joeun asked. He did not seem to realize they were pajamas. Without looking up, she took them wordlessly. She slipped on the trousers and belted her top over them. The faint scent of Toda made her heart lurch, but she pressed her lips firmly together.

"Here, take this," Joeun said, passing her a hat of woven straw. A thin, net-like cloth was sewn to the brim, and Elin examined it curiously. Joeun picked a pair of gloves off the floor and handed them to her. "Put on the hat and gloves when we go out back. They'll be too big for you, but better too big than too small."

"What is this?"

"It's a shield to protect you from my little treasures. I won't spoil the surprise by telling you anything more." He winked and went briskly out the door. Elin followed obediently, hat and gloves in hand. Once outside, she gasped. Mountains so tall they seemed to pierce the sky towered in the distance. Just looking at them made her dizzy. They looked too enormous to be real, a stark contrast to the gentle green hills rolling before her. Against the blue sky, their white-crowned peaks stood out sharply, caressed by wisps of cloud that looked like snow spray.

"Is this your first time to see the Afon Noah, the Mountains of the Gods?" Elin nodded. "That's the wall that separates the world of the gods from the world of men. It's said that the ancestors of the Yojeh once lived on the other side."

Elin stared wordlessly. So that's the Afon Noah. She could hardly believe it. Here, right before her eyes, was the range built to shut humans away from the world of the fearsome gods that peopled the myths called the Afon Kahlo, tales which her mother had told her so often. So it really existed.

"Your eyes are going to pop out of your head if you keep staring like that." Joeun laughed. He rested his hand on her shoulder. "They've been there since the beginning of the world. They're not going to disappear just because you take your eyes off them for a moment. You'll have plenty of chances to look at them all you want. But first, come and see my treasures."

She followed him behind the house and through a copse until they emerged into a large, sunlit clearing. Beneath the broadleaf trees stood several boxes resting on brick platforms. Their tops were covered with straw. Bees buzzed around the boxes in the rear, but Elin could not see any around one box that stood in the sunlight. Joeun frowned and stopped. He laid a restraining hand on her arm and said, "Wait here."

The words had no sooner left his mouth than a black, smoke-like cloud rose from the strangely silent box. But it was not smoke. It was bees: tens of thousands of them—an astounding sight. They rose into the air, circling slowly, their wings thrumming.

"Oh no. This is bad . . ." Joeun muttered. "They're swarming! Did I miss a queen cup?"

The cluster circled toward them with a deafening drone. Terrified, Elin was about to fling her arms over her head and crouch down on the ground when Joeun grabbed her elbow. "Don't make any sudden movement. Put your hat on very slowly."

Teeth chattering and hands shaking, Elin raised her hat to her head. Her stomach cramped, and she broke into a cold sweat, certain that the bees would attack her at any moment.

"Don't worry," Joeun whispered. "As long as you stay still, they won't hurt you." Humming loudly, the thick blob hovered over their heads where they stood motionless and then moved on, the air vibrating with the sound of millions of tiny beating wings. Elin's skin crawled. Finally, the lead bees came to rest on a thick tree branch, and the others followed suit. Soon a huge, squirming lump of black and yellow enveloped the branch.

Joeun let out his breath slowly. "It's all right now. You can move, but slowly, okay?" Elin, too, had been holding her breath, and now she let it go. "Once they've landed on a branch like that they'll stay there for at least half a day. As long as there's no aggressive movement nearby."

While she listened to Joeun explain, Elin stared in fascination at the squirming lump. Now that she was no longer afraid of being stung, the huge swarm's strange behavior excited her curiosity.

"Why did they stop on that branch?" she whispered. "Does it have nectar?"

Joeun responded with a smile in his voice, "No. They didn't gather there to collect nectar. They've discarded their old hive and are traveling with the queen to find a new home."

Elin looked up at him in surprise. "There's a queen in there?"

"You saw the big bee that flew at the back of the swarm, didn't you? That's the queen bee. When the hive becomes overcrowded, she leaves a young queen bee larva in the original hive and takes about half the worker bees with her to find a place to build a new hive."

There was something not just frightening but incredibly powerful about the swarm's perfectly ordered flight. "So will they go on a long journey?" Elin asked.

Joeun laughed quietly. "I certainly hope not, because if they do, I'm going to starve. I clipped the wings of the queen bee to prevent them from getting away. It's not really fair I suppose, but it will keep her from flying very far. Come give me a hand, will you? I have to get a new beehive ready."

Elin followed him back to the west side of the house and noticed a stable and a goat pen. The animals watched with interest as they approached. That must be Totchi and Noro, she thought, although she wasn't sure which was which. Joeun continued around the house to a shed on the north. The uneven coats of thick white plaster on the walls announced the workman to be an amateur. The building was full of tools and equipment, and the shelves on the north wall were lined with clay jars. It was dimly lit by a single window with a raised shutter, and the air inside was cool.

Joeun picked up an empty box and frowned. "Oh, that's right. This is the only usable hive left right now." He gestured with his chin to the back of the shed. "I'm going to carry this box outside. Could you bring that black jar for me?" Elin turned in the direction he indicated and saw that there was, indeed, a small black jar on the shelf. Instead of a lid, it appeared to have handles.

"Is that . . . a sprayer?"

Joeun looked at her in surprise. "Yes, but how did you figure that out?"

Her mother had used one much like this to spray ointment onto the Toda when their hides had been scratched. In her mind, Elin saw her mother's white hand gripping the sprayer. She followed Joeun outside without answering, carrying the sprayer in both hands. They walked as far as the meadow. There, Joeun rested the hive on the ground and took off the lid. He pulled out many boards, each covered in the same strange pattern. Noticing that Elin was staring at them, Joeun explained, "These are comb frames, where the bees live. Give me that sprayer, please."

She handed him the contraption and he began spraying something onto the frames and into the box. A sweet, slightly fermented fragrance wafted toward her. She had expected it to smell like medicine, and she looked at Joeun in surprise. "It smells good!"

He smiled. "It does, doesn't it? I just hope the bees think so, too."

"Oh! I see! You're scenting this hive so that the bees will want to live in it. Because bees are attracted by the smell of flowers."

He looked at her curiously. "How old are you?"

"What? . . . Oh. Ten."

"You certainly don't talk like a ten-year-old."

She blinked at him. Then she blushed, recalling that Saju had once told her, "You talk like a grown-up."

Seeing her flush, Joeun said, "I wasn't criticizing you for being cheeky or anything, so you don't need to feel bad. To tell the truth, I'm quite impressed." He smiled again and shook the sprayer. "But unfortunately, you guessed wrong. This isn't what will encourage them to live here. It's the sugar water that I'll spray in here after that will draw them in. I applied this particular concoction for a different reason. Can you guess what it is?" Then he laughed. "I'm betting you can't."

Elin stood beside him, holding each frame as he sprayed it, but all the while she was wondering why he needed to spray everything with such a strong scent. Did he want to make them drunk? As she pondered this question, a certain scene leapt into her mind. When an old Toda had died and a young Toda was being moved into the same Pond, her mother and the Stewards had smeared the gluey membrane of the dead Toda onto the young one.

"Uncle Joeun . . ." she murmured.

"Yes?"

"Did another swarm of bees live in this box before?"

Joeun's hands stilled, and he looked at her. "Why do you ask?"

She said uncertainly, "I thought that perhaps you were trying to erase the scent of other bees with this spray . . ."

He groaned. "I don't believe it! You guessed it. That's exactly what it's for, to erase another smell."

Elin's face lit up in a smile. Raising his eyebrows, Joeun grinned back. "Ah. You smiled," he said as he began spraying the frames again. "You look very happy when you smile, you know.

"You're right. Each hive of bees has its own distinctive scent. That's how they can distinguish members from their own hive. But I'm not erasing the smell of bees. I'm erasing the smell of their bitter enemy. A very stinky toad called a gosu got into this box. By the time I noticed, the bees had already fled. I washed and dried the inside, but bees are very sensitive to smell." He brought the tip of the sprayer close to her nose so that she could smell it. "This liquid was distilled from nafalan flowers, which honeybees love. Interestingly, it even calms bees down when they're excited. So I thought I'd try and see if it'll cover up the smell of the gosu . . . But still, I'm impressed that you guessed what it's for. Were your family beekeepers?"

Elin shook her head and looked down at the ground. Silently, Joeun chided himself. Idiot. There you go again . . . Just when the sun starts to shine, you go and cast a cloud over it. For this child, any talk of her family was like touching a tender wound. He knew this, but his curiosity kept getting the better of him, making him say one thing too many. That's a bad habit. I'm too impatient. She was extremely sharp. If he tried to pry, she would notice immediately. The best way to put her at ease was to let it be and forget trying to find out more.

"Right then. It's time to put the frames back in. Give me a hand, will you?"

Elin nodded.

3

ROYAL JELLY

How on earth is he going to get that swarm into this box? Elin wondered. While she watched with keen interest, Joeun put on the gloves and netted hat that she handed him and carried the box to the tree, placing it under the branch that was now black and swollen with the escaped bees. He had sprayed the inside of the box with sugar water and put some honey in it as well. He went back to the shed once more and this time returned with a large bag, a hatchet, and a step.

"If you want to watch, that's fine, but don't come any nearer than this," he said. Then he walked over to the branch and placed the step beneath it. Stepping onto it, he raised the large bag slowly up toward the squirming mass of bees.

He's going to put them in that bag! She cringed. Surely that would anger the bees. They might attack him.

Slowly the bag enveloped the black lump. The branch was fairly high, so even when standing on tiptoe, Joeun could not capture the entire mass. This did not seem to concern him, however, for when most of the bees were in the bag, he quickly pulled the mouth closed and raised his hatchet. Bringing it down where the bark was clear of bees, he chopped the branch off and let it slide into the bag. The remaining bees buzzed about excitedly, but Joeun paid no attention. Throwing the hatchet to the ground, he climbed off the step with the bag in his hand and pressed the mouth of it against a small slit near the bottom of the bee box.

From where she was standing, Elin could not see clearly, but it looked like the bees were crawling out of the bag and into the box. Even so, many still buzzed in the air. She shrank back, keeping her eyes on Joeun. For a long time, he stood watching the entrance to the box. Finally, he put the bag down on the ground and walked slowly over to her. "We're done. Let's have some lunch."

"What?" she exclaimed in surprise. Could it really be all right to leave the beehive entrance open? "But won't they escape?"

Joeun laughed. "No need to worry. Come back after lunch and you'll see. They may be flying about outside right now, but by then they'll be snug inside the hive."

Elin looked at the box. Bees were crawling in and out of the hive, and many more were flying about in agitation. They had flown off in search of a new home. Wouldn't they rather run away than be shut up in a box once again so close by? They might be enjoying the sugar water right now, but once it was gone, wouldn't they leave?

Joeun put a hand on her shoulder. "If it bothers you that much, why don't you stay and watch? I'll go back to the house and call you when lunch is ready. But you'd better come when I call . . . And don't go near that box."

Elin nodded. Once he had left, everything seemed suddenly very quiet. There were only the sounds of the breeze rustling the branches and the bees humming. She watched them move. Then suddenly her eyes opened wide. The bees that had been flitting back and forth around the box began to drop toward it, one after the other, as if drawn by a magnet. When they reached the entrance, they folded their wings and streamed inside, as if to say, "We're home." Before she knew it, not a bee was left. She stared at the box, spellbound. This, she thought, was true magic. What on earth could they be doing in there? They had set off on a journey to a new land. Were they now consoling each other, saying, "I guess this place will have to do"? And how did that huge black swarm fit in there? She longed to peek inside . . .

Joeun had told her not to go near the hive. But as long as she didn't touch it, if she just peeked inside that opening without startling the bees, perhaps she could see something. She glanced behind her and then moved stealthily toward the box. It was very quiet. She crouched down and peered inside the long, narrow slit that served as an entrance. It was so dark that she could not see anything. Or maybe she could. Something was moving. Was it bees? She could hear a whirring of wings. What were they doing?

She tilted her head and strained her eyes, trying to see inside, when suddenly someone grabbed her shoulder. Startled, she was about to scream when a large hand covered her mouth, and she found herself tucked under an arm and carried away. Joeun did not set her down until he reached the house. "I told you not to go near that box!"

Elin bowed her head. "I'm sorry."

"Honeybees rarely sting people, but if they're excited or think you're an invader, they will defend their hive with their lives."

"I'm sorry."

She looked so contrite that Joeun relaxed. "Honestly," he said. "You scared the wits out of me!" Then he asked her gently, "Did it seem so strange that they should all go quietly into the box?"

Elin responded in a small voice, "Yes . . . They left a box just like it because they didn't like being trapped inside. So why did they go into another one as if they were going home?"

Joeun smiled. "That's because it is home. For worker bees, wherever the queen bee decides to live is home."

"Oh!" Elin looked up. "Did you say that we were done because you saw the queen bee go inside?"

"That's right. If the queen bee is content with the box, the other bees will follow. A bee's loyalty is even stronger than ours. They never rebel against their leader. Sometimes it's almost spooky to watch . . . It's as if they're being pulled into the hive by a string, every single one of them."

Elin remembered how they had all flown out together in a single swarm—and how they had all crawled back into the queen bee's box, as if under a spell. "I wonder if the queen bee uses some kind of magic," she said.

Joeun laughed. "She just might. After all, many mothers seem to have supernatural powers."

"Mothers? Is the queen bee a mother?"

"Yup. She's the mother of every single bee in that hive."

"Really?" Elin's eyes widened. "All of them? You mean that queen bee gave birth to all the bees in that box?"

"Hard to believe, isn't it? But it's true. There are tens of thousands of worker bees in there, but every one of them is her daughter. The worker bees

47

are all female, but they don't lay eggs. They just work the whole time, collecting nectar. Only the queen lays eggs and she does so by the tens of thousands."

Elin stared at him with her mouth open. She felt goosebumps rising on her skin. How incredible! A single queen bee could lay thousands of eggs. The daughters born from those eggs became worker bees and spent their whole lives working. How different the relationship between a mother bee and her children compared to Elin's relationship with her mother. As she imagined the queen bee laying eggs and her daughters emerging from them, she was suddenly puzzled.

"That's strange."

Joeun raised his eyebrows. "What is?"

She looked at him. "If the worker bees are her children, they should be like her, so why aren't they queen bees, too?"

"Hmm." He looked at her for a moment and then gently pushed her shoulder. "Let me show you something." He led her to the same shed where he had stored the box and sprayer. Inside, he lifted up a slatted wooden platform and leaned it against the wall. Beneath it was a trapdoor set into the floor, which he raised, revealing a hole. Lying on his belly, he reached in and pulled out a small black jar. After removing the tightly fitting lid, he beckoned to her.

"Come and look." Peering inside, Elin saw what looked like a thick, slightly yellowish paste. Joeun took a small spoon and scooped out a little. "Taste it."

Elin licked the spoon. At first, she thought it was sweet, but the sourness that followed stung her tongue and throat. "Yuck!" She stuck out her tongue and screwed up her face. An overpowering odor clung to her mouth and nose.

Joeun began to laugh. "Sorry. Was it that strong? Here. Chase it down with this." He took a jar of honey off the shelf and let her lick some off the spoon. It took away the sourness, but the smell, which slightly resembled goat's milk, lingered in her mouth. "This is tabu chimu, or royal jelly. Bee larvae fed on this turn into queen bees." He closed the lid tightly. "When they think it's time for a new queen bee, the worker bees prepare special receptacles called queen cups. These are the cradles in which queen bee larvae are raised. The queen bee lays eggs in the cups and when they hatch, young worker bees come to give them royal jelly, which they secrete from their own bodies. That's how new queen bees are raised."

He replaced the black jar of royal jelly in the hole and lowered the trap-door. Then he grinned. "Let me tell you a secret. I can make queen bees."

Elin frowned, wondering what on earth he could mean. His grin deepened.

"This is how it's done. I take some beeswax and press it into a mold that resembles a queen cup. Then I put a frame between the part of the hive where the honey is stored and the part where the queen bee is, so that the queen can't get into the upper part of the hive. The worker bees get quite upset by her absence. When I see that they are so anxious for a new queen bee that they can't stand it anymore . . ." He stood up, went over to the shelf and came back with a slender wooden implement with a tiny scoop on the end. "I use this to extract a worker bee larva and transfer it to the queen cup that I made. As soon as I do that, the workers become very busy. When the egg hatches, they start feeding it royal jelly. A bee larva raised on royal jelly will grow into a splendid queen bee."

Elin frowned. "Really? You mean that the egg of a worker bee is identical to the egg of a queen bee?"

"That's right. The only thing that makes a difference is whether or not the bee is raised on royal jelly. Tabu chimu has a strange, magical power to transform an ordinary worker bee into a queen."

The odor that lingered on her tongue suddenly seemed very strong. Frightened, Elin stuck out her tongue and felt it. "Will my tongue be all right?" she asked. "Nothing strange will happen to it, will it?"

Joeun burst out laughing. "No, no. Relax. Your tongue isn't going to turn into a queen bee. In fact, this is what saved your life. When you were in bed with that high fever, I gave you royal jelly mixed with honey and juice to drink." He waved the little spoon with which he had given her a taste. "You should be grateful. Tabu chimu is a powerful elixir that promotes longevity, and it's really expensive. How much do you think that little spoonful you licked costs?"

Elin drew in her breath and stared at him. He whispered dramatically, "A whole gold piece."

"Really?" She stared at him in astonishment. "A—a gold piece?" That amount of money would buy three chunks of top-grade bee. the size of an adult fist. The amount of royal jelly she ate had only been as large as the tip of her baby finger. How expensive! That meant that Joeun had spent a fortune to make her better. She paled and felt her stomach grow cold. She could not possibly repay him.

"Joeun . . ."

"What is it? Don't you feel well?"

She shook her head. Her face tense, she said almost in a whisper, "Joeun . . . I don't . . . have any money."

He looked at her in surprise. Then his face grew serious and he reached out his arms and grasped her by both shoulders. "I'm so sorry. That was stupid of me. I blabbered away without thinking." He looked her straight in the eyes and spoke slowly and deliberately. "I have no intention of taking any money from you. I would never do something so cruel. I may not be rich, but I'm not poor either. I don't have any family of my own to support. The amount of food you eat or the medicine you need is nothing. Don't worry."

But his words could not reassure her. Elin's mother had given Saju's parents several big silver pieces in return for taking care of her. She knew that it wasn't right to take advantage of someone who wasn't family. But she had no home to return to. If he did not let her stay, she would have nothing to eat and nowhere to sleep.

She cast down her eyes, feeling alone and helpless, and her mouth twisted as she forced back the tears that rose in her eyes. Placing both hands before her on the floor, she bowed. "I . . . have no home . . . to go back to. I have no money either." Her voice sounded very distant to her ears. "But I can cook. And I can sew. I can take care of the goat and the horse. I will work hard . . . So please let me stay here."

For a moment, Joeun was at a loss for words and could only stare at the little girl, who trembled as she pressed her hands against the floor. He was amazed that someone so young would think about the need to pay him to take care of her. He had never met a child like her before. There had been plenty of ten-year-olds where he used to live, but they were innocent and carefree, ignorant of the suffering in the world and obliviously dependent on the adults around them. Were all children of the artisan class like Elin? If so, they were far more mature than the youth of the nobility or of upper-class professionals. Yet, despite her maturity, she did not seem to intuit what an adult like Joeun really felt. He had already made up his mind to take her in, yet she couldn't see that.

Almost six years had passed since a painful incident had driven him from his family and forced him to live alone as a beekeeper. There had been times when he had found this existence lonely. He had never raised a girl before, but Elin seemed more capable for her age than any of the boys he'd taught, and she was very smart. He was pretty sure he could take care of her—that is, of course, if she really was all alone in the world.

Something very unusual had happened to her. He was sure of that. If he adopted her, it could lead to trouble. Rather than getting carried away by his feelings, he should probably think this over more carefully. But he was already fond of Elin, even though they had only spent three days together. He did not want to let her go. If her parents did show up and take her away, he knew that he would miss her. Yet she seemed unaware of how he felt. She kept a firm distance, seeing him as a stranger and the care he gave her as a debt that must be repaid. Just patting her on the head reassuringly would not ease her mind.

"Elin," he began, and she raised her face. "Do you know how much people pay to stay somewhere overnight when they're traveling?" Elin shook her head, her face tense. "The price is usually a single small piece of silver . . . Do you know how much a child hired as a servant to work in the hall of a noble or a merchant is paid?"

Again Elin shook her head. "The going rate is about fifty copper pieces, or half a small piece of silver. So if you stay and do the housework for me, you can think of your pay as fifty copper pieces. Now, the cost for lodgings, that's for adults. For children, it's half the price. So if you do the housework, we'd be even, because the amount you would get paid is the same as the amount you would spend to stay overnight. What do you say? Is it a deal?"

Elin's face brightened instantly, and she smiled at him.

"All right, then. That settles it. Once you're completely better, I'll expect you to work hard, okay?"

Elin nodded emphatically.

TWO

THE SOARING BEAST

I

OF BEES AND HARPS

Despite being the busiest season, spring made the heart of a beekeeper like Joeun dance. As flowers burst into bloom, honeybees flitted about gathering nectar to deposit in the hexagonal honeycomb cells. Once the liquid inside evaporated, they capped each cell with white beeswax. Bee colonies thrived and expanded at this time of year. Although this meant that beekeepers had to guard against swarming, more bees meant more honey, and more honey meant more income. But first the honey had to be extracted from the comb.

Joeun and Elin rose early each morning. If the sky was clear, they eagerly set to work. First, Joeun would slide a honey knife from the bottom to the top of the comb, removing the wax seal so neatly that it made Elin itch to try. Then he would place the honey-filled comb, frame and all, into a large, barrel-like contraption and crank the handle on top. As the barrel began to spin, golden honey flowed out from the bottom. Elin's job was to strain the thick liquid through a clean cloth into clean jars and close the lids. If she worked hard, she was rewarded with a generous spoonful of honey.

While freshly extracted honey was delicious, what really surprised Elin was the taste of pollen, which the honeybees also collected and stored in the comb. She had been intrigued by the bright pollen balls that clung to the bees' legs when they returned to the hive, but she had never dreamed that the pollen was edible. She tried some at Joeun's urging and was amazed to find it sweet and delicious. Watching her eyes widen, Joeun had smiled knowingly. "I bet only beekeepers know how good that tastes," he had said. "It ferments and sours within just a day or two, you see."

They worked from dawn to dusk without a break and woke each day to find more work waiting. For Elin, it was all new and fascinating. Every night sleep overtook her as soon as she crawled under the covers and every morning there was more to do. As the days passed, the raw agony of loss slowly dulled. Still, on rainy or slow days, loneliness would suddenly overwhelm her and not even Joeun's presence beside her could ease her heart. Nothing could fill the space left by her mother's absence. When the tears welled up inside, she went to the stable and crouched down to weep beside Joeun's gentle mare, Totchi, who stood placidly munching hay. Perhaps Joeun knew why she went away, but he said nothing and just let her be.

As spring slowly moved toward summer, Joeun gradually came to the conclusion that Elin had been telling the truth about having no home and no family. She had obviously lost her parents in some very cruel way, but at least no one seemed to be pursuing her. Once every seven days he took the mare and traveled a toh (about an hour) to the crossroads on Kojon Way where a weekly market was held. There he would sell his honey and buy supplies. One day, he offered to take Elin with him, and she jumped at the chance. Clearly, she was not afraid of being seen.

Quiet by nature, she stayed by his side even when they reached the town, gazing with shining eyes at the banners and the wares in the stalls. The merchants who knew Joeun were curious to see him with a girl who obviously had Ahlyo blood in her veins, but all he would tell them was that he had taken in the daughter of a friend. When he bought her a pretty dress with a flower-embroidered collar such as the local girls liked to wear, she thanked him with pleasure. But her face did not light up the way it had on the way to town when she had seen a leaf-shaped beehive hanging from the branch of a long-leafed hoaku tree. He concluded that she was more drawn to living creatures than to clothes or accessories.

She could watch the entrance to a beehive for hours, forgetting time. Once, a new queen bee emerged from the hive, piping its beautiful high note, and he had seen Elin's eyes fill with tears and her cheeks flush with emotion. She wandered about the fields, following the bees, and when she returned, she would relate with excitement that the hives of bees in the wild differed from one species to another, as did the flowers from which they collected nectar. But she did not come rushing back out of breath to report on every little discovery like other children would have done.

At first Joeun thought it was because she was not used to him, but as time passed he realized that whenever she made a discovery, it was her habit to ponder it on her own. While emptying the ashes from the hearth or shoveling manure from the goat pen, her mind appeared to be full of questions and speculations, and she often muttered to herself. Joeun found that eavesdropping could be quite interesting. Once while watching the honey drip slowly from the extractor, she had murmured, "It's really not at all like nectar." As he cranked the handle, Joeun's ears had pricked up, but Elin did not even seem to know that she was talking out loud. With her eyes fixed on the flow of honey, she continued, "But the color of the honey when the saloh flowers were blooming was different from the color when the nosan were in blossom . . . so I suppose it must be flower nectar after all."

Joeun could not keep quiet any longer. "Why are you wondering about whether or not this is flower nectar?"

Elin looked up with a startled expression and then flushed. After a moment's silence she said, "The other day I licked the nectar from the flowers that the bees like. It was sweet, but it didn't taste at all like honey."

Joeun looked at her in surprise. Now he understood what was puzzling her. It was such an obvious question that he could have laughed out loud, but instead he was intrigued that at only ten she was wondering why honey did not taste the same as the flower nectar from which it was made. "I see. That's true. So what is honey, then?" Realizing that he had fallen back into his old habit of teaching, he paused momentarily, but Elin did not appear to notice.

Her expression intent, she said, "Honeybees fill their bellies with nectar and then spit it out when they reach home. So I thought the honey must be the nectar mixed with their saliva . . ." She paused and Joeun waited, wondering what else was puzzling her. She cocked her head and continued. "But they fly such a long way. I followed them. They went to a meadow so far away that by the time I reached it, I was tired and out of breath. Bees are tiny, right? Much smaller than me. So that meadow must be even farther for them." Joeun was so absorbed that his hand paused on the handle. "My mother told me that people and animals don't eat just so that they can grow. They need food to give them the energy to move. That's why they get really hungry if they move a lot or walk a long way. If that's true, then how can these honeybees survive? They fly so far to eat nectar, but then they fly all the way back home and spit up what they've eaten.

"And what about that honey? It would take a lot of spit to make it so thick and dark . . . but bees are so little they must have hardly any spit at all. If they cough up that much, wouldn't they shrivel up and die? How can they fly about as if it didn't bother them at all?"

Suddenly realizing that he had stopped his work, Joeun hastily began cranking the handle. "That's not an easy question to answer," he said. "I promise I'll teach you everything I know, but for now you must be patient because first we've got to extract the honey. Wait until we finish."

From that day on, Joeun took every opportunity that arose to share all he knew about honey with Elin. Her appetite for knowledge was like that of a newborn chick searching for food. But he only realized how extreme her desire was one rainy day when it was almost summer. He had ridden to town to make a deal with a trader, leaving the house in Elin's charge. On the way home, it had begun to rain and by the time he reached the house it was pouring. The last time he had been caught in a sudden downpour, Elin had come down the road with an umbrella to meet him. He had been expecting her to do the same today, but even when the house came in sight, she still did not appear.

He led Totchi into the stable, where he rubbed her down and gave her some hay. Then he walked to the house. Even at the entranceway, not a sound could be heard from inside. He opened the door anxiously, wondering where on earth Elin could have got to on such a miserable day, only to see her sitting in the far room beyond the earth-floored kitchen. She had her back to the door and did not turn around even when he entered the house. Walking quietly up behind her, he peered over her shoulder to see what she was doing and raised his eyebrows in surprise. She was totally absorbed in one of his books—a medical tome on poisons. Her head was moving slowly as she followed the words on the page, and she seemed to be murmuring something.

"Hey there," he said. She started and whipped around to stare up at him. The blood drained from her face. "I'm sorry!" She seemed to be expecting a severe scolding for taking a book without asking permission.

Joeun sat down in front of her and took the book in his hand. "No need to apologize . . . but can you read?"

Elin nodded.

"Did you go to school?"

She shook her head. "My mother taught me."

Joeun waved the book in front of her. "Your mother taught you well enough to read something as difficult as this?"

Elin hunched her shoulders. "It was too hard. I couldn't read a lot of the words."

Joeun smiled. "I see. That's a relief. To tell you the truth, you gave me goosebumps. I come home on a dark, rainy day to find a ten-year-old girl totally absorbed in *The Book of Poisons*." Elin ducked her head sheepishly. "This is a textbook for sixteen-year-old youths of the upper artisan class. If you had been able to read it effortlessly, you would have to forgive me for thinking you were some kind of supernatural creature." The color was returning to her face, and he looked her in the eye. "But you were really concentrating, weren't you? You didn't even hear me come in. Was it that interesting?"

Elin nodded, wondering how she could possibly explain. She had discovered Joeun's extensive book collection the other day when he had gone into town to trade. It had been raining, and she was bored. She had opened the cupboard in the living room with the intention of mending Joeun's clothing. To her amazement, the cupboard, which was large enough to walk right into, was jammed with stacks of books. Never in her life had she seen so many books in one place. She knew she shouldn't touch his things without asking, but she could not resist. She just had to know what kind of books they were.

She had taken them out one by one so as not to disturb the order, looking at the titles with rising excitement. There were books full of stories, books about honey, books about different countries . . . It was like having a pile of treasure right in front of her. There had been no time to read before Joeun returned home, so she had been longing for a chance to be alone in the house ever since. Today, as soon as he had left, she opened the cupboard and pulled out the books. She knew that she only had until he came back, but still it took her a long time to decide what to read. She had begun reading the medical book quite by accident.

After thumbing through several books to see what they were about, she had noticed the heading "Change in Odor" in this one. Instantly, she recalled her mother wading into the Pond to see why the Toda had died. Elin had asked her why their odor had changed but her mother had looked shocked and warned her to tell no one. Why had she told her not to tell? Why had the Toda's odor changed? As she pondered these questions, another memory surfaced in her mind—something her mother had said when they shared their last meal together: Toda living among men grow weak.

"Think about it. What can Toda in the wild do naturally that Toda raised in the Ponds can't? I'm sure you'll find the answer for yourself one day. But when you do, don't tell anyone. Not until you understand why you shouldn't tell them what you know."

These words had stuck in the back of her mind. When she had seen the heading, she had hoped to find a clue to this riddle. But there were so many unfamiliar words that she could not grasp the meaning, no matter how many times she read it. Still, she had understood one thing. Poison changes body odor. The book had said that you could identify what poison had killed someone by smelling the person's mouth. This made her think. Her mother had told the inspector that the Toda had died of poisoning. Perhaps the poison had caused their smell to change. She was just starting to think this over when Joeun had returned. She could not tell him why she had chosen this particular book to read, so instead, she kept her head bowed silently.

Joeun closed the book with a snap. "Do you want to learn how to read this kind of thing?"

Elin's heart gave a great thump, and she raised her face abruptly. "Yes."

He gazed at her steadily and then smiled. "All right then. I'll teach you whenever we have a break in our work."

At one time in his life, Joeun had thought that there was no greater joy than teaching an uneducated child who was so much slower than his classmates that he was convinced he was a failure, and seeing his eyes light up with comprehension and the realization that he could do it after all. When he began to teach Elin, however, he discovered another joy: that of teaching a child with extraordinary potential.

In addition to living creatures and books, Elin discovered yet another passion—the harp. One day when they went into town to buy supplies for the summer, they came across a band of traveling musicians who visited a few times a year. They were just setting up their instruments on a rug spread out under the bright blue sky. "Would you like to stay and listen for a bit?" Joeun asked. Elin looked up at him and nodded.

The troupe gave a fine performance, presenting a repertoire that ranged from melancholy love songs to dance tunes. Elin listened as if entranced. As they walked along the mountain path toward home, Totchi bearing their luggage, she began singing one of the love songs the musicians had performed. "Frogs chirrup in the moonlit night, in the dawn mist the bird's song flows, oh how it flows, disturbing the still night . . ." As the song reached its climax, Elin sang soulfully, "Don't weep, dawn bird, don't weep, for I'll recall your voice from last night . . ."

"Elin, do you understand what that song means?"

"He's asking the bird not to cry, right?"

Joeun choked on a laugh and shook his head. "Never mind," he said. "You'll understand soon enough . . . Everyone knows that song around here, but I didn't realize it was popular in Aluhan territory, too."

Elin blinked. "Really? I never heard it before."

Joeun looked at her in surprise. "What? But you were just singing it."

Elin frowned, obviously confused. "Because I heard them sing it."

"You can sing a song you've only heard once?"

Elin did not know what to say. That particular song had stayed with her because it had been pleasing to her ear, but whether she could remember any song in the same way, she was not sure. As they walked along, Joeun kept glancing at her as if thinking about something. As soon as they reached home, he opened a cupboard and pulled out a small harp.

"I haven't taken this out for some time . . ." he muttered. He plucked the strings one by one, listening intently and loosening or tightening the small screws on the frame. Finally, he nodded to himself and then looked at Elin. "Do you know this song?" he asked. The tune he played conjured up an image of gentle spring sunlight. She shook her head.

"No, I never heard it before."

"No? It's a nice tune though, isn't it?"

Her eyes shining, Elin said, "Yes . . . And you play really well!"

Joeun laughed. "I fell in love with the harp when I was twelve. My father permitted me to play as a hobby, but when I stopped being content with merely playing and began learning to build my own harps from an instrument maker, he put his foot down, demanding to know if I planned to become a musician. This harp is one that I made. It has a good sound, doesn't it?"

Elin nodded. Joeun strummed the harp, effortlessly plucking out light reels that made her want to dance and tunes that made her think of gazing up at the moon in the night sky. She leaned forward eagerly, moving her head in time to the music and humming along.

"Elin, try humming this one," Joeun said. He played the song that he had played first, the one that made her think of spring sunlight. When he finished, Elin hummed the tune perfectly from beginning to end. Joeun was amazed. What surprised him most was not the fact that she could hum a song that she had only heard twice, but that she reproduced the notes in the same pitch as he had played them, without any trace of hesitation or uncertainty. Joeun's harp teacher had once praised him for having an excellent ear for music, but Elin's sense of pitch clearly surpassed his own.

From that day on, he began to teach her the harp. Just as he had expected, she proved to have an exceptional ear for music and the ability to reproduce a tune accurately after hearing it only once. However, her ability did not extend to composing new pieces of music. She was drawn not to composing music but to creating sounds. She was fascinated by the fact that the sound of the harp changed subtly depending on how it was strung, the type of wood used, and the shape of the instrument.

When Joeun taught her the basics of harp making, she threw herself into making harps of all shapes and sizes out of different kinds of wood. Of course, she could not make harps as exquisite as those of an instrument maker, but her enthusiasm for harp making was to last for many years.

2

THE SUMMER SHACK

Summer arrived. The shadows of the trees stood out starkly in the bright sunlight and cicadas sang from dawn to dusk. Joeun lived in the highlands, higher than the village where Elin had lived with her mother, and the dry air and cooler evenings made summer much more pleasant. One day, after the saloh flowers by the lake had faded and the yellow nosan flowers that had blanketed the fields were beginning to fall, Joeun went to the nearest farm and borrowed a horse. He and the farmer had a long-standing agreement that once the farmer's wheat had been harvested and the next crop of beans had been planted, Joeun could rent the horse until the fall.

Upon his return, Joeun uncovered a cart that had been securely wrapped in waterproof cloth, brought it out into the sunlight, and began cleaning it. Just then, Elin ran up. "Did you finish taking care of Noro and Totchi?" Joeun asked. When she nodded, he handed her a rag. "In that case, help me clean this thing. If you notice any loose or twisted boards, let me know."

Nodding once again, Elin clambered inside and began rubbing the sides of the cart with the rag. The bed of the cart was far longer than those she was used to seeing. "What are you going to put in here?" she asked.

"All of the hives, along with our food and bedding."

Elin paused to stare at him. "What? Are we going somewhere?"

Joeun grinned. "We're going to follow the flowers. All the way up the mountain. I have a summer shack about three-quarters of the way up. In summer, the slopes are covered in flowers like fujak and sasha. It's quite spectacular." Seeing her face light up, he continued, "At least that will give you something to look forward to while you work. We have an awful lot to do before we go!"

It was only at dawn five days later that they finished closing up the house and loading the cart with all the hives and luggage. After hitching up Totchi and the other horse, Joeun began leading them along the mountain trail, through the morning mist. Elin followed after the cart, herding the goat, Noro, ahead of her with a small switch. Their pace was fairly slow as they had to be careful not to jar the hives too much. Although the trail was covered in summer grass and shaded by trees, Elin was soon drenched in sweat. Gnats tried to crawl into her eyes and mosquitoes hovered around her sweat-soaked skin with a high whining sound.

They had covered the hives with wire net so that air could pass through, but Joeun still sprayed the hives frequently with water to keep them from getting too hot inside. When they came to a spring burbling from the rocks, Joeun stopped the cart. Elin cupped the water in her hands and gulped it down. It was so cold it numbed her fingers, but she felt much refreshed after washing her hands and splashing her neck. When she ducked her head under the stream of water and then shook her dripping hair, Joeun laughed. "Just like a pup. How about behaving a little more gracefully? You're a girl after all."

Elin grinned and shook her head vigorously. "I'd rather be a puppy."

Smiling, Joeun looked at his little charge, with her darkly tanned skin and stick-like limbs. He could not braid her hair, so he had cut it at collar length, which made her look like a boy. "You're impossible!" His heart filled with tenderness. What a priceless gift he had been given.

They continued along the mountain trail, stopping occasionally to rest. It was not until the sun began sinking low in the sky and the orange-tinged light slanting through the branches struck the trunks of the trees that they stumbled out into the open. Elin gasped in wonder. Before her stretched a gentle slope carpeted in a profusion of colorful flowers that finally dropped away into nothingness. Rosy clouds drifted slowly by, grazing the edge of the cliff. A hush fell as the cart came to a standstill. The only noise to be heard was the soft rustle of grasses swaying in the wind and flowers brushing against one another. Beyond the deep valley that lay beneath the meadow, the snow-capped peaks of the Afon Noah soared. Standing in the field, where only the voice of the wind could be heard, Elin felt as though she had wandered into another world.

"Let's get a move on," Joeun said, laying a hand on her shoulder. "It's not much farther."

The summer shack was less than half the size of the house Joeun lived in from fall to spring. The boards he had tacked over the door last fall were still in place, undisturbed by animals. "Here we are at last," he said. He pounded his back with his fist and then stretched his arms above his head. "After you've put the animals in the pen, look after the horses. I'll set up the hives and then unboard the door and sweep out the chimney."

"All right."

Nights on the mountain were chilly, even in midsummer, and Joeun knew they wouldn't be able to sleep without a fire going in the hearth. But as birds frequently roosted in unused chimneys, his first task was to clean out any nests. Although he had always been strong and healthy, this annual move was exhausting and from the age of fifty-five, it had begun to drain his strength more every year. Last year he had been too tired to sweep out the chimney and had just wrapped himself in a blanket for the night. That wouldn't do this time, though, not with Elin here. He endured this hardship each summer not just to get more honey, but because he liked this place.

I wonder how many more years I'll be able to do this.

Gazing out over the meadow bathed in the light of sunset, he felt some of his fatigue lift. Rainfall had been plentiful this year, and the field was thick with flowers. The bees would gather lots of nectar. This year he intended not only to make honey, but also to collect herbs for medicine.

Once he had found chigo growing on this very mountain. The root of the plant was a miracle cure for inflammations of the internal organs, and it brought a high price because it only grew in steep, inaccessible ravines. The place where he had seen it was a sheer bluff, and he would have to be very careful if he were to gather any. One slip and he'd be at the bottom of the valley. Wild Toda lived in the river that flowed through it. Of course, if he fell, he would be dead anyway. Still, it was worth trying. Just one small chigo root would bring him a large gold piece.

Until now, he had only had to feed himself. When he grew too old to move, he had thought that he would just lie down in this meadow to die while watching the clouds drift in the sky above. But now there was Elin. In six or seven years, she might marry. She would need a proper dowry if she were to wed into a good family, and clothes and furniture to start a new household.

Even as this thought passed through his head, however, something told him that she would never live the life of a normal girl. She was too unusual. He had become even more aware of this when he had begun teaching her to read. *If only she were a boy . . . *he thought *. . . and not part Ahlyo.* Then he could have used his connections from the past to get her a place at the school in the capital. Every time he thought about how her potential might blossom with a proper education, he was overcome with frustration . . . But *I'll have to worry about that later.* Either way, he would need money. He did not mind this. In fact, the thought gave him energy and drive. The desire to set her on the road to happiness consumed him, just like it had when he had cradled his own child in his arms for the first time.

Their days in the summer shack passed quietly and midsummer approached. One evening as they were eating dinner, Joeun said, "You're used to living here now. You won't mind if I go away for a day or so, will you?"

"No, I'll be fine."

"Good then. I'll leave the place in your hands tomorrow. Be sure to take good care of it."

"Of course."

Joeun raised his eyebrows. "Nicely said . . . but don't you try touching the bees just because I'm not here to see you." She started, and he frowned sternly. "Did you think I didn't notice? I've no idea why you would even want to, but you're just dying to touch one, aren't you? I've seen you squatting in front of the hive debating whether to reach out a finger or not. Some people have died just because they've been stung, you know. Don't take it lightly, you understand?"

"Yes." Elin bowed her head, rubbing her thumb against her forefinger.

If he knew that she had already been stung, she thought, he would really scold her. The short bristles covering the honeybees were so even they looked like they had been cropped with a razor. Longing to know if they felt soft or coarse to the touch, she had reached out ever so carefully to gently stroke one. But as soon as she had touched it, it had buzzed into the air and stung her forefinger . . . How it had hurt! And the pain did not ease no matter how she licked it or sucked on it.

That in itself had been hard enough to bear, but the worst part had been finding a stinger-less bee dead upon the ground when she went out the next morning. Joeun had told her that a honeybee dies after it stings, but it was only when she saw the little corpse lying motionless on the grass that she had understood what it really meant. She could not name the feeling that rose in her breast. It was as if a tiny hole had pierced her heart and a cold wind blew through it. She had stood for a long time staring at the tiny body while the other bees, apparently oblivious to their sister's death, flitted about.

Joeun watched Elin as she sat frowning, her head bowed. "You sometimes do the craziest things, you know. Leaving you behind on your own makes me quite nervous. Ah! One more thing! Don't you dare crawl under Totchi's belly." Elin flinched at this. When she had heard that Totchi was a mare, she had crawled underneath her, wondering if she had an udder that could be milked. But she had no idea that Joeun had seen her. "Totchi is docile. That's why you weren't kicked, but even Totchi will kick and buck if a fly bites her in the wrong place." He peered into her face. "Elin, look at me." She raised her head. "Listen," he said, gently but sternly. "There is a big difference between people and animals. Don't ever forget that. Totchi is a gentle mare. She's used to you and to me. She's like family. But if a wasp stung her and she was startled by the pain, she could kill you with one blow of her hoof. A person stung by a wasp would go crazy with pain, too, but they would never kill their friend because of it. A horse can't make that distinction."

As she listened to his words, Elin was overcome by a strange sensation. Her mother, she remembered, had said something very similar.

"Do you understand?" Joeun demanded.

"Yes."

He nodded and his expression softened. "All right then, tomorrow I'm leaving the place in your charge." He took some cheese from a wooden plate, stuck it on a stick, and began to toast it in the fire.

Watching him, Elin asked, "Where are you going?"

"Hmm? Oh, I'm going to look for herbs."

"Herbs? Aren't you feeling well?"

He smiled. "No, no, not for me. I'm going to sell them. Have you ever heard of chigo root?"

Elin shook her head.

"It's great for curing inflammations of the internal organs. A root this big"—he made a small space between his thumb and his forefinger—"sells for one large gold piece."

"Really? A whole gold piece!"

Joeun laughed and skewered another lump of cheese on a stick. "Yes, really. That's a pretty good price, wouldn't you say? Mind you, chigo is tricky to get because it grows in deep ravines where it 'thrives on the breath of the Toda,' as they say. It might take me more than a day to get some, so don't worry if I'm not back by nightfall tomorrow." Having stuck the skewers into the hearth, he raised his face to look at her and stopped in surprise. She was staring at him, her face bloodless. "What's wrong? Do you feel sick or something?"

Elin shook her head. In a faint voice, she finally managed to say, "You're . . . going to where there are Toda?"

Joeun blinked and looked at her for some time. Then he raised his brows and smiled. "So that's it. You're worried about me. Well, thank you. But there's really nothing to worry about. I'm used to hiking around here, and I won't be going down into the valley. So just relax and take care of the house for me."

Elin nodded, but the fear that rose inside her like a dark cloud could not be banished by his words. The smell of Toda filled her nostrils, and the writhing swarm of Toda swallowing her mother filled her sight. Joeun went to bed soon after, intending to rise early the next morning, but although she lay down, Elin could not sleep. Even if he didn't plan to climb down into the valley, what if he slipped?

Then he would be taken by her greatest fear. He would be killed in no time, just like her mother. Her mother. Who she had thought would be with her, always.

What if he doesn't come back? A trembling spread from the pit of her stomach and seized her body.

3

THE SOARING BEAST

Joeun rose just as the dark sky paled toward dawn and dressed quietly so as not to wake Elin.

Lying motionless in her bed with her eyes closed, Elin listened to the faint sounds of his movements. Finally, he shouldered his pack and went out the door. No sooner did she hear the door click shut than Elin threw back the covers and leapt out of bed. She moved swiftly, following a plan she had worked out during the night. As soon as she had dressed, she grabbed the remaining cheese and fahko from last night's supper off the shelf and shoved them into a pack. Throwing this over her shoulder, she stealthily opened the latch.

It was not yet fully light, but she could make out the black shape of Joeun in the distance as he walked through the bluish darkness. She hurried after him. The first part of the journey was through the meadow and if he turned around, he would see her. But she would worry about that when it happened.

If he had not been thinking about something else, Joeun would probably have sensed that he was being followed. But as he walked along the rugged mountain trail down toward the valley, his thoughts were far away.

I wonder if Elin was ever attacked by Toda . . . Her face had been so pale when she had asked if he was going to where there were Toda. He had assumed she was worried about his safety, but in retrospect there must be more to it than that. When he had found her lying on the lakeshore, she had been caked in a glue-like mud that reeked of Toda. Anyone who got close enough to get that coated in slime ought to have been eaten alive. Anyone but a Rider, that is. He frowned at this thought. *Wait a minute. That's a possibility I hadn't considered.*

Although the Yojeh did not own such base creatures as the Toda, he had heard that the Aluhan, the Grand Duke, who was not bound by sacred rules, had skilled beast handlers called Toda Stewards to raise and train them. *She came from Aluhan territory and she seems to be from the skilled classes . . . Was she the child of a Steward? But the Toda Stewards swore allegiance to the Aluhan alone. Surely they would never mix blood with an Ahlyo. Oh dear, that child remains a mystery.*

Morning came, but it was a dark day. Heavy clouds flowed across the sky. His prayers that it would not rain must have fallen on deaf ears, for by the time he neared the ravine, large drops had begun to fall. In moments, it was pouring as if someone had upended a barrel in the heavens. He fled into the shelter of a large tree and wondered whether he should turn back or not. If it had continued to rain, he would have given up and gone home. But the downpour gradually dwindled to a gentle drizzle tapping on the leaves, the clouds lifted, and the summer sun showed its face at last. The soggy ground would hamper his footing, but it seemed too much trouble to turn back after coming all this way. He swung his pack onto his shoulder and returned to the trail, wiping away large drops of water that slipped from the leaves of the trees onto his face.

The rustling of a bird or animal in the brush behind him caught his attention. Wildlife must be on the move again after the storm, he thought. In addition to the pack slung over his shoulder, he carried a small pouch tied to his waist, and from this he pulled a pungent fruit, the strong odor of which repelled most wild creatures. He squished it in his hand and rubbed the juice on his clothes. The smell conjured up the face of the old man who had generously shared his knowledge, teaching Joeun everything from bee-keeping to walking the mountains. Without him, Joeun doubted that he could have made a living as a beekeeper. He offered a silent prayer for the repose of the man's soul and set off again.

At last, the forest came to an end and a deep ravine appeared ahead. The cliff had been hollowed out so that it curved like a deep bowl, far below which ran a muddy river. It must have rained at the headwaters, for the river was fuller than he remembered. He walked slowly along the edge of the cliff, thick with grasses, looking carefully for each foothold.

Last year, he had come out of curiosity, wondering if any valuable herbs grew here. When he had chanced to see chigo blooming at the base of a large soshu tree halfway down the cliff, it had already been dusk and there had not been enough light for him to find his way down. Besides, the spot where the plant grew was impossible to reach without a rope, and he had not thought gathering the root to be worth the effort.

This time, however, he had come for the express purpose of collecting the plant and was better prepared. The soshu was just where he remembered, and he put down his pack and took out a sturdy rope. Wrapping one end around the trunk of a firmly rooted tree and securing it tightly, he tied a small stone to the other end and threw it toward the soshu tree. It fell among the bamboo grass. Joeun grasped the rope and began climbing backward down the cliff, placing his feet carefully. He had descended about twenty paces when suddenly the rock beneath his right foot crumbled, followed almost immediately by the rock under his left foot. With his hands still clinging tightly to the rope, his body swung hard against the cliff, knocking the wind out of him. Pain seared his hands where the rope burned, and he let go with a cry. He began sliding down the rock face, his belly scraping against stone. Reaching out to grasp a bush, he smashed his chin on a branch instead. Sparks filled his eyes. Losing consciousness, he slid helplessly down the cliff.

Something touched his chin, and a sharp pain shot through his head. He groaned and opened his eyes. His blurred vision cleared, and he saw Elin's worried face, streaked with mud and tears, peering down at him. "Joeun! Joeun!"

He gazed up at her blankly for a moment and then opened his mouth to speak, only to feel pain racing through his jaw. He reached up automatically to touch it, but a little hand caught his own and held it firm. "Don't! You've got a bad cut there, so don't touch it." She pushed against his hand with all her strength.

Joeun moved his lips gingerly, tears starting in his eyes. "Where am I?"

"Halfway down the cliff," Elin answered, choking back sobs. "So please don't move . . . There's a ledge here, but there's only enough room for the two of us. Whatever you do, don't move!"

With his eyes, he told her he had understood. Her lips began to tremble, and she burst into tears. "I thought . . . you were dead!" Relief washed through her, releasing all the fear and adrenalin inside her. Shaking violently, she threw her head back and wailed, and as she did so, the terror that had gripped her gradually lessened its hold. After weeping until she had no more tears left, she took a deep breath and wiped her face vigorously. Looking into Joeun's face again, she asked, "Are . . . Are you all right?"

Once again, he answered with his eyes. He hurt all over, but judging from the fact that he could wiggle his fingers and toes, he had not injured his spine or broken any bones. His wits had returned, and he now realized his predicament. He may not have broken any bones, but his legs and back had taken a beating. He wouldn't be able to climb the cliff for a while. He must have lain unconscious for some time. The sun was already starting to set.

Trying to move his arm, he noticed for the first time that he was covered in a blanket.

"What's . . . this?"

"Your blanket. It was rolled up under a tree, so I tied it to my back before I climbed down."

"You . . . what?"

"It's not that heavy. I brought food and water, too." She raised a flask and smiled proudly, crumpling her tearstained face. Joeun had had no idea she was following him, but now he was glad that she had.

"Can . . . you . . . climb up . . . the rope?" he murmured, trying not to move his jaw. Elin nodded. "Take the blanket . . . and sleep under . . . the tree . . . at the top . . . It'll be . . . dark soon."

Elin shook her head. "No. I'm staying with you."

"Stupid . . . It's too . . . narrow . . . What if . . . you fall?"

"I won't. It's wide enough."

He gave up and let her have her way. The temperature dropped rapidly as the sun set. Even though Elin covered both of them from head to foot in the blanket and pressed her body close, it was too cold to sleep soundly. Many times Joeun woke in the night and each time Elin helped him up so that he could relieve himself. Each time he stood up, agony shot through his back and legs. Even worse than the pain, however, was the fear of falling from the ledge. In the darkness, he could not see where the rock shelf ended. How he wished he could sleep through until morning.

As the long night drew to a close and dawn was just beginning to break, Elin started awake, disturbed by a familiar musk-like odor. At first, she thought it must be the old nightmare that haunted her mind, but when she poked her head out of the blanket she knew it was no dream. The scent of Toda pervaded the icy dawn air. Fear strangled her, and her pulse raced. Gently, so as not to wake Joeun, she moved her head and looked over the edge, but all she could see was a rock ledge like this one farther down the cliff. In the dimness, she could just make out the dark shadows of some bushes and a few logs, probably washed up by the surging river, lying on the ledge. Yet each puff of wind carried the distinctive scent of Toda.

Suddenly, something moved at the edge of her vision. Casting her eyes in that direction, she froze. Faintly but surely, she saw one of the logs moving. Her spine grew cold. They were not logs after all. They were Toda: three of them . . . What, she wondered, could they be after?

As she watched, they began inching slowly but steadily toward what appeared to be a thicket of brush. Squinting, she saw something stirring inside it. What on earth could it be? An animal? Or perhaps a hatchling? That must be it. It wasn't brush but a bird's nest.

As soon as she recognized the nest for what it was, she realized something very odd. Toda were huge beasts, large enough for a Warrior to ride. Having ridden one herself, she knew that their heads were as big as her body. Yet the hatchling in that nest was far larger than any Toda head. Could there really be a bird that big? She had never seen even a full-grown bird larger than herself, let alone a hatchling. And this definitely appeared to be a baby. Although it flapped its wings occasionally, its movements were still clumsy and immature.

Where was its mother? By now, the Toda had crept very close. Soon they would pounce upon the hatchling and rend it from head to foot. Elin grimaced. Her heart went out to it. It was only a baby. How awful to die like that . . . She longed to do something, but she knew only too well that she could not stop Toda just by throwing stones at them. They reared their heads and poised to strike.

It'll be killed! She screwed her eyes shut.

At that moment, a piercing whistle split the air. The complex modulation of notes reminded Elin of a finger flute. She jerked her head up to gaze toward the sound. Although the sky was still a deep ultramarine, sunlight rimmed the mountain peaks above in a halo of pale gold. In the midst of that light, a dark speck appeared and hurtled downward, gliding on giant wings. Still whistling, it swooped past her head, casting a dark shadow.

Elin stared so intently that she forgot to blink or even to breathe as she branded its shape on her brain. It was no bird. Gigantic wings, as wide in span as the rock ledge, needle-sharp fur of dazzling silver, a fearless wolf-like face, huge, sharp-clawed feet . . .

A gust of wind stirred by the creature's wings swept up Joeun's blanket, and Elin grabbed it hastily. The winged beast sped smoothly through space, sinking down upon the Toda. To her astonishment, the Toda had turned away from the nest and rolled onto their backs with their bellies exposed, as if to say, "Here I am. Eat me." Then followed the strangest hunt she had ever seen.

Not once did the Toda raise their heads, even when the beast attacked. Snatching one in its jaws, like an eagle scooping up a snake in its beak, the creature tore it to shreds. Toda scales were impervious to arrows, yet the beast's fangs bit through them as if they were made of soft leather. In moments, all three Toda had been ripped to pieces.

Caught in a shaft of morning light that passed over the mountain ridge, the beast blazed silver. Elin stared transfixed at the godlike figure feasting on Toda as if they were sacrificial offerings.

And that song . . . She remembered her mother placing her fingers against her lips and whistling a melody that was now imprinted indelibly on her memory. The beast's song had sounded so similar. Why had the Toda responded like that? If that sound could control them, then why didn't they close their earflaps to block it out? Or did the sound penetrate through their mouths even when their earflaps were closed?

Once it had finished eating, the creature began preening its fur just like a cat, rubbing its bloodied muzzle against its breast. Then it folded its wings. At that moment, a strange sound, like that of a harp being strummed, reached Elin on the wind. *Lon-lon-lon* . . . It must be the creature's cub. The baby flapped its wings in appeal and cried again. The mother beast responded with the same harp-like sound. *Lo, lolon, lolon.* Then it walked over to the nest, opened its mouth, and began feeding its young. The tenderness with which it folded the cub within its wings and fed it was a far cry from the fierceness with which it had devoured the Toda.

Joeun sat up slowly behind her. "Joeun," she whispered. He nodded and peered carefully over the edge.

"A wild Royal Beast."

"Really?" Elin stared at it, fascinated. So this was the Sacred Beast that the gods had bestowed on the Yojeh as a sign of her royal sovereignty. Elin had heard that many of these Royal Beasts were raised under the protection of the Yojeh. If their number decreased, it was believed that disaster would overtake the land.

"Yes. That's a Royal Beast," Joeun murmured. "I've seen them in the capital . . . But I never thought that I would see one in the wild. They're very rare, and I've heard their numbers are declining because they only bear one offspring at a time. Yet for some reason the ones raised under the care of the Yojeh never bear young. They have to capture cubs in the wild and bring them to the Royal Garden to maintain their numbers." He sighed. "I wonder how on earth they manage to take them from under the wings of such fearsome mothers as that."

By noon, Joeun had regained quite a bit of movement. Although steep, the cliff face was not vertical, and he could climb it using the rope if he went one step at a time. Elin went first to find footholds, and Joeun followed after, placing each foot where she had shown him. When they reached the top, the relief was so great that they both shook from head to foot. Feeling exhausted and lethargic, they packed up and silently headed home.

As they walked along the narrow trail, Elin's thoughts remained fixed on the Royal Beast, on its bright silver body glinting in the sunlight, on its song that reminded her of her mother's finger flute. It used it to immobilize the Toda. Does the Royal Beast's song freeze Toda, just like the Rider's soundless whistle? No. It wasn't the same. When the Riders blew their Silent Whistles, the Toda turned as stiff as logs. They didn't turn over and lie defenseless, exposing their bellies like that. In her mind, Elin saw her mother whistling through her fingers. The Toda had stopped instantly, en masse, and looked at her intently, like loyal hounds listening to their master. Then one of them had swum up, as if obediently following her orders, and had let Elin ride him when her mother had hoisted her onto its back. Her mother had manipulated the Toda with her finger flute . . . And the Beast had manipulated the Toda with its song.

Were the sounds it made like a language to the Toda? She suddenly remembered that the morning the Kiba had died, the other Toda had whistled for a long time. That sound, too, had resembled the finger flute. Both her mother and the Royal Beast had used complex modulations . . . If that was the language of the Toda, could she, too, make them obey her by reproducing the same sounds? A shiver ran down her spine.

If I could make the Toda obey me by whistling . . . If I could do the same thing my mother did . . . Could I control the Toda?

She tripped over a root and almost fell, returning with a jolt to reality. Joeun turned to look back at her. "Are you all right?"

She nodded. Seeing his pale face, she thought he should be worrying about himself, not her. "Do your legs hurt?"

Joeun gave a short laugh. "My legs hurt. My back hurts. My jaw hurts . . . I hurt all over, but there's no way I want to spend another night out in the open. Tonight I'm going to curl up in my nice warm bed and sleep soundly."

He turned around and began walking again. Following behind, Elin let her thoughts return to her mother; to the smell of waterweeds in Lagoh Marsh; to her mother's cold cheek pressed against hers in the frigid waters as she held her tight.

Whenever she felt lonely, Elin recalled this scene, as if pulling it out of her breast pocket to look at it. But something about it had always bothered her. Her mother's face before she blew the finger flute. Clearly she had been torn, frowning as she struggled to decide. Then, as if pushing her doubts away, she had said, "Elin, you must never do what I am going to do now. To do so is to commit a mortal sin." And placing her fingers to her mouth, she had commanded the Toda with her music and saved Elin's life.

But what sin had her mother forbidden her to commit? Had she meant that Elin must not try to control the Toda with the finger flute? If so, why? Why was that such a terrible crime? Her mother had hesitated to use it even to save Elin's life . . . Anguish spread through her chest. In the end she chose to save me. Yet her hesitation, however slight, showed how great a sin it must be . . .

Each time Elin reached this conclusion, the question that she had tried so hard to bury in the depths of her heart raised its head. Her mother could control the Toda. If so, then she must have been able to save her own life,

75

too. Then why did she choose instead to give herself to the serpents? Why had she chosen death instead of life together with Elin? She desperately wanted to believe that this wasn't true. But no matter how she suppressed it, she could not banish this thought from her mind.

She sighed. There were so many things she wanted to ask. Her mother had left so many unanswered riddles. She wanted to understand what her mother had meant, to know why she had done what she did. Then her memories would no longer be clouded by cold strands of doubt; then she could love her mother without question . . .

The image of the beautiful Royal Beast tenderly cradling its cub under its wing rose into her mind. As it swooped down from the heavens, had it hesitated to control the Toda in order to save its young?

Such were her thoughts as she gazed up into the sky softly tinged with twilight.

THREE

THE GIFT OF THE CUB

I

SWIFT-FOOTED IALU

By the time Ialu laid his piece of sandpaper on the floor, the afternoon sun slanting through the window had turned the color of pale honey. He ran a finger softly along the top of the meticulously sanded drawer and sensed from the touch that it was good. This was the last one. He picked it up and slid it into the dresser. It slipped in snugly, as though sucked inside, and the bottom drawer popped out with a puff of air. Ialu smiled. It was done.

He took the broom from where it leaned against the wall and began sweeping up the wood shavings on the floor. Just then he heard a knock at the door.

"It's me, Yantoku, the cabinetmaker. I've come to deliver your order." Although Ialu recognized the gruff voice of his foster brother, he did not unlock the door immediately. Instead, he stood inside the entrance, listening intently for anything out of the ordinary. Only then did he slowly open the door.

A large man with a ruddy complexion stepped inside bearing lumber in his arms. No sooner had he entered than Ialu closed the door and latched it firmly. Yantoku raised his eyebrows. "As cautious as ever," he said in a teasing tone. "There's no one out there, you know." Ignoring this remark, Ialu led him into the back room. When Yantoku saw the chest of drawers, he laid his load on the floor and went to kneel in front of it. Stroking the wood with knowing hands, he checked the workmanship. Then, still kneeling, he looked over his shoulder at Ialu and grinned.

"Nicely done. No one would doubt me if I told them I'd made it myself. Impressive work from someone who isn't even a carpenter by trade."

"That's because it's just a hobby," Ialu responded quietly. "I can work on it as long as it takes to make it right."

Yantoku stood up, one hand still resting on the dresser. "Right, then. Let's leave it at that. Otherwise I won't be able to hold my head up as a carpenter." He stroked the top once more and then cocked an eyebrow at Ialu. "Are you sure you won't take any payment for it? Work of this quality would fetch at least ten large gold pieces, but you only let me pay for the materials. Don't you want even some of the profit?"

Ialu shook his head. "I don't do this for the money. I do it because I like making things. It gives me pleasure, and if it brings you some profit at the same time, what could be better?"

Yantoku frowned. The room in which they stood was empty but for the dresser and Ialu's tools. Dust motes drifting through the air glinted in the late afternoon sunlight. It seemed to him more like a prison cell than a home. He could not help feeling sorry for his foster brother. *But I bet I'm the only person in the world who pities a member of the Se Zan, the impenetrable shields who guard the royalty . . .*

Ialu was the third-born son of Yantoku's neighbor. He and Yantoku had been raised like brothers among the tumbledown shacks on the back streets behind Sakkala, home to the poorest craftsmen in the royal capital. Ialu's mother had been sickly, and all her children but two, Ialu and his younger sister, had died soon after birth. When Ialu was born, she had been unable to nurse him, and Yantoku's mother, who had just given birth to Yantoku, had suckled them both, holding one in each arm.

Though he was a man of few words, Ialu's father had been a skilled cabinetmaker who had won favor with the master carpenter. If things had gone on without incident, Ialu would have inherited his father's trade, taken a bride, and been raising his own kids by now, just like Yantoku. The day that had so radically changed Ialu's life remained vividly imprinted on Yantoku's memory.

They had been eight at the time. He and Ialu had left home a little before noon bearing packed lunches for their fathers. The two men were working on the interior of a new house being built for a rich merchant. Ordinarily, the boys would rather have played than run errands, but delivering lunch was an important task, and they headed straight for the west side of town where the wealthy merchant class lived.

It was a fine day, and the sun was hot. Puffy white clouds swelled in the blue sky, and the trees that lined the boulevards of the west district cast dark shadows against the white walls of the manors. Ialu and Yantoku had just turned a corner and come into view of the house where their fathers were working when the ground heaved under their feet and began to sway violently, as if some giant creature were shaking itself beneath them. The boys tumbled to the ground. Crawling on all fours, they raised their heads and saw the building begin to tilt. Then, with a shriek of wood against stone, it collapsed. A cloud of dust rose in the air, enveloping the wreckage.

Only when the dust began to clear did the two boys come to their senses and run toward the heap of rubble. Choking on the dust that clogged their noses and throats, they screamed for their fathers as though half crazed.

Yantoku's father had been lucky. He had been standing in the garden when the quake hit. Though covered in a shroud of ash-like dust, he had escaped with only a few scrapes. Ialu's father, however, lay buried beneath the debris. The crimson blood spurting from his nose and mouth seemed strangely vivid against his dust-smeared face.

Ialu froze at the sight. Then he shouted, "I'll get a doctor!" and, turning on his heel, broke into a run. Taken by surprise, Yantoku turned to race after him, but he could not catch up. Ialu ran as if a fire was on his tail, and the distance between them only widened. Still, Yantoku managed to keep him in sight until he reached the main avenue. Just as Ialu's small figure stepped into the street, disaster struck. A horse galloping down the road stumbled on a crack caused by the quake. It crashed to the ground, upsetting the carriage behind it. A horse-drawn coach careening down the street from the opposite direction collided with the overturned carriage in a thunder of noise and slowly toppled over.

Yantoku stared in horror. Ialu was right in the path of the falling coach. Just as it came down on top of him, he kicked the ground with his right foot and pitched forward, twisting his body. Somehow he managed to slip through the tangle of harnesses and wreckage and shimmy over the belly of a horse where it lay convulsing on top of the heap, its legs flailing in the air. Then he leapt off onto the other side and disappeared from sight, leaving Yantoku staring in amazement.

Yantoku was not the only one who had witnessed Ialu's spectacular feat. A member of the Se Zan just happened to be passing and saw it too. Impressed, he hunted Ialu down patiently, arriving at his house five days later while the family was still in the midst of the funeral rites. The elegantly garbed Se Zan offered Ialu's astonished mother enough money to support the family for life, in return for apprenticing Ialu. To his mother, who had lost the family's breadwinner and been left with a baby and an eight-year-old son, this proposal seemed their only hope.

The Se Zan were living shields, existing solely to protect the Yojeh and her family. To guard against any vulnerability, they were forced to sever all ties with their own families and were forbidden to marry. Duty required these solitary warriors to lay down their lives for those they guarded. In return, regardless of the rank into which they had been born, they were treated as nobility and given the honor due to the Yojeh's most loyal subjects. Those who gave their sons into service as Se Zan were rewarded with a large sum of money. Ialu's mother had had no choice but to agree.

Yantoku could still remember the day Ialu had left the home in which he had been born, his hand held firmly by the Se Zan. Yantoku had wept loudly, but Ialu had not uttered a sound. Biting his lip, eyes on the ground, he had left the alleys of Sakkala without once looking back.

They did not meet again until twelve years later. By then, Yantoku was a cabinetmaker in his own right, and he and his father ran a small shop. One day, Ialu had walked in by chance. When he realized who had come out to serve him, his expression hardened, and he made to leave, but Yantoku grabbed his arm. Fortunately, his father had not been in the shop that day, and the apprentices had gone off for lunch. He pleaded with Ialu to stay, promising that he would not tell anyone that they were foster brothers and offering to give him news of his family. Thus began their clandestine friendship.

Ialu, however, appeared to regret having given in to Yantoku's pleas and remained vigilant about concealing their friendship. When Yantoku had teased him for his caution, Ialu had responded without anger. "In my world, compassion is viewed as a weakness that can be used to one's own advantage. There are people out there who would use your life and the lives of your loved ones to bargain with me if they knew that we were close. If you value your family's happiness, don't get involved with me any more than you need to."

The last twelve years of Ialu's life must have been completely different from mine, Yantoku thought. Although there were traces of the old Ialu around his mouth and eyes, at times he exhibited a coolheadedness that reminded Yantoku of a well-honed blade.

Ialu removed his sawdust-covered tunic, folded it and placed it by the wall. Then he turned to Yantoku. "I'll be off duty again in ten days. You can come and get the dresser then, around noon. Bring an apprentice to help you if you want. But make sure you don't tell him my name."

"I know, I know. You don't have to keep warning me . . . Are you leaving for work at this time of day?"

Ialu nodded as he pulled an indigo cloak, the kind worn by artisans, off a hook on the wall. He never wore his uniform until he was inside the palace. Instead, he dressed as a craftsman, his face concealed beneath a conical straw hat, and mingled with the other tradesmen who frequented the palace. As Yantoku turned to depart, leaving Ialu to change, he heard Ialu say, "Take care."

Yantoku grinned. "Of course."

The sky deepened slowly to the blue of twilight, leaving a single streak of sunlight on a cloud. The smell of grilled fish and smoke from the kitchens hovered in the narrow lane through which Ialu walked. He stepped out into a broad avenue crowded with people heading home from work and rowdy groups of men off for a drink at the taverns in Lasan district. Passing an alleyway, he heard shouting. A cluster of men were cursing and kicking a huddled form in the shadow of a stack of wine barrels. A youth of just fifteen or sixteen lay curled up on the ground to protect his stomach from their feet. Ialu frowned but slid his eyes away, pressing his lips tightly together.

Just then he heard familiar footsteps threading their way through the throng. He continued on without slackening his pace. "Hey!" A hand grasped his shoulder. He came to a halt and turned to face a tall, powerfully built man dressed much like him. The faint scent of the perfume used by women in the red light district still clung to his clothes. It was his colleague, Kailu. He regarded Ialu with raised brows. "You're coldhearted. Are you just going to pretend you don't see that?"

Ialu returned his gaze coolly without responding. Kailu clicked his tongue in disgust. "So that's how it is. Well, I don't need your help anyway." He turned on his heel, but Ialu grabbed his elbow.

"Kailu, leave it."

Kailu glared at him. "I'm off duty. Don't try to stop me."

Ialu shook his head. "We are never off duty." The blood rose to Kailu's face, and a muscle in his jaw twitched. "Tomorrow the Aluhan arrives in the capital," Ialu continued. "Anything could happen. Surely you haven't forgotten Ossalu? If you still insist on going despite that, then do as you please." He removed his hand from Kailu's elbow, and Kailu shook his arm in irritation.

"I'm not so stupid as to let an assassin disguised as a hoodlum kill me like Ossalu," he snapped. Still, he turned away from the alley and fell into step beside Ialu. The two walked silently up the gentle slope toward the palace. The forest surrounding it was covered in a soft halo of new leaves backlit by the dwindling glow of dusk.

As they walked, Kailu blurted out, "What a lousy way of life."

At this, Ialu came to an abrupt halt. Kailu, who had kept on walking, turned to look at him. "What?"

"If you don't like it," Ialu said in a low voice, "then get out. Now. Renounce your vows. You can't possibly do the work of a Se Zan with any trace of doubt in your mind."

"But—"

Ialu cut him off. "There's no point in continuing if you feel that way. You'll just be miserable, right?"

Kailu returned his gaze steadily. "What about you, then?"

A sad smile touched Ialu's eyes. "Me? I've killed too many people to let myself doubt now."

Silenced, Kailu followed him. He had never heard his comrade talk like this before. Ialu had a quiet air, reminiscent of a forest in winter. When dressed in tradesmen's clothes, he looked like nothing more than an ordinary craftsman. No one passing them now would ever suspect that this was the swift-footed Ialu. But as soon as he was on duty, he became an agile warrior. True, he had killed more men than any other Se Zan . . . But that was because he was the first to notice danger and therefore the first to dispatch an adversary. The assassin was usually dead before anyone else realized what was going on.

There were times when Kailu was sure his comrade must have eyes in the back of his head. Not having killed yet, he had envied Ialu's prowess. Until now. In the dying light, the long shadows of the trees fell across Ialu's back. Kailu watched him wordlessly as they walked toward the palace.

2

THE YOJEH AND THE ALUHAN

Shunan felt the breeze caress his cheek as he descended from the carriage. As it passed, it rustled the newly unfurled leaves on the branches, causing the light to shimmer. Before him spread a forest so silent it was hard to believe the bustle of the city lay just behind him. Birds warbled somewhere deep within.

This was the Immaculate Forest—the forest where the Yojeh resided—and there was something decidedly sacred about it. Standing on the white path that led to the palace, Shunan placed both palms to his forehead and bowed low in reverence.

His thoughts were disturbed by the sound of his father clearing his throat. Assisted by a member of his retinue, the Aluhan stepped down from the coach and, turning his sullen face toward the palace, bowed formally. From this point onward, not even the Grand Duke was permitted to ride in a coach: He must proceed on foot. He set off with his son down the stretch of white sand, his guards walking in front and behind. A large procession of attendants followed silently, bearing gifts of precious metalwork, elaborate brocades, and clocks ornamented with coral and pearl, brought all the way from the seat of the Aluhan to celebrate the Yojeh's birthday. The soldiers who had accompanied the Grand Duke thus far remained behind with heads bowed as the procession disappeared into the forest.

The white sand path glittered in the sunlight that filtered through the trees. After walking for some distance, the palace finally came into view. It was a maze of buildings, extending far behind the visible façade, with walls of huge planks of unvarnished wood and connecting passageways roofed in blue ceramic tiles. There were no ramparts nor any gates or guards to protect it. Each time he came, Shunan found himself in awe. Although rebuilt only fifty-seven years ago, it looked ancient, more like a shrine to a god than the seat of a ruler.

The palace in which he had been born and raised was at least ten times the size, and its luxurious interior had been crafted by the finest artisans. A deep moat guarded its walls, vigilant soldiers manned its stout ramparts round the clock, and forbidding gates towered at its entrance, impressing upon any would-be enemies the castle's impenetrability.

With his eyes fixed on his father's back, Shunan's thoughts turned to what he knew must be on his father's mind. The heavy sacrifices made by generations of faithful Aluhan for its protection were the sole reason the Yojeh's palace required no defenses. "The Yojeh's subjects," his father often said, "dismiss us as upstart warriors tainted with blood. But without us, they could enjoy no peace nor remain safe from the aggression of their neighbors. We willingly ride the Toda, which they consider unclean, and defile ourselves with blood, so that this country may prosper and the Yojeh may live enshrined in this sacred forest without sullying her hands."

This, Shunan knew, was true.

Long ago, when the Yojeh's ancestor had first appeared, the kingdom had been on the verge of extinction. The crown prince of that era had feared his younger brother would rise up against him when he took the throne, so he slew him and massacred his followers. His nephew, however, escaped, and when he reached manhood, he led the nobility against the king to avenge his father's death. The two sides were evenly matched, and many died in the prolonged struggle, including the king and his nephew. When the land teetered on the brink of destruction and the people's spirits lay broken, Jeh, the Royal Ancestor and the first Yojeh, crossed the Afon Noah into the corpse-strewn plains.

Wherever Jeh went, a Royal Beast hovered protectively overhead, and whenever she came to a river, the Toda bowed their necks before her, forming a bridge for her to cross. To the local people, this tall woman with her shining hair and golden eyes appeared to be a noble goddess. They prostrated themselves before her and begged her to stay and live among them. This plea she granted. Like a loving mother, she gathered together all the nobles, craftsmen, merchants, and farmers who had been scattered by the war, and rebuilt the country from its foundations. This was the beginning of the Divine Kingdom of Lyoza.

Peace reigned for many long years, lasting until the rule of the Royal Ancestor's great-granddaughter. Then, the neighboring kingdom of Hajan rose up to invade Lyoza. Jeh's great-granddaughter, however, refused to fight back. Under the law of the gods, it was an unpardonable sin to stain one's hands with another's blood; anyone who violated this law was forbidden to pass into the paradise of Afon Aluma after death. Rather than let her people suffer the consequences of such a heinous crime, the ruler offered to surrender herself to the enemy. One of her retainers, however, stopped her. This was Yaman Hasalu, Shunan's ancestor. "Even should you give your life," he reasoned, "your sacrifice would be meaningless, for the Hajan will never understand why you would do this. It is your people who will suffer if the Hajan conquer us. Allow me to accept defilement in order to defend this country. I swear I will live thereafter in exile so that no stain shall fall upon the royal capital. For the sake of your people, I beg you to give me the divine treasure, the Toda Whistle."

Deeming his intentions to be sincere, Jeh's great-granddaughter granted his wish. Yaman led his troops to the great Amasalu River and used the whistle to ride the Toda through the waters and over land to destroy the Hajan army. Once he had vanquished the enemy, he kept his vow and, without returning to the capital, went to live on the other side of the mountains so that Lyoza would remain undefiled.

Touched by his faithfulness and sincerity, the ruler of Lyoza interceded on his behalf, granting him laku la, absolution for deliberately choosing defilement to protect the lives of others. Through her intercession, those who fought to save their people could now be cleansed at death and enter Afon Aluma, wrapped in pure light. She bestowed upon Yaman the title of Aluhan, Grand Duke, and allowed him to govern a region across the mountains.

The first cracks in this relationship emerged in the time of Yaman's grandson, Oshiku Hasalu. Oshiku reared herds of Toda and organized the Toda Riders into powerful fighting units. With these, he subdued neighboring countries, expanding his domain and accumulating wealth. Each time he swallowed up another kingdom, he sent the ruler of Lyoza gold, silver, and jewels, as well as many rare and precious treasures. The ruler, however, considered such trophies to be unclean and refused to accept them.

She also commanded Oshiku to stop invading other lands, but he refused to obey. The countries surrounding Lyoza, he argued, were just waiting for a chance to attack. True peace and security could only be obtained by subjugating these territories and spreading the belief that killing was a sin. Besides, more territory would give the people access to a greater variety of goods, and more subjects would mean greater prosperity for all.

Although at first the ruler of Lyoza dismissed this reasoning as dangerous, she could not ignore the fact that many of her subjects were secretly migrating across the mountains. With its broad and fertile plains crossed by numerous rivers, the Grand Duke's territory covered the best farmland, and under his policies, bustling towns sprang up and trade thrived so that even the common folk prospered. In comparison, the land where the ruler lived was mountainous, harvests were erratic, and trade was far from robust. When she learned that some of her people were almost starving, the ruler relented. She stopped rejecting Oshiku's gifts and instead accepted them, to share with those who lived on her side of the mountains.

At some point, the people began to call this army-less ruler the Yojeh. They continued to worship her as the soul of their country—the pure one who brought the kingdom divine protection. For this reason, her subjects referred to the goods they gave her as "offerings" rather than as "tax." In her hands rested the authority to make final judicial decisions, and it was she who commanded district and central officials and who governed affairs of state.

It was the Aluhan, however, who controlled the army and held the wealth of the country in his grasp. With this division between authority and power, friction was inevitable. Those who lived in Aluhan territory had come to see themselves as the backbone of the country. After all, it was they who shed their blood and deliberately accepted defilement so that Lyoza could prosper. It rankled that the officials dispatched by the Yojeh and the people living in her territory, despite being noticeably poorer than those in Aluhan territory, looked at them with disdain and called them "Wajaks" for staining their hands with blood and intermarrying with those they conquered.

Discontent gave birth to a rebel group known as Sai Gamulu, literally "blood and filth," whose members wished to see the Aluhan made king of Lyoza. They blamed the divisions in the country on the Yojeh and saw her as an obstacle to development. To eliminate her and place the Aluhan on the throne, they believed, was the only road to prosperity for the Divine Kingdom. It was a thwarted assassination attempt that finally caused the Yojeh to acquire her own bodyguards.

The incident occurred during the reign of the Yojeh Sheemiya, grandmother of the current Yojeh, Halumiya. Had it not been for a faithful servant, who shielded her from an assassin's blow at the cost of his own life, the Yojeh would have died. Worse still, her attackers set the palace on fire. Once again, it was through the desperate efforts of loyal servants that she managed to escape alive. Three-year-old Halumiya was rescued along with her, but the Yojeh's daughter, Meemiya, perished in the flames.

This tragedy shook the kingdom of Lyoza to the core. It signaled the end of an era in which the division between authority and power lay hidden beneath a veneer of friendship, and exposed the strained relationship to the light of day. The fact that anyone would want their ruler dead shocked not only those who lived in Yojeh territory, but also those who lived in Aluhan territory. While they might resent being looked down upon, the majority revered the Yojeh as a pure and selfless descendant of the gods.

The Yojeh summoned the Aluhan, Lamashiku, to her palace and announced that if he insisted on killing her people and trying to control the country for personal gain, she would revoke laku la. This caused Lamashiku to tremble with fear. To die without being cleansed from defilement was to be condemned to Hikala. And besides, he, too, revered the Yojeh. The Aluhan already had wealth and power. While he might covet the throne, he knew that without the support of the gods, kingship would be far too heavy a burden for him to bear. He swore to the Yojeh that he had no ambition to rule and no connection with the Sai Gamulu. In fact, he vowed to hunt down and execute those misguided souls.

But the Sai Gamulu could not be rooted out. Like a rotting swamp in which rank foam oozes to the top, sympathy for the cause continued to fester beneath the surface. The invisible group of assassins survived like a smoldering fire, slipping beneath the blanket intended to smother it only to burst out elsewhere. Its members swore an iron oath never to reveal their allegiance to it, even on pain of death. People from all walks of life, from farmers and merchants to the Yojeh's own retainers, were rumored to have joined its ranks. The diverse backgrounds of those who died trying to kill the Yojeh seemed to verify this. The movement was also intimately connected to the nobility and high-ranking officials. For those hindered from increasing their wealth because the Yojeh judged such intentions to be impure, the Sai Gamulu were very convenient assassins.

Clearly, the awe in which the Yojeh was held as the descendant of the holy one who first crossed the Afon Noah was no longer enough to protect her. Sheemiya therefore chose from among her most faithful servants those who excelled at martial arts, and assigned them to protect her and her granddaughter Halumiya, the future Yojeh. This was the origin of the Se Zan.

Shunan was acutely aware of where he stood in the history of his country, and of the responsibility he was expected to bear. As the eldest son, he must succeed his father as the Aluhan. The brooding face of his younger brother, Nugan, left behind in their castle, flitted through his mind. Though Nugan never said so, Shunan knew that he must curse his position as the younger son, fated to spend his life in service to his elder brother. But in this age, when dissension could be felt even among the common people, the rank of Aluhan was not as enviable as Nugan imagined. Though Shunan knew his father's wishes and why he valued his eldest son, in his own heart, he harbored a different dream.

As he followed the lady-in-waiting along the wooden corridor, moving ever deeper into the palace, a gleam of anticipation kindled in his eyes, and he could not keep his heart from racing. In a few moments, I'll be in the presence of Princess Seimiya. Has she changed in this last year? In the dim light, Shunan, young heir to the Aluhan, prayed his father would not notice the blush that rose in his cheeks.

When the Aluhan and his eldest son were ushered into the dining room, Yojeh Halumiya was already seated at a large dining table laden with food for the celebration. With her were her granddaughter, the princess Seimiya, and her nephew, Damiya. Ialu and the other Se Zan stood behind the Yojeh and the princess, their eyes sharp and alert, ready to protect them at a moment's notice.

The Yojeh and her family rose, smiling in welcome. "Aluhan, Shunan," the Yojeh said. "Thank you so much for coming." It was her sixtieth birthday, but despite her white hair, she stood tall and straight, and her skin was so smooth it was hard to believe her age.

The Aluhan and Shunan knelt before her, pressing both palms to their foreheads as they bowed low. "Great Yojeh Halumiya, allow me to congratulate you on the anniversary of your birth," the Aluhan said in his deep voice.

"Thank you . . . Now please, let us dispense with protocol. Come to the table. They served the dishes a little too soon. We'll have to hurry if we are to eat before the meal grows cold."

Shunan rose with his father and sat down in the place prepared for him. The Yojeh spoke kindly and easily to everyone, as if they were family. Her manner differed entirely from any of the rulers he had met during his travels with his father. She has no need to maintain her dignity through formalities, Shunan thought. Even when she smiled with the warm affection of a grandmother, something in her golden eyes naturally subdued people. Her granddaughter Seimiya had inherited this same air of being wide open to all those she met without allowing familiarity. But Seimiya, who had just turned sixteen and had yet to acquire the Yojeh's life experience, had a fresh, almost precarious quality that reminded him of a butterfly newly emerged from its cocoon.

Shunan suddenly noticed that the princess had turned her brown eyes and bright smile on him, and he felt his heart begin to beat wildly.

The Yojeh looked him up and down, her expression gentle. "What a fine young man you've become, Shunan," she said. "It's hard to believe that the little boy you once were has already turned twenty. No wonder I'm growing old. You're a head taller than your father, too."

"Thank you," Shunan responded, feeling nervous. "I passed Father in height three years ago."

Damiya, the Yojeh's nephew, said with a grin, "You've grown in more than body, Shunan. The look you gave Seimiya just now is proof that you're a man."

It was just the sort of remark Damiya would make. He loved to make light of everything, but his words wiped the smiles from the faces of Shunan and his father. The Aluhan turned to him with frowning eyes and opened his mouth to speak when Seimiya said in a clear, light voice, "You know what Uncle Damiya is like, Shunan. Don't pay any attention. He just loves to tease. I've told him a hundred times to stop, but he never listens." With this she glared at Damiya, who merely smiled and raised his eyebrows.

The rank of Yojeh was passed from mother to daughter—a tradition derived from the first royal ancestor, the tall, stately woman who had come from beyond the Afon Noah. Thus, even though he was the Yojeh Halumiya's own nephew, Damiya could never succeed to her position. Far from being troubled by this fact, however, he appeared to relish the carefree nature of his standing. Though close to thirty, he remained single. Tall and handsome and fond of women, he was notorious for his affairs, not only with aristocratic widows but also with common maids. Yet even should such dalliances result in the birth of a daughter, no one but Seimiya's daughter would have the right to become the next Yojeh.

Damiya used his relatively unfettered position to advantage, traveling widely in place of the Yojeh. He had visited the Aluhan's castle many times. His observations were extremely helpful to the Yojeh in making decisions. The Yojeh's line produced mysteriously few offspring, only one or, at the most, two children. Seimiya was the only daughter of Halumiya's only daughter. She had lost both parents ten years ago in an unfortunate accident when their carriage had crashed into a tree, and since that time, her grandmother, the Yojeh Halumiya, had raised her as if she were her own daughter. Whereas Halumiya was broad-minded and decisive, Seimiya was more reserved and inclined to mull things over carefully. Damiya was the one person with whom she could relax. Although he was, accurately speaking, her cousin rather than her uncle, they were on such comfortable terms that she called him "Uncle."

Damiya might appear flippant on the surface, but he was quick-witted and adroit at drawing out those things that Seimiya found difficult to confide in her grandmother. He would point out an aspect that she had not considered and turn her worry into laughter. He insisted that one was bound to find a better solution by being optimistic and carefree than by worrying all the time. But Seimiya could not adopt such an easygoing attitude—not when she considered the damage that she, as the designated future Yojeh, could cause to the entire nation by a single mistake in judgment.

Nor could those around her help being cautious in the way they treated her. The man she married would be the father of the next Yojeh, and therefore the Aluhan could not dismiss Damiya's jest lightly. Scowling, he gave Damiya a hard stare. "It's true my son is now a grown man. No man could look upon the princess's beautiful face and not be affected. But I'll have you know that my son knows his place."

Halumiya sighed. "Of course, Aluhan. We've never doubted that. Come," she continued brightly, "let's think of other things. It's my sixtieth birthday after all—although I'd rather not announce my age very loudly." She turned to her chamberlain. "The preparations must be ready by now. Open the big window." The chamberlain raised his head and signaled to the servants aligned on the south side of the banquet room. The window opened with a loud noise, and the bright spring light flowed into the room. Shunan squinted his eyes against the glare.

Petals fluttered into the room, carried on the cool breeze. The sasha trees that lined the edge of the enormous garden were in full bloom, their branches bowing under a profusion of delicate white flowers. The whole garden was bathed in a soft light, as if to celebrate the sixtieth birthday of this frank old woman born in the spring so many years ago.

3

THE GIFT OF THE CUB

A banquet had been laid out in the garden on tables set in a semicircle facing the hall. There, the many nobles who had gathered to celebrate the Yojeh's birthday were seated in order of rank. Food-laden plates were being carried to the tables, and the assembled guests were enveloped by the delicious aroma, which mingled with the fragrance of the flowers. A white felt carpet had been spread over the lawn in the center of the garden where graceful maidens waving pink silk ribbons danced to the lively accompaniment of a band of musicians. The capital's best jesters had also been gathered, drawing laughter with their banter and keeping the party well entertained.

Evening approached, and the Golden Hour arrived, when the world was bathed in a golden glow. Dawn and sunset represented the boundary between the Time of Life and the Time of Death; that point in time when spirits were most fulfilled. The musicians and dancers withdrew, and the white carpet was removed. A solemn mood fell over the banquet. The Yojeh rose and stepped up onto the broad dais that overlooked the garden. The people bowed their heads. Raising her arms wide, she closed her eyes and began reciting a prayer of gratitude to the gods who ruled heaven and earth for protecting her for sixty long years.

When she opened her eyes, the sound of a flute could be heard from deep inside the garden. Everyone turned to look as several strong men appeared pulling a huge cart. It rumbled as it rolled into sight. More carts followed until sixteen carts had formed a line, leaving ample space between each one. The crowd stirred, and those sitting in the back rose partway out of their seats, straining to see the creatures within. Sixteen Royal Beasts, their wings catching the golden light, faced the Yojeh. Their feet were chained securely to the carts and, although they occasionally flapped their wings, they did not fly into the air.

Even when raised from birth by human hands, Royal Beasts could never be tamed. Yet captive beasts never flew, even after their wings were fully formed. They simply sat there, awesome and silent, emitting an aura distinct from any other beasts. The fact that their handlers stood alert and ready to use the Silent Whistle at any time was because they knew only too well just how fearsome they could be. There was no guarantee that they would not rip their chains asunder should something upset them.

All the guests at the banquet had seen a Royal Beast before, yet today the murmur of the crowd was louder than usual. There was a cub among the others. It seemed very young, still covered in downy fur and only as tall as the bellies of the mature Beasts on either side. It appeared to be very uneasy. Brought to an unfamiliar place, it now found itself exposed to the eyes of many strangers. It flapped its wings repeatedly and kept turning its head, gazing around anxiously.

Putting down his glass, the Yojeh's nephew Damiya walked over to the Yojeh and bowed. "Most honorable Aunt, please accept this birthday gift from your unworthy nephew."

Her eyes still on the beast, the Yojeh murmured, "So you are the one who captured this cub."

"Yes. I present it to you with a prayer for a long-lasting reign."

The Yojeh nodded. "Thank you."

Ialu watched the entire banquet as though he were gazing at a moving picture. It was a method he had acquired naturally once he began guarding the Yojeh as a Se Zan. Mentally he stepped back and opened himself to everything around him, never letting any single point capture his attention. When he allowed himself to feel the whole picture like this, even in the midst of the confusion of this banquet, he could sense the instant something was out of place, like a post disturbing the flow of water in a stream.

Today, too, he watched. But when the Royal Beasts appeared, he could not help but look at them, despite the knowledge that any distraction would give enemies an opening. They were beautiful beasts, yet the sight of them always inspired in him a feeling of pity. The young ones in particular wrenched his heart. Ialu slid his eyes away and glanced at the Yojeh. Her expression startled him. For a brief instant, pain crossed her face. Her look was not that of someone who found power in bending these Royal Beasts to her command. Feeling that he had seen something he shouldn't, Ialu turned his gaze straight ahead and pulled himself together, opening his senses once again to his surroundings.

The presence of the cub among the Royal Beasts disturbed the air. The other Beasts beat their wings and swayed from side to side, as if the cub's anxiety was contagious. Each time the large wings flapped, blossoms fell from the sasha trees lining the edge of the garden and swirled in the air, concealing the crowd and the banquet in a blizzard of petals. Ialu frowned. He did not know what, but he had felt something . . . Wings rising, up, then down . . . A blizzard of petals . . . A space, wide open, just above the cub, which stood shorter than the beasts around it . . . He saw the Beast Handler on the far right raise the Silent Whistle to his lips. It made no sound, but in the next instant, the Royal Beasts stopped moving.

Just as their wings froze, something glinted in the top of a sasha tree behind the beasts. Ialu nocked an arrow to his bow and leapt out in front of the Yojeh, shooting toward the tree. At the same moment, a shaft loosed by an invisible assassin nicked the cub's shoulder and then sank into Ialu's abdomen. The cub's shrieks shook the garden as blood spurted from its shoulder. A black shadow fell from the sasha tree, landing with a thud like soft, ripe fruit.

"Ialu!"

He heard someone shout his name, but the arrow lodged in his stomach made it impossible to breathe. A cold sweat broke out on his face and he crumpled to his knees, his mouth open. He could not breathe. He grasped the arrow shaft in his hand and wheezed as air rattled in his throat. Everything seemed to be turning dark.

"Ialu! Ialu!"

Listening to his name, he slipped into the blackness.

When his mind rose at last from a pit of spinning darkness, his body felt numb and leaden.

Someone spoke. "Are you awake?"

Ialu opened his eyes and focused on the owner of that voice. A doctor looked down at him. "Can you hear me?"

Ialu blinked to show that he could. His stomach felt as stiff and hard as a board, and the pain was both dull and sharp. He did not feel like speaking.

"You're going to be all right," the doctor said cheerfully. "You were incredibly lucky. The arrow lodged itself in the muscle without even grazing any of your organs. It must have lost some of its momentum when it struck the Beast . . . You owe that cub your life, you know." He went on to explain how he had treated the wound and how long Ialu would need bed rest. Then he took a spoonful of tisane and tipped it into Ialu's mouth. "Swallow that carefully, like you're licking something, so that it doesn't get into your lungs."

Ialu did as he was told, swallowing slowly, only to feel hot pain run through his stomach. The thought that he would have to endure this agony every time he tried to eat or drink was depressing. The doctor told him to get plenty of rest and then left the room. There must have been a sedative in the tisane, Ialu thought. He was overcome with a drowsiness that sucked him back down into darkness. As he descended that dark slope, the events before and after the assassin loosed his arrow played out in his mind. Those scenes bothered him. He had had a vague feeling that something was out of place at the time, and now it came back to him distinctly.

The Beast Handler. Why had he blown the Silent Whistle? And why had his eyes been drawn to that particular Handler, the one on the far right of the Beasts?

The last thing he remembered before everything dissolved once again into darkness was the blood spurting from the cub's shoulder and the sound of its scream.

While the Royal Beasts were being presented to the Yojeh on her birthday, the Toda were being paraded in the Aluhan's castle far away. The Aluhan's younger son, Nugan, had been left in charge during his father's absence. He stood watching the parade, his back erect, leaning on the hilt of his favorite sword, a crude and hefty weapon, the tip of which rested on the ground. In the courtyard, the Toda changed battle formations to the beat of a drum. With each movement, dust whirled in the air and their sweet, musk-like scent wafted toward him. The heat of excitement stirred within him every time he smelled it. He found it far more thrilling to watch the Toda devour their prey than to embrace a woman.

If only I could use the invincible Toda as I pleased. Then we'd have nothing to fear from any other country.

As a child, Nugan had worshipped the first Aluhan, Yaman Hasalu, the hero who had arisen to save the Yojeh and this country, who had ridden the Toda across the plains to destroy the enemy, not for personal gain but for the ruler and her people. His way of life had been so pure and beautiful. The first time Nugan had heard the story, it had moved him to tears, and his whole body had trembled with emotion. Laying a large hand on his head and stroking his hair, his father had said, "Grow up to be like Yaman." But at his coming-of-age ceremony, when Nugan had voiced his longing to emulate his hero, his father had snorted. "Are you still talking such nonsense?" he had jeered. Nugan vividly remembered the burning rage he had felt.

Unable to direct his anger at his father, he had vented it in military training. The Yojeh's nephew, Damiya, happened to be visiting. One day, while watching Nugan practice, he seemed to intuit Nugan's feelings. Nugan could recall the day Damiya had first spoken to him as if it were yesterday. He had never really liked the man. While he respected the sacred blood that ran in his veins, he scorned his slender build and effeminate beauty, not to mention the fact that his frequent visits were attributed to a dalliance with one of the castle chef's daughters.

But that day, he had found Damiya to be far more broad-minded than he had ever guessed. "When people are exposed to corruption for so long," Damiya had said with a friendly smile, "it's only natural that they are ashamed to have lofty aspirations. What really matters is the degree to which you can maintain such aspirations despite the corruption around you . . . Nugan, don't ever lose your admiration for Yaman Hasalu."

Nugan still treasured those words in his heart. How could anyone consider it immature to admire the life of Yaman Hasalu? Now he understood that his father and brother, far from being wise and noble, had ulterior motives. While on the one hand they condemned those assassins who sought to remove the Yojeh as disloyal, on the other, they let them carry on without interference. Obviously, they must secretly hope to take the Yojeh's place one day. Nugan could not bear the thought that he, who had inherited the true spirit of the Aluhan, should be forced to live as their vassal for the rest of his life.

If only I could hate my brother, he thought. Then he could dream of deposing him and succeeding to his station. But he loved Shunan. Although his brother's patience toward his own selfishness and defiance frequently annoyed him, Nugan found it impossible to dislike him. Whenever he thought about hating his brother, his mind always went round in circles, as if he were lost in a maze.

The demonstration finished and Nugan was turning to go back into the castle when a Toda merchant who had been waiting on the edge of the courtyard approached him. "Your pardon, my lord," he said.

Nugan stopped and looked down at him. "What do you want?" he asked.

The man bowed low and held out a letter. "I was asked to deliver this message into your hands. Please take it."

Nugan frowned as he took it. It had no seal or other mark to identify the sender. He ripped it open roughly and spread out the neatly folded sheet of paper. As he read it, a strange light began to gleam in his eyes. By the time he had finished reading it, his face was white. He folded it up again and slipped it into the breast of his robe. Then he looked at the bearer. "And just what is your relationship with the sender?" he asked.

"I humbly beg your pardon, but I am not permitted to speak of that."

Nugan glared at this impudence and said in a low voice, "I could have you apprehended and tortured to get that information from you, you know."

The man's face stiffened, but he answered quietly, "If you did so, the sender would interpret that to mean that you reject his proposal. Is that what you wish?"

Nugan clenched his fists. He must judge carefully where the path before him might lead. He must avoid making a hasty decision. Yet even so, he felt a rush of exhilaration, as if he had finally glimpsed an exit from the maze in which he had been trapped.

FOUR

KAZALUMU, THE ROYAL BEAST SANCTUARY

I

JOEUN'S SON

The foal staggered up onto spindly legs and thrust its head under its mother's belly. Butting its nose against her teat, it began guzzling milk. Joeun's face relaxed. He glanced at Elin where she stood beside the foal. "Thank goodness that's over," he said. "They should be all right now."

He had been reluctant for the mare to foal, but Elin had insisted that it wasn't fair to prevent Totchi from experiencing motherhood. She now had three hives of her own, and the income from the honey they produced was hers. When Joeun learned that she had set aside enough to pay for a stallion to service the mare, he finally relented. The owner of the horse Joeun borrowed each summer came to help them when Totchi's time drew near. It was just bad luck that on the very day the mare went into labor, the farmer's son had cut himself with a hoe. Joeun and Elin had been up all night trying inexpertly to help with the mare's first foaling.

"You've got straw in your hair," Joeun said. Elin smiled and reached up to pull a wisp of straw from her head. She had grown considerably taller in the last four years. Although her limbs were still as thin as sticks, her slim figure was becoming more feminine. Joeun watched her as she smiled fondly at the foal and its mother, and realized once again that she was changing from a child into a woman.

Each time he noticed, he worried that the absence of a mother in her life might be a bad thing. She did not seem aware that she was steadily climbing the ladder to womanhood. Although old enough to wear her hair up, she still cut it in a shoulder-length bob, and she insisted on making her clothes from his hand-me-downs because, as she put it, "I won't have to worry about getting my clothes dirty."

Looking at other girls her age in town, he worried that he had failed to raise Elin properly. But how could he help her be like them when he had never raised a daughter of his own? If she was still like this when she reached marriageable age, he wondered if she would ever find happiness. Though not beautiful, her features were fresh and pleasing. Yet she had a certain air that kept others at a distance, and when lost in thought, her stillness—like a lake deep in the mountains—made it hard to believe she was only fourteen. Still, she was never moody, and her smile was like a ray of sunshine that pierced the clouds and lit up the world around her.

"You must be tired," Joeun said. "Go wash up and get some sleep."

Elin shook her head. "I want to stay a bit longer. You should get some rest yourself."

Joeun stretched, with a groan. "All right, I will then. I must be getting old. When I was younger, missing a night's sleep never bothered me . . . Don't overdo it though, Elin."

She nodded and began rubbing the sweat gently from Totchi's neck.

Joeun stepped out of the stable into the brilliant sunshine and drew in a deep breath of spring air fragrant with the scent of warm earth and soft green buds. At that moment, a fierce pain shot from his chest to his back. It was as if someone had clamped his heart in an iron fist and was squeezing it tight. Unable to breathe, he clasped his hands to his chest and fell to his knees in the grass. Cold beads of sweat dripped down his face as he struggled against the pain. Slowly the agony dissipated, but the dark cloud of fear that spread through his breast in its wake kept him on his knees.

The pain he had just experienced was no trifling matter. Recently, he had noticed his heart racing at times, for no reason, and occasionally felt short of breath or a pressure in his chest. But that violent pain had been a clear warning that something was wrong. He put his hands on his knees and rose slowly to his feet, wiping the sweat from his forehead with his hand.

Perhaps I'm getting closer to the end than I thought. Will death come for me like that, suddenly, without warning? He stood numbly in the yard bathed in spring light. If it does, what will happen to Elin? Though mature for her age, she was still a child. He pressed a hand to his mouth and closed his eyes. He could see all too vividly the bleak future that awaited a girl as young as her if she were cast out into the world without a protector. He had better consider to whom he could entrust her care when he died. He had expected to have more time than this, but clearly he had better think about it now, and without delay.

He opened his eyes and crossed the yard with heavy steps. As he went round the corner of his house, he was startled by the sound of a horse snorting. Someone was standing in front of the door—a young man, dressed in clothes that would normally be seen only in the capital. At the sight of his face, Joeun stopped in his tracks.

"Asan . . ."

A frown creased the young man's forehead. The two stood motionless, staring at one another. Finally the young man spoke.

"Hello, Father."

When Elin met the young man who was Joeun's son, she saw in his face an old, familiar expression—the one she had seen on her grandfather's face every time he had looked at her or her mother, a mask that concealed the same thought. What is an Ahlyo doing here, acting as if she were kin?

She bowed her head to the floor in formal greeting. "Pleased to meet you," she said. "I'm Elin." Asan nodded brusquely and then turned to speak with Joeun without addressing a single word to her.

"Father, please think it over. Mother and I aren't the only ones who have been waiting all this time for your reputation to be restored. The teachers and students at the school are longing for you to return, too." Joeun sat with his head bowed and stared at the floor without responding. "Tosalielu has agreed to restore your honor. This is a wonderful opportunity. Takalan has been ruined, charged with treason against the Yojeh. He'll never meddle in the affairs of the school again. Please, Father! Come back. It's what everyone wants!"

Joeun raised his head and gazed at his son. "Would you give me some time to think about it?"

Asan scowled. "But, Father! What's there to think about? You were the headmaster of the most prestigious school in the kingdom. Do you intend to live out the rest of your life secluded in the mountains like this?" A trace of a smile crossed Joeun's face as he regarded his son. With an exasperated look, Asan thrust his chin in Elin's direction. "If you're worried about the girl, I'll convince Mother for you. We can take her in until she comes of age and then find her a husband from the artisan class. As a foster daughter of the Tohsana family, she should have no problem making a match."

Joeun turned his eyes on Elin. She looked down and did not meet his gaze. He remained silent for a long time, but when he spoke, it was only to say once again, "Let me think about it."

Asan left, promising to return in ten days' time. After calmly finishing the day's work and clearing up after supper, Elin slipped out of the house and went into the stable. She hung the lantern she carried on a post, and the foal blinked as though dazzled. It was already surprisingly steady on its legs. Totchi nuzzled it lovingly. As Elin stood leaning against the railing, gazing at the pair, she heard footsteps. Joeun came up beside her and rested his elbows on the top of the railing. The two stood silently for some time just watching the foal with its dam.

Finally, Joeun broke the silence. "Forgive Asan, Elin. He has never lived anywhere but the school in the capital. He's an honest man, but he cares a bit too much about honor and rank . . ."

Elin turned to look at him. "You were the headmaster of a school?"

Joeun smiled. "I never told you, did I? . . . I guess because when I met you, I felt that I was starting my life over. I decided then and there to forget the twenty years I had spent as a teacher and the other twelve as headmaster at Tamuyuan, the school for boys of the skilled artisan class. I made up my mind to spend the rest of my days as an ordinary beekeeper, adopting the speech and attitudes of a peasant."

He paused to rub a hand over the old scar on his chin and then continued quietly. "I like teaching children. I didn't become a teacher just to follow in my father's footsteps. For me, it was a calling. Of course, because I liked it, I was passionate about it. I'm pretty sure I was considered a good teacher. Otherwise, why would I be appointed headmaster at only forty years of age? Everything in my life seemed perfect . . . until that one incident."

Joeun shifted his eyes to the foal without seeing it. "A teacher should treat each pupil fairly. But teachers are only human. It's hard not to give more attention to students who excel at their studies, especially if they are good people. One of my students was a boy named Neekana. He wasn't from a wealthy family, but he was extremely bright and had a cheerful disposition. One of my other students was Saman, the son of a wealthy bureaucrat named Takalan. I just could not like Saman, even though I knew that as a teacher I should treat all my students equally."

Joeun frowned. "He lied so smoothly, you see, as if he were telling the truth. Cruel lies intended to get others into trouble. He was jealous and had an excessive amount of pride . . ." He paused, as if to swallow a bitter taste that rose in his mouth. "The marks on the final exams determined whether the young men in the graduating class could assume the job or post that they desired. Saman, of course, intended to become a high-ranking bureaucrat, just like his father. But his marks were far below standard. It was my job to grade the final exams. When Neekana received the highest mark, it made me very happy. He, too, had been aiming to become a bureaucrat, and with that mark, he would have no problem."

Joeun's mouth twisted. "But the night before the grades were to be announced, Saman and his father came to my house. Saman accused Neekana of threatening him. Neekana, he said, had told him not to answer the questions correctly, that if he got a good grade on the exam, Neekana would tell all Saman's friends about the lies he had told. I laughed out loud. Neekana was far smarter than Saman. Why on earth would he need to threaten him? The idea was ridiculous. I said as much, although more gently than that, because his father was there. But his father was furious. His son, he insisted, could not possibly be lying. Why would Saman tell a lie that revealed he had deceived other students? He demanded that I fail Neekana and give his son the grade he needed to become a bureaucrat. I refused adamantly."

He closed his lips and fell silent for a moment. Then, forcing the words out, he continued. "That night, Saman killed himself." Elin looked up at Joeun with a start. There was a darkness in his expression that she had never seen before. "Takalan blamed me. He claimed that if I had believed in his son, Saman would not have killed himself. He said I was unfit to be headmaster of Tamuyuan because I clearly favored Neekana over his son. Prince Tosalielu, who owned the school, had no choice but to dismiss me from my post."

Joeun looked at Elin sardonically. "To be honest, I still think that Saman killed himself out of spite. Governed by his inflated pride, he would have fiercely resented the fact that I didn't take his words seriously. I think he killed himself to hurt me for not believing him, to make me pay for it . . . But, Elin, that is precisely the kind of person a teacher really needs to teach." His eyes were filled with pain. "I did everything I could to protect a capable student, but I abandoned Saman without a second thought, simply because I disliked him. Even after he died, I still could not stand him. And I would certainly have abandoned him again if the gods had turned back time. Knowing that about myself shocked me far more than my dismissal."

Totchi snorted loudly, and Joeun turned his eyes back to the horses. After some time, he spoke again, slowly. "I want to stay here and live with you like this. But, to be honest, I'm torn. The school, like the rest of society, is fraught with power struggles. It can be a pleasant place if you have the backing of a powerful teacher. But those who study under someone like me, under someone who falls from grace, are relegated to the lowest positions in the hierarchy. I wonder whether it is really right for me to pursue my own happiness when my former students may be suffering for my failure."

He turned to face Elin. "Would you mind very much if I were to ask you to live as my foster daughter in the capital?"

Elin gazed back at him wordlessly. *Joeun wants to go home.* He himself had not yet realized it, but to her it was clear. The way he talked had changed when he spoke of his past. She had known this day would come. Over the years, she had come to understand how society worked, and it had become clear to her that Joeun had not been born a beekeeper. The wide range of subjects he taught her every night, even his ability to play the harp, indicated the depth of his knowledge and education. No one from the peasant class would have been permitted to study these things. Although Joeun had never spoken of leaving, Elin had prepared herself long ago for the possibility that they would part. It was not that she had foreseen it. Rather, she had prepared herself in self-defense—so that when the time came, she would not be hurt. Since the day her mother had been torn from her, she had lost any faith that happiness was eternal and unchanging.

Change, she knew, was something that came suddenly. But though it might come without warning, she never wanted to taste again the sorrow she had felt at the loss of her mother. She had therefore been careful to keep some distance between herself and Joeun. Had he understood?

She loved him. She wanted to live with him forever. But her spirit drooped at the thought of living in the capital with Joeun's son and family, of feeling like a burden and being married off to some unknown artisan. In her childhood, she had learned all too well what it meant to marry into that class. The only woman in her village who had become an artisan in her own right had been Elin's mother. If she married one, she would be expected to bear the man's children, serve him, and take care of his house for the rest of her life. This held no attraction for her at all. She did not want that kind of life, even if refusal meant parting with Joeun and living alone.

There's so much more I want to learn, so many questions I want to find answers for.

One of these as yet unanswered questions was why her mother had believed controlling the Toda was such a mortal sin. She had mulled over her mother's words and recalled the look on her face again and again.

Now she thought she could understand, at least a little, what she might have felt.

When Elin watched the honeybees or other creatures in the wild, when she observed the diversity of their life cycles and the astounding precision of their habits, there were times when she felt herself become a prick of light in the vastness of the night sky, times when all living things, people, beasts, and insects, dwindled to equal points of light twinkling in the darkness. Having felt the world from that perspective, having held this vision in her mind, there were moments when the practices of a beekeeper struck her as loathsome—especially the way beekeepers made royal jelly. The liquid that the worker bees wrung from their bodies to make a new queen was traded for large sums of money. A teaspoon was worth a small gold piece, and Joeun deftly manipulated the bees to make it. Royal jelly was a good product and a good medicine. That's why he did it, and, of course, that wasn't bad. But every time she watched him control the bees, she recalled the dark expression on her mother's face as she had rolled the Toda Whistle in her palm.

Had her mother been feeling the same way, that it was wrong to manipulate other living things? Had she felt herself to be just one of countless pinpricks of light in an infinite expanse of darkness? Had she seen that the Toda, too, were dots of light? Was that why she had felt it was a sin to treat them that way?

Why are Toda the way they are? Why are we humans like this? Questions like these teased her mind. Perhaps there were no answers, but she wanted so much to find them.

"Uncle Joeun . . ." she said. "Is there a school in the capital where girls can study?"

A look of sadness crossed his face. "There are . . . but they're all designed to train girls to be good wives to members of the nobility or high-ranking artisans. Even if you went, I can't imagine that you would be satisfied with what you learned." He sighed and shook his head. "If only you were a boy . . . I don't know how many times I've thought that. If you were a boy, I'd enroll you in Tamuyuan without hesitation, regardless of whether Asan or anyone else objected."

Sometimes daughters of the nobility were permitted to study at Tamuyuan, but very few, and Elin, who came from Ahlyo stock, would certainly not be allowed in. Joeun reached out a hand and stroked her hair. "So you don't want to come and live with us in the capital?"

Elin bit her lip to keep it from trembling. Keeping her head down, she nodded. "I was very happy living with you . . . I wish we could go on this way. But if that's not possible . . . I . . ." She took a deep breath and went on. "I want to live by myself . . . I don't want to live in the capital in your house as a foster child and be married off."

Joeun closed his eyes and nodded once. "Yes. I can see that. You're not the type of girl who would be happy as the wife of an artisan." Yet deep inside was the thought that even such a fate was better if it meant Elin would not be left alone when he died. He could not help but feel that his son's arrival on the very day that he had felt so ill was an act of fate. He sighed again. "What are we to do, I wonder?"

From the moment she had met Asan and sensed that the time of parting was near, Elin had been rolling an idea over in her mind. Since that summer four years ago, she had been drawn to the Royal Beasts. Or perhaps obsessed with them was a better description. Every year when she and Joeun returned to the hut in the mountains, she had gone back to the cliff to watch them. Joeun had scolded her countless times, but she could not resist. One day, he had exclaimed in exasperation, "I once knew a woman just like you, who was possessed by these Beasts."

She looked up at him now and said, "Uncle Joeun . . ."

"What?"

"You told me once that you knew someone who worked in a sanctuary for Royal Beasts. A woman. You said that she was a beast doctor."

Joeun blinked. "Ah. You mean Esalu, at the Kazalumu Sanctuary. They call it a sanctuary, but it's really where they take care of injured beasts until they die." He could see his friend's face in his mind. She had been admitted to Tamuyuan, even though she came from the lower ranks of the nobility. Sallow-skinned, with angular features, she could not have been called pretty even in flattery, but she had been extremely clever, and the two of them had become fast friends.

"Esalu. Hmm." He frowned and his expression grew thoughtful. "I see. A beast doctor. Yes, that's a possibility I hadn't thought of. It's a high position, but because exposure to blood is defiling, women are allowed to assume that rank. And you might be very well suited to it.

"As for Kazalumu Sanctuary, children come from all over the country hoping to become doctors. They study while taking care of the Royal Beasts, so it would really suit you as a place to live." Even as he said this, however, he still looked concerned. "But it's a hard job, heavy labor with few rewards. If anything happens to one of the Beasts, the doctor may be blamed . . . and in some cases, even sentenced to death."

The image of her mother being dragged before the inspector jumped vividly into Elin's mind, and a cold pain shot through her chest. Yet, almost simultaneously, another image surfaced in her memory—her mother's pale hand slowly and gently caressing the huge flanks of the Toda, her mother's face as she gazed at them . . .

Then, like a bright flash of light, she remembered—she had always longed to be like her mother, to gain knowledge, and to use it to help the beasts.

I want to become a doctor and care for the Royal Beasts. The thought spread inside her like fire through an open field.

She raised her head. "Uncle Joeun, my mother was a beast doctor."

Joeun's eyes widened. "What?"

"But she only treated Toda. I was raised in a village of Toda Stewards in the Tohan district on the western edge of Aluhan territory . . ."

With her eyes cast down, she began to tell him the tale that she had concealed for so long in the depths of her heart. She told him how her mother, who had belonged to the Ahlyo, had wed the eldest son of the village chief and given birth to Elin. For this she had been cast out of the Ahlyo. But because she had excelled at healing, she had been entrusted with the care of the Kiba, the most precious of the Toda herd. When the Kiba were found dead one morning, she had been blamed and sentenced to a brutal death. Elin told him how she had tried to save her mother, but instead had been placed upon a Toda, wrenched away, and carried to this land. Elin told Joeun everything—everything except the fact that her mother had used a finger whistle to control the Toda. Somehow it did not feel right to share that.

Joeun listened openmouthed. "So that's what happened." He shook his head. "You've finally solved that riddle for me. When I found you, you were covered in glue-like mud and Toda slime. I had always wondered how on earth that was possible . . . Now I see . . ." Her past had been far more painful and cruel than he had ever imagined. He looked at her steadily. "But if that's the case, wouldn't you hate to become a Royal Beast doctor?"

Elin shook her head. "No. I loved to watch my mother when she cared for the Toda. She was the best doctor in the village . . . I always wanted to be like her."

Joeun looked into her clear, shining eyes and nodded. "All right, then. I'll ask Esalu."

2

THE ENTRANCE TEST

The rain that had fallen incessantly since morning finally ceased when the carriage carrying Elin and Joeun reached the Kazalumu highlands. The clouds chased across the sky by strong winds still glowered darkly, but they were brightening at the edges, and patches of blue sky peeped through the gaps. Cloud shadows flowed across the gently sloping highlands, caressing the meadow. A high fence surrounded the Royal Beast Sanctuary, but its height was barely noticeable in the vast area it enclosed. The sanctuary was almost as large as the highlands.

There was another Royal Beast sanctuary located nearer to the capital on the Lazalu highlands. Sick and wounded beasts, however, had to be kept separate to avoid tarnishing the purity of the Yojeh and bringing misfortune. These "damaged goods" were kept at the Kazalumu Sanctuary, a day's carriage ride from the capital, where they were tended until they died. A boarding school had been annexed to the sanctuary to train aspiring beast doctors. Schools in the capital, like Tamuyuan, only accepted applicants from the upper class. There, outstanding students could ascend to the coveted rank of "grand master." At Kazalumu, however, students were from the artisan class and, although they could become beast doctors, they would never rise higher than that. Still, children came from all over the country, hoping to receive credentials that would guarantee a living in their homelands.

Funded by the Yojeh, students were provided with free tuition, as well as free room and board and uniforms, which made Kazalumu very popular with parents from the poorer classes. Over a hundred hopeful applicants arrived each year, but the Yojeh's funds could only support a maximum of sixty students in total, and the income received for veterinarian services from the district's livestock farmers was barely enough to cover the teachers' salaries and living expenses. Only fifteen or so students graduated each year. This meant that only fifteen new students could enter. Consequently, the exams that determined who would enter were extremely tough.

As soon as he had decided what to do with Elin, Joeun had jumped into action. First, he had written to his old school friend, Esalu, explaining the situation and asking permission for Elin to take the entrance exam. In the two weeks it took to receive a reply, he had arranged for another beekeeper to buy his hives, while at the same time preparing Elin for the exam.

Spring seemed to fly by. When Esalu's letter finally arrived, Elin could not keep her knees from trembling as she watched Joeun break the seal. The answer was brief, penned in a script so bold it was hard to believe it had been written by a woman. The official entrance exam, Esalu wrote, only took place in the summer. However, three students had been expelled for misconduct that spring. For this reason, and the fact that the request was from Joeun, she would be willing to conduct a special entrance exam for Elin. But it would be very strict. To be accepted, Elin would have to achieve marks as high as the student who had ranked third in the regular exam. Elin could come on that condition.

Elin and Joeun had spoken very little during the journey to Kazalumu. A mixture of sadness, hope, and anxiety had made their hearts too full for speech. As they alighted from the carriage in front of the school, the fragrance of damp grass stroked their cheeks. Dark clouds, blown on the wind, raced above them, pierced by a shaft of sunlight that sparkled on the rain-wet meadow. In the midst of that vast plain stood Kazalumu Boarding School.

The school was composed of three large, two-story buildings, their walls so weathered by wind and snow that the wood had yellowed. The dark thatched roofs were covered in moss and dotted with flowers that must have sprouted from wind-blown seeds. From deep beyond the great wooden doors came the faint murmur of voices, but, perhaps because classes were in session, it seemed far too quiet for there to be sixty students.

Joeun laid a hand on Elin's shoulder. "You don't need to worry. The entrance exam is for twelve-year-olds. You'll do fine. If you relax and stay clearheaded, you'll pass for sure."

Elin nodded, but her mouth felt very dry. While she tied the reins to the post beside the gate, Joeun struck the rusted copper bell that hung nearby. It made such a dull noise that Elin wondered if anyone would ever hear it, but soon the great doors creaked open, and a tall figure appeared from within, wearing ankle-length trousers beneath a stained, knee-length white apron. At first, Elin thought it must be a middle-aged man, but when the light struck the person's face, she realized it was a woman. She came toward them and Elin caught the faint scent of animals from her clothes. Although she did not seem to be that old, the woman's short-cropped hair was sprinkled with white, and her tanned face was laced with wrinkles, reminding Elin of beef jerky. The woman shot back the iron bolt in the gate and opened it, beckoning them inside.

"It's been a long time, Esalu," Joeun said. "You haven't changed a bit."

The woman smiled. "I've aged, Joeun . . . And it looks like you've gotten quite brown." Then she ran her eyes over Elin. "So you're Elin, are you?"

Elin placed her palms to her forehead and bowed. "Yes, I'm Elin. It's an honor to meet you."

Esalu nodded. "You're very tall. I heard you were fourteen but you seem more like sixteen."

Joeun patted Elin on the shoulder. "She's too thin. These last two years she shot up in height. She used to be such a little thing that a puff of wind would have blown her away."

Esalu nodded once again. "Come," she said. "Let me show you around the school." She turned toward the entrance, and they followed after her. After being outside on the open plain, it took their eyes a moment to adjust to the dim light inside. The corridor smelled of ancient wood mingled with the sunny scent of boys, a combination that for Joeun brought back a flood of memories.

Removing their shoes in the dirt-floored entranceway, they slipped on the indoor shoes they had brought with them. Esalu gestured for them to follow her, and they began walking along the wooden floor of the dimly lit corridor. They could hear the voices of students responding to their teachers from the rooms on the south side of the corridor. The north side was also lined with rooms, but they appeared to be empty.

Esalu came to a stop before a sliding door at the end of the hallway. A sign above it announced in faded letters HEADMASTER'S ROOM. She put her hand on the door, but Joeun hastily stopped her. "Esalu, wait a second," he said in a low voice. "Who's the headmaster now?"

Esalu raised her brows and slid back the door. On the far side of the room, a sliding door with paper panes had been pulled back, allowing a soft light to pour inside. But the room was empty.

"I've been the headmistress for the last two years," Esalu said. "Didn't you know?"

Joeun looked at her in surprise. "Really? . . . I thought you had no interest in politics."

Esalu laughed. "This isn't Tamuyuan. No one with any ambition would stay here long. In Kazalumu, the position of headmaster is filled by someone who has no ambition and is willing to stay for life."

From the moment she entered the room, Elin's eyes were riveted to the north wall. Built-in bookshelves extended along it, holding a library that far exceeded Joeun's collection. Thus preoccupied, she missed the shocked expression on Joeun's face. For any school, the headmaster's room proclaimed its wealth and status. The position of Kazalumu was obvious at a single glance, and Joeun could not conceal his astonishment at the room's austerity. He knew that Esalu had never been interested in luxury or fancy trappings, but the sparse furnishings in the barren room were plainly cheap and worn. A large wall clock stood beside the bookshelves, ticking loudly as it marked the passage of time. Thick woven carpets lay on the floor. At the far end, facing the door, was a single low desk and legless chair. Four more low desks, each with two legless chairs, were arranged around a hearth embedded in the center of the room. A small stack of coals glowed red with flames in the hearth, and an earthenware teapot with a wisp of steam rising from its spout sat on a metal brazier above it.

Esalu gestured to the chairs by the hearth. "Have a seat while I make some tea." Seeing the look on Joeun's face, she smiled. "There's no maid to serve tea here. And even if I had the money to hire one, I'd spend it on taking in another student instead." She poured the tea deftly and served them. Then she looked at Elin. "Whether you pass or fail, you must stay here tonight with Joeun. I'm sure you're tired after the journey. You could take the test tomorrow if you'd rather."

Elin placed her cup on the table. Perhaps because she was excited, she didn't feel tired. Nor could she bear the thought of waiting in suspense any longer. "If possible, I would rather do it now."

Esalu nodded. "All right, then. We'll do that. But first drink your tea. It should help you relax a little."

The hot tea had a pleasant citric aroma and a slightly sweet taste, and it warmed Elin up from the inside. Her fingers stung where they held the hot cup. Although it was spring, the journey across the highlands in the rain had been very cold. She had only realized how frozen her hands were when she had picked up the cup. Just as Esalu had said, by the time she had finished the tea, she was feeling more relaxed and able to register the furnishings and her surroundings.

"That's brought the color back to your face," Esalu remarked. "Shall we start, then? Joeun, come over here please."

Joeun stood up ponderously, cup in hand, and went to sit down beside the headmistress's desk. Esalu then took three sheets of paper, a pot of ink, and a pen from her desk and placed them in front of Elin. "Go ahead. The amount of time you have to complete it is one toh."

When she saw the writing that filled the thin sheets of paper, Elin's heart began to pound almost painfully. Her tongue clung to the roof of her mouth and her mind felt numb. She took a deep breath and looked at what was written. The first page was all mathematical equations, the second was questions about the life cycles and habits of various animals, and the third was essay questions. The answer to the first question came to her, and she felt herself relax. From then on, she was oblivious to everything around her. When she had completed the last page, she checked her answers one more time and then quietly laid her pen on the desk.

"Are you done already?" Esalu asked. "Only half a toh has passed."

Elin blinked. She had no idea how much time had passed. All she knew was that she was finished. Even if she tried, she would not be able to think of anything more to write. She rose and, walking over to the headmistress, handed her the test. Picking up a pair of reading glasses from her desk and placing them on her nose, Esalu began reading.

The ticking of the clock, which Elin had not even heard before, seemed to echo loudly in the room, and the sound of the steam rattling the lid of the kettle set her nerves on edge. Esalu read swiftly through the first two pages, placing them one by one on the table as she finished. But she spent a long time reading the essays on the third page. When she finished, she looked not at Elin, but at Joeun. "So . . . I can see why she's such a favorite of yours."

A smile spread slowly across Joeun's face. "What do you think?"

Without answering, she placed the test paper on the desk and tapped it with her knuckle. Then she stretched and looked up at Elin. "For your studies, you can start in the intermediate level with students your own age instead of the novice level. But for your practical lesson, you'll start off mucking out the stalls of the Royal Beasts and other animals along with the twelve-year-olds. All right?"

After a pause, Elin nodded. "Yes, thank you."

"That's settled then. I'll introduce you to the other students this evening at dinnertime." Then Esalu smiled. It was only when Elin saw her smile that it really sank in. She had been accepted into the school. All the tension drained from her body and she could not keep her voice from trembling. "Tha-thank you so much."

Esalu reached for a rope that hung down from a small hole in the ceiling and pulled it. Shortly after, they heard a knock on the door.

"Headmistress, it's me, Kalisa."

"Come in," Esalu said, and the door opened to reveal a woman slightly younger than the headmistress and so stout she looked like she would burst. "This is our dorm mother," Esalu said. "She serves as a mother to all sixty of our students."

Kalisa smiled brightly. "Rascals is what they should be called. Really, they're a lot of work, but somehow or other we get along . . . Oh, there I go, forgetting to introduce myself. I'm Kalisa. You're the new student, are you?"

Elin bowed formally. "My name is Elin. I'm pleased to meet you."

Kalisa's smile grew broader. "My goodness. What a proper greeting. It's so nice to have girls. Can you clean, do laundry, sew?"

Before Elin could reply, Joeun said, "She did all the housework in our home. She won't be any trouble to you, don't worry."

"Splendid! The boys are so lazy sometimes. You know, Headmistress, we should really start recruiting more girls."

Esalu laughed and laid a hand on Elin's shoulder. "Let Kalisa show you around the school. Kalisa, I'm going to put her in the intermediate class. You take her to her room and tell her everything she needs to know about living here."

Kalisa's eyes grew round. "You're going to skip to the second year, are you? You must be very bright!" Then she smiled at Joeun. "Don't worry. I'll take good care of her."

Joeun bowed deeply. "Thank you very much."

"You're welcome," Kalisa replied. "Come along now, Elin."

"But her belongings are still in the carriage," Joeun protested.

"No need to worry about that," Esalu said. "I'll get the custodians to help bring her things in. You'll stay here tonight, too, won't you? Elin can stay with you in the guestrooms tonight instead of the dorms."

"Really? That would be wonderful."

Once Elin had followed Kalisa out of the room, Joeun turned to Esalu and bowed. "I can't thank you enough. I know I was asking you a big favor to make this exception, and I really appreciate you giving her a chance."

Esalu picked up Elin's test papers in her hand and passed them to Joeun. As he began reading through them, she said quietly, "In thirty years of teaching, I've seen a lot of good students, so it's no surprise for me when one of them gets every question right except for a small calculation error. But to be honest, her answer to that essay question astonished me."

Joeun put the first two sheets on the desk and began to read Elin's essay on "Why do you want to be a beast doctor?". The gist of her answer was this: "I am fascinated by the mystery of why things are the way they are, whether living or inanimate. I want to understand. Why is the smallest honeybee so incredibly efficient? Why is there so much diversity even among bees of the same hive? When I start thinking about things like this, my mind is filled with questions. I want to know why living things are the way they are, including me.

"Unlike people, beasts do not use language. In order to care for them, we must study them continuously and look at every aspect. I am sure that whatever I learn about beasts will help me to learn about the things I want to know."

Joeun rested the paper on the desk and looked at Esalu.

"You're a teacher to the core, aren't you?" she said. "You may have left the school, but when you discovered such an able pupil, you couldn't resist teaching her, right?"

Joeun shook his head. "No, it wasn't like that. I didn't 'discover' her. She walked into my life out of the blue." He told her everything, from the day he had rescued Elin to what she had told him about her mother. When he finished, it was late afternoon, and the sunlight slanting through the window had turned to gold.

Esalu frowned slightly and said in a low voice, "I see. So that's her background. She has a stillness that is unusual in a girl of fourteen, and I guess that explains why." She looked down at the floor and murmured, "So her mother broke the Oath of the Ao-Loh."

Joeun raised his brows. "Ao-Loh?"

Esalu's head jerked up as if she had been startled. "What? Oh, I was mumbling. I said that her mother broke the vow of the Ahlyo, the People of the Mist. If you look at her eyes, you can tell at a glance that she has Ahlyo blood. I have very firmly told everyone here, including the students, that if Elin joins this school, they are all to ignore the fact that she is part Ahlyo, so you needn't worry on that account."

Joeun's face relaxed. "Thank you. I'm relieved to hear that."

Esalu smiled faintly. "Whether Ahlyo or Wajak, and regardless of whether she's a girl or of low rank, as long as she has the desire to help the Beasts and the brains to do so, she has what it takes to belong to this school." For an instant, Joeun glimpsed in her expression the stubborn fierceness of the girl he had studied with so long ago.

3

YUYAN

Eight paper lanterns hung from the ceiling of the spacious dining hall, casting a soft light over the students sitting at the long tables. The simple fare laid out before them was at least plentiful. As Elin was led to her seat, she felt the eyes of every boy in the room follow her, and the pressure of their gazes weighed on her chest. She had never seen so many boys gathered in one place in all her life, nor had she ever been stared at in such a way. She was never able to recall how Esalu introduced her to the students or what she had said herself.

When she sat down, she was surprised to find a girl in the seat beside her. Large-boned and tall, the girl was smiling broadly. "Now isn't this grand!" she exclaimed in an unfamiliar lilting accent. "Another girl!" Grabbing Elin's hands in her own, she continued, "Until you came, I was all on my own, a wee little girl among all these boys. But now look at this! I've been sent a friend!"

Stunned to receive such a profuse welcome from a complete stranger, Elin looked around in confusion, but the boys were all grinning.

"What do you mean, 'wee little girl'?" one of them teased.

"Yeah, you eat more than the rest of us put together, you lazy old thing."

Ignoring them, the girl shook Elin's hands vigorously and said, "My name's Yuyan. Do say you'll be my friend." Her warm hands were large enough to envelop Elin's. Looking at her wide-open smile, Elin found herself smiling in return.

"My name's Elin. And yes, let's be friends."

Yuyan's eyes seemed to sparkle with joy. "There now, look at that lovely smile! You seemed kind of grownup and quiet for a while there, but when you smile, well, you're actually pretty cute." Then, turning to the boys, she demanded, "Don't you think so, too?" The boys just kept on grinning, but something in their expressions reminded Elin of the way a mischievous older brother might look at a younger sister. "Come on, then, dig in!" Yuyan cried. "Dig in! Before dinner gets cold!" And before the students or even the teachers had picked up their chopsticks, she had begun shoveling food into her mouth.

When a startled Elin turned her eyes from Yuyan to look at those around her, the boys laughed and then nodded at her, as if to say, "Go ahead. Eat your supper."

From his seat beside the headmistress, Joeun watched Elin begin to eat and breathed a sigh of relief. Elin was bright, but she tended to remain aloof. And she was of Ahlyo blood. His greatest fear had been that she would feel left out at the school, but it looked like there was no need to worry.

As if reading his mind, Esalu said, "She'll be fine with Yuyan in her group. Yuyan's like a ray of sunshine. She does tend to be a bit hasty at times, but she's comfortable with anyone and makes others feel comfortable with her."

Watching the sturdy girl chattering as she ate, Joeun nodded. This was the right decision. The thought spread through him, dissolving the weight that had burdened his mind since the day his son had appeared. He felt light at heart, but it was a lightness tinged with sadness.

The next day, Elin wept when Joeun rode away in the cart. What could she say to him? How could she express all the feelings that filled her heart for this man who had rescued her from the lakeshore and raised her as if she were his own child? All she could do was to bow her head low and listen to the sound of the cart's wheels growing fainter in the distance. She felt as if the happiness of being held and protected by him, the joy of their life together, was receding with him.

So much about life at Kazalumu was unfamiliar that at first Elin was bewildered. To her surprise, the hardest thing to get used to was keeping in step with the crowd of students with whom she now lived. In the dormitory, she was required to do everything at the same time as everyone else, from rising in the morning to going to bed at night. With Joeun, as long as she finished the jobs she was responsible for, she could do what she liked, but here she had almost no time for herself.

Classes covering new material were interesting, but she found those covering subjects that she had already studied with Joeun boring. When a class was stimulating, she still had to struggle because so many questions popped into her mind. With Joeun, she had been free to ask questions whenever they occurred to her, but here it seemed that no one had anything to ask. She hesitated to raise her hand when all the other students just sat and listened in silence. She found the practical lessons in caring for sick animals hard, too, because the students were only expected to remember what the teacher told them and to repeat the same tasks over and over. She could not stop to observe an animal more closely whenever something puzzled her. It was simply not allowed.

One night, Yuyan peered into her face with an anxious expression. "What's wrong, Elin? You seem awful tired and a wee bit pale, too."

Unlike the boys, who slept in large communal rooms, Elin and Yuyan had a small room of their own, because they were the only girls in the entire school. Before, Yuyan had had the room to herself, and Elin had worried that the sudden appearance of a roommate might have made her feel crowded. In fact, however, she seemed to be genuinely pleased. Rooming with her, Elin realized that she was indeed a very easygoing and kindhearted person. Her only faults were a remarkable tendency to jump to conclusions and her habit of talking, loudly, in her sleep. There were times when Elin was jolted awake in the middle of the night by her friend shouting outrageous things, but the next morning the two girls always had a good laugh over what she had said. As the days went by, they became such good friends that they felt as if they had known each other all their lives.

When Yuyan expressed concern for her like this, Elin was sorry that she was such a poor talker. Unaccustomed to sharing her inner thoughts and feelings with others, she had trouble knowing how and when to confide in her friend. Yuyan, who had been raised in a mountain village on the northern edge of the Yojeh's territory, appeared at first glance to be unconcerned by what others felt, but in fact she was quite empathetic and quick to notice when anyone was anxious or in distress.

"I s'pose it's only to be expected. After all, you've been gathering up Beast dung with the young ones. They're such a noisy bunch, you must be exhausted."

Elin smiled and shook her head. "No, really, I quite enjoy working with the younger kids . . . That's not what's bothering me." Hesitantly, she shared her discovery that she found it hard to adjust herself to the pace of others.

Yuyan listened, her eyes wide, as Elin haltingly explained her confusion and her struggle to cope. When she finished, Yuyan gave a low whistle. "You've got to be kidding. That's what's bugging you? Now who would've guessed just from looking at you? The boys're always talking about how mature you are. They think you're pretty special to fit right in even though you came in the middle of the term."

Elin was amazed. It had never occurred to her that others would see her that way.

Yuyan laughed. "What? You mean you didn't even notice? The guys can't take their eyes off you, Elin. You've got Ahlyo blood, right? It makes you kind of mysterious, sort of special, you see." She spoke frankly. "Y'know, Elin, the headmistress told us to ignore that you're part Ahlyo, but I think she's expecting an awful lot. It's only human to notice when someone's different, right? If it were me, I'd say that instead of ignoring it, we ought to tell people not to be so dumb as to take those differences in the wrong way. That's what really counts."

Yuyan had been gazing steadily at her the whole time she was speaking, and Elin nodded. "I think so, too. That's far more important."

Yuyan's face lit up. "You see? Take me, for instance. I talk funny, right? The guys used to laugh at me when I first came here, but then—you know Kashugan?"

Elin blinked and had to think for a moment before she recalled a tall boy with a long face. "Ah! I know who you mean. The one whose sash is always crooked."

Yuyan laughed. "Yup. That's him all right. No good at tying his sash. But, what I was trying to say was, one day he told the others that they weren't right to laugh at me. He told them the way people speak depends on where they're brought up. 'You wouldn't like it if someone laughed at the way your folks spoke either,' he said."

Elin smiled. "Really? He's very kind, isn't he?"

"You bet! And isn't that just the nicest thing someone could do? So, Elin, I'm not going to ignore the fact that you're part Ahlyo, because it makes no difference what color your eyes are. You are who you are, and that's all that matters."

Elin was startled to find her eyes filling with tears. Before she could stop them, they were flowing down her cheeks. Looking flustered, Yuyan clasped

Elin's hand. "No, don't cry now. Please don't cry. I'm sorry. I'm always too blunt."

Staring at the ground, Elin shook her head. "I'm sorry." She wanted desperately to stop her tears, but it was impossible. She wiped her eyes roughly and shook her head repeatedly. For the first time in her life, she realized how deeply she had been hurt by people's reactions to her Ahlyo heritage. The way her grandfather and Joeun's son had looked at her had cut her to the core.

Yuyan's truly amazing, she thought. Her grandfather, who had stood by and let the Toda attack his grandchild, might have the high rank of Chief Steward, but compared to Yuyan, he was no better than trash. Elin wiped her eyes again and looked at Yuyan. "Thank you." No other words came to her, but Yuyan, her eyes full of tears, nodded.

4

THE BEAST WHISTLE

Despite Yuyan's concern, Elin really did not mind collecting dung with the first-level students or mucking out the stalls of the sick animals entrusted to the school from neighboring farms. True, at just twelve years of age, the younger students were still a bit immature. They complained boisterously that the manure was "gross" and "stinky," and their idea of cleaning was to spread the muck around rather than to make things cleaner, so that Elin usually ended up finishing the job herself. Yet she found this job a welcome diversion.

What made her happiest was the fact that she got to see the Royal Beasts every day. Only the older students were permitted to care for the Beasts, but while the creatures were let loose in a large pasture during the day, the younger students gathered the dung from their quarters and spread out fresh straw. Whenever she saw the Beasts in the distance, Elin felt her heart sing. They stood in the gently rolling pasture, napping in the warm spring sunshine and flapping their wings leisurely every so often. When she first saw them, something about them seemed different from the Royal Beasts that she had observed every year in the wild. Yet at the time she could not put her finger on what it was.

"Royal Beasts never grow accustomed to human beings." Their teacher drilled this lesson into them. "They may seem calm and peaceful, but when roused, their rage is terrible. You must never let down your guard when you approach them." In a quiet voice, he related the tale of a boy who, thirteen years ago, had approached too close to a Royal Beast. He had been torn to shreds in seconds. The first-level students shuddered at this story. As she listened, Elin recalled the scene she had witnessed on the rock ledge several years ago. For fangs that could slice effortlessly through the impervious scales of a Toda, a human body would seem as soft as lard.

"You must never go near the Royal Beasts until you are in the upper level and have acquired enough knowledge and experience. Do you understand?" So saying, the teacher slowly drew a small whistle from his robe. Elin's eyes opened wide in surprise. It looked just like the one that her mother had used. "This is a Silent Whistle. It makes no sound even when you blow it, but it will cause the Royal Beasts to freeze. The upper level students carry one with them at all times and use it when there is a need. This is the only tool we have with which we can control the Royal Beasts. Remember that."

One student raised his hand. "How far does the whistle reach?"

"About ten paces. If you are farther away than that, you should assume that the whistle won't have any effect."

Elin felt as though the teacher's voice was coming from very far away. She had never dreamed that people would manipulate Royal Beasts with the Silent Whistle, just like the Toda. Her heart sank as she listened.

The first time she saw the whistle being used was about a month after she had come to the school. In the morning, the weather was fair, but a little after midday, dark clouds suddenly covered the sky and strong gusts of wind began to blow. Elin's group was laying out straw in the Beast quarters when a burly youth came racing inside and yelled at them to hurry.

"Quick! There's a thunderstorm coming and the Beasts will be back soon."

At the sound of thunder, Royal Beasts instinctively sought shelter, which in the Sanctuary meant the stables rather than a rocky ledge under an overhang where they would have roosted in the wild. The older students, who were aware of this habit, feared that they might be trapped inside when the Beasts returned. The younger students hurriedly finished laying the straw and were about to leave when the youth, who had been watching the pasture, pushed them back. "Wait! Don't go out yet! One of them is almost here." He glanced at his companion. "It's all right to use it, isn't it?"

The other nodded. "It's an emergency. Do it."

The first youth raised the whistle to his lips and blew on it sharply. It made no sound, but looking out of the window Elin saw a Beast that had been running full tilt toward them stop dead in its tracks as if it had hit an invisible wall. It toppled slowly over, and remained as still as stone, even when it struck the ground. Lightning flashed across the sky, and the inert Beast glowed white in the darkness. A heavy rain fell, pummeling its body and drenching its fur, yet still it did not move.

Elin felt goosebumps rise on her skin. The sight chilled her to the bone. She had seen her mother blow the whistle and freeze the Toda many times, but never before had she felt like this.

That whistle kills the Beasts. These words flashed through her mind like lightning.

Within less than ten han (about ten minutes), the Beast began to twitch and, under the anxious gaze of the students who had escaped outside the enclosure, it slowly rose and made its way inside. But those words and the image of its motionless form, struck by the rain, remained seared on Elin's mind long after.

The words rose into her mind again one day near summer as she stood leaning against the fence and watching the Royal Beasts. By this time she had realized what was so different about the Beasts at the sanctuary—their fur. They lacked the dazzling brilliance that had radiated from the wild Beasts as they soared overhead, backlit by the morning sun. The fur of the Beasts here was dull and lackluster, a far cry from the breathtakingly beautiful radiance of their wild counterparts.

Was it because they were hurt or diseased? Or did the Beasts change when raised in captivity? The teachers had taught her that when raised by men from infancy, they never flew. As she gazed at the Beasts standing in the pasture and recalled the powerful strokes of the wild Beasts' wings as they had sped through the sky, a cold, dry wind seemed to blow through her heart.

The words her mother had said as she threw the Silent Whistle into the fire came back to her now. "It's not taking care of the Toda that I mind . . . It's that whistle. I've always hated using it. I hate watching the Toda freeze whenever I blow it . . . To see beasts controlled by humans is a miserable thing. In the wild, they would be masters of their own destiny. I can't bear watching them grow steadily weaker when they live among men."

Lost in the recollection of her mother's face in the hearth light, of her low voice as she spoke, Elin did not notice that someone was approaching, even when the sound of footsteps was right behind her.

"You're watching the Beasts?"

The sound of Esalu's voice jolted her back to the present. The headmistress stood beside her, gazing at the Beasts. "I often see you standing here watching. Do you like them?"

"Yes."

Esalu shifted her gaze to Elin's face. "You don't seem very happy when you look at them, though."

At first, Elin did not know how to respond, but then she remembered how Joeun had described the headmistress. She was possessed by the Royal Beasts, he had said. Before she knew it, she had blurted out, "Because I feel sorry for these ones that are raised in captivity."

Esalu raised her eyebrows. "Why do you say that?"

Elin turned away from Esalu to look at the Beasts. "I've seen them in the wild. Their fur isn't dull and lifeless like this. They soar in the heavens on their powerful wings, and their fur gleams like silver in the sun."

Esalu's eyes widened. "You what? You mean you've actually seen Royal Beasts in the wild?"

Startled by the force of her voice, Elin turned to look at her. "Yes."

"Where?"

Her tone was sharp and Elin felt her throat tighten. "Mount Kasho. There was a nest on a precipice overlooking a ravine."

Esalu frowned. "Mount Kasho? What were you doing so deep in the mountains? No one lives up there."

"We were beekeeping. Joeun's summer hut is up there. We spent every summer on the mountain."

"Ah, I see." Esalu's expression relaxed. "Yes, beekeepers have to follow the flowers up the mountain in summer, don't they?"

Why had Esalu reacted like that? Elin wondered. "Is there something wrong with seeing Beasts in the wild?" she asked.

Esalu shook her head. "No, not at all. In fact, it's very fortunate. You see, it's extremely rare for anyone to see wild Beasts. I doubt if anyone but the Beast Hunters has ever seen them. When I was younger, I wanted to find some so badly that I climbed quite a few mountains myself, but I never saw any. I sought out the Beast Hunters as well, hoping that they would tell me where to look, but for them, that knowledge is like a goldmine, and they weren't willing to share it with anyone."

She looked at the Beasts standing in the pasture. "Is their fur really that different from those in the wild?"

"Yes. The fur of wild Beasts shines in different shades depending on the light that hits them. The color looks different in the morning light than at noon. But the fur of the Beasts here never changes. Perhaps they're missing some essential element in their fur that makes it shine."

Esalu remained silent, as if lost in thought, her eyes on the Beasts. Then she raised her arm and pointed at each one in turn. "That one on the left flapping his wings, that's Naku. He has weak intestines and needs a special diet. Tosaku beside him has a tumor in his large intestine and probably won't last more than a few months. Sattoku on the right has a disease that softens the claws and fangs."

She turned to look at Elin. "It could be that their fur doesn't shine because they're ill . . . Or it could be something more than that." She watched Elin intently, obviously thinking, and then said in a quiet voice, "If you observed the Royal Beasts here carefully, do you think you would be able to identify other differences between them and Beasts in the wild?"

Elin returned her gaze. "I don't know . . . I can't tell unless I try."

A smile crept into Esalu's eyes. "Well said. Let me change my question then. Would you like to find out what the differences are?"

Elin felt her pulse quicken. "Yes."

Esalu nodded and then gestured with her chin. "Follow me then." She began walking toward the Royal Beast quarters. Elin thought she was going to go inside, but instead she passed by the entrance and, going around the wall, headed down a small path through a wood where she had never been. The deep green leaves on the branches fluttered over their heads. Once through the wood, another building for housing Beasts appeared ahead.

A sturdily built young man was just coming out of the door. He bore a pail in one hand and a bucket of dung in the other. Noticing Esalu, he stopped and stood respectfully. Esalu looked into the pail.

"It didn't drink much, did it?"

The young man shook his head, his expression gloomy. "No, it didn't. I prepared the tokujisui potion just as you told me to, but the cub wouldn't even try it."

Elin started and looked at the bucket. Tokujisui? Was it the same potion her mother had given the Toda? Or was that the name for any concoction of nutrients dissolved in water?

She shifted her feet to get a better look, but as soon as she moved, Esalu said, "Do you want to see?"

Elin blushed. "Yes."

"Then go ahead."

Elin peered into the pail. The color of the liquid was similar to the potion used for the Toda. She brought her face close and smelled it. There was no mistake. It smelled the same as the Toda potion.

After watching Elin's expression wordlessly, Esalu asked quietly, "Can you tell what's in it?"

Elin hesitated for a moment. If she answered, she would have to tell Esalu about her mother. She looked up and when her eyes met the headmistress's, she realized immediately that Esalu already knew. She knew that Elin's mother had been a Toda Steward. Joeun must have told her.

"The stewed roots of atsune and lakalu weeds mixed with secretions from togela bugs . . . If this were for Toda, I would say that it has more lakalu than usual."

The young man holding the pail stared at her, but Esalu nodded. "That's right. I increased the amount of lakalu weed because it stimulates the appetite. But it looks like it didn't work." Esalu looked at the young man. "Thank you. You can go now. Leave the bucket of dung there."

The young man kept looking at Elin, but after setting down the bucket, he bowed and left. Esalu knelt on the ground and, taking a wooden paddle from the side of the bucket, began examining the contents. Elin crouched down to watch. After spending some time carefully checking the droppings, Esalu glanced at Elin.

"Did you notice anything?"

"The color is paler than the dung of the other Beasts. There's no grass stems mixed in with it, and it looks pretty soft. If this is the amount collected in one day, it's not very much. And the fact that there is a high fur content is also a concern."

Esalu's eyes narrowed. "So you've been examining the droppings you collect every day, have you?"

Elin blinked, wondering why on earth Esalu would need to ask such a question. "Yes. I thought that's why we collected them in the first place."

"But your teachers never said that, right? They just told you to gather the dung and clean their quarters."

Elin thought for a moment and realized that this was true. She had never seen any of the first-level students examining the dung.

Esalu smiled faintly. "When first-level students finish the year, they have to take an exam in order to graduate from this task. The teacher questions them verbally about the condition of the droppings for each one of the Beasts they cared for. Almost all the students are taken by surprise. They have no inkling of the important information to be found there. They are shocked at their own ignorance. And that is a very good lesson for them."

"I had no idea." As a child, Elin had accompanied her mother every morning when she went to the Toda Chambers, and the first thing they did was examine the trough filled with dung. Her mother had explained carefully and methodically how she could tell, just by looking at it, the condition of each Toda. Something akin to pain spread through Elin's chest. Everything she would learn here would be sure to bring back memories of her mother. She was following in her mother's footsteps.

Looking at Elin's downcast face, Esalu said, "I hear your mother was a Toda Steward."

Elin looked up. "Yes."

"So she was training you to become a Toda Steward, too, was she?"

Elin shook her head. "I don't know. She never mentioned it to me." Esalu watched her wordlessly, and looking at her face, Elin was suddenly exasperated. It was as if the headmistress were trying to determine what was inside her by feeling her through a thick cloth. "My mother was a Toda Steward, but when we parted, I was only ten years old. To be honest, I never had a chance to learn what kind of creatures Toda are, or the meaning of my mother's work. When I was little, I was always with her, so I remember what she did, and when I asked questions, she always answered thoroughly. That's why I knew what was in the tokujisui. But I don't know anything more than that. I have nothing but hatred for those who sentenced her to death, and certainly no loyalty to them."

Esalu gazed steadily back at Elin, whose eyes were filled with anger. Then she said quietly, "Don't misunderstand me. I heard about your past from Joeun, but I hold no prejudice against you just because you are the daughter of a Toda Steward."

"Then why—?"

But Esalu stopped her with a gesture of her hand. "I queried you in that way for a different reason. But I don't intend to tell you about that now. I'm sure we'll have another opportunity someday."

Frowning, Elin stared at her. If there was one thing she hated, it was ambiguity.

Her expression serious, Esalu continued, "Neither Royal Beasts nor Toda are mere animals. They are political tools tied to the very core of this country. Whether they like it or not, anyone deeply involved in their care has no choice but to become involved to some extent in politics. And in politics, there are many secrets. To reveal one's hand carelessly can lead to unforeseen consequences."

"But that's got nothing to do with me," Elin insisted.

"Really? Then let me take you at your word."

Although Esalu had said she would trust her, Elin sensed that her words still held hidden meaning. She glared at her, anger rising in her stomach, but Esalu ignored her. Standing up, she brushed the dirt from her knees. "Come with me," she said. "Don't say a word until I speak to you, and keep your footsteps as quiet as you can."

She removed a treatment kit from a cupboard beside the entrance and went inside the building. Following her, Elin was shocked. The interior was as dark as if someone had poured ink over her eyes. The other Beast quarters had a window in the ceiling that could be raised to let in light and, unless the weather was very bad, it was always left open, even at night. But the windows in this one were all shut tight, and no light penetrated except from the entrance.

The smell of Beast permeated the darkness. As her eyes adjusted, she could make out latticed bars covering the walls and ceiling, like a prison cell. Deep inside, she could see a form. It was nothing more than a huddled shadow, but even so she could tell that it was much smaller than the other Beasts. It must have raised its head, sensing their presence, because she saw two golden eyes gleam in the darkness.

5

LIGHT

Esalu walked over to the wall and began moving something. There was a creaking of wood, and a shaft of sunlight suddenly penetrated the darkness. The headmistress must have raised the window in the ceiling slightly. A whimpering sound, almost like a baby crying, issued from the cage when the light touched its depths. The dark shadow huddled in the corner flapped its wings frantically, but its right shoulder sagged unnaturally and its right wing did not rise as high as its left.

It wasn't even full grown.

The Beast was just a cub that should still have been protected by its mother in the nest. Its frantic movements dislodged a blanket covering its back. Its cries were so heartrending that Elin pressed her hands over her ears.

Esalu came up beside her. Raising the Silent Whistle to her lips, she blew on it gently. Instantly, the cub froze, its wings still partly raised and its golden eyes staring fixedly ahead. Esalu handed the whistle to Elin and said quietly, "If it starts to move while I'm in the cage, blow it."

Then she lifted the latch on the door and went inside, carrying a box of medical supplies. First she examined the creature thoroughly from head to foot. Although still an infant, it was already taller than her, and she had to reach up to look at its right shoulder. She checked the wing joint as well, and Elin noticed a brown stain on the fur there. That must be where it had been hurt.

Esalu opened her box, removed a large pair of scissors, and began wielding them with both hands, clipping the fur around the wound. Taking out a jar of disinfectant, she spread it on the exposed flesh. If the cub unfroze now, Esalu would be ripped to pieces before she could escape. Elin held the whistle to her mouth and watched the entire process with bated breath. She noticed other bald patches in the creature's fur besides the area around the wound.

Has it been biting itself?

She knew that horses would bite themselves repeatedly when frustrated or depressed and suspected the cub must be doing the same. That would explain why there had been so much fur in its dung.

Esalu finished her treatment swiftly and pulled the blanket back over the cub with a tenderness that was hard to imagine from her daily behavior. Once she had finished tucking the blanket around it, she ducked back out through the door of the cage. After lowering the window once more, she nudged Elin, and the two moved out of the stable, which was plunged once again into darkness.

While Esalu was putting away the box of supplies, Elin asked, "Why is it so afraid? Because it was wounded?"

"Don't you know what happened last month at the Yojeh's birthday celebration?" Esalu asked as she closed the door of the shed.

"No."

"I see. Joeun seems to have lived like a hermit, so I suppose you never heard the news." She wiped her hands on her apron and turned to look at Elin. "An attempt was made to assassinate the Yojeh at that banquet."

"What?" Elin was rendered speechless. The word "assassinate" seemed so alien to the word "Yojeh." Who in this world would contemplate killing a god? Why would they even consider such a thing?

Seeing the shocked expression on her face, Esalu challenged her. "Didn't Joeun tell you anything?"

"No . . ."

"I guess he really did intend to leave the world behind then. He probably didn't want to tell you how perverse society can be." She sighed. "But if you are going to live here in the Beast Sanctuary, you will need to be well informed about what's going on and the corruption out there. I'm sure your instructors will find opportunities to explain things in more detail. All you need to know right now is that some people have been trying to kill the Yojeh for many years."

"But who?"

Esalu's smile deepened. "After what we talked about earlier, this is a bit awkward to say the least, but it can't be helped. Those who seek to take the Yojeh's life belong to an organization called the Sai Gamulu, which literally means 'blood and filth' . . . They wish to see the Aluhan crowned king."

Elin felt her skin grow taut. She had often heard people in the Toda village complain that people from Yojeh territory treated them with contempt. The resentment they harbored had very naturally been imprinted on her own mind, and she was therefore well aware that there was some animosity between the Wajak, who lived in Aluhan territory, and the Holon, who inhabited Yojeh territory. But she had always assumed that this friction existed only between the two peoples. She had never dreamed that anyone would actually want the Yojeh killed and the Aluhan crowned king in her place.

If the rift between the two was that deep, then surely it was very unwise for a daughter of the Stewards who raised the Aluhan's Toda to be staying at a sanctuary for Royal Beasts, the very symbol of the Yojeh. That would certainly explain Esalu's attitude toward her. But if so, then why had she agreed to let Elin enter the school?

Esalu, who had been watching Elin's face, said quietly, "I can pretty much guess what you are thinking, but let me tell you this. I do not doubt you or feel any hostility toward you for being the daughter of a Toda Steward . . . At the same time, however, I think it is best that you do not tell anyone else, not even Yuyan."

When Elin said nothing, Esalu drove home her point. "You will come to understand the situation in this country in due time. I am telling you not to speak to anyone about this until you can grasp the situation and judge for yourself. Do you understand?"

Elin knew that she was right. It would be a mistake to tell anyone before she knew what was going on. "Yes, I understand," she answered.

Esalu nodded. "All right then. But we were talking about Leelan."

"Leelan? Light?"

"Sorry. That's the name of the cub in there." Esalu turned her eyes toward the Beast quarters. "Leelan was a birthday gift presented to the Yojeh by her nephew. The first time it was ever exposed to a crowd of people was in the garden at the banquet. The assassin was hiding in a tree behind it and the arrow intended for the Yojeh grazed the cub's shoulder while it stood frozen by the Silent Whistle."

A chill spread through Elin's chest. In her mind's eye, she could see the paralyzed Beast. It had been torn from the protection of its mother's breast only to be thrust before a huge crowd in the bright light of day. How frightened and confused it must have felt. Had it cried out in fear, searching for its mother without understanding what was happening? In the midst of that terror, how had it felt when the arrow suddenly sliced its shoulder?

"What's the matter? You're not crying, are you?" With a look of surprise, Esalu peered into Elin's face.

Elin averted her eyes. The sudden and violent surge of emotion that had risen inside her was unsettling. She knew all too well what it was like to want to curl up in fear and wail like a baby—the terror that comes from being suddenly wrenched from one's mother, the confusion at being abandoned in the middle of a vast darkness without a clue of what to do . . . Was that cub once again gnawing on its flesh in the darkness? Was it biting itself repeatedly, tormented by feelings it could not suppress?

She looked up as a strong hand gripped her shoulder. "Elin, get a hold of yourself. What's wrong?"

She brushed away her tears. "Nothing. I just felt sorry for Leelan."

Esalu seemed taken aback. "I can see why you might pity it . . . but you shouldn't let yourself get so emotionally involved. You can't make accurate judgments without keeping your distance and remaining objective." She sighed and muttered. "I thought you were more levelheaded than that, but I guess I was wrong . . . I was thinking of asking you to observe Leelan, but perhaps I should reconsider."

She can't be serious! Elin thought. How could anyone possibly remain objective if they knew what Leelan has been through? If she and that boy taking care of the young Beast can't feel its pain, then they don't understand it at all. They haven't a clue of how petrifying it is to be suddenly separated from one's mother and to find oneself totally alone.

She closed her eyes and took a deep breath. Then, opening her eyes, she said quietly, "Miss Esalu."

"Yes?"

"I don't think that objectivity necessarily guarantees accurate decision-making."

Esalu frowned. "What do you mean?"

"I think that keeping your distance can also mean that you stop feeling things."

Esalu gazed for some time at the red-eyed girl in front of her before she finally spoke. "I see. You have a point. Are you claiming that when you observe Leelan, you can empathize and remain objective at the same time? That sounds good in theory; whether it can actually be done is another matter."

Elin rubbed her eyes. "I don't know . . . But I want to try."

Esalu shrugged. "All right then. Try. But there's not much time, so you had better be very diligent."

"There's no time?"

"That's right. That young Beast hasn't eaten a thing since the day it was injured."

"Since the day it was injured? So it hasn't eaten anything for over a month."

"Royal Beasts can live a long time without food, but Leelan is only a cub. If it would just drink some tokujisui . . . Even that would help."

At the word tokujisui, Elin felt a twinge of distaste. She searched her memory for the cause and recalled something her mother had told her. Tokujisui, she had said, makes their fangs harder and their bones larger than Toda in the wild. But at the expense of other parts. Elin raised her face to look at Esalu. "I have a request." Esalu looked at her questioningly. "I want to observe Leelan in my own way. Would you let me do that?"

"What do you mean?"

"Please excuse me from classes, practical lessons, and chores. Just for one month. That's all I need. I promise to make up for the extra work I cause the other students when I'm finished. And I'll sit for my exams and take the training tests at the same time they do. So please, just for one month, let me concentrate on nothing else but Leelan."

Esalu frowned. "How exactly do you intend to 'concentrate' on Leelan?"

"I will stay here day and night. I'll even eat my meals in the stable to let the cub get used to my scent. Other than that, I will just do whatever comes to mind from watching it . . . And there's one other thing . . ." Elin clenched her fists and gazed straight at the headmistress. "If while I'm doing this, the cub begins to eat meat and fish like the offspring of Royal Beasts in the wild, please let me continue to care for it after that." She was so desperate she could feel her legs shaking. "If I am able to help Leelan recover, it will be proof that I chose the right method, won't it? So please, let me try."

"You certainly are taken with that cub, aren't you?" Esalu said sharply, brushing back a strand of hair from her forehead. "But let me warn you: Royal Beasts will never, ever be tamed by humans. No matter how much care you devote to that young one, it will never get used to you. You will never be special in its eyes. If you approach it with such foolish illusions, you will be torn to shreds. Don't ever forget that."

Elin recalled the sting of the honeybee she had once tried to touch so long ago. *Esalu is probably right. I chose to empathize with Leelan of my own free will, but even if I stake my life on caring for the cub, there is no guarantee that it will respond in kind.*

"I understand what you're saying," Elin said. "But how can I find out without trying?"

Esalu's expression remained cold. "Death by the fangs of the Royal Beasts is not the only risk we take when we care for them," she said. "If there is any fault to be found in our care, we could be charged with disloyalty to the Yojeh and thrown in prison. That is why not even the senior students are given full authority to care for them. If anything should happen, it is I who must bear the blame, and therefore the students follow my orders, serving as my hands and feet. Do you have any idea how insolent you are being? You have essentially declared that you believe you can take better care of that Beast cub than me, despite the fact that I have studied Royal Beasts for the past forty years and have been involved in their care nonstop for three decades."

Elin's heart beat loudly and her face stiffened. With trembling lips, she looked down at the ground.

Esalu continued quietly, "You are smart. Your mother, a Toda Steward, trained you well to develop your talents, and you were fortunate to be mentored by Joeun, a superb teacher. No doubt that's why you feel you can do what others can't . . . I, too, have felt that way. It will be better for you to find out quickly that you are not so special after all." She sighed. "You can take care of Leelan for one month in the way you deem fit. However, there is one thing that you must promise me, to protect Leelan from any failure on your part."

Elin raised her face slowly and looked at Esalu. With a stern expression, the headmistress removed the Silent Whistle from her robe. "When you open the door to the cage, you must always blow on this whistle. Never be overconfident. Swear to me that you will act only when you are sure of what you should do."

Elin put her hands to her mouth. "Yes. I swear."

"Come to my office later. I will explain in detail how to care for Leelan. But I will be the one to treat the wound, so don't even try to touch it."

"Yes, Headmistress."

Esalu nodded and handed the Silent Whistle to Elin.

Thus began the days that were to dramatically change Elin's life.

6

TOMURA

"That's amazing! Unbelievable!" Yuyan exclaimed. At the sound of her excited shout, the boys remaining in the classroom during the break looked over in surprise. Yuyan threw her arms around Elin. "You must be the first kid in Kazalumu history to jump straight to the upper level."

"Yuyan, wait. I'm not . . ." Elin interjected hastily, but her friend did not hear her.

"Well done, Elin! This is just so exciting! But, you know, I'm gonna miss you. We won't be taking classes together anymore I guess." She squeezed Elin so tightly that Elin blinked in surprise. Frantically, she tried to correct the misunderstanding.

"Yuyan, you've got it all wrong. Listen . . ."

But now the boys rushed over and joined the commotion. "Are you really skipping to the upper level?" they asked.

Elin tried to shake her head as best she could while still trapped in her friend's embrace. "No, I'm not! Yuyan misunderstood . . . Yuyan, please! Let me go! You're strangling me."

This time Yuyan must have heard her because she released her reluctantly. "What's there to misunderstand? You said the headmistress gave you a Silent Whistle, right? And you're not coming to classes or doing chores anymore, right?"

Free at last, Elin drew a deep breath. Sparks danced before her eyes. Pressing a hand to her forehead, she looked around at her classmates. "I'm sorry. I should have explained more clearly . . . The headmistress gave me permission to take just one month off to observe a Beast cub in the stable back in the woods. I'm not skipping any grades."

As she was talking, the door to the classroom slid back and a tall, sturdy young man came in. When she saw his face, Elin faltered. It was the same one who had been taking care of Leelan. He came over to where they sat and glared down at Elin, his face rigid.

"Do you have some kind of connection with the headmistress or something?" he demanded. His voice sounded strained. He was obviously struggling to keep his anger from showing.

Elin shook her head. She felt her pulse quicken and her stomach cramped. "Connection? I'm not related to her, if that's what you mean . . . My foster father is a friend of hers, but . . ."

His eyebrows shot up. "Have you no sense of shame? How could you use that kind of influence to take over my job? Without experience or training, you could end up harming that cub, you know. Can't you tell right from wrong?"

Elin felt the blood drain from her face. She tried to speak but found it hard to breathe. In a faint voice, she managed to say, "No, you've made a mistake. I didn't use any connection to get permission to care for Leelan."

He gazed at her steadily, his frown deepening. "Then why did the headmistress take my job and give it to you?"

"Because I've seen Royal Beasts in the wild."

He looked taken aback, his eyes widening. The students sitting around Elin also looked startled. "Really? You've seen Royal Beasts in the wild?"

Elin nodded. "Yes. I was raised by a beekeeper. Every summer we went into the mountains, following the flowers, to places where most people never go. We ran into wild Royal Beasts when we were collecting herbs on a steep cliff. There was a nest halfway down with a mother and her young."

Some of the anger left the young man's eyes. "But what does the fact that you've seen Royal Beasts in the wild have to do with caring for Leelan?"

Elin's voice was dry and hoarse. "The headmistress asked me if I would like to find the differences between Beasts in the wild and those in captivity, and I said yes, I would."

There was a long silence. He regarded her thoughtfully, one hand absently stroking the newly grown fuzz on his chin. "Are you sure that's all?"

Elin frowned in puzzlement.

The young man looked as if he were debating whether to say what was on his mind or not, but then continued. "Come on. There must be more to it than that. You're an Ahlyo. Didn't she give you the job because you have some kind of special knowledge?"

Elin's chest felt as if it had been pierced with a thin blade. Unable to speak, she shook her head mutely.

"You deny it? But you knew what was in the tokujisui. And not just for the Royal Beasts, but for the Toda, too."

A look of surprise crossed the faces of Elin's classmates. There was a ringing in Elin's ears and the color seemed to drain from everything around her. A cold sweat sprang up on her forehead as she raised her face to look at the young man. "That's . . . not because . . . I'm an Ahlyo."

She did not want to talk about her mother. But how could she make him understand without telling him? She stared at him dumbly, her mind blank, unable to find any words to say. Suddenly a warm hand grasped hers and squeezed it firmly. Startled, she turned to see Yuyan nodding at her reassuringly. She felt her frozen body loosen, and sound came rushing back . . . As she relaxed, she remembered what Esalu had told her and looked squarely at the young man.

"I can't tell you right now why I know what's used in the Toda's toku-jisui. The headmistress told me that I was not to talk about it." The young man looked dissatisfied, but Elin plowed on. "She told me I should not even tell my friends. She said that when I grow up and understand the world better, I'll know how to explain it properly, and that I shouldn't tell anyone until then."

"Not even me? She didn't say that, did she?" Yuyan demanded, looking forlorn. At the sound of her plaintive voice, so different from the tense conversation that had preceded it, the heavy atmosphere in the room seemed to shift.

Elin bowed her head. "I'm sorry, Yuyan, but she specifically said not to tell you."

Yuyan cocked an eyebrow. "Well, that's not very nice. But I suppose it can't be helped. Besides, it's kind of an honor to be recognized as your friend by the headmistress. And you will tell me someday, right?"

Elin nodded.

The young man looked down at the two girls with the expression of one who has just had the wind taken out of his sails. Finally, he said in a gruff voice, "Well, I guess if the headmistress knows why and still entrusted you with Leelan's care, then it's not my place to complain." He bent down to look Elin straight in the eyes. "But remember this. Leelan is very precious to me. That cub is as fragile as glasswork that could break at any moment. Can you guess how I feel about having to relinquish it into your care before it has been cured?"

Elin remained silent.

"If anything happens to Leelan, I'll never forgive you. Keep that in mind and take care of that cub as though your life depended on it." With this parting shot, he stood up and left the room.

The door slid closed with a sharp click. At the sound, Elin started and charged out of the door. She had to run to catch up to his long strides. "Wait . . ." she called out. The young man stopped and turned.

"What?"

Elin searched frantically for words. She had thought she wanted to apologize, but when she saw his face, she realized that a simple apology was meaningless. She had stolen Leelan from him. When she had pleaded with the headmistress to entrust her with the young Beast's care, she had not spared a moment's thought for the sorrow it might cause this young man. She deserved any abuse he might throw at her.

Yet, even so, she could not bear to leave Leelan alone like that in the darkness. If this young man and the headmistress continued to use the Silent Whistle every time they went into the cage, that Beast would die. They might scoff at her if she told them, but she was sure of this. If she really wanted to help Leelan regardless of what others might think of her, then it was selfish to seek forgiveness. Still, she did not want this young man to think that she had asked the headmistress for the job so that she could win her favor. She wanted him to know that she also cared about Leelan.

Although he was looking at her with a frown, he did not rush her. She swallowed and said the first words that came to her. "I felt sorry for Leelan . . . I was taken from my mother, too . . . when I was little."

The young man's brows twitched.

"Leelan is still at the age when Beasts should be sheltered under their mothers in the nest. I could imagine how it must have felt when it was torn from its mother, without any warning." Elin forced herself to go on. "In the wild, the Royal Beast I saw nurtured her young tenderly, just like humans, so . . ."

"You've said enough," he said. "I understand already." He turned to leave.

"Please. Teach me," Elin blurted out. "About Leelan."

The young man turned slowly to look at her.

Taking a deep breath, she repeated, "Please, teach me what you know about Leelan."

A bitter smile touched his eyes. "You've got some nerve, haven't you? Is that what you want? To build your house on the foundation I made? Are you that desperate for recognition?"

Elin shook her head. "I just want Leelan to eat, to come out into the light of day instead of staying huddled in the darkness. I only have one month . . . You said that Leelan was precious to you. You are the one who knows that cub the best. So please teach me."

He gazed at the girl for some time, her eyes huge and bright in a pale face. She's a selfish little brat who would do anything to get her way, he told himself. Yet he could not feel angry with her. The dark rage that had smoldered in his stomach just moments before had suddenly been stilled. If Leelan were to be entrusted to this girl's care, then she would need detailed instructions so as not to do anything careless. He rubbed his chin.

"Come with me. I'll show you what to do."

Elin's face lit up. "Thank you!" she said, and followed after him.

The young man frowned. He wanted to believe that she had taken over his job in order to show off, but when he saw the light in her eyes, he found that he couldn't. He had heard the passion in her voice when she had said she wanted to see Leelan eat. She was not lying when she claimed that she cared.

To be honest, he had grown weary of caring for the cub. Despite his efforts, it had never warmed to him, but always responded with fear and hostility. He had been proud when the headmistress had assigned him to its care. She had believed in his ability, and he had longed to fulfill her expectations. He had also sincerely pitied the Beast cub and wanted to help it. But no matter what he did, it refused to eat. These last few days, all he had been able to think of was what would happen to his reputation if Leelan should die while under his charge. When he had suddenly been relieved of his duties, he had been angry and wanted to let the girl know what he thought. At the same time, however, he had no desire to wrest his job back from her.

If he had had any confidence that what he was doing for Leelan would make a difference, he would have refused outright when the headmistress had asked him if he was willing to let someone else take over. The truth was that he had accepted because he no longer knew what to do. Perhaps the headmistress had realized how he was feeling. Perhaps she had been willing to let this girl try because she, too, was at a loss.

Just one month . . . What might happen in a month? If the cub continued to refuse its food and the tokujisui, it would surely die. If it died while under this girl's care, he could not be blamed. Although he knew it was cowardly, this thought passed through his mind. Still, who knew what this girl was really capable of? Perhaps she could use the mysterious knowledge of the Ahlyo to save Leelan.

He found he did not mind that thought at all. If it meant that he could see Leelan napping in the sun, then he would be willing to endure the mortification of this girl succeeding where he had failed.

The sound of her voice brought him back to the present. "Um, would you mind telling me your name? I'm Elin."

"Oh, uh, yeah. I'm Tomura."

7

LIGHT FROM BELOW

"You want to remove the wall of the stable?" Esalu stared at the young man standing in front of her. "Why?"

Tomura looked slightly flustered. "Because Elin asked me to. She said the angle of the light that comes through the window is a problem. She thinks it frightens Leelan."

Esalu pushed back an unruly strand of hair. "What do you think?"

Tomura frowned. "I don't know. On the one hand, I doubt whether something like that would matter . . . but, you know, that girl's different, so the things she says make me wonder."

"What do you mean she's different?"

"She spends all her time in the Beast quarters. She has her friend save food for her and when she goes to the dorm to have a bath, she gathers up as much as she can carry and takes it back with her. She's been there five days already, and the only time she leaves is to take a bath or use the toilet. She spends the rest of her time with Leelan. She wraps herself up in a blanket and just sits there watching."

Esalu laughed. "So she's bathing, is she? When she said she wanted Leelan to get accustomed to her scent, I thought she wouldn't even wash."

"She does. I met her on the way to the bath. She said that Leelan doesn't seem to react much to smell, but she thought it might be better not to let it detect her body odor." He reddened. Honestly, she was really just a kid, not a girl. Talking about things like that didn't seem to embarrass her at all. "Anyway, I've been checking up on her every day, just to make sure everything's all right. Usually, she doesn't pay much attention, but today she actually came out of the stable to talk to me. I was wondering why when she asked me to remove the wall. Or rather one of the planks. At the level of the water basin."

"The water basin? Ah, I see. That's quite low down. So she's asking you to remove a board near the floor."

"Yes. She said she wants to try introducing light from below Leelan rather than from above."

Esalu stroked her chin. She thought she could guess what Elin was thinking. "I see . . . That should be all right. Go ahead and do what she asked. Can you do it yourself, or should I ask one of the custodians?"

"No, I can handle it. Those boards aren't even part of the stable. They were just tacked on later because Leelan was so upset by the light. I just need to remove the nails." He bowed briskly and left the room.

Strangely, the more Elin grew accustomed to the darkness, which at first had been impenetrable and smelled of Beast, the more comfortable it began to feel—despite the fact that she had found the darkness frightening as a child, and that she still did not like it even now. Standing with the blanket wrapped around her, she discovered that her mind felt full of peace, as if she were drifting on the bottom of a pool of warm water. There were times when she was not sure if she were sleeping or waking.

Leelan must want to be immersed in this warmth. The cub had not eaten for a long time, so perhaps it spent all its time dozing. It was very quiet on the other side of the bars.

When Elin had first begun observing it, the cub had appeared to be distracted by her smell, her presence, her breathing. It had stirred frequently, and Elin could hear it tearing out its fur. But by the second day, these sounds had almost ceased. Watching day and night, she gradually began to sense when it woke up and when it went to sleep. The door of the stable was left open, and there was enough light to see the cub's form vaguely. When the light that filtered through the door took on the clear transparency of dawn, Leelan would begin to move. It drank water and discharged body wastes so punctually each day that these actions seemed to be timed to the sound of the school bell.

As she watched, Elin explored the things she noticed in her mind.

Its scent was not as strong as the other Royal Beasts. Was this because it was slowly approaching death, its life force gradually waning? Why did it drink water but avoid food? It had been weaned already and had been eating meat like the other Beasts until it was shot at the banquet. Why?

At first, just as Tomura and Esalu had instructed her, Elin had used the whistle whenever she entered the cage to bring the cub food, change its water, and clean away its dung. She had thought that this was unavoidable. But when she left the cage and watched to see if it ate, she noticed that it began gnawing violently at its fur as soon as the paralysis wore off, almost as if it thought there was some evil creature inside and was trying to rip it out and kill it. Elin had not used the whistle since.

The cub's wound had already closed, and Esalu had told her that she would not be coming to tend Leelan's wound for a week. Although Elin had pointed out that the right wing still drooped as though it hurt, the headmistress had said, "If you hurt your leg, you'd use it cautiously, too, at first. You might even limp for a while after it heals." She had given Elin seven days to do what she liked before she came to check on the cub again, but had warned her to tell her immediately if she noticed any change in its condition.

Seven precious days. For that time at least, Elin decided to refrain from using the whistle and devote herself to watching the cub. She could open the door and push water and food in as far as she could by hand. The cub's urine would drain away naturally on the slanted floor. Although she didn't like the idea of leaving the stall dirty, after some anxious consideration, she decided that a few days would not hurt. After all, Leelan did not produce much dung right now anyway.

Soon after, the cub stopped biting itself almost entirely, although Elin was still not completely sure if this was related. As she watched the motionless figure, she tried to imagine what it was thinking. It must perceive sounds and sights quite differently from human beings. Still, we must have some things in common, too. Surely feelings such as our longing to be cuddled by our mothers and our sadness when we are left alone must be similar?

The dark stall must remind Leelan of the warm darkness beneath its mother. If so, then wouldn't light remind it of its mother's absence? Wouldn't it bring back those fearful memories of waiting alone and afraid in the nest without its mother's body protecting it, and of being captured by the Beast Hunters?

But without light, Leelan could not see her food. Tomura and the headmistress had said that other animals could recognize food by smell and that Royal Beasts were no exception, but Elin sensed that this was not so. Of course, smell was important, but wouldn't being able to see it be important, too? When Elin closed her eyes, she could detect food with her nose. But it was hard to tell if it was safe to eat without seeing it. It would take courage to put it in her mouth. If, like Leelan, she were already terrified by everything around her, if any little thing startled or frightened her, wouldn't she be even more afraid to eat something that she couldn't see?

When she had ignored Joeun's scolding and gone repeatedly to watch the Royal Beasts, she had been impressed by the mother's keen eyesight. Soaring in the heavens, it seemed to spot prey from an incredible distance and would swoop out of the sky to hurtle unerringly toward it. Then, returning to its nest where its cub waited, it would bob its head up and down with the prey gripped in its fangs and make that distinctive harp-like sound—*lon, lon, lon.* The cub would respond with its own cry and then devour the meat.

What would happen if she waved the meat up and down in front of Leelan instead of just placing it on the floor inside the cage?

Elin tried hanging the meat from the end of a broomstick and waving it through the bars, but as usual there was no response. The light from the door did not reach far enough inside the cage for Leelan to see it clearly. Placing the broom and the meat on the ground, Elin sat down and sank her chin into her hand. If only there was a bit more light . . .

In the evening, the light slanting through the door reached as far as Leelan's feet, yet the cub did not seem alarmed . . . Elin suddenly opened her eyes. Maybe it wasn't afraid because even when protected beneath its mother some light would have reached its feet. Only when the mother stood up and stretched her wings would it have been exposed to light from above. For Leelan, maybe light was something that should come from below.

When she shared this idea with Tomura, who had come to check up on her, his thick eyebrows came together in a frown. "You want me to remove a board from the wall? . . . I can't do that without permission." He had stalked off grumbling to himself, but it appeared that he had indeed gotten permission, for he returned that afternoon with some tools.

"Please be as quiet as possible," Elin said.

"I don't need you to tell me that." He picked up a long iron crowbar and carefully began pulling out the nails while Elin went inside the stable and watched Leelan. After the last nail had been removed, Tomura slid one end of the crowbar between the planks and put his weight on it. There was a creaking of wood as the plank came loose and then the afternoon sun spread across the floor. Elin held her breath. The shaft of light reached up the Beast cub's legs all the way to its belly, but although it lowered its head slightly and blinked repeatedly, it did not flinch.

Elin let out her breath. Her hands were shaking.

Thank goodness . . .

Leelan had shown no fear. Just as she had thought, it was the angle of the light that was important. It was just a small thing, but the fact that her idea had hit the mark made her so happy she wanted to jump up and down. Quietly she went outside.

"How did it go?" Tomura asked, tapping his boot with the end of the crowbar. The expression on Elin's face told him the answer.

"It's not scared. The light comes all the way up to its belly, but it looks calm."

Elin beamed, and Tomura smiled back, perhaps because it was the first time he had seen her smile like this. "Really? That's great."

Elin nodded. "Yes. With that much light, it will be able to see the food. I'm going to wave the meat in front of it."

Tomura looked exasperated. "You're still saying that? It can detect food by the smell. It knows there's food there but just won't eat. That's why we've been having so much trouble trying to care for it."

"Yes, I know . . . But I'm still going to try."

Elin went to the shed behind the dorm and got a spear that the students used for fishing. Balancing a hunk of meat on a broom handle and waving it up and down had proven quite difficult. This time she would skewer it to the end of the spear. She stuck a piece on the spear point to see how it worked and found that it was surprisingly heavy. She had difficulty waving it, and the meat slipped off as soon as the point angled slightly downwards. She would have to cut it smaller. She tried a hunk half the normal size and found that this was more doable.

Tomura was still there when she returned to the stable. He grinned when he saw her newly invented tool. "Ah, I see what you've done. At least it's better than that broom you were using."

Elin blushed and took the fishing spear into the stable. Tomura stood beside the door and peered inside. Although he had only removed one plank, there was enough light now that he could see Leelan from the doorway.

The cub seemed to be used to Elin. When she came into the stable, it merely raised its head without flapping its wings. She approached the cage softly. Where should she put the spear through the bars to make the movement look natural to Leelan? How would its mother have done it? She closed her eyes and conjured up the image of the mother Beast tenderly caring for its young on the rock shelf. With the prey in its mouth, the mother had bobbed her head as if bowing deeply, dropping the food from the cub's eye level down to its legs . . .

Elin opened her eyes and pushed the fishing spear through the bars at chest height. Using the crossbar of the cage as a lever, she raised the meat to Leelan's eye level and then dropped it down to its feet. The cub moved its head, following it. Then it brought its face close as if to sniff it.

Leelan's smelling it! This was the first time Leelan had shown any interest in food. Standing with bated breath, Elin heard a sound like that of a harp string being plucked. *Lon-lon-lon.*

It's talking! But it was different from the wild cub's cry of joy before devouring its mother's offering.

The cub raised its head and looked at Elin, meeting her eyes and staring straight at her. This, too, was a first. It kept repeating that singsong call. And as it did so, it tilted its head, looking first at the meat and then at Elin.

It's asking me something. Elin's pulse quickened. What could it be asking me? How should I answer it? I've got to do something or . . .

But she did not know what to do. She stood frozen, unable to move, and as she stared at Leelan, she saw the light gradually fade from the cub's eyes. It ceased its cries. Its eyes shifted away from the food, and it returned to the same posture as before.

Hot tears burned inside Elin's nose and trickled from her eyes. Leelan had spoken to her, but she had been unable to answer. If she had, Leelan might have eaten. She had been so close . . .

Elin shook the spear, dropping the meat at Leelan's feet, and then withdrew it from the cage. When she went outside, Tomura's face was full of excitement and curiosity. "It looked like Leelan sniffed the meat."

Elin nodded without speaking. Tomura frowned. "And didn't it make a strange noise?"

Elin blinked. "Strange noise?"

"Like a harp being plucked."

Elin stared at him. "But that's how Royal Beasts communicate."

Tomura's eyes widened. "What? I've never heard any Royal Beast make that sound before. Do they sing like that in the wild?"

"You mean the Royal Beasts here don't?" Elin asked in surprise.

"No. The cubs make a noise like a baby crying and the adults make a sort of groaning sound. But that's the first time I've ever heard one make a sound like that."

Elin stared blankly at the stable, her mouth still partly open. The pair of Beasts she had watched on that rock ledge had frequently communicated in that singsong way. She had never imagined that the Beasts here would not. But now that she thought about it, she realized she had never heard the Beasts in the meadow or Leelan call like that . . . until today.

She stood lost in thought, absently stroking one ear. Why had the cub made that sound? And why hadn't it done so before?

"Hey, are you listening?"

She started at the sound of Tomura's voice and opened her eyes. "Oh, yes, sorry. What were you saying?"

Tomura rolled his eyes. "I asked if Royal Beasts sing like that in the wild. You haven't answered me yet."

"Oh, yes, they do. Frequently. But I wonder why the Royal Beasts here don't," she muttered to herself. Lowering her head, she went back into the stable, still stroking her ear.

Leelan had turned once again into a motionless shadow. The meat lay untouched on the ground like a piece of stone. The cub must be hungry, so why wouldn't it eat?

Elin hunched down and rested her chin on her knees. Any creature, no matter what the species, would eat if it were starving, because not to do so would mean certain death. What on earth could be strong enough to suppress even the impulse of hunger? What was going on in the cub's mind? What was it thinking? Humans sometimes took their own life by choice. Were there animals that could do that, too?

But Leelan was asking me something . . . The cub had sniffed the meat and then looked at her and cried . . . as if asking her whether it was all right to eat . . . If she had been able to say yes, in the language of the Royal Beasts, would it have eaten?

Elin crossed her arms on top of her knees and buried her face inside them. The Beasts communicated in a language different from that of humans; their thought patterns must be different, too. If she could understand their language and their way of thinking, maybe she could convince Leelan to eat. But that would involve tremendous effort. Could Leelan survive for as long as it would take Elin to find the key?

Long ago, when she had lost her own mother, she had not eaten for two full days, yet she had not felt hungry. Maybe once one passed a certain point, the body's natural instincts became so distorted that, oblivious to hunger, one gradually grew weaker, both physically and mentally, slowly disintegrating toward death like a pile of sand.

Raising her head, she looked at the shadow huddled on the other side of the bars. Would that cub, its life upset by the tragedy that had overtaken it, die confused in this darkness, never eating, unaware that it was starving? Probably yes, as long as Elin remained unable to answer its question.

A sharp pain shot through her breast, as if she had been stabbed with a needle, and in its wake came a hot rush of sadness. Maybe I'll be too late.

That night Elin skipped supper. She simply had no appetite. Curled up in her blanket, she lay on her side, but for a long time she could not sleep. When she finally dozed off, her mind was filled with dreams.

One image ran through her brain repeatedly: the Royal Beast flying home to its young. Singing tenderly, *lon, lolon, lon . . . lon, lolon, lon*, it waved a chunk of meat before its little one. The cub sang back, adoringly, then bobbed its head and attacked the meat. For some reason, it kept looking at her while it sang. *Lon lon.* As the sound echoed in her ears, the scene changed to Joeun's house. Joeun was proudly showing her his harp and plucking the strings. The tone, he told her, could be changed by rubbing the strings slightly as one stroked them. He plucked a string, *lon*, and at that sound, Elin's eyes flew open. For a moment, she stared into the blackness. Then, throwing off her blanket, she jumped up and dashed out of the stable.

PART TWO

THE ROYAL
BEASTS

FIVE

TURN OF FATE

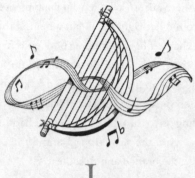

I

THE VOICE OF THE HARP

Propelled by the inspiration from her dream, Elin burst from the stable and raced through the dark forest to the dormitory. The moon had already set, and only the stars glimmered through the thin clouds. There was not a light to be seen in the dormitory. The black shape of the building huddled against the darkness. Everyone must be asleep by now, she thought.

She tried the back door, but it was locked and would not budge. She paused for a moment, biting her lip. She couldn't bang on the door to wake the dorm mother at this time of night. But when she thought of Leelan's condition, she could not bear to wait until morning. With only the starlight to guide her, she made her way to the west side of the building. The room she shared with Yuyan was on the second floor, but the window was dark. Yuyan, too, must be asleep.

A windbreak had been planted near the building, and a branch from one of the trees almost reached her window. Yuyan had once joked that when she and Elin became young women, boys might climb it to court them. Elin rubbed her hands together. She was a good climber. Although there were no branches to give her a foothold on the lower trunk, she had often climbed trees like this with the boys in her village.

She slipped her feet out of her shoes and undid her sash. After tying the hem of her robe at her waist to keep it from flapping open, she wrapped one end of the sash around her right hand, put it behind the trunk and grasped the other end with her left hand. Gripping both ends firmly, she leaned back and hopped onto the trunk. Then she shimmied up the tree like an inchworm, slipping the sash up the trunk and then following with her feet, over and over again. Soon she had reached the thick branch that stretched toward her window. Holding on to the trunk with her left hand, she whirled her right hand in the air to wind the sash around it and then used both hands to pull herself up onto the branch and straddle it.

Looking along it, she saw that it was too thin at the end to bear her weight for very long. She would need to wake Yuyan up first and get her to open the window before she went that far. She broke off a long, thin branch and, holding it at arm's length, tapped it against the window. The sound was muffled by the leaves at the tip, but after tapping three or four times, she saw a shadow move inside.

"Who's there?" It was Yuyan. Just as Elin opened her mouth to answer, however, her friend spoke again. "Kashugan? Is that you?"

Elin almost dropped the stick she was holding.

"You shouldn't be here . . ." Yuyan whispered hoarsely. "I mean I'm glad you like me, but we're still at school, you know."

Elin's mouth hung open as she stared at Yuyan's shadow. Suddenly, a fit of giggles seized her. She clapped a hand over her mouth and shook so hard that she almost lost her balance. Roughly reminded of where she was, she froze, then hastily clutched the branch. This was no time to laugh. If she stayed here too long, the branch might break. She slid gingerly along it and said in a hushed voice, "Yuyan, sorry. It's me, Elin. Open the window."

Yuyan stopped pleading with Kashugan abruptly and wrenched the window open.

"Elin?"

"Shhh!" Elin quickly hushed her. "Sorry I woke you up. Move. I'm going to jump."

After making sure that Yuyan was out of the way, Elin crouched like a frog on the branch, then leapt toward the window and, grabbing the ledge, propelled herself inside. Her feet hit the floor with a loud thud. The two girls remained motionless, listening intently to see if anyone on the floor below had woken up. Fortunately, there was no sound.

"Elin! What's going on?" Yuyan whispered.

"I'm sorry. There's something I need right now, but the back door was locked."

Yuyan let out a deep breath. Stroking her chin and trying to act casual, she said, "So, um, you didn't hear me say anything, did you?"

"No, nothing at all . . . Not even the name Kashugan." As soon as the words were out of her mouth, Elin doubled over, clutching her stomach and quivering with suppressed laughter.

Yuyan gave her a playful kick. "Hey! How dare you laugh at me?" She pummeled Elin's back with her fists, then hugged her as the two of them rolled on the floor, breathless with laughter.

Footsteps thundered up the stairs, and the door slid open with a snap.

"Just what do you think you're doing? It's the middle of the night!" Kalisa, the dorm mother, stood in the doorway. She must have jumped out of bed, because she was still in her nightdress.

The girls hastily knelt on the floor. "Sorry!"

When she saw Elin, Kalisa's eyebrows flew up. "Elin? I thought you were staying in the stable. I'm sure I locked the doors. How did you get in?"

Elin cringed. "I'm very sorry . . . There was something I really needed . . . I didn't want to disturb you, so I climbed in the window."

"The window? But this is the second floor!" She must have noticed the branch outside the window then, because she suddenly lost her voice. After a moment, she said, "You didn't . . . Well . . . In all my twenty years as a dorm mother, you're the first girl who has ever snuck in by climbing that tree." She gave Elin a stern look. "How could you be so reckless? I thought you were a good girl, but I guess I was wrong. I'll let you off this time, but don't you ever try that again! Do you hear me? Think what could have happened if that branch had broken."

"I promise. I won't do it again."

Kalisa sighed and left the room, shaking her head.

Alone again, Elin and Yuyan looked at each other. Their fit of hysterical giggles had passed, leaving in its wake a gentle tickle of amusement in their bellies.

"So what did you come back for?"

Yuyan's question reminded Elin of why she was here. She jumped to her feet and opened the door to her closet. Behind her, she heard the sound of two stones being struck together to make a spark, and within moments, Yuyan had lit a lamp. Elin pulled out the bag containing her small harp.

Peering over her shoulder, Yuyan said, "What's that? Oh! A harp!"

Elin stroked it softly. Of the three harps she had once made with such passion, this was her favorite. When she had lived with Joeun, she had played it often in her spare time, but for the last two months she had not even touched it. Since coming to the school, all her energy had been spent on getting used to her new life.

"I made this myself," she murmured as she stroked it.

"You made it? That's amazing. I never knew you could make a harp."

"It's nothing compared to what a craftsman could do." She began plucking a few phrases of a favorite tune and noticed that the strings had loosened since she had last played it. It sounded slightly different from the pitch of the Royal Beasts in the wild.

"That's lovely," Yuyan said with a blissful smile, but Elin shook her head.

"No, this won't do." She frowned as she plucked the strings one by one. While the tone was similar to the sounds the Royal Beasts had made, it was not quite right. To Leelan, it might not sound like the same language.

When she shared this thought with Yuyan, she looked puzzled. "But why wouldn't it work?" she asked. "It might be a little different, but wouldn't it still be recognizable? I mean, look at us. You and I don't have the same accent, but we still understand each other."

"I know. But somehow I don't think it's going to work. We can recognize words as words because we can tell the difference between sounds like 'eh' and 'lee.' Human languages have an incredible number of very distinct sounds. But the Beasts only seem to have a few. The differences are in pitch and length, and the echo after the note, as well as the order in which those sounds are made. But the differences are so slight that, at first, the notes sound the same. If the Beasts can pick up meaning from such tiny differences as these, then even the smallest deviation might make a sound meaningless."

Yuyan grunted. "Well, I guess the only way to find out is to try it and see," she said.

Elin nodded. There was no guarantee that she could even tune her harp close enough to those notes. It would be a long process, and there was no time to waste on complaining about it. She would just have to try. She stood up.

Yuyan looked startled. "You're not going back there now, are you?"

"Yes, I am."

Yuyan frowned. "Elin, you just can't let something go once you get started, can you? But you're not indestructible, you know. Remember to take care of yourself, will you?"

Elin smiled. "Thanks, Yuyan."

Leelan did not budge, even when Elin opened the stable door and walked inside. Her heart began to pound as she readied her harp and faced that black shadow. Taking a deep breath, she plucked the string that was closest to the sound she remembered, a low middle tone. The note reverberated in the silence.

Lon . . .

The Beast cub moved faintly, as if the sound had disturbed its sleep, but it did not open its eyes or show any interest. Elin tried a few more times, but the cub only shifted slightly, as if annoyed, without opening its eyes.

Elin's shoulders slumped, and she exhaled slowly. She had expected a more dramatic response. While she knew the sound was not exactly the same as the mother Beast's, she had expected Leelan to respond, just as a person in a foreign land might turn to look if she heard a word that resembled her own language.

I guess I was wrong.

She crouched down. The disappointment was worse because she had put so much effort into this. Still cradling the harp in one arm, she pulled the blanket around her and curled up inside. She had barely noticed the hard, cold floor before, but now it seemed to bite into her shoulders. She hugged the harp to her chest, as if to stem the despair that beat in her heart, and closed her eyes. Once Elin fell asleep, her dreams were disjointed and meaningless.

When she woke, the morning light was shining into the stable. She was trembling with cold.

I forgot to put the plank back on the wall. The draft must have chilled my neck and back. I'll have to remember to put it back on tonight.

She had slept with the harp in her arms, and it had left a mark imprinted on her chin. She stroked the spot thoughtfully and raised her eyes to look at Leelan. As usual, the cub sat motionless. The straw beneath it was filthy. If she couldn't do anything else, she might as well clean its stall. It was unfortunate that she would have to use the Silent Whistle, but it would be worse to leave the stall like this.

She sat up and hugged her knees. Still cold, she kept the blanket wrapped around her and touched the harp. Did the sound that the cub's mother made come from its chest? If so, perhaps it was not a clear, ringing tone, but rather duller, resonating inside its body. She might be able to reproduce that sound if she loosened the string a little. She plucked the string absently.

Lon . . .

Leelan's eyes popped open. Elin started and stared at the cub. Its blinking, golden eyes were fixed on her.

Elin plucked the string once more. The cub was still staring at her. It did not react any further, but she had clearly gotten its attention.

What? . . . Why?

It had not responded at all last night. Why was it responding now? What was different? Yesterday it had been sleeping. Maybe it hadn't heard her. Had it responded now because it was awake? Or . . .

Elin looked at her hands. She was holding the harp inside the blanket. She felt the hairs rise on the nape of her neck. Maybe that's why . . . Had the muffled sound from under the blanket been closer to how the note sounded in its mother's body?

Elin closed her eyes and plucked the string again. She listened intently. Yes, it's close.

It was much closer to the sound she remembered, but something still wasn't quite right. Leelan seemed to feel the same way. Now that it had grown used to the sound, the cub closed its eyes, as if it were tired. Elin bit her lip. Leelan had reacted to the harp. If she could just produce the same sound as its mother, she was sure the cub would respond to her. But how could she do that? When she plucked the harp inside the blanket, it was muffled, but the sound she remembered had more resonance. If she could just get a little more tension, if she could pluck the string inside something like a drum, she might get closer. She stood up with the blanket still draped over her shoulders.

"You want permission to leave the school?" Esalu had just returned to her office after breakfast. Resting one hand on her desk, she lowered herself into her seat and looked up at Elin. "Where do you want to go and why?"

"I want to go to the town at the bottom of the hill. I saw an instrument maker there when Uncle Joeun and I were passing through on our way here. I'd like to go as soon as possible."

"You want to go to an instrument maker?"

Elin licked her lips. "There's something I want to try."

Esalu watched her as she explained what had happened since yesterday. The girl kept running her thumb over a red mark on her chin, as if nervous about what the headmistress would think. When she had finished, the only sound in the room was the ticking of the clock. Esalu brushed a strand of hair from her forehead. "I had heard that Royal Beasts make that kind of sound. You remember that I once went to see some Beast Hunters?"

"Yes."

"Well, at that time, a veteran hunter told me that Royal Beasts in the wild make a different sound from those in captivity. He, too, said it sounded like a harp string."

Elin nodded. "Yes, it does."

Esalu continued to gaze steadily at her. "But even if you can reproduce that sound, isn't it a bit simplistic to think that you'll be able to communicate with a Royal Beast?"

A faint blush crept into Elin's cheeks. "I'm not expecting to be able to talk to Leelan with a harp," she said passionately. "Beasts don't think or feel the same way that people do. So even if I could understand the words they used, I don't think I could have a conversation with them. But it should still be possible to communicate very simple things, just like with a dog or a horse. If a dog is trained to understand the command to wait, it will wait until we tell it to eat. I've heard that Royal Beasts are very smart. If that's true, then we should be able to teach them at least the same things that a dog can understand."

Esalu shook her head. "Elin, dogs live in packs that have a very clear hierarchy. Communication with members of the pack is crucial. If they recognize a human as their master, they will obey. Bonds of trust can be formed . . . But Royal Beasts are not the same. They don't live in packs; they're solitary creatures. They will never grow accustomed to people, and they will never form bonds of trust."

"But the Beasts I saw in the wild often spoke to their young. Dogs or horses tend to communicate more through touch, but the Royal Beasts seemed to communicate through that harp-like sound quite a lot."

Esalu's eyes narrowed, but Elin leaned forward. "Miss Esalu, you told me to look for the differences between Royal Beasts in the wild and those in captivity. Well, this is a remarkable difference. I want to know why. Why don't Beasts in captivity make the same sounds as Beasts in the wild?

"Also, Leelan was definitely asking me something. I want to know what it was trying to say."

Esalu ran a finger across her lips and gazed blankly at the bookcase, as if pondering something. "All right," she said finally. "Go ahead and try it." She pulled open a drawer and took out a piece of paper with some writing on it and a bag of coins. "Use these. There are fifty copper pieces in here. If that's not enough, give them this promissory note. It should be worth the loan of a small piece of silver because it's from the school. But don't buy anything that costs more than that."

Elin bowed happily. "Thank you so much!"

Esalu nodded without smiling. "Can you ride a horse? It will take two toh on foot."

"Yes, I can ride."

"Then ask one of the custodians to lend you a horse. Be careful, and make sure you're back before curfew."

"I will."

2

TURNING POINT

A shadow fell across Elin's hands. "There you go again, making something weird. What's that?" She did not look up. Although she heard Tomura's voice, it registered as meaningless sounds rather than as words. Her full attention was focused on trying to decide whether to directly cover the wooden frame of the harp in leather, or to bend a curved bamboo piece along either side of the frame and stretch the leather around them.

She had not been able to get as much leather as she would have liked. If she made a mistake, she would have to go back and buy more. While it would be more work, it would be easier to adjust the sound if she stretched the leather across an outer frame of bamboo. This would also mean that she could use the leather as a single large piece. Then, if that didn't work, she could try the other method and cut the leather into smaller pieces without worrying about running out.

"All right, then. That's decided," she murmured. She picked up two thin bamboo sticks she had gotten from a bamboo artisan. From the instrument maker, she had managed, after much persuasion, to purchase a piece of unscraped cowhide for making drum leather, as well as a piece of scraped hide that had already been stretched and dried across a drum shell. The latter would resonate better, but Elin decided to try the unscraped cowhide first.

It was too dark in the stable for this job, and she was longing for some sunlight, so she had spread a cloth on the grass outside. It was a bright sunny day, warm enough to raise a light sweat as she worked, and a reminder that spring was almost over. She clamped the bottom end of the bamboo frame between her toes and placed the top end against the harp, nicking the spot with her knife to mark it. It was not just the strings but the wooden frame of the harp that resonated. What she was about to do would change her harp permanently. The thought that it would never sound the same again brought a twinge of regret.

She continued working steadily. By the time she had finished, the late afternoon sun had dyed the world with golden light. A leather pouch, curved by the bamboo, now stretched around the right side of her harp. Placing it on her knees, she closed her eyes and plucked a string.

Lon . . .

Resonating within the hide, the sound was muffled. Elin frowned with concentration, eyes still closed as she followed the note. It was close, much closer than before. There was a slight difference in pitch, but the way it resonated was very like the sound that the mother Beast had made. A slow smile spread across her face. This just might work. If she adjusted the tuning slightly, she should be able to get even closer to the sound she wanted.

She let out the breath she had been holding and opened her eyes. They felt raw, and the muscles at the back of her skull were so tight, they gave her a slight headache. She looked around and frowned in puzzlement. A breeze passed gently across the twilit meadow. Somehow, she had had the impression that Tomura was standing beside her, but no one was there. In fact, he had left long ago in disgust because, no matter what he said, Elin only responded with vague noises. She had no recollection of when he had come to stand beside her or when he had left.

Her back and knees were stiff from sitting so long. She grimaced as she stood up. Holding the experimental harp, she looked toward the stable.

Considering Leelan's physical condition, she should really test it now. But her legs would not move.

What if this doesn't work either? She sighed. She would call it a day and try tomorrow when it was light. It was almost time for Leelan to sleep anyway. She knew that she was just avoiding it, but still she packed up her tools silently and returned to the dormitory for supper.

"Miss Esalu! Miss Esalu!"

At the sound of Tomura's urgent voice outside her door, Esalu stopped writing and raised her head. "Come in."

No sooner had she spoken than the door slid open violently. Tomura burst into the room, his face pale except for two bright spots on his cheeks.

"What's wrong?" Esalu asked, frowning.

With trembling lips, Tomura said, "The cub . . . It's eating. Leelan is eating!"

Esalu's eyes widened. "What did you say?"

"Please, come. Come and see."

Esalu rose and ushered Tomura, who was all but hopping up and down, out of the room. When the cub's stable came into sight, the first thing she noticed was a large hole in the wall. Following her gaze, Tomura hastily explained. "Oh . . . I should have reported to you sooner, but I widened the hole yesterday. Elin asked me to."

"That must let in a lot more light. Doesn't it frighten Leelan?"

"No, not at all. Leelan's not afraid of light anymore."

Esalu pursed her lips and approached the stable door. It was much brighter inside than in the other stables. The acrid smell of dung and urine stung her nostrils, but this barely registered. The sight before her brought her to a standstill, her heart in her throat.

Elin was standing on the other side of the bars, face to face with Leelan. In her hands she held some strange instrument with which she produced a soft sound. *Lon, lon.* The Beast cub held down a large piece of meat with its feet and bobbed its head up and down as it tore off chunks and swallowed them.

Esalu stared, forgetting to breathe. The early summer light shone brightly on the filthy straw, on the giant cub, and on the slight figure of Elin, who only came up as high as the cub's shoulder. With each jerk of Leelan's head, dust particles danced in the air.

Elin's face was expressionless, her eyes half closed as if all her attention was focused on the sounds she was making. Leelan gobbled down the last lump of meat and then cried in a wheedling tone. *Shashasha.* Elin walked slowly backward, plucking her harp—*lon, lon, lon*—as if in response, and then ducked her head through the gate of the enclosure. She did not close it, but instead stood on the other side of the bars, quietly and slowly plucking the string. The cub's head swayed as if in time with the harp. Then its eyes grew glazed and sleepy, just like a baby with a full belly and no fear in the world.

Only when its eyes closed did Elin put down her harp and shut the gate. When she picked up her harp again, expression finally returned to her face. As she met Esalu's gaze, her eyes filled slowly with tears. Weeping soundlessly, she walked over to Esalu, and the three left the stable without uttering a word. Once outside, Esalu placed a hand on Elin's trembling arm. "You did it, Elin," she said huskily, then could say no more. Tears pouring from her eyes, Elin nodded.

The three of them sat down on the grass beside the stable.

"So, Leelan responded to your harp just as you thought," Esalu murmured. She ran a hand over the instrument with the hide frame.

"Yes . . . Two days ago, when I plucked the strings in the stable, Leelan looked at me as if surprised. And began making a noise that seemed like a response."

"What did you do?"

"I tried answering back."

Esalu frowned. "But how? Could you understand the meaning of the notes?"

Elin wiped the tears from her cheeks and shook her head. "No. But I remembered a sound that the mother Beast used to make and tried to reproduce it." She adjusted the harp on her knee and plucked a string.

Lon, lolon, lon . . . Lon, lolon, lon.

"The mother Beast often sang like that when cuddling her cub in the nest . . . And when I played those notes, Leelan gave a cry that sounded like a baby asking for more attention."

Esalu leaned forward. "You mean 'shashasha,' right? I've never heard a Royal Beast make that sound. Is that what it means?"

"I think so. Because, in the wild, the cub would rub its nose against its mother when it made that sound . . ."

For the last two days, Elin had played the harp frequently in the stable, focusing her thoughts on reassuring the cub. It's going to be okay, Leelan. You're safe now.

And every time, the cub had made that coaxing sound. Later, it had begun to rub its head against the bars of the enclosure, as if trying to get closer to Elin. It was at one of these moments that she had asked Tomura to enlarge the hole in the wall. Even when its whole body was bathed in light, the cub had not seemed to mind. Not only that, but whenever Elin returned after leaving the stable for meals, it had cried and flapped its wings, just as the wild cub in its nest had done when its mother returned.

This morning, she had been stunned to see it making the same motion the wild cub had made when it wanted to be fed. Now, she had thought. I'm sure it will eat if I feed it now.

But she could not play the harp and wave the meat on the end of a spear at the same time. She had hesitated, but if she let this moment pass, the chance might never come again. Quicker than thought, she had jumped to her feet and opened the gate. Placing a lump of fresh meat inside, and then, plucking the harp to soothe the cub, she had stepped into the enclosure. Tucking the harp under her arm for a moment, she had picked up the meat, raised it to the cub's eye level, and then had placed it at its feet.

Just as before, the cub's head had followed the meat down to the ground. Smelling it, Leelan had looked at Elin and cried uncertainly. *Lon, lon, lon.* Elin had held her breath and plucked out the response. *Lon, lolon, lon . . .*

A light had gleamed in Leelan's eyes, as if the chains on its mind had sprung open. It had bit the meat ferociously, ripping off chunks and gobbling them up.

Esalu had been listening intently, but at this she looked shocked. "Elin!

How could you! Thank goodness you were spared this time, but you should never, ever go near a Beast that hasn't been immobilized."

Elin winced at the violence of her tone. "Yes, I know. I thought the same thing afterward. I'm sorry."

Esalu shook her head slowly and sighed. For some time, no one said a word. Only the sound of the breeze stirring the treetops could be heard in the quiet meadow.

"Outrageous," Esalu whispered finally, and Elin braced herself for another scolding. But the headmistress's expression was gentle. To Elin's surprise, she saw admiration in Esalu's eyes. "You really are an outrageous child, you know," Esalu murmured. "You've done something that no one has ever achieved before."

Much later Elin was to ask herself many times, what was the turning point? Was it the afternoon she had begged Esalu to let her care for Leelan? Or the night she had decided to use her harp to respond? Or was it . . .

And every time she came to the same conclusion. There had been many turning points. Some fate had forced upon her, while for others, she had forged the path herself. But one thing was certain: That particular morning represented a major change in her life.

3

THE DECISION

The Beast cub first ventured out into the sun three days after it began to eat. It had been fasting so long that Elin was worried it would not be able to digest the meat, but it was blessed with good health and steadily recovered without vomiting or getting diarrhea.

When the custodian slid back the large door to the pasture, Leelan ran out into the sunlight on slightly wobbly legs. Located in the highlands, the Kazalumu Beast Sanctuary was mostly meadow, and was bordered by a forest and a river on the far end. The main meadowland, which was the area near the stables, was dotted with large ponds formed by groundwater welling to the surface. These made perfect bathing pools for the Royal Beasts.

Elin and the others watched from a distance as the cub approached one of these ponds on its unsteady feet. It crouched at the edge and drank, then jumped in with a vigor that made those watching gasp. Leelan, looking very pleased, splashed about so exuberantly that Elin, Tomura, and even Esalu could not help grinning.

"Royal Beasts like to keep clean," Tomura said with a laugh. "So I guess it makes sense that having a bath would be the first thing it would do."

"Do you think it could drown?" Elin asked, but Tomura shook his head.

"No, the pond's not deep enough. You don't need to worry."

Squinting against the sun, Esalu watched the cub. Finally, she nodded and said, "It looks like it'll be all right. While it's outside, you two go and clean that stable. I have a meeting now, but if anything happens, be sure to let me know right away."

After watching her stride off into the woods, Tomura turned his gaze back to Leelan. The cub splashed, and drops of water sprayed through the air, glittering like jewels in the sunlight. At last, it climbed out of the pond, drenched and dripping, and sat down in a sunny spot, where it closed its eyes contentedly.

"I feel like I'm in a dream," Tomura said as he watched the cub. "I can hardly believe that that's Leelan over there basking in the sun . . . You're amazing, you know. And I'm not just saying that." Startled, Elin looked up at him. "I mean, you actually did it." He raised his eyebrows and looked down at her. "Even if, for example, you had used some secret of the Ahlyo—"

Elin frowned. "But I never—"

Tomura raised his hand. "Wait until I finish. What I wanted to say is that I would still respect you, even if you had known and used those secret ways." She blinked as he continued calmly. "It's your determination—your absolutely crazy determination—that I respect. For the last twelve days, the only thing you have thought about is Leelan. I have never seen anyone so totally focused as you." His mouth twitched in a smile. "Not to mention your wacky ideas . . . Watching you made me realize that worrying about what

169

other people think really holds back the imagination. You're just totally oblivious to all that. You say the craziest things and never even consider whether people will laugh at you. That's why you come up with ideas that no one else would ever dream of."

Not knowing how to respond, Elin stared at the ground. Tomura patted her shoulder with a large hand. "Time to get to work on that stable, don't you think? I'll rake out the dirty straw, and you run water over the floor, okay?"

Elin looked up in surprise. "What? No, wait. I can do the straw."

Tomura laughed. "It's okay. I'm faster than you anyway." He strode off toward the toolshed. Elin started to follow him, but then turned to take one last look at Leelan. When she saw the cub dozing in the sun, its head nodding, she felt something warm rise from her middle and spread slowly to every corner of her body. The cub was napping in the sun . . . Time, which had come to a halt, had begun to move again. Elin smiled and ran to catch up with Tomura.

The headmistress's office was not that large. When all ten teachers gathered there, it felt quite stuffy. Esalu, however, always held meetings in this room because she found it easier to concentrate here than in the spacious dining hall.

The entire teaching staff was already there when she entered. Some had been puzzled by the urgent summons, and Yassa, her assistant, was in the middle of explaining the situation. The faces they turned to her betrayed their excitement.

"Sorry to keep you waiting," she said.

When she had sat down at her desk, Yassa asked, "How did it go? Did you let it out into the meadow?"

"Yes. It was a little shaky on its feet, but it went out and bathed."

Yassa smiled broadly. "That's wonderful!"

Esalu turned to look at the others. "As I'm sure Yassa has just told you, Leelan has begun to eat and is recovering steadily. I called this meeting today to consult about this matter."

She paused for a moment, but just as she opened her mouth to continue, another teacher cut her off. It was Losa, a middle-aged man with a biting tongue that made students keep out of his way. "Before you continue, may I be allowed to speak?"

"Of course."

"I know that Professor Yassa was still in the middle of explaining, but have you heard the rumor that has been circulating among the students?"

"What rumor?"

"That the child of the Ahlyo has used their secrets to treat Leelan. I told the students not to be ridiculous and reprimanded them severely. However, if I may be so bold as to say so: In my humble opinion, the reason such rumors arose in the first place is because you, the headmistress, entrusted that girl—who is only in the second level of middle school—with the care of a Beast cub. That was a blatant display of favoritism."

Esalu's lip curled. "Yes, that is most certainly what sparked the rumor. But clearly, my decision was not a mistake, at least in terms of Leelan's recovery."

Losa opened his mouth again, but Esalu silenced him with a wave of her hand. "Let me hear your thoughts and questions later. First, let me explain how this all came about." The teachers sat up straight. "You're all aware of the circumstances in which Leelan suffered physical and emotional wounds, so there's no need to confirm those details. The cub showed an extreme aversion to light and had not taken any food or tokujisui for over a month. The situation had reached the point where the cub might have died had it continued to refuse food and drink for another two weeks. This is something that we had all discussed many times, but none of us were able to find a solution. Are you with me so far?"

They all nodded, and she continued. "The reason I chose a girl who was only in the second level to care for Leelan is because I saw a clue to a solution within the knowledge she possessed. Not because she was Ahlyo," Esalu said, looking pointedly at Losa, "but because she had observed Royal Beasts in the wild."

A murmur of voices rose from the assembly. Most of them were learning of this for the first time. Esalu looked around the room, and everyone fell silent again. "The girl, Elin, has observed Royal Beasts in the wild. In addition, she has outstanding powers of creative thinking and observation. This is something those of you who have taught her already know, and it also makes clear why Joeun, who for many years served as the headmaster of Tamuyuan, thought she was so special. I decided that if our traditional approaches had failed, we had nothing to lose by letting her try."

Losa scowled, but many of the other teachers were nodding, particularly those who had taught Elin.

"The first thing Elin discovered was the reason Leelan was afraid of light. She reasoned that for a cub that was used to being in the nest with its mother, light would ordinarily come from below. Being exposed suddenly to light from above would mean that its mother was gone. She asked me if she could remove the boards at the bottom of the stable wall, and I said yes, because I thought it was an excellent idea. And it worked. Leelan was not afraid of light that gradually entered the stall from below."

The teachers' faces registered surprise. Esalu nodded and continued. "Even from this one idea you can see how innovative Elin is . . . I'm ashamed to admit it, but until she said she wanted to remove those boards, I had never even considered the angle of the light."

A rueful smile touched her eyes. "Perhaps it would be more accurate to say that there is a gap in our knowledge, rather than in our ability to think creatively. Because Elin had seen Royal Beasts in the wild, she knew how a mother and cub live in the nest. We, however, don't even know that much. We, who have been entrusted by the Yojeh to care for the Royal Beasts, simply do not know."

A heavy silence fell over the room.

"But—" Yassa began.

"Yes," Esalu said, nodding. "There's nothing we can do about that because we are strictly bound to follow the Royal Beast Canon. Royal Beasts are the symbol of the Yojeh's sovereignty, and when they come under the care of humans, the Canon must be followed to the letter. Every item of their care is recorded in minute detail from what to feed them to the type of straw used in their stalls. The Canon states that Royal Beasts must always be given tokujisui and that we must use the Silent Whistle when we approach them."

Esalu looked at each of them in turn. "That is precisely why it never occurred to us that there might be any other way of raising them. There was no room for us to discover new ideas. But Elin, who is still only in the second level, does not know the Royal Beast Canon. The Royal Beasts that she knows were those she saw in the wild when she went deep into the mountains with her foster father, Joeun. So she treated Leelan not like a Beast in captivity, but like a Beast in the wild. She remembered how the cub demanded food from its mother and what made it feel safe and calm. That's where she got her ideas."

She rubbed her arms. "It made my hair stand on end to hear that the child had walked into the enclosure without using the Silent Whistle. Instead, she plucked a harp that she had altered to sound like the mother Beast. She got close enough to touch the cub when she fed it."

The teachers looked astonished, and Losa exclaimed, "But that's impossible. You mean the rumor is true, then? She used the secret ways of the Ahlyo?"

"Professor Losa," Esalu said with an exasperated expression. "Didn't you hear a word I said?"

Losa looked offended. "What do you mean by that?"

"Exactly what I said. Why do you think that I have just explained in such great detail how Elin came up with her ideas? I was demonstrating that it was not the secrets of the Ahlyo that helped her to heal Leelan. Far from it. Rather, she succeeded because she could examine the problem through the lens of her knowledge of the Beasts in the wild, without being restricted by the Royal Beast Canon as we are. Now is it clear?"

Losa flushed bright red. "I know that. But being able to come up with an idea like imitating a mother Beast on a harp does not make one capable of actually doing it!"

Esalu shifted her gaze ever so slightly, a sign Losa's sharp eyes did not miss. He continued, "You see I'm right, don't you? She couldn't have done it without some special skill. There must be something behind this—something like the tricks that the Ahlyo are said to use."

Esalu stopped him with a movement of her hand. "Just a moment, Professor Losa. It's perfectly natural for you to think that . . . Or rather, I should say that that is precisely why I called this meeting. I knew that some people would think like this." Her expression was stern as she gazed at them. "We must urgently consult about whether or not to report to the palace the fact that Elin did not use the Silent Whistle, and that instead she found a way to communicate with a Royal Beast using a harp."

The teachers looked at one another and began talking among themselves, filling the room with the clamor of their voices. Losa waved his hand as though to cut through the noise and declared in his shrill voice, "But there's no question about it! We cannot possibly fail to report a matter of such grave importance."

Esalu thumped on her desk for silence. She waited for the clamor to recede like the tide pulling back from the shore, and then spoke. "First, think calmly about what would happen if we were to report this to the palace. Until now, we believed that the Royal Beasts would never become accustomed to man. The only method we knew by which we could control them was the Silent Whistle. And all it does is immobilize them. It does not communicate our intentions. Elin has overthrown these assumptions."

"Yes, and that's exactly why—"

Esalu interrupted, her voice like thunder. "Hold your tongue until you have heard me out!" Everyone jumped at the fierceness of her tone. Esalu glared at Losa, her eyes aflame. Words flowed from her as though bursting through a dike. "If we report this to the palace, naturally it will cause an uproar. I will most certainly be accused of failing to obey the tenets of the Royal Beast Canon. I would readily accept that. From the moment I adopted this course of action, I planned how to explain myself. But my greatest concern is for Elin—for this girl that we accepted into our school as our responsibility. It's Elin who I fear for!"

She slammed her hand on her desk. "She has done nothing wrong. Her only crime was to long, with all her heart, to cure Leelan. To do that, she spent twelve solid days and nights with that Beast cub, and because of that effort, she has done what we could not. She has achieved the impossible!

"But there are many who will not believe that this is the result of her efforts. They will look at the color of her eyes and connect her achievement to the blood that runs in her veins." She seemed to be struggling to keep the anguish from her face. "If someone else had also been able to control Leelan as Elin did, I would not be so worried . . . But both Tomura and I tried it. We plucked the harp the same way she did, but the cub only listened. It did not respond the way that it did to Elin."

The expressions on the teachers' faces revealed mixed emotions. Esalu watched them with her right hand pressed against her temple. "Yes, you see. Just as you are now thinking, anyone who hears this will feel that Elin must be different from us. But, you know, I don't believe that that's the case. I ask you to think about this objectively as beast doctors. From Leelan's point of view, yes, Elin is special. But that's not because she's an Ahlyo. It's because she managed to make Leelan see her as its mother.

"Think about it. It's as if Leelan has been reborn. The cub was lost in the terror of darkness, with no mother to respond to its cries. And who was it who responded as its own mother had? Elin. It was Elin who gave it food, while reassuring the cub that it was safe to eat."

Yassa stroked his beard. "You mean it's a type of imprinting?" he murmured.

Esalu nodded. "Most likely. Our knowledge of the Beasts is limited, so it's hard to say for sure, but I believe that that's highly probable."

A young teacher spoke, his face thoughtful. "But many cubs that age have been brought to our sanctuary and raised here, yet there has never been any report of this kind of imprinting."

Esalu turned to look at him, brushing an unruly strand of hair from her face. "What is the procedure you use to feed the cubs?"

He looked surprised, as if he were wondering why she would ask such an obvious question. "I leave the food in the cub's enclosure while it's out in the meadow. If it's raining, or if for some other reason I can't let the cub outside, I blow the Silent Whistle and paralyze it before leaving the meat inside."

Esalu nodded. "Exactly. Now imagine what that looks like to the cub. Food is placed in its enclosure when it's not there, or food appears before its eyes while it lies paralyzed. How could a cub possibly see us as a mother figure who feeds it?"

"Oh," the young teacher whispered.

Esalu continued in a quiet voice. "We've never tried to have any intimate contact with the Royal Beasts. We care for them for decades and nurse them when they die, yet we never establish the type of relationship with them that we would with a cherished dog or horse . . . And as long as we follow the procedures dictated by the Royal Beast Canon, we never will establish such a relationship." The teachers stared at her silently, as if pondering this new perspective. "Elin, who does not know the Canon, cared for Leelan as she would have for a dog or horse. As a result, she is the first person in the entire nation to have succeeded in bonding with a Royal Beast."

Esalu's face was tinged with sadness. "But in the eyes of the statesmen in the palace, this result will have an entirely different meaning. They will rejoice to know that the Royal Beasts can be controlled. And they will try to use Elin for their political schemes because of her special power." Esalu's voice grew hoarse. "When I think of how they will treat her—this unique young woman, who is so clearly of Ahlyo lineage—I am overcome with fear.

"If she becomes the focus of such attention, she cannot fail to attract the notice of the Aluhan and his people. Remember, the Royal Beast, the only living creature capable of devouring the Toda, symbolizes the ascendancy of the Yojeh's power over the Aluhan. I am sure that even you can guess what would happen then."

A heavy silence enveloped the room. Esalu whispered, "If I had known that that child would do something so unorthodox, I would never have entrusted Leelan into her care. But regret will not turn back time. All I can do now is find a way to protect her.

"Let me ask you once again," she said quietly. "Do you think we should report what has happened to the palace?"

Despite the sunny afternoon, at sunset, clouds moved in to cover the sky, and night brought with it a driving rain. Elin crouched on the floor of the stable as always, watching Leelan sleep while she listened to the rain strike the roof.

At suppertime, Esalu had explained to the entire school how Elin had helped Leelan recover. Her explanation had been very clear, and so convincing, it squashed for good the rumor that Elin had used Ahlyo magic. When she had finished, Esalu had called on everyone to guard the story within the walls of Kazalumu. If people from the palace were to learn of this tale, she had said, they would find an excuse to take Elin and Leelan away to Lazalu, the official Beast sanctuary. She had begged them to vow to protect their classmate and the Beast cub and prevent that from happening.

When she had finished speaking, everyone—teachers and students alike—had risen to their feet and, placing their hands over their hearts, had vowed to do so. At the sound of their voices, which had shaken the dining hall, Elin had felt for the first time in her life what it was like to be protected by friends. A hot rush of joy spread through her as Yuyan's hand squeezed hers and her fellow students beamed at her.

But when the meal was over, Esalu had summoned her to her office. There she had learned the other meaning concealed within this vow, and the knowledge made her skin crawl. The Royal Beasts that devoured the Toda were the symbol of the Yojeh's power, Esalu had explained, and her ability to manipulate them would make her a crucial pawn in the eyes of both the Yojeh and the Aluhan. It had never occurred to Elin that the bond between her and Leelan could be seen in that way. Esalu had once told her that the Royal Beasts were political creatures, but now, for the first time, the reality of those words pressed against her heart.

That's what Esalu was protecting us from by making the whole school vow to keep Leelan's story a secret.

Elin covered her face with her hands. *It's all so stupid,* she thought. Royal Beasts eat Toda because that's what they were born to do, just like horses eat grass. How could anyone claim that this gave them the right to rule the country? In her mind's eye, she saw the face of the inspector who had sentenced her mother to death. His reasons had been ludicrous, yet he had spoken as if what he was doing was for the highest good. "The most important qualification for the care of the Toda," he had shouted, "is unwavering loyalty to the Aluhan!"

Mother . . .

Unlike her grandfather, she was sure that her mother had looked after the Toda for their own sake, not for the sake of the Aluhan. Otherwise, she would not have loathed the Silent Whistle or tokujisui. Had she cared about the Toda the same way that Elin cared about Leelan? Had she wished that these creatures, who were born in the wild, could live as nature had intended them to live?

Elin's hands slid slowly from her face. The damp night air touched her cheeks. No matter what happened, she would stay true to her heart. It was no concern of hers what the Yojeh or the Aluhan hoped to achieve through their struggle for power. Even if it should put her life in danger, she would not bend in her resolve. Regardless of what the Royal Beast Canon said, she would never make Leelan drink tokujisui, something a Beast in the wild would never touch. Nor would she ever use the Silent Whistle.

She had shared these feelings with Esalu, although she did not tell her about her mother. Esalu's expression had seemed dark, as if she were pondering something, but she had agreed. "Because," she had said, "I promised to leave the cub in your care if you could make it eat again."

Elin had always thought of Esalu as an intimidating woman, and had suspected her of having hidden motives. To her surprise, however, the expression that had flitted across her face at that moment had reminded her of her mother.

A strong wind shook the Beast stable, and the rain lashed against the walls. The sound must have startled the cub, because its eyes popped open. It stood up, making an anxious sound in its throat, and tottered over to the bars to butt its head against them. Without thinking, Elin rose and, putting her arm through the bars, reached up to rub Leelan's cheek. Its fur, which she was touching for the first time, was far softer than she had imagined.

The cub's eyes narrowed, and it rubbed its cheek against her hand, crying plaintively. Affection welled up inside her. How she wished she was big enough to wrap her arms around this poor, frightened little cub.

4

THE LAST LETTER

Leelan grew rapidly. So much so that Elin noticed changes almost daily. The Summer Trials, exams that determined which students could go on to the next level, were approaching, and she could not afford to spend so much time with the cub. But when she was not there, Leelan wandered about the meadow forlornly, crying and searching for her, and this made it hard for her to focus on her studies.

Kazalumu School could not afford to let students stay any longer than necessary. Those who failed their exams had to leave. If their parents were wealthy enough to pay for tuition, students who failed could stay on for an extra year, but Elin had no intention of asking Joeun for money. Of course, Yuyan helped Elin to catch up on her studies but, much to her surprise, Tomura also came to her rescue. He would have to take the Graduation Trials very soon, which ought to mean that he had no time to spare for anyone else. But he did not seem in the least concerned when he was tutoring her. His claim that he was an exceptional student must be true.

Somehow she managed to make it through the Summer Trials, and then the long summer holidays began. Students were allowed to return home, except when they were in charge of the Royal Beasts and any sick animals from neighboring farms. Most students could not wait to be reunited with their families, while their parents, who needed every pair of helping hands during the busy farming season, were just as eager to welcome them home.

When Elin found out that she could go home for the holidays if she chose, the thought of visiting Joeun passed through her mind. But when she considered how he might greet her now that he had returned to his old life in the capital, she did not have the courage to put that thought into action. And then there was Leelan. If she left the cub behind, someone might use the Silent Whistle. In the end, she contented herself with writing him a long letter. She wrote about life at the school, about Yuyan, and many other things, but she did not mention Leelan, just in case Joeun's son read it. Only a few months had passed since she and Joeun had parted, but the days they had lived together now seemed like some distant dream. She found this both strange and sad.

Yuyan left for her home far away, complaining repeatedly about how much she would miss Elin. Even though she knew that she would see Yuyan in the fall, the room seemed huge and empty without her.

Tomura had passed his exams at the top of his class and was now a qualified beast doctor. He told Elin that he was going to stay in Kazalumu for a year starting in the fall, and help care for the animals while he thought about what to do next. Having graduated with the highest score, he also had the right to remain at the school as a teacher. He had told her frankly that he was considering that option.

With far fewer people, the school was very quiet. The Kazalumu highlands remained fairly cool even in summer. Still, the sultry hum of cicadas could be heard from the forest bordering the meadow, and Elin found herself drenched in sweat every time she cleaned the stables.

Freed from her studies, she spent all her time with Leelan, from early morning until late at night, as if they were parent and child or siblings. One day, she realized something astonishing. Leelan seemed to understand what she was saying—not everything, in the way that a human would, but without a doubt, the cub recognized and understood certain words.

She was cleaning the stable when she first noticed this. Leelan came back before she was finished and was about to come inside. Without thinking, she shouted, "Stay outside! I'm not finished yet!" Instantly, Leelan halted at the doorway. The cub poked its head inside to see what she was doing, but did not come in. At first, Elin could not believe it. She finished cleaning, wiped the sweat from her forehead, and placed a lump of meat in its stall.

"It's all right. You can come in now," she said. As soon as she had spoken, Leelan rushed inside. Elin felt the hairs rise on the nape of her neck.

The only possible explanation for the cub's behavior was that it had understood what she had said. When she thought about this, she realized that it was not so strange. After all, dogs, when trained, could understand such commands as "Stay!" so it made sense that Royal Beasts could, too. But the thought of the possibilities this opened up made her tingle with excitement.

How much language can Royal Beasts understand? she wondered. If she combined harp notes with words and gestures, Leelan might be capable of understanding quite a lot.

From that day onward, she threw herself into teaching Leelan words. Once she started, it was soon obvious that Leelan picked up meanings much more quickly and intuitively than a dog or a horse. Not only that, but the cub watched her closely and tried to mimic her. Perhaps Leelan was observing her facial expressions, gestures, and tone of voice just as intently as Elin had been doing with Leelan in order to guess how the cub was feeling. Royal Beast cubs spent most of their time with their mothers, learning one-on-one how to survive, so remembering the mother's gestures and tone of voice must be very important.

At the same time, Elin was struck by the enormity of the responsibility she had taken on. Is it really all right for me to act as Leelan's surrogate mother? After pondering this for some time, she decided to consult Esalu.

Esalu listened carefully to her concern. When she spoke, her expression was grave. "I see." She paused and stroked her chin. Then she raised her eyes and looked at Elin. "So you're worried that if you try to serve as Leelan's mother, the cub won't learn how to live or communicate as a Royal Beast, and instead will learn to communicate with humans. Is that correct?"

"Yes. If I go on like this, the cub will learn the words that I speak, but not the language of other Beasts."

A sad smile crossed Esalu's face. "Elin, you don't need to worry about that."

"Really? Why?" Elin asked.

"Because the cub will live and die here . . ." Esalu said quietly. "It was a gift to the Yojeh. It will never be returned to the wild. You have forgotten that."

Elin felt as if she had been punched in the chest. Stunned into silence, she could only stare at Esalu.

She did not remember bowing or leaving the room, or even walking down the corridor. When she saw Leelan standing in the bright summer sun, a fierce sorrow surged within her. Even if she never used the Silent Whistle and never gave the cub tokujisui, in the end, Leelan could still never live as Beasts did in the wild. The cub would have to live here to the end of its days. She wept soundlessly, the tears pouring down her cheeks.

Not long after, Elin's letter to Joeun came back in an unexpected way. One evening, as she was feeding Leelan, one of the custodians came and told her that Esalu wanted to see her urgently. She washed her hands quickly and hurried to the office, but when she asked for permission to enter, the voice that responded sounded so husky that she thought it must be someone else.

When she entered the room, Esalu gazed at her steadily with red-rimmed eyes and flushed cheeks. "Come here, Elin," she said.

Elin walked over to her, and Esalu handed her a thin envelope that lay on top of a parcel. Elin's name was written on it in strong black script. She turned it over and saw that the sender was Asan Tohsana. A chill pierced her heart. With trembling fingers, she opened the envelope and extracted the letter, spreading it open. The first line leapt out at her.

My father, Joeun Tohsana, passed away yesterday morning from a heart attack.

The sentence rang repeatedly in her mind. Her brain seemed to have gone numb. No matter how many times she tried to read the rest of the letter, her eyes just slid over the words. She did not realize that she was crying until Esalu gently took the letter from her hands. "May I read it?" she asked.

Elin nodded. Esalu quickly read it through. "Very brief, isn't it? He wrote only the bare minimum . . . What a heartless son." She sighed and gripped Elin's shoulder. "You must be brave, Elin."

Hearing the huskiness in Esalu's voice, Elin felt the truth sink heavy in her chest: Joeun was gone.

His face, his voice, rose in her mind. She would never, ever see him again. Even though she had hoped someday to surprise him by showing him Leelan. Even though she had been aiming to graduate at the top of her class so that she could see the pride in his face and hear him praise her. Even though she had been planning to thank him on that day for taking her in, to tell him that her life had been happy because of him.

She had not told him any of the things that really mattered. And now he had left her without any chance to do so.

Elin covered her face with her hands and wept aloud. Esalu came around her desk and embraced her awkwardly. She held her until she stopped crying. "Don't cry, Elin," she said. "Joeun told me how happy he was to have lived with you. He was so proud of you. So don't cry anymore." She let her arms fall and opened the large parcel that lay on her desk. "Look. Joeun left these for you."

Inside the brown waxed paper were the books that Elin had discovered in Joeun's closet and read in secret.

"Isn't that just like him?"

Elin did not answer. She rested her forehead on the books and wept again.

Joeun's son, in accordance with his father's will, had sent the books to Elin and Esalu after the funeral, along with the simple note announcing his father's death. It was very clear that he wanted nothing to do with the Ahlyo girl that his eccentric father had taken under his wing. Still, because of Esalu's prestige, he would have done what was proper for Elin if she had asked him. Elin, however, had no intention of meeting him ever again. She felt no desire to have a guardian other than Joeun. She was no longer a child. Fortunately, she did not need to worry about food, clothing, or shelter until she graduated, and by then, she would be old enough to take care of herself.

Watching the sky darken to twilight, Elin thought of the summer days she had spent with Joeun. And it gradually dawned on her how incredibly lucky she had been. If no one had found her on the bank where the Toda had left her, she would probably have died. If the person who had found her had been cruel, who knew what kind of misery she might now be living in?

She saw Joeun's smiling face in her mind's eye. Yes, she had been happy. Those days with him were like priceless gems.

When I grow up, I'll go back to the meadow on Kasho Mountain where Joeun had his summer hut.

She would lie in that meadow full of flowers he had loved so much, look up at the sky, and speak with him. She would tell him how grateful she was for all he had done, how much she had longed to see him, how she had spent her days, and how she had grown up . . . She would live in such a way that Joeun would declare, "Well done, Elin, well done. You've lived your life well."

She stood in the meadow gazing up at the sky until the clouds streaming across it turned from smoky gray to a deep, dark blue.

5

WOUNDED

Summer had passed, and the students were just returning when the Beast cub began to shed its baby fur. Beneath the soft down, a thicker coat with a brilliant sheen was beginning to emerge, but the effect was marred by shaggy clumps of partly shed fur clinging to its body.

"Oh, poor Leelan! What a sorry sight," Yuyan exclaimed. She had just returned to the school and was visiting the stable for the first time.

"Don't say that, Yuyan. It takes years for Royal Beasts to fully mature and develop a full adult coat. But at least she'll have shed her baby fur soon. Then she'll look prettier."

Yuyan's brows flew up. "She? You mean Leelan's a female?"

"Yup. I just found that out recently."

It was only when Royal Beasts shed their baby fur that it became possible to determine their gender. Esalu had taught Elin how to check, and she had been thrilled to find out that Leelan was female.

"She may be a girl, but she's a raggedy one, that's for sure," Tomura remarked as he passed by with the medicine box.

Yuyan burst out laughing. "She sure is. A raggedy girl. You couldn't have put it better, Tomura."

It was true. Leelan did look very raggedy. Elin struggled not to laugh. "You're so mean," she teased, and then turned to Leelan. "Don't you pay any attention to them. Just wait until you get your coat. Then they'll see."

Leelan raised her head and looked at them, as if she knew they were talking about her. Then she began scratching vigorously, making a rumbling noise in her throat. The matted clumps must be irritating her. Wisps of downy fur whirled in the air.

"Now if she were a dog or a horse, we could groom her with a brush," Tomura said.

"That's an idea," Elin murmured. She turned abruptly and ran over to the toolshed. Although a dog brush would be too small, a horse brush just might work. When she returned with the brush, Tomura and Yuyan gave her a startled look.

"What on earth are you planning to do?"

"Do you expect me to sit by quietly while you call my little girl raggedy?" Elin said, grinning at Yuyan as she climbed over the fence. She walked over to Leelan, feeling her friends' eyes on her back as they watched her anxiously. The cub made a plaintive sound as she approached. Spreading her wings, which had grown significantly, she hopped up and down, stirring up a cloud of fur in Elin's face.

Elin covered her face with her arm. "Leelan! Stop that! Stay still, will you?" Although she still cooed impatiently, Leelan did as she was told, folding her wings and lowering her head to nuzzle her cheek against Elin's shoulder.

"I don't believe it . . ." Yuyan looked stunned. "Who would have thought a Royal Beast would do that . . . She's acting like a pet dog or cat."

Tomura nodded. "I know what you mean."

Elin raised the brush to Leelan's nose so that she could smell it. "I'm going to brush your fur with this, so stay still." Leelan sniffed the brush inquisitively, but when Elin began running it gently over her lower back, she seemed to like the sensation and began purring happily. "You're just too big, Leelan. It will take me all day to groom you using a horse brush. We'll have to make one your size."

She kept brushing as she talked, working up to Leelan's belly and chest, but when she slipped the brush under the wing joint, it caught in a tangle. It must have hurt. With a squeal of pain, Leelan bared her razor-sharp fangs. Before Elin could react, they had nicked her left earlobe and shoulder. Heat shot across her skin, as if she had touched a pair of red-hot tongs. She leapt away with a scream. Staggering backward, she fell to her knees on the grass. Blood dripped down her face. Blood dyed the grass, spreading slowly around her. A single thought blazed through the confusion in her mind. She raised herself to one knee and twisted her body to look back at Tomura.

"Don't!" she yelled. "Don't blow the whistle!"

Tomura, who had just been reaching for his Silent Whistle, froze and let his hand fall. Elin pressed her right hand against her ear and stood up. She felt no pain in her shoulder. Or rather, she felt no sensation at all, as if it were numb. "Whatever you do, don't blow the whistle!" she shouted again. Then she tried to turn back to Leelan.

The cub was frightened. Panicked by the smell of blood and Elin's reaction, she flapped her wings frantically.

I must scold her, Elin thought. I must teach her right now that her fangs can hurt us.

But when she saw the blood dripping down her arm, she lost her voice. Her heart raced, and the world around her seemed unsteady. There was a ringing in her ears, as if cicadas were humming in her head. Silver specks of light flickered in front of her eyes, and she broke into a cold sweat. Turning her back on Leelan, she began tottering toward her friends. Dimly, she noticed that they had climbed over the fence and were coming toward her, but everything appeared blurred.

I must not fall.

If she did, Leelan would panic.

She forced herself on, dragging one foot in front of the other. Relief washed through her as she felt Yuyan and Tomura support her on either side. The ringing in her ears became a roar, and the world went dark.

When she opened her eyes, she wondered for a moment why she was lying on a soft mattress. She let her gaze wander over the ceiling. The clear light of an autumn afternoon shone through the window. A dull pain throbbed in her left ear and shoulder. She moved her head slowly, wincing, and saw someone sitting by her pillow. It was Esalu. When she saw the disgusted expression on her face, it all came back to her.

"Honestly, Elin," Esalu grumbled. "What a stupid thing to do."

Elin's face twisted. When she thought of how she had sauntered so confidently up to Leelan with that brush in her hand, she felt so ashamed, she wished she could disappear. How was Leelan feeling right now? Yuyan and Tomura must be worried sick, too.

She pulled the quilt up over her head and hid her face. She wept, not so much because of the pain, but because of her stupidity.

"Now don't you go hiding under those covers," Esalu said sternly. "You'll just make the cut on your ear worse. You've got three stitches in your earlobe and eight in your shoulder, you know." She pulled back the covers roughly. "If you're ashamed of what you've done, then just make sure you never do such a foolish thing again! This time you got away with a cut on your ear and shoulder, but if those fangs had been even slightly to the right, they would have sliced your jugular. If that happened, you'd be dead. Royal Beasts are not pets. You were so cocksure of your bond with Leelan that it blinded you to the obvious risk!"

Elin was sobbing so hard that she could barely breathe, but she nodded.

Esalu sighed. "I have to admit that I'm partly to blame. I overestimated your ability. Leelan has almost matured into an adult now. I think it's better if you don't touch her anymore."

Elin opened her eyes and stared at Esalu. "No . . . I won't stop."

Esalu glared at her. "I don't care whether you like it or not. No means no. Whether Leelan means to harm you or not, she could cut your throat and kill you just by baring her fangs."

Elin shook her head as best she could without lifting it from the pillow. Struggling to suppress her sobs, she said, "I . . . know that. I . . . promise . . . I won't be . . . careless again . . . But if I . . . distance myself from Leelan . . . it won't be fair . . . She sees me as . . . her mother . . . Please . . . let me stay . . . by her side . . . until she's ready . . . to be independent."

Esalu frowned and looked at her for a long moment. Finally, she said with a sigh, "If you insist on seeing Leelan so subjectively, you're going to get yourself killed one of these days. You've fallen into the same delusion that afflicts so many people who care for creatures. You think that this was just a freak accident, don't you? That as long as a fluke like this never happens again, Leelan will never hurt you. Because you're special to her."

Elin's face crumpled. Watching her, Esalu said softly, "It may be true that to Leelan you are like a mother . . . But a beast is always a beast." She broke off and rubbed her face with her hand. Her eyes were blurred with fatigue. She looked at Elin and asked, "Do you know what it takes to make a beast obedient?" She did not wait for an answer. "Beasts obey anyone they perceive as stronger than themselves, anyone they see as superior. For a beast, the most important thing is the ability to discern how strong others are. You studied that, right? Beasts that live in packs or herds measure each other's strength and decide who is stronger. The weak obey the strong.

"In the world of beasts, strength and weakness are unforgiving measures that determine survival. A runt will not receive food from its mother. It will be kicked from the nest by its siblings and left to die. A weak male will never have the chance to mate and leave offspring in this world. The weak cannot protect their territory.

"In a one-on-one relationship, it's only natural for beasts to measure which one is the stronger."

Esalu pulled the Silent Whistle out of her robe and shook it in front of Elin. "You hate this, I know. But the Royal Beasts are far superior to us in strength. This is the only thing that can convince them of our superiority, despite our physical weakness." She threw the whistle on top of Elin's chest. "If you see yourself as Leelan's mother, then train her. While she is still young, drill into her the fact that you are superior, so that she learns to obey you without question . . . If you don't, when she grows up, there will inevitably come a time when you can no longer control her."

Esalu's eyes had a cold glint that would tolerate no argument. "The feeling that all creatures share in common is not love. It's fear, Elin. Engrave that on your bones. If you continue to dream and nurture this illusion in your heart, your eyes will lose the ability to see the truth. Those wounds are a good lesson. Decide right now to abandon that dream. Be objective and logical, and learn to keep a proper distance, to take a stand."

Elin slid her hand out from under the covers and grasped the Silent Whistle. She stared at it for a while, but then held it out. Esalu looked at her silently, and Elin returned her gaze.

Finally, Esalu said in an exasperated tone, "Write your will then. Write that if you die, it was your own fault—that it was due to your own stupidity. Say that the headmistress is not to blame for your mistake. Write it and give it to me when you're done." And with those words, she left the room, an angry scowl still on her face.

Esalu might just have been venting her frustration, but when Elin was able to get out of bed, she really did write a will. She did not address it to anyone in particular. She merely wanted to record her feelings, because if she were to keep getting close to the Royal Beast, she might lose her life at any time. When she recalled the moment Leelan's fangs had sliced her ear and shoulder, her stomach knotted. If they had touched her neck or midriff . . .

She did not need Esalu to warn her. She was terrified to the core. For the first time in her life, she was afraid of Leelan. Yet she still could not bring herself to use the Silent Whistle to "train" the cub. As she wrote her will, she remembered Joeun's warning.

"Listen. There is a big difference between people and animals. Don't ever forget that. Totchi is a gentle mare. She's used to you and to me. She's like family. But if a wasp stung her and she was startled by the pain, she could kill you with one blow of her hoof. A person stung by a wasp would go crazy with pain, too, but they would never kill their friend because of it. A horse can't make that distinction."

It was true. There was a huge gap between beasts and humans. She had a bad habit of taking that gap too lightly, such as the time she had killed a honeybee by trying to stroke it. These wounds were a warning stamped on her body so that she could never forget.

Still, she did not think that Esalu was right. Fear could not be the only emotion that living creatures shared in common. The feeling that she sensed Leelan had for her was far warmer than that. How could she use the Silent Whistle if she wished to teach Leelan that violence was wrong? Using the whistle would be like beating her with a whip, and she could not bear the thought of training her like that.

Not wishing to give the will to Esalu in person, she put it in an envelope with the headmistress's name on it and placed it in Esalu's shoe cupboard. She did not know if Esalu had read it or not, for she never mentioned it, but she did not stop Elin from going to Leelan once her wounds were healed.

SIX

FLIGHT

I

QUICKENING ANXIETY

By nature, Shunan was a light sleeper. And sleep did not come easily right now. His mind was busy with many thoughts, for he knew it might not be long before he must take his father's place as Aluhan. For that reason, he had chosen to wander through the palace gardens tonight. Although he pitied the guards who must stay with him so late, he found his thinking was sharper when he paced back and forth gazing at the thin clouds veiling the moon.

For the last few years, two concerns in particular had occupied his mind. One was the movement of the Lahza, the horse riders who were spreading across the eastern plains, swallowing up the many tribes that lived there. In the past, they had been just one small tribe among many, but now they had amassed more than a hundred tribes and were building a formidable nation. Their frequent raids along the eastern border of Lyoza were proof that they had ambitions regarding this land.

Up to now, the Toda Warriors had repelled them every time. But the Toda were few in number. With incursions so frequent, the Aluhan could not rely on Toda troops alone, and recently he had begun recruiting large numbers of soldiers from the common people. This only increased the commoners' discontent.

And that was Shunan's second concern. His people shed their blood to protect this land, yet instead of the respect that they deserved, they were viewed by the Holon with fear and contempt, and were suspected of plotting to kill the Yojeh. Why are we the only ones to lay down our lives in defense of the kingdom? This was the doubt that festered in his people's minds, and it was turning slowly into discontent and a deep-rooted bitterness.

That's what is breeding assassins in our midst, yet every attempt on the Yojeh's life increases the Holon's fear and hatred for us . . . The longer this goes on, the more entrenched this vicious cycle will become. If we don't break free of it, there will be no future for our country.

But to choose the wrong way to do so would cut even more deeply into the fabric of the nation. No matter what, they must avoid acting hastily. Shunan's father, however, suffered from an old illness that was growing steadily worse, and Shunan feared that he would force himself to take action before he had resolved the doubts in his mind. He knew full well that if his father should commit the act of brutality he was contemplating, it would not be from self-interest, but rather to protect the future of his sons. But the method he was considering would be a colossal mistake.

The problem was the shape their country should take. He and his father were both in agreement on the ultimate goal. What they did not agree on was how to get there. Shunan was sure that his father's approach would not bring about a better future.

He claims that the Yojeh's authority is all froth and no substance, but he doesn't realize that the structure of that power is laid deep within his own mind.

And that is why coercion and force were the only solutions his father could see. If he knew what Shunan was thinking, his eyes would pop out of his head, and he would undoubtedly declare it impossible. He would have good reason, too. Anyone would agree, whether they were Holon or Wajak. His brother Nugan, who believed that the true way of the Aluhan was to swear fealty to the Yojeh and accept defilement on her behalf, would blaze with anger and denounce his idea as a desecration.

But this country will only be reborn when we succeed in destroying the invisible yet rigid power structure embedded in people's minds.

Shunan was aware that his people trusted him, and he believed that he could do what it took to fulfill that trust. But if Lahza became a powerful kingdom, it would no longer be possible for the Aluhan's people alone to defend this country. Should that day come, their survival would depend upon their ability to unite their two territories.

He came to a halt at the edge of the pond and looked up at the moon. There is only one way to bind our two peoples together. But how was he to share this feeling, to communicate his thoughts to her? His mind had been focused on this problem for some time. Once and only once, he had summoned the courage to convey to her what he was thinking. Her response had been curt—a natural reaction. But if he failed to change her concept of "natural," there could be no future for this country. To communicate with her would be dangerous, like walking a tightrope, but it would have to be done.

While Shunan was gazing up at the moon in the palace garden, Ialu was lurking in a back alley in the capital. Ever since the attempted assassination on the Yojeh's birthday four years earlier, he had been following a hunch. No one knew the true nature of the Sai Gamulu. Had the assassin really been a member, or was someone using its existence as a cover for their own assassination plot? If his suspicion proved to be right, it would mean that someone was trying to kill the Yojeh for a very different reason than the Sai Gamulu.

He tensed as he felt someone approaching. A dark figure emerged far down the street and moved toward him. As soon as he saw the outline of the person's face by the faint light of the moon, the tension drained from him. It was one of his trusted men who was helping with the investigation. The man bowed slightly.

"How did it go? Did you find anything?"

He nodded. "It may not be directly related to the same incident, but I uncovered something disturbing as I was checking up on the merchants he deals with."

The demand for wild Toda eggs had risen dramatically over the last few years due to frequent skirmishes with the horse riders of Lahza, and many men had begun collecting the lucrative eggs, despite the risks involved. Most people in this trade were Wajak, not only because Toda were considered unclean, but also because they were bought by the Aluhan. Recently, however, some Holon had become involved. Wild Toda lived in the remote mountain rivers and swamps of Yojeh territory as well, so it was no surprise that people would be drawn by the promise of high profits. But to sell the eggs, they needed a connection with the Toda traders of Aluhan territory. According to Ialu's subordinate, one merchant who served as a middleman had dealings with the person he suspected.

"Toda . . ." Ialu whispered. The man in question ought to have no relation to Toda at all. If he were indeed trying to gather fighting serpents, then Ialu could perceive a dreadful possibility. "Thank you. You did well. I'm impressed that you were able to find out that much in such a short time. Please keep your eye on that merchant. See if he is not only selling eggs but is involved in raising them somewhere as well."

Whenever her maidservant Nami brought some of her mother's baking, Seimiya's heart beat faster, as if she had just run a race. As the official taster who protected the Yojeh's only granddaughter from poisoning, Nami was highly trusted, and no one thought of inspecting the food she brought. But once, a letter had been hidden within one of her baked goods.

When she had given it to Seimiya, Nami had been prepared to die. She had waited until they were alone and then, her face deathly pale, she had presented it to Seimiya and told her that during her holiday the Aluhan's eldest son had come to her alone one night. With a grave expression, he had told her his vision of how the Yojeh could be saved from assassination and the nation spared from division.

With trembling lips, she had said, "Lord Shunan told me that he intended to kill me if I objected. But although I am not wise, I think his idea is the best way to save the Yojeh. I know that if others heard what he suggested, they would be furious. But for me, the only thing that matters is your life and the life of the Yojeh." A light had kindled in her eyes as she gazed at Seimiya. "You have the Se Zan to protect you, but in the end they are only human. There is no guarantee that they will be able to stop every assassin that comes. I . . . I am afraid. I'm afraid that one day, both of you . . ."

Seimiya, her face bloodless, had grasped the girl's trembling arms. "That's enough, Nami. I understand. . . . But the road he proposes is unthinkable. He must know that. So why did he even suggest it?"

The blood that ran in her veins was not that of ordinary people. It was sacred, inherited in a direct and unbroken line from her ancestor, who had been born in the land of the gods far beyond the Afon Noah. It was this that made the Yojeh the soul of the nation. The most important duty of a woman born to that line was to protect its sacredness. That was why they often married an uncle or a cousin. If the women in the Yojeh's line married men without that ancestry, even members of the nobility, the sacredness of that blood would be watered down.

She could not help being attracted to Shunan. If only I had been born a noblewoman instead . . . What joy she would have felt to receive this letter had that been the case. She had bitten her lip at this thought. She hated to give in to self-pity, no matter how small.

Looking sternly at Nami, she had said, "I understand why you did this. But you must never again bring me such a letter. Were anyone to find out, it would indeed divide this country, so make sure that you never mention it to anyone."

"Yes, my lady," Nami had replied anxiously.

In the four years since that time, there had never been another letter, but whenever Nami brought her mother's baking, Seimiya could not help but remember Shunan's proposal.

Nami was just pouring tea into a fine china cup when she heard the voice of a young Se Zan outside the door.

"Lord Damiya is here. Shall I let him in?"

Seimiya raised her head and nodded. Nami opened the door, and Damiya walked in bearing a large box. He must have just returned from outside, for he was cloaked with the smell of wind—a scent that raised Seimiya's spirits. Whenever she saw her uncle, he reminded her of a fresh breeze blowing through a stuffy room—bright and bracing, but with a hint of danger, as if he might carry her off to some forbidden place.

"My dear Seimiya, how are you today?" He smiled and made to place the box on the table. Nami hastily pushed the tea and sweets to one side, and he nodded to her before gently putting it down.

"What have you brought me, Uncle? Knowing you, it's bound to be something strange."

Damiya looked at her in mock offense. "Strange? Now when have I ever given you something strange? Here, take a look." He lifted the lid and gestured toward the box.

Seimiya gasped. Inside lay a perfect replica of the palace, along with the gardens and the forest surrounding it. Surely this must be what it would look like from the sky. The model was so exquisite, she could hardly believe it was man-made, but she gave him a playful glare. "Dear uncle, you're still bringing me toys, as if I were a mere child."

Damiya reached out a hand and caressed her cheek. His touch was so gentle, it was as if a wing had brushed her face.

"If I thought you were a child, I certainly wouldn't bring you something like this. Only a grown woman could appreciate such fine craftsmanship. You know perfectly well how much talent has gone into this, don't you?"

Seimiya cast down her eyes, her heart beating quickly. She strove to keep her voice calm so that he would not know how his touch had unsettled her. "Of course, I do."

He took her hand gently in his and placed her fingers on the tips of the wooden trees. They tickled like the hairs on a calligraphy brush, and she tensed.

"It's amazing, don't you think? See how soft they are. If the gods reached out to touch the trees in the forest, I bet they'd feel just like this."

Seimiya endured the tickling in her fingertips as she listened to his voice.

Four years had passed since the autumn Elin had first arrived at Kazalumu School. Every fall, the trees hedging the highlands turned bright gold in a blaze of color against the distant snow-topped ridges of the Onolu Mountains. The sight always took her breath away. But autumn did not linger in the highlands. It sped away, followed by the cruel winter.

The snow-laden wind that blew from the northwest collided against the mountains, dumping heavy snow on the north face. Fortunately, this meant that not much snow fell on the highlands, which were on the southeast side. But the chill of the wind, freed from its burden and whistling lightly down from the mountains, penetrated to the bone.

By the winter solstice, snow fell even in Kazalumu, fluttering down to cover the meadow, the stables, and the school in a thin white blanket. While Royal Beasts did not like rain or thunder, they were impervious to the cold. Regardless of whether the meadow was covered in snow, as long as it was sunny, they went outside, their breath frosting the air.

Leelan had matured into a full-fledged, well-proportioned Royal Beast. But what everyone admired most was her fur. Tomura, who was now a teacher, was fond of remarking to his colleagues that even the coats on the Beasts at the Lazalu Sanctuary could not compare in beauty to hers. He need not have bothered, as they were already staunch admirers.

One day, Esalu stood watching Elin with Leelan. She remembered Elin telling her that the fur of wild Beasts seemed to change color depending on the light. True to those words, Leelan's fur shone golden at sunset and silver in the morning. But what caused this difference? Several things came to mind, but two of these seemed particularly significant. Since Elin had begun to care for her, Leelan had never been immobilized by the Silent Whistle, even though it was used regularly on the other Beasts, nor had she drunk any tokujisui.

If those are the differences that cause her fur to shine like that . . . why on earth would the Canon dictate that we care for Beasts in a way that dulls their fur? For many years, Esalu had wondered if there wasn't some hidden purpose behind the Royal Beast Canon. I wonder if the warning which that man gave me has something to do with this.

Once, long ago, while searching for Royal Beasts deep in the mountains, she had met a tall stranger, an incident which she had never mentioned to anyone. When she had first learned that Elin had seen Beasts in the wild, she had feared that she might have some connection with him. Having observed her for the last four years, however, Esalu had discarded that suspicion and was now convinced that, just as Joeun had said, Elin knew nothing of the vows the Ahlyo kept, even though she was of Ahlyo blood. If she had been bound by those vows, she would never have deviated from the Canon.

The encounter remained clear in her memory—the tall man's cold green eyes and his robe that was as gray as the mist, the dim light among the trees that had surrounded them, the smell of damp moss.

When he had learned that she was a teacher at the Royal Beast Sanctuary, he had warned her, "You must stop looking for Beasts in the wild. From the moment a Beast falls into the hands of men, it is bound by Aoh, the Law. Without Aoh, Beasts are dangerous. You, and those like you, whose duty is to bind them to the Law, must not see them in the wild."

When Esalu had asked him why, he had answered coldly. "You are an intelligent and enthusiastic scholar who raises the Yojeh's Beasts. To see them in the wild would kindle a flame in your heart that could trigger the most fearsome calamity. I'm sure you find that hard to believe, but I know what you do not. I beg of you, please heed my warning. Do you wish to cause a disaster for which you would never forgive yourself?"

She had not wanted to bow to an Ahlyo prophesy that made no sense, but the cold fear that had gripped her was still firmly rooted in her mind. She had felt as though the Ahlyo were always watching her, and so had not gone hunting wild Beasts again.

What could be so dangerous about seeing Royal Beasts in the wild? she had wondered. What was the Law meant to protect, and how was that connected to the Beasts? It had made her angry to think that those who dedicated their lives to caring for the Royal Beasts were not allowed to know. The idea that people would keep others ignorant in order to protect something was abhorrent. Sound judgment could only be made once one knew all the facts. To conceal them would prevent people from making an informed decision.

Who is trying to keep us ignorant? She did not think that the wandering Ahlyo had that kind of power. And besides, the Canon was supposed to have been written by the first Yojeh. Could it be the Yojeh?

For years, she had had no way of finding out, but then Elin had come along. In her naivety and ignorance of the Law and the Canon, she had burst through the rules with ease. At times, the sight of her with Leelan filled Esalu with foreboding. Will something terrible happen if we continue raising Leelan like a Beast in the wild? Leelan already stood out from the other Beasts in the sanctuary. If she continued to mature like this, would it cause some disaster? The Ahlyo had tried to stop Esalu from even seeing wild Beasts. What had he feared?

Esalu was aware that part of her wanted to learn what that danger was, and that this was one reason she had given Elin free rein. At the same time, however, she was afraid to put Elin at risk just to satisfy her own curiosity. Perhaps she should tell her everything. Even if she did, Elin was unlikely to change how she cared for Leelan because of what the Ahlyo had said. After all, this was the girl who had written her will so that she could stay with Leelan. Still, she could not bring herself to reveal to Elin that it was the Ahlyo's warning she had feared all these years.

Leelan spread her wings, and Elin's slender figure seemed suddenly even smaller. Esalu stood and stared for a long time at the girl as she reached up, without the least trace of fear, to stroke the Beast's chest.

2

FLIGHT

When the New Year's break came and Kazalumu was once again deserted, Elin breathed a sigh of relief. During the last four years, a disturbing idea had been germinating in her mind. Most people would probably have dismissed it as nonsense; but those who did not might be alarmed. She did not even feel comfortable sharing it with Yuyan.

As Elin had come to know Leelan better, there were times when the Beast's intelligence amazed her. In certain ways, Royal Beasts were very like humans. She did her best to prevent others from noticing these things, but by spring of her first year, Leelan could understand almost everything Elin said. She had not only mastered the "words" that Elin had created from variations of *lon*, the Beasts' harp-like cry, but she also used them to convey what she wanted.

The first "sentence" she had communicated had been very simple— "back," "itchy," "scratch." Elin, however, had been stunned. What she had just heard seemed impossible. She had taught Leelan sounds for different parts of the body, such as back, head, shoulder, and feet. She had also taught her sounds for "hurt" and "itchy," and for "touch" and "scratch." But she had never shown her how to put those sounds together to make a sentence. Instead of merely mimicking Elin, she had combined sounds on her own to convey where she itched and what she wanted done about it.

Elin knew that dogs and horses could understand some words and convey what they wanted to some extent, but only through sounds they already used, such as barks or whinnies, along with body movements and facial expressions. They did not use a language composed of arbitrarily combined sounds. Leelan, however, not only used the "words" that she had been taught, but had figured out how to combine these to convey a complex wish. She had grasped the sounds and the semantic rules that Elin had created and had used them to produce language. In no time at all, the two were communicating quite naturally—Elin speaking to Leelan in human speech, and Leelan responding with harp-like cries . . .

There were times when Elin felt that she had opened a forbidden door. Honeybees built hives, marvelous structures that humans could never hope to imitate. In the same way, all wild creatures used innate, yet astounding, capacities to build the environment in which they lived. But she could not help thinking that what Leelan had done surpassed the bounds of nature.

Or could it be that Royal Beasts in the wild also modulated their cries to make conversation? If so, then they were much closer to humans in their thought processes than anyone had believed. And if that were the case, then why had no one ever had a conversation with one, despite the fact that Beasts had been raised in captivity for several centuries?

This point struck Elin as very unnatural. When she had first noticed Leelan's ability, she had reread the Royal Beast Canon. The first Yojeh must have known what Royal Beasts could do when she had written these rules, and it was then that the idea came to Elin: Did the Yojeh deliberately design the Canon so that no one would ever communicate with the Beasts? Elin's heart had grown cold at the thought. If that was her intention, then I may be making a terrible mistake . . .

She did not know why it would be taboo for people to speak with Royal Beasts. But if the hidden purpose of the Canon was to prevent this, what would happen if the Yojeh or those around her discovered what she was doing? What if not just Elin but Esalu and everyone else at the school got into trouble? This was her greatest fear, and the reason she was so careful to conceal the fact that she and Leelan could communicate.

When anyone else was around, she hardly spoke to Leelan at all. The harp was a bit safer because no one else could understand, but even then she tried to use it when no one was there, limiting any conversations with Leelan to times when they were far from the school, such as when they were in the shadow of the forest or at the river. She had to be discreet, however, because people like Professor Losa might get nosy if she seemed to be keeping Leelan out of the way.

For this reason, she felt a tremendous load lift from her shoulders whenever there was a holiday.

Leelan wanted to go out every day. "I'm not like you. For me, snow is cold," Elin grumbled, but Leelan ignored her. She hopped lightly on her hind feet, moving with ease across the snowy fields. Her favorite spot was the ravine through which the river flowed. She could spend most of the day perched on a crag just listening to the water murmuring.

But the cold bit through Elin's leather boots and fur-lined coat, freezing her to the bone, and her feet sank in the powdery snow, making it a struggle just to walk. She had to stop frequently and stretch the kinks out of her back. Leelan could have raced ahead, but she always stopped, waiting patiently like a mother for her child. This made Elin wonder when Royal Beasts normally left the nest.

Leelan looked and sounded far more like the wild Beasts than those at the sanctuary, and she appeared to be full grown. Yet she still could not fly, nor did she show any sign of wanting independence or of going into heat. When did wild Beasts reach maturity and set off to stake out their own territory? Did being raised by humans delay growing up?

When I graduate . . .

Elin's dream was to study Royal Beasts in the wild and compare their behavior with those at the sanctuary. To do that and remain in charge of Leelan, however, she would have to win the right to stay at the school by placing first in the Graduation Trials. Yuyan assured her that even if she did not place first, she would still be able to stay, precisely because of Leelan, but Elin did not want special treatment. She did not want to owe anything to anyone.

These were the thoughts in her mind as she tramped through the snowy meadow. The land began to slope gently downward, and the forest came into view. The custodians kept the trees well trimmed to make it easy for the Royal Beasts to pass through it. Unlike the deciduous forest bordering the southeast edge of the highland, the wood here on the northern edge was filled with dark green conifers, which kept the ground virtually bare of snow.

The wind dropped when they entered the trees, and the air felt warmer. Except for the occasional thud of snow sliding from a branch, not a sound could be heard, not even birds calling. Inhaling the tangy scent of the forest, Elin followed Leelan to the ravine, where a steep cliff overlooked the river below. In summer, they could climb down, but in winter, the icy snow clinging to the rocks made it far too dangerous.

Leelan's favorite place was a ledge that jutted out over the ravine. Exposure to the sun kept it free of snow, and a rock outcrop sheltered it from the wind. When Leelan perched on the ledge, Elin nestled like an egg between her legs to warm herself. She was sure that Esalu would have a fit if she saw them like this, but Leelan had learned a lot and now knew that Elin could be easily harmed. Once she was warm again, Elin pulled a book from her cloak and began to read. Leelan's chest rumbled like a bellows as she rested in the sunshine, looking blissfully content.

"That, good."

Elin raised her head at the sound of Leelan's voice. "What's good?"

"That."

Elin turned her eyes to follow the Beast's gaze and saw a single bird floating in the air. It did look nice and plump. "You're right. It's probably very tasty. But you can't catch it."

"Why?"

"Because it's flying."

Leelan made a cooing sound in her throat. "Fly?"

Elin put her book away and stood up. Spreading her arms, she waved them up and down, mimicking flight. Leelan spread her wings and flapped them, but nothing happened.

"Back, neck, itchy. Scratch."

Elin sighed. "The back of your neck? I can't reach. Bend down, will you?"

Leelan crouched and bent over.

"I'm going to climb up, so don't move, all right? Even if it hurts, don't shake me off." Leelan was three times taller than her, which made Elin feel like a tiny bug whenever she climbed onto her back. She gripped Leelan's fur to hoist herself up.

"Where? Here?" She noticed a spot on Leelan's neck where the fur was ruffled. She began to scratch it, and Leelan purred ecstatically.

Suddenly, Elin lurched. For an instant, she thought Leelan had moved, but then she knew what it was.

Earthquake!

The trees whipped back and forth, and snow cascaded from their branches. She could hear the rock ledge groan beneath their feet. Never had she felt such a strong quake before. Leelan gripped the ledge with her claws and spread her wings as she struggled to stay upright. Elin closed her eyes and clung desperately to her neck. With a terrible sound, the ledge beneath them snapped, then crumbled, and Leelan, whether through quick thinking or pure instinct, kicked the ledge with her feet and beat her great wings.

Elin felt her body rise, and a blast of wind tore at her hair. Beneath her, she could feel Leelan's powerful muscles moving rhythmically. The wind on her face was so strong that she could barely open her eyes, and even when she did, all she could see was sky.

We can't be . . .

Gripping Leelan's neck tighter, she shifted slightly so that she could look down. The sight made her gasp.

We're flying! . . . We're flying through the sky!

The river looked like a narrow ribbon. The snow-covered woods and fields, brilliant in the sunlight, extended far into the distance. Elin could feel Leelan's joy as she thrust through the air on her great wings. She moved as if she could see the wind and the layers in the atmosphere, as if she knew instinctively which currents to use and which to avoid.

"Happy, happy, happy . . ." she crooned as she soared through the heavens.

It was all Elin could do to hang on. Wind roared past her ears. She could not bear to look down, and the knowledge that there was no earth beneath their feet made her tremble. She forced the thought from her mind. She could hardly breathe, but when she raised her head for air, the wind hit her so hard she almost let go. Hastily, she buried her face in Leelan's neck. This offered some relief, as the force of the wind now pushed her against Leelan's back, but there was nothing she could do to alleviate the cold. Icy air flowed across her, her hands grew numb, her teeth chattered, and tears welled in her eyes, which were screwed shut.

"Leelan . . . Leelan!" She screamed. "Down! Leelan, please! I'm cold!"

Leelan, drunk with elation, did not respond at first. Only after Elin had shouted repeatedly did she begin slowly to descend. Wings widespread, she glided down onto the snow-covered meadow. The impact as Leelan's feet hit the ground was painfully jarring. Somehow Elin managed to disentangle her frozen fingers from Leelan's fur and slide off her back. Unable to move, she lay huddled on the ground, shaking uncontrollably.

Leelan whimpered anxiously, peering at her, then gently lowered herself on top of her, like a mother Beast warming its young. Even when the Beast's warmth had seeped through her body, Elin could not stop shivering, and her hands shook as she pressed them against her mouth. When her trembling finally ceased, all strength seemed to have been leached from her body, and she lay curled fetus-like beneath Leelan's soft, warm belly for a long time.

At last, she crawled out, but remained crouched in the snow, eyes blank, oblivious to Leelan's cries. It was only when she slowly raised her head and saw Leelan's face that emotion returned.

"Happy, happy, happy." Leelan's eyes were shining, and Elin could see that she was bursting with joy. A grin spread across her face.

"You flew . . ." Her eyes burned with the tears that trickled down her cheeks.

"Flew! Flew!" Leelan cried, her head raised to the sky, but then she stopped abruptly and stared toward the forest.

"What's wrong?"

Leelan's hackles rose, and she made a rumbling noise in her chest that Elin had never heard before. What could be the problem? Elin followed her gaze. At first, she could see nothing. Then, squinting her eyes, she realized that what she had taken for the shadow of a tree was actually a man. She leapt to her feet.

Tall, dressed in gray, he stood beneath the trees watching them. Perhaps because she had seen him, he began to walk slowly toward them. Snarling, her fur standing on end, Leelan moved in front of Elin, as if to protect her, but the man showed no sign of fear as he approached. His eyes were invisible beneath the gray hood. Taking something from his cloak, he brought it to his mouth. Elin started.

"No!" she cried, just as he blew the Silent Whistle. Leelan's snarls ceased, and she stood frozen in place, her fangs bared and wings slightly raised. The man walked past her as though she were merely a statue and stood before

Elin. Now she could see his face clearly. He looked to be in his mid-forties. Within the shadow of his hood, his green eyes shone coldly.

"There's no mistake. You must be Sohyon's daughter. You look so like her."

Elin stared at him blankly.

"We need to talk. Come into the forest where the trees are denser. The Beast can't follow us there."

3

THE SIN OF THE AHLYO

As she followed him, Elin had the strange feeling that she was walking in a familiar dream. He belonged to the Ahlyo, her mother's people, and seemed to know her mother well. Perhaps he was kin . . . Her heart beat in her throat and her mind was spinning. She barely felt her feet touch the snow.

The man strode ahead into the forest. When he was deep enough among the trees that they could not be seen from the meadow, he stopped and turned to her. Then he spoke. "This is your first time to see me, but I have been watching you from a distance for several years. You and the Beast."

Elin's lips felt stiff as she spoke. "Watching . . . us? . . . But why? Who are you?" For the first time, she saw a flicker of expression in his eyes.

"Even your voice is like Sohyon's," he whispered. He gestured for her to sit on a dry log and sat down beside her. "Your mother and I were of the same clan. You wouldn't know because you weren't raised among us, but each clan is divided into two kinship groups. She and I belonged to opposite groups, or Toh no Hara." A sad smile touched his lips. "We choose our life partners from our clan's Toh no Hara. Sohyon was to be my wife."

Elin stared at him, forgetting even to breathe. He smoothed the expression from his face, as if to rein in his emotions. "But it wasn't because you are Sohyon's daughter . . . I was watching you because, four years ago, a Spirit Beast warned us about you."

"A Spirit . . . Beast?"

The man stared off into space. "Long ago, our ancestors committed a great sin in a far distant land beyond the Afon Noah. In their remorse, they placed a curse upon themselves so that their descendants would never make the same mistake. The curse was such that, when they died, their souls would not cross into the heaven of Afon Aluma, but would remain here as a Spirit Bird to warn us should anyone use the Handler's Art. The Spirit Beast cannot speak to the people of this world, but the Spirit Bird can. It lives within the Spirit Beast and becomes its voice . . . It warned us that someone had used the Art to communicate with the Royal Beasts."

Elin imagined the spirits of her ancestors hovering in the snow-scented gloom of the frozen forest. She hugged her arms against her body. Had they been watching her the whole time? Were they still watching her even now?

"At first we thought that Sohyon must have taught you the Art. You cannot imagine how shocked we were when we realized that you weren't using the skills passed down among our people."

He gazed at her face. "Along with the Law, we are drilled in the Art from the time we are very young—so that it will never be used again, so that our people will never forget the past and rediscover it. Yet you developed it on your own."

His voice was hoarse. "We do not possess the kind of magic that we are rumored to have. All we have are the skills passed down by our ancestors from a land that once flourished beyond the Afon Noah. We have no special powers at all. Yet you, without any knowledge of those skills, developed the Art from nothing."

He placed a hand over his face. "Our despair was deep. How, we wondered, could someone acquire this ability naturally? Is it impossible to prevent disaster even by sealing away our ancient skills? Is this how someone sets off down the path to destruction—without even realizing that she is doing so?"

Elin stared at her fingers. White and trembling, they seemed to belong to someone else.

Clearly, by "Handler's Art," he meant her ability to communicate with

Leelan. He thinks that what I've done is wrong. Is it really so terrible as to cause my mother's people despair? Why do they think it's a sin?

Deep inside, she heard her mother's voice, the words she had spoken just before she had used the finger flute to control the Toda. "Elin, you must never do what I am going to do now. To do so is to commit a mortal sin."

Now, with a sudden flash of understanding, she realized what her mother had meant. She was speaking to the Toda with her finger flute. And she was warning me that to do so is a crime . . .

A pain stabbed her heart. To communicate with the Beasts, to tell them what she wanted and direct their actions: Her mother's people called this the Handler's Art—and they considered it a mortal sin.

"Why?" Elin whispered. "Why is it a sin to speak with the Royal Beasts?"

The man did not answer immediately. He rubbed his face with a rough and bony hand as if searching for words. Finally he sighed and said, "Even if I told you, it would sound too simple. How can I possibly convey to you the true horror when you have never seen the other side of the Afon Noah? You would never believe that speaking with the Beasts could have such terrible consequences." He raised his eyes and looked at her. "But, still, I must try . . . When I saw the Beast fly today, I knew that I had no choice.

"I should probably kill you and the Beast now to avert future disaster. Our people have vowed, however, never to take a life for any reason except for food. All we can do is to share what we know and pray that you will make the right decision . . ." He gripped his knees. "Daughter of Sohyon, I beg you to listen carefully to my words. And then I implore you never to let that Royal Beast fly again. Return it to the shelter of the Law. This is the wish of your mother's people. We beg you to understand, and pray, with body and soul, that you will make the right choice." Then he began his tale.

When he finally finished, he stood up and walked off into the forest. For a long time, Elin sat on the log as if stunned.

The story he had told her was indeed horrific. But just as he had warned her, it sounded like something that had happened long ago. Although she now knew what had happened in the past when people had manipulated Royal Beasts and Toda, she could not see how her conversations with Leelan, or for that matter how her mother whistling to the Toda just once, could cause such a disaster. Surely there would need to be a complex combination of factors to cause something like that. Had the Ahlyo blown the episode out of proportion because following the Law was the very reason for their existence?

Elin buried her face in her hands. Mother, did you believe your action was a mortal sin and try to pay for it with your life? Was that why you threw away the chance of a future with me?

She had no memory of when she stood up or how she left the forest. When the bright, snow-cloaked meadow came into view, she heard a keening wail rend the air, and sound came rushing back. She dashed out of the trees into the meadow.

Leelan, wings spread wide, was stamping her feet and crying in anguish. Running over, Elin hugged her and, burying her face in her warm, glossy fur, burst into tears.

How could it be a crime to speak with Leelan? Why was it wrong for Leelan to soar through the heavens? How could something that brought such joy possibly be a sin?

Elin felt Leelan's warmth against her cheek, and her heart cried out.

I won't stop Leelan from flying. No matter what they say, I refuse to bind her with the Law.

"She what? Leelan flew?" Esalu's brows shot up as she listened to Elin's stumbling account of what had happened.

"Yes. During the earthquake, the ledge we were on crumbled and . . ."

Esalu stared at her openmouthed. "Well. Who would've guessed . . ." she whispered, absently running a hand through her graying locks. Then her expression sobered. "It's unheard of for a Beast in captivity to fly. Absolutely amazing. But we're going to have to make sure she doesn't escape from the meadow."

"I know. I was worrying about that, too. I don't think she would actually try to run away. And even if she left the meadow, she'd come back. But if she happened to have some kind of accident while she was gone . . . Just the thought makes me shudder."

"You're right there, Elin. We have to be prepared for every possibility. Because she's a Royal Beast." Esalu pressed her fingers against her forehead and thought. After a long moment, she raised her eyes and looked at Elin. "You said you rode on her back, didn't you?"

"Yes."

"In that case, maybe you should start flight training."

"What?" Elin blurted out. "Flight training?"

"Yes. Train her not to fly unless you are on her back. Teach her that even if she flies, she must come back here. Drill it into her body and mind so that it becomes a habit." Esalu laughed at Elin's stunned expression. "You're lucky it's the holidays. Make sure she's trained before the other students come back."

"Er . . . Headmistress Esalu . . . it was actually . . . quite terrifying to ride on Leelan's back when she was flying."

Esalu raised her brows again. "Well, I certainly never expected to hear you say that you were afraid of anything." Then she grinned. "I'm just teasing. Of course, we'll have to figure out a way to make it safe. Perhaps we can make some kind of leather harness, like a saddle on a horse. I'll talk to the custodians and get their help." She seemed to be struggling to keep her features calm and impassive, but a gleam of excitement shone in her eyes. Elin grinned at the sight, and elation spread through her. The heaviness that had filled her heart since meeting the Ahlyo finally evaporated.

Esalu liked to put her ideas into action immediately. She marched Elin off to the custodians' office to explain what they needed, and found the men relaxing around the hearth. After listening to Esalu's rapid-fire explanation, they looked at one another.

"What should we make?" one of them asked.

The chief rubbed the stubble on his chin thoughtfully. A darkly tanned man well on in years, he was popular with the students for the clever toys he made in his spare time. "Ain't no time to make nothin' from scratch," he said. "If the girl's gonna train the Beast before the others get back, we've gotta use somethin' ready on hand. We could try a saddle, but most are made for horses, not the back of a Beast . . . I'm thinkin' we might wanna try a quilt saddle."

"Ah . . ." Understanding lit the faces of the others. Such saddles were common in areas with harsh winters. Made of a large piece of cowhide that wrapped around the horse's flanks and was secured with a strap under the belly, they resembled a quilt, which was where the name came from.

"That'd be easier to fit on the back of a Royal Beast. We just need longer cinch straps to fasten it with. We'll need to figure out how to attach reins to the cinch, too, though the Beast might not fancy that. It won't do for the girl to fall off, either, so let's try fixin' metal rings to her belt and the saddle to hold a good strong lifeline. That'll make it easy to fasten and unfasten." The gleam in his eyes made it clear that he loved his craft. "Now who'd have thought that one day we'd be makin' a saddle for a Royal Beast?"

The result was a very sturdy and well-crafted saddle. The only drawback was its weight. While that would be no problem for Leelan, Elin was the only person who could approach her without using a Silent Whistle, and this meant that she would have to saddle the Beast by herself.

"You sure you can hoist that thing?" The chief custodian's brow furrowed at the sight of Elin balancing the saddle on one shoulder.

"Yes, I'll be fine." In reality, she was doubting whether she would be able to lift it onto Leelan's back, but there was no time to fix it. She would just have to make do.

Leelan raised her head as Elin drew near and watched her with interest. "What?" she asked.

Elin let her sniff the saddle until she was satisfied and then explained what it was for. She wondered if Leelan could understand the complex explanation, but when she told her to bend down so that she could put the saddle on her back, Leelan turned about and crouched down without question.

It made Elin feel strange every time Leelan responded like this, but she shook her head to chase the thought away. Placing the saddle on her knees, she swung it up and spread it over Leelan's back. Leelan craned her neck around at the sudden weight of it, and Elin ducked under her belly and fastened the two straps securely.

"I'm going to climb up, so don't move," Elin said. She shimmied up Leelan's back, settled herself onto the saddle, and thrust her toes into the stirrups. The chief custodian had fitted them perfectly to her feet. She felt much more secure sitting in a saddle. She grasped the end of the short life-line and clipped it on to a metal ring on her own belt. Then she took the reins, which were attached to the cinch crossing Leelan's chest, and wrapped them around each hand.

"Fly!" she shouted. Before she had time to catch her breath, Leelan had kicked the earth beneath them and launched herself into the sky. Elin's head whipped back, making her dizzy. The wind pressed against her chest and pushed her backward. Hastily, she pulled herself forward to nestle against Leelan's back, just as she had done on their first flight. The wind roared in her ears and her hair tangled, but with the stirrups, reins, and life-line, she felt very safe.

Finding an updraft, Leelan spiraled higher and higher, then joyfully slipped into a glide. Elin's heart froze when she looked down, and she found Leelan's descent gut-wrenching, but the gooseflesh thrill of flying far out-weighed her fear.

Pressing her cheek against Leelan's back, she smiled. She could hear the bellows-like sound of Leelan's breathing and sense her ecstatic joy.

Hands shielding their eyes, Esalu and the chief custodian stood for a long time watching the Royal Beast soar through the heavens with Elin on her back.

4

THE MALE BEAST

When the snow covering the meadow had melted and birds once again darted through the air, a horse-drawn cart bearing a Royal Beast lumbered into the Kazalumu Sanctuary.

"I've never heard of a mature Beast being captured in the wild before," Yuyan said as she placed her hands on top of the railing and stretched over it to peer into the meadow. The students were all clustered at the fence, watching the custodians bring in a Beast paralyzed by the Silent Whistle. Elin was standing beside Yuyan.

"The Hunters made a mistake," Kashugan remarked casually. Recently, he seemed to be wherever Yuyan was. Whenever they were alone, Elin teased her, but Yuyan responded sagely that it was hard to be so popular.

"They were trying to capture a cub in the nest. The parent came back and crashed into the cliff when they blew the Silent Whistle." He gestured as he spoke, making it seem as if he had actually been there when it happened.

Royal Beast Hunters were bound by strict rules that forbade them to kill a wild Beast under any circumstances. To have accidentally injured a mature one was shameful. They had retrieved the wounded Beast with the cub because they certainly could not leave it there. The wounded adult had been brought to Kazalumu while the cub was sent to the official sanctuary.

"So the mother was protecting her cub . . . We'd better fix her up quick so she can get back to her little one."

"You're wrong there, Yuyan. That's the father."

"The father?" Yuyan's eyebrows flew up.

"I heard them say it's a male."

Yuyan stared at Kashugan. "Where do you get that kind of information?"

Kashugan laughed a little bashfully without answering.

The Royal Beast had been transferred to a large cart built for Beasts. Even wounded and frozen, its beauty far surpassed that of the other Beasts in the sanctuary.

On the night of the next day, Elin was summoned to Esalu's office. When she walked in, the headmistress put her cup of tea down on the table and looked up.

"Ah, Elin. Sorry to summon you so abruptly."

Elin shook her head. "Is there something I can do for you?"

Esalu gestured for her to sit down. "You know a Royal Beast was brought here yesterday. We're calling it Eku, meaning male, for sake of convenience. Anyway, every time the effects of the Silent Whistle wear off, he goes into a violent rage. At this rate, even if we treat his wounds, they're just going to open up again."

"Ah . . ." Elin nodded, recalling what Leelan had once been like. Whenever she had woken after the Silent Whistle, she had gnawed furiously on her own fur. Just like Leelan, the new Beast, Eku, had been hurt when the Silent Whistle was used. Perhaps he associated the memory of the whistle with his injury and was reacting to it.

"So I wondered," Esalu said, adjusting her reading glasses, "if you'd like to try using your harp on Eku."

Elin frowned as the words of the Ahlyo flashed through her mind, but she pushed them away. "I don't know if it will work, but I'll try."

Seeing Esalu's eyes gleam with the pure curiosity of the scholar, Elin felt her own heart begin to race.

I wonder if a wild Beast will respond to the harp, too . . .

As Elin approached the stable, a thudding sound jarred the pit of her stomach. Eku must be throwing himself against the wall. The harp was crooked under her arm, and she slipped it into her hand as she hurried inside. Frowning, the teachers stood looking through the bars at the raging Beast. When they saw Elin, their faces lit up with keen interest, and they stepped aside to let her through.

Eku was in a miserable state. With his wings spread wide for balance and his broken leg dangling awkwardly, he hopped on his sound leg and hurled himself against the bars. With each impact, the bars groaned, and dust trickled down from the ceiling.

"What do you think? Can you do it?" Esalu whispered.

"I don't know . . ." Elin answered in a low voice. "But I doubt that he'll even listen to the harp right now. He's too excited." She looked at Esalu. "Give me one night. Let me stay here with him."

Esalu seemed to guess what she really wanted. "All right," she said. "Listen, everyone, let's leave this to Elin and go outside. If any of you feel the need to watch, you can, but to help Eku calm down, I think the fewer people in here the better.

"Elin, what about the light? Shall I turn it out?"

"Yes, please."

Esalu nodded and, blowing out the lantern, she ushered the teachers out the door. Even after they had left, Eku continued to storm about the cage. Elin sat with her back against the wall and watched. He was big. A whole head taller than Leelan perhaps. If he broke the bars, she would be torn to shreds in seconds . . . For the first time in a long while, she felt a lump of fear in her stomach. Motionless, she watched, waiting for the Beast's anger to dissipate.

Past midnight, Esalu slipped in quietly. Eku, most likely exhausted, was fast asleep and snoring faintly. Esalu sat down beside Elin and wrapped a blanket around her shoulders. The two of them spent the rest of that long night cuddled in their blankets, nodding off occasionally.

When day began to dawn, Elin took out her harp and started to pluck it quietly, mimicking the sounds that Leelan made when she was feeling content and lazy. The Beast opened his eyes and raised his head, looking surprised. Esalu opened her eyes, too, but she kept quiet. The Beast listened for some time, and then began to make a slightly higher pitched sound in his chest. Elin smiled. It was the sound that Leelan made when she came too close to another Beast in the meadow. Elin thought it indicated lack of hostility.

Restraining her excitement, she plucked out the response repeatedly as she stood up slowly. The cooing of the Beast and the thrumming of her harp intersected and then resonated. The sound gradually faded, and the Beast no longer raised its hackles when she approached. She picked up a lump of meat containing a sedative and, opening the door, threw it inside. The Beast, which had been fasting ever since it was captured, devoured it in a single gulp.

Elin helped set the bones in the sleeping Beast's leg. "It's broken in two places," she murmured.

"Yes. Thank goodness it's a simple break. He should heal quickly." Esalu worked deftly and, in no time, the leg was splinted and bound. By the time they left the stable, they could hear the breakfast gong. As they walked toward the school, Esalu asked, "What does that sound mean?"

"You mean the one I played? I think that the Beasts use it to show they mean no harm. I've heard Leelan make that sound when she gets too close to other Beasts."

Esalu said thoughtfully, "That's interesting, isn't it? We've been taught that the Royal Beasts don't live in packs, yet if they communicate like that, checking for the presence or absence of hostility, and allowing those that intend no harm to approach, they may have more interaction than we thought. They may even form a sort of pack, but one that's spread out over a much wider territory."

Elin nodded. She had been mulling over this idea for quite some time. "Yes, I've been thinking the same thing. I'm not sure how to describe it, but Leelan often explains what she wants with quite a bit of detail. If Royal Beasts really are solitary, they shouldn't need such sophisticated ways of communicating."

"Really? That's fascinating . . . There's so much we just don't know about them. They're like a blank sheet of paper. The more we observe them, the more we should be able to learn."

Elin felt a warm thrill course through her. It was true. The more she learned about them, the more she discovered new things, and if she could study them in the wild, she would be bound to learn even more.

When the school came into sight beyond the forest, Esalu said, "Your harp communicated to that Beast, even though you were not imprinted on his mind from infancy."

"Yes. But that's because it's a very simple sound. Just like mimicking a greeting will communicate in a foreign language."

Esalu looked up at Elin. "Do you think that if I tried it, it would work for me, too?"

"Yes, probably . . . If you had never used the Silent Whistle on Eku."

Esalu frowned. "Oh . . . right. I did use it. Do you think he remembers?"

"Yes, Royal Beasts have excellent memories. I believe that they remember very clearly anyone who has used the whistle on them.

"Still, thinking of Leelan, even if someone has used the Silent Whistle once or twice, how that person treats the Beast afterward might change the response."

"I see . . ." Esalu nodded and gazed at Elin. "It's worth a try anyway. Would you teach me how to make those sounds?"

Elin blinked. She had prepared herself for the day when she would be asked this question. But now that the time had come, she found that it was not easy. If she taught Esalu, sooner or later people would realize that anyone could communicate with the Beasts . . . and that might trigger a catastrophe. If the spirits of her ancestors were still watching her, would they tell the Ahlyo what she had done?

Elin stood still. She could not refuse without explaining why. While she hesitated to tell her what she had learned from the Ahlyo, she could not bear the thought that Esalu might assume she wished to keep the skill to herself. And besides, Esalu had a right to know. If Elin was to continue using the Art to treat Royal Beasts like this, then she must consult her properly, at least this once.

She turned to face her. "It would be easy for me to teach you, but before I do, there is something you need to know." She was not sure where to start and, in the end, she took a long time in the telling, but Esalu listened without uttering a word. When she was finally through, Esalu sighed.

"So that's what he meant . . ." she murmured. She rubbed her hands over her face, as if she were scrubbing it. Then she looked up at the sky and said, as if to herself, "So that's what he meant by a 'catastrophe.'" She looked at Elin and smiled. "I met an Ahlyo once, too. Deep in the mountains . . ."

"I see . . ." Understanding dawned in Elin's face. "So that's why you seemed suspicious of me when we first met."

Esalu's smile deepened. "Yes. I should have told you much sooner, but I just couldn't bring myself to talk about it. I'm sorry it took me so long, but now I'm glad I've told you."

She looked back at the Beast stable and said quietly, "Your fear may be justified . . . It may be better to keep the Handler's Art to yourself. If people knew that anyone could use it, others would be sure to try and control the

Royal Beasts." Her eyes shifted back to Elin, and a look of concern crossed her face. "But when I think of you, it seems to me that that road could be very dangerous. There would be less risk to you if it were a skill that anyone could use."

Elin shook her head. "I would rather that the risk was mine alone. My mother's people pleaded with me, yet I made the decision to ignore them, even though they were desperate. I just can't bear to confine Leelan within the narrow cage of the Law to avoid some future catastrophe that might never happen. But if my actions might bring about such a disaster . . ." Her voice grew husky. "Then when it comes, I will not hesitate to lay down my life, if I believe that could avert it."

Esalu gazed at Elin's bloodless face—the well-defined features held a stillness that seemed beyond her eighteen years. She reached out and gently touched her hand. It was trembling slightly, and she gripped it firmly. "All right. I respect your commitment. But we must be careful not to let others know that you can use the Art."

Elin felt the warmth of Esalu's dry hand against her own. Her throat constricted, making it impossible to speak. She gazed at Esalu, noting that her hair was peppered with gray these days, and bowed deeply.

5

FLIGHT OF TWO BEASTS

Eku recovered quickly and, within half a month, was completely healed. The teachers involved in his care could not hide their astonishment. Elin always accompanied them when they treated him, calming him with her harp so that she could feed him a sedative concealed in a lump of meat. It was her idea to use a slow-acting sedative rather than one that put him to sleep right away, and he ate eagerly, unaware that the meat had anything to do with him falling asleep.

Whenever Elin went to Leelan's stable after assisting with Eku's treatment, Leelan seemed very interested in her. She sniffed her intently until she was satisfied, and then turned away with a contented expression. Elin also noticed that the fur on Leelan's chest was taking on a pinkish hue. When she asked Esalu about it, however, Esalu said that she had never seen this in any other Beast.

Once sure that Eku was completely healed, the teachers decided to let him out into the meadow. He had only been brought here for healing, not as a gift to the Yojeh. Now that there was no longer any worry that he might die, they could free him. "Besides, he eats almost twice as much as the other Beasts," Yassa remarked, voicing what they all felt. Kazalumu Sanctuary had a hard enough time making ends meet. It could not afford to feed a Royal Beast that received no funds for its care from the Yojeh.

Elin was standing beside Leelan when they opened the stable door to let Eku out. It was a warm spring day, and the morning dew sparkled whenever the sun poked its face from between the thin stream of clouds. Eku appeared in the doorway and hopped out into the meadow, squinting as if to accustom himself to the light. He spread his wings wide, raised his head, and sniffed the air. At that moment, Leelan, too, raised her wings and sniffed.

Elin looked up at her in surprise, and then around at the other Beasts in the meadow. Although they looked at Eku, they just stood there, without sniffing. Leelan began making a strange cooing sound in her breast. Elin gasped. The fur on her chest, which had been a pale red, was now bright crimson, as if blood had spurted across it. And that was not all. She was exuding a strong, sweet scent.

Eku raised his head to the sky and gave a high-pitched trill. *Li, li, li, li, li, li.*

Immediately, Leelan responded, trilling an even higher note. Eku flew into the sky with powerful strokes. Leelan ran forward and launched herself into the air. As if pulled by a thread, the two Beasts became a single dot in the sky, flitting above and below one another in a strange dance. Radiating a hard light, they flew along the edge of the silver clouds, ripe with the sun. Leelan's chest gleamed like a bright red jewel.

Before the eyes of the speechless watchers, Leelan and Eku mated.

The confirmation of Leelan's pregnancy threw the school into an uproar.

"We can hardly keep this a secret from the palace," Yassa remarked, and Esalu could only nod in agreement. The number of Beasts under the Sanctuary's care was reported to the palace and meticulously recorded, and that number determined the amount of funds the Sanctuary received. If Leelan gave birth successfully, they would have to report her cub to the palace. As Yassa had said, they could not possibly hide what had happened. Not only that, but Eku had not returned to the wild. He had remained instead by Leelan's side, as if to protect her, and they would have to explain why they needed to apply for funds to feed him, too.

The night that the teachers decided to report Leelan's pregnancy, Elin was summoned to Esalu's office. The headmistress sat at her desk as usual, but she could not hide the fatigue in her eyes. Elin knelt before her and bowed her head to the floor.

"I'm very sorry."

That was all she could say. It should have been her who faced the great wave that would soon engulf Esalu, but even if she told the inspector that everything had been her decision alone, as the head of the school, Esalu would still be held responsible.

"Look at me, Elin," Esalu said gently. "There's nothing to be sorry for. You only did what I have always longed to do myself."

Elin looked up at her in surprise and saw that she was smiling.

"I went searching for Royal Beasts in the wild because I wanted to see what they were really like. But I gave up because I was afraid, and so I wasted my youth. When you came, Elin, it seemed like fate was giving me another chance. And you succeeded beautifully." Elin stared at Esalu, whose eyes now brimmed with tears.

"To see Royal Beasts mate and bear young . . . I never dreamed that such a day would come. I can never, ever thank you enough." Her voice shook, and she wiped her eyes with a wrinkled hand. "You've done what no one else before you could. This is an outstanding achievement, worthy of the highest praise . . . It makes me boil with anger to think that we can't simply celebrate your success."

Elin looked down to hide her tears. The dream that she had cherished for so long—for Leelan to fly, mate, and bear young, just like Beasts in the wild—had finally come true, yet she could not rejoice, and that was so frustrating. It was a huge comfort to her just to know that Esalu shared this feeling.

The headmistress sighed. "When I saw Leelan mate, a riddle that had puzzled me for many years was finally solved . . . Royal Beasts mate in flight."

Elin nodded and wiped her tears with her hands. Looking at Esalu, she said, "I was surprised, too. I think from what I observed standing beside Leelan that the scent of the male may have brought her into heat."

"That's right. Both she and Eku sniffed the air, didn't they?"

"Yes. Then Leelan's fur suddenly turned bright red, and she gave off a very sweet scent. I think those must have been signs that she was ready to mate. Now that I think of it, whenever I visited Leelan after being with Eku, she sniffed me. It was around that time that the fur on her chest began to change color, too."

"I see. So the scent of a mature male brings a female into heat." Esalu's gaze shifted to her desk. "But the other Beasts showed no interest whatsoever."

There were three other females in the Sanctuary in addition to Leelan, and they had all been sunning in the meadow. Elin shivered at the thought that, even though they could smell Eku, they had not responded at all.

Esalu murmured as if to herself, "What could be the reason? What prevents the other Beasts in the Sanctuary from going into heat? The Silent Whistle? The tokujisui?"

"I think it's the tokujisui."

Esalu looked at her in surprise. "Are you sure?"

"There could be other factors involved, so I can't be certain, but I think that tokujisui is definitely one factor . . . The night before they took my mother away, she told me that tokujisui made the Kiba's fangs harder and their bones larger than Toda in the wild, but at the expense of other things."

Even when she tried, Elin could no longer remember her mother's face. The one thing she did remember clearly were the words she had said. "She told me to think about it. She said that there was something Toda in the wild do naturally that those raised in the Ponds can't. She said that I'd find the answer for myself one day. But then she warned me not to tell anyone the answer, not until I could understand why I shouldn't tell them what I knew . . ."

Her throat closed, and her words faltered. She clenched her teeth to hold back her tears. Then, taking a deep breath, she said, "When I saw Leelan mate, I knew exactly what she had meant. I knew what Beasts in the wild do as a matter of course that Beasts raised in captivity can't."

She lifted her eyes to look at Esalu. "Horses and cows raised by men still bear young. It is only Royal Beasts and Toda that become barren . . . And only Royal Beasts and Toda are given tokujisui."

A heavy silence fell on the room. The only sound to be heard was the night wind rattling the window.

Someone, long ago, had devised an ingenious way of preventing both Royal Beasts and Toda from reproducing, one which concealed this motive so that not even those caring for them realized what was happening. But why? Was it to prevent the catastrophe that the Ahlyo had described? But it had been the first Yojeh, not the Ahlyo, who had written the Royal Beast Canon.

A thought rose into Elin's mind, and she paused in shock. If what the Ahlyo had told her was true, they had come from beyond the Afon Noah—just like the first Yojeh . . . A chill spread through her chest. What if the first Yojeh had experienced the same catastrophe and had felt the same way as the Ahlyo? . . .

Looking up, she saw that Esalu was watching her. "I have a request," Elin said, with a very pale face. "Don't keep my existence a secret."

Esalu's eyes widened slightly. "What did you say?"

"I don't want someone else to take the blame for what I've done while I hide. If the Canon was intended to prevent a catastrophe like the one the Ahlyo fear, then the Yojeh will be very angry that we allowed the Beasts to breed." She leaned forward, but Esalu interrupted her before she could continue.

"Elin, just a minute." A smile touched her face. "I'm glad you're taking this seriously, but in this, you are still inexperienced. Is that what you were worried about? I'm not concerned about that in the least." Elin blinked, looking puzzled. "What happened here was a coincidence," Esalu said. "We tried very hard to save the life of the Beast cub, and, lo and behold, she happened to bear young . . . Why would the Yojeh reprimand us instead of celebrating?"

Esalu's smile broadened when she saw the blank look on Elin's face. "Don't you see? We may be scolded for not following the Canon, but for those who work in a Beast sanctuary, the top priority is to save the life of the Beasts. So the fact that our efforts were aimed at healing Leelan is a given. But more than that, the true purpose of the Canon is a secret. No one has told us the reason for it, so we can't possibly be blamed." She laughed, but then her expression sobered.

"You must not show yourself in public . . . What we need to worry about is what happens after people know about Leelan. You understand, don't you?"

Elin nodded.

Just as Esalu had said, when the news reached the palace, Leelan's pregnancy was hailed as a promising omen, and the Yojeh's praise and congratulations were conveyed to the Sanctuary. Kazalumu rose instantly to fame, and the Yojeh substantially increased the amount of funds awarded to it, much to the delight of staff and students. As the students were fond of noting, thanks to Leelan, they now got an extra side dish every evening.

The fact that a Royal Beast gifted to the Yojeh was now pregnant cheered the hearts of her people. Recently, the only news seemed to be bad news, such as attempts on the Yojeh's life and ominous increases in the Aluhan's forces, which they claimed were needed to defend the borders against marauders. Wherever people gathered, they spoke of Leelan's pregnancy as a sign of good fortune.

And the person most excited by the news was the Yojeh herself.

Pregnancy for a Royal Beast lasted longer than for humans. By the time the swelling in Leelan's belly began to show, it was time for Elin, along with Yuyan, Kashugan, and her other classmates, to sit for the Graduation Trials. Having been so busy with Leelan, she had barely had time to study and went into the exam feeling quite anxious. When the results were announced and she found that she had passed at the top of her class, she stood for a moment staring at Esalu's face in stunned silence.

Then Yuyan raised her hands and began clapping enthusiastically, and the whole room erupted with applause. Elin walked toward the front as if in a dream, hardly feeling her legs move. It was only when she felt the touch of the diploma in her hands that joy finally welled up inside her.

Esalu smiled. "Congratulations, Elin! You worked so hard for this, didn't you?" Elin pressed her trembling lips together and bowed deeply. It was a hot summer's afternoon, and the incessant sound of the cicadas in the trees outside poured like rain through the open windows of the dining hall.

That summer was a season of joy mingled with sorrow. The graduating students, who had spent the last six years in the dorm, must now leave the nest, each to begin their own path in life. Yuyan had decided to return home and become the village beast doctor. Letters from her family and relatives spoke longingly of her return. Not only her village, but three others in the same remote valley had no beast doctor to care for their livestock.

"Everyone's counting on me," Yuyan said with a grin. But when the day of her departure finally arrived, she clung to Elin and wept bitterly, as if they would never see each other again. Elin, who found it hard to express her feelings so freely, could find nothing to say. She just stood there, tears streaming down her cheeks. Her pain at this parting was even deeper than her friend's. The thought that she and Yuyan would never share the same room again seemed to open a gaping hole in her heart through which a cold wind blew.

Yuyan's family came to get her, but Elin had no mother or father to greet her or to rejoice in the fact that she had come first in her class. Once Yuyan left, she would have no one to whom she felt this close. If Joeun had still been alive, he would have grinned and hugged her tightly. . . . If only he were here. She could not help missing him.

When Yuyan and the others had left, Kazalumu was so quiet it seemed deserted. At first, Elin was plagued by a hollow sense of loneliness, but the summer was so busy and her work so demanding that this feeling gradually faded. For one thing, she could not rely on Esalu or the other teachers for advice, as none of them knew how to care for a pregnant Beast either, and she was frequently overcome with anxiety. For another, she not only had to prepare for the Entrance Trials at the end of summer, but in addition, from the fall, she would begin teaching for the first time.

From the day she was officially appointed a teacher, Elin wore the Silent Whistle around her neck every day. It was her duty as a teacher responsible for the lives of her students, but she kept it concealed inside her robe because it bothered Leelan. Esalu said nothing, although Elin was sure that she must have noticed.

When the highland breezes had once again turned cooler, a horde of children, their faces taut with excitement, invaded the school. Although Elin was used to new students entering at this time of year, it was one thing to welcome them as an older student and quite another to greet them as a teacher. The thought that, in the eyes of these young twelve-year-olds, she appeared to be a teacher filled her with a strange mix of pride and embarrassment.

She was charged with teaching first-level students about the lives and habits of beasts, birds, and insects. It was a beautiful autumn day when she first stood at the podium. Sunlight spilling through the window cast the shadow of the window frame on the floor. Ten students sat up straight and tall, their eyes riveted to her. They must be curious because I'm a new teacher, she thought, and this made her so nervous that her voice shook. Later, she realized that it had been their first class, too, and they had probably been just as nervous as she. Nor would they have known that she was a new teacher. To them, she was just one of many. Although this did not dispel her shyness at being seen as a teacher, to her surprise, she really enjoyed teaching them.

She did not have Yuyan's gift for speaking and creating a cheerful atmosphere, but the children listened eagerly when she shared her personal experiences about what she had learned or what caught her interest. Once she overheard a student in the hall say, "I love it when Professor Elin talks about when she was a child. That's the best part, don't you think?" This made her so happy, she felt like jumping up and down.

As she taught, a longing began to grow in her heart. She wanted to share with them the mystery of the creatures that lived in this world. She wanted them to feel the shiver of excitement that she felt when learning. At the same time, however, the act of teaching frightened her. As a student, all she had needed to do was to think and question. If her idea was right, she would be able to prove it in time, and if it was wrong, she could correct it. But as a teacher, she needed to believe that what she said was correct, so that they could memorize it with confidence. Yet, even while she taught, she could not help questioning whether or not the things she told them were true.

When she shared this with Esalu, the headmistress said, "The knowledge we teach is simply the truth as we know it at a particular time. What we believe to be true now may be exposed as error through the discoveries of succeeding generations. That's how human knowledge has been renewed throughout the ages. Remind your students of this every chance you get.

"A good teacher is not one who never doubts, but rather one who strives to keep on learning despite the doubts in her mind. At least, that's what I think."

Elin's days as a new teacher flew by. As spring approached, it became increasingly difficult to balance teaching with her care of Leelan. Noticing Elin's pallor, which was obviously due to lack of sleep, Esalu arranged to have another teacher take over her classes temporarily. As Leelan's time drew closer, Elin almost never left the Beast's stable. However, one day, on her way back to the dormitory for a change of clothes, she ran into her students as they were leaving the dining hall after breakfast.

"Professor Elin!" one of them called out in a high-pitched voice.

She stopped and turned, and was surrounded by first-level students.

"Is the Beast cub going to be born soon?"

Elin smiled. "Not yet. It will need to get a lot warmer first. But her belly's already very big."

The children's eyes shone. "I wish we could see. Professor Elin, can't we go and look?"

Elin shook her head. "I'm sorry, but no. This is Leelan's first pregnancy, and she's quite nervous. Please let her be."

The shortest boy grabbed her hand. "Professor Elin, is it true that you can talk to the Beasts?"

Elin felt as if something cold had brushed her heart. She did not answer immediately, and, seeing her expression, one of the boys put his hand across the other's mouth. "We're not supposed to talk about that, remember? The older boys said."

The other boy glared at him and shook his hand away. "But—"

He would have continued protesting loudly, but Elin placed her hand on his shoulder. Pressing a finger against her lips, she said, "Quiet please."

She looked at the faces of her students, staring up at her in silence, as if in awe, and the thought spread through her that she could not keep her ability a secret forever. It was close to a miracle that the school had managed to conceal it at all when so many people lived here. Such a miracle could not last. Like water percolating through an earthen wall, the day would certainly come when her secret seeped into the outside world.

"It's true that Leelan and I can communicate certain words to each other," she said. "I learned to understand her a little because I spent all my time with her, day and night, when she was a cub. But this isn't something you should talk about lightly. It's quite complicated. The older students were right when they told you not to mention it. Don't ever tell anyone outside the school that I can speak with a Royal Beast . . . Will you promise me?"

The students frowned, as though puzzled, but they nodded. Looking at their faces, Elin felt that it could not be much longer before her secret was known. And she was right.

SEVEN

AMBUSH

I

THE YOJEH'S VISIT

The Yojeh's visit to Kazalumu Sanctuary was planned for the tenth day of Tosalu Balu, the month of early summer, around the time that Leelan's cub would be weaned.

From the day she was born, the Yojeh had never set foot outside the palace grounds, and her announcement that she was going to Kazalumu caused an uproar. The ministers, her granddaughter Seimiya, and her nephew Damiya joined forces to convince her to abandon the notion. If she were to leave the palace, they insisted, it would be far more difficult to protect her. But the Yojeh would not listen.

Damiya suggested that if she wished to see Leelan's cub that badly, they could have it brought to the palace, but she retorted that she did not want to see a Royal Beast dragged into her garden. Such stubborn insistence was very unlike the usually rational and considerate Yojeh, but her longing was acute and stemmed from the fact that, unlike her forebears, the risk of assassination had prevented her from setting eyes on the country she ruled. In the end, all who opposed the idea gave in.

After that, the discussion focused on planning their travels and how to protect the Yojeh and her procession. The Kazalumu highlands were about one day's travel from the capital. They had decided that the Yojeh would stay one night at the manor of the Lord of Kazalumu. However, traveling by horse and carriage on the unpaved highland roads would be very hard on her at her advanced age.

"There's no choice on the way there because the terrain is all uphill. On the return journey, however, the best solution might be to travel to the town of Salano and, from there, take a boat down the river." This proposal came from the Lord of Kazalumu, who had offered her his manor on the way there.

"But she might feel queasy," one of the ministers protested. "And besides, traveling by boat is dangerous."

The Lord of Kazalumu shook his head. "That river is very broad and flows slowly, so there is no fear of capsizing. Many elderly people prefer to travel by river than by horse because it's much easier on the body than bumping over rough roads in a horse-drawn carriage.

"As the river flows all the way to the capital, I believe that going by ship will be less strenuous than other forms of travel."

Trial runs by both boat and carriage were undertaken, and it was confirmed that boat was easier, just as the Lord of Kazalumu had said. The Se Zan were split in two, some to accompany the Yojeh and the rest to remain in the palace to guard Princess Seimiya. Ialu was to be in charge of protecting the Yojeh.

It was on a bright, cloudless summer day that the Yojeh left the wood surrounding the palace, and the air was fresh with the scent of green leaves. People eager to see the procession lined the road and strewed flowers before her carriage wherever she went. The entourage proceeded to the Kazalumu highlands without incident. The Yojeh, for whom this was the first long journey of her life, was certainly tired when she reached the lord's manor, but she was treated to such a warm welcome, and had such a good night's sleep, that she felt refreshed by morning.

Gazing at the vast green meadow from the carriage window, the Yojeh exclaimed with childlike excitement, "What a lovely place!"

A leisurely wind pushed cloud shadows slowly across the field, while birds flitted between earth and sky, chirping merrily. Flowers, yellow and white, dotted the field and swayed in the breeze. But when Kazalumu School came into sight, the Yojeh's face clouded.

"My goodness . . . What an old building. I never thought it would be so plain."

Her nephew, Damiya, who sat across from her, smiled dryly. "It's a sanctuary for Beasts that are ill. Naturally, the official Royal Beast sanctuary in Lazalu is much grander."

The Yojeh frowned. "Then we'll have to think of a more fitting treatment for Kazalumu. After all, they have achieved what the grand Lazalu Sanctuary could not."

Damiya grinned. "I'm sure your gracious words will send this lot into ecstasy."

Ialu rode ahead, intent upon the surroundings. Although he had posted many guards around the highlands, in a place as open as this, it would be quite possible for an assassin to kill one of his men without being noticed, and so he remained vigilant as he escorted the carriage.

The entire school, from the teachers to the students to the custodians, were dressed in clothes specially ordered for this day. Tense and nervous, they stood to attention to greet the Yojeh. The twelve-year-olds, their cheeks flushed, burst into a song of welcome.

The Yojeh smiled as she listened. When the song came to an end, a middle-aged woman, who appeared to be the headmistress, stepped forward. She delivered a speech of gratitude for the honor of this visit in prim and proper language befitting her station. She then gestured for the Yojeh to proceed toward the stables.

It was a fine day, and the Yojeh could see the Beasts in the sanctuary napping here and there in the sun. Her eyes crinkled in a smile as she watched them from outside the fence.

"They look so content. The grass must feel very warm and cozy on such a sunny day."

The headmistress stopped just before the rolling meadow and said, "If it would please Your Majesty to look in that direction, you will see Leelan, Eku, and their cub, Alu, just over there."

"Oh my!" the Yojeh exclaimed. "So there they are! Why, what a darling little cub!"

Hearing her excited cry, the others also looked toward the meadow. There, indeed, stood two large adult Beasts with a small cub at their feet. The grand chamberlain who had accompanied the Yojeh frowned, however, and turned to Esalu.

"But they're so far away," he said. "We can't see them very well from here. Why didn't you keep them in the stable?"

"If we kept them inside on a sunny day like this, they would make a great fuss to go outside. We let them out because if they threw themselves against the stable walls, they could injure themselves." Esalu responded with firm composure, and the grand chamberlain fell silent.

The Yojeh, who was a head taller than the headmistress, smiled down at her. "I see . . . But as the chamberlain said, it is a bit far. We have come all this way to see them. Could we not be allowed to go a little closer?"

Esalu shook her head. "I beg your pardon, Your Majesty. Royal Beasts never become truly accustomed to people and . . ."

But Damiya interrupted. "What could be the problem? Her Majesty only wishes to go a little closer. Surely the Royal Beasts would never harm the Yojeh. And even if some problem occurred, you could use the Silent Whistle."

Ialu noticed the frown that flickered across Esalu's face at his words. But Damiya missed this reaction entirely as he turned to Ialu. "Our dear swift-footed Ialu, it is the Yojeh's wish. It won't matter if we go beyond the fence and get a little closer, will it?"

Ialu thought a moment, and then asked Esalu, "If several people with Silent Whistles stand ready, would they be able to stop the Beasts for certain?"

Esalu said reluctantly, "Yes, I believe so, but I still cannot recommend it. Besides, if too many people approach at once, Leelan may become agitated."

Ialu nodded. "In that case, choose a few teachers who are accustomed to handling the Beasts to accompany the Yojeh with their Silent Whistles ready. From our group, only the Yojeh, Lord Damiya, and I will go." He turned to his men and gave them instructions, while at the same time checking his bow.

As Esalu was selecting the teachers to accompany the Yojeh, Ialu noticed something unusual. Instead of being focused solely on the Yojeh, the eyes of the teachers and students, who were keeping their distance, kept flitting elsewhere. Following their gaze, Ialu's eyes fell upon a tall woman. She appeared to be a young teacher. She wore the same uniform as the others, but of all those assembled, she was the only one who never even looked at the Yojeh. In her hands she bore a strange-looking harp partially covered in leather, and she stared steadily at the Beasts with their cub. This bothered him, but as he sensed from her no hostility or intent to harm, he shifted his attention outward to the whole picture.

Esalu, who up to that point had been very efficient and quick, seemed to be having trouble selecting the teachers. She said something to the teacher beside her. He turned on his heel and began making his way through the students, heading toward the young woman. When he spoke to her, she listened carefully, then began to speak. The teacher, obviously her senior, listened to her, nodding frequently. Ialu thought that he would bring her, too, but when she had finished, he came back alone.

"What message did you give that girl?" Ialu asked.

Esalu raised her face to look at him. She mumbled at first and then said, "Well, er, she's the teacher in charge of Leelan, you see, but she has a cold, so I asked her to leave this to us and not to come any closer."

The teacher returned and whispered something to Esalu. She nodded.

"All right. I see . . . But you've told her not to come this way just to be on the safe side, yes? Good." Esalu then turned to the Yojeh. "Your Majesty, I beg pardon for the delay. The preparations have been made. Allow me to serve as a guide. I must ask Your Majesty not to make any loud noises or sudden movements."

The Yojeh's attendants looked offended, but the Yojeh nodded magnanimously. They entered the meadow through a place where the fence swung into the field. Ialu walked in front, opening his being to every sensation around them, and placing himself between the Yojeh and the Beasts.

The two adult Beasts raised their heads and looked toward them, as if wondering what was going on. The cub, which stood between its father's feet, extended its neck just like its parents and watched them approach.

"It's adorable," the Yojeh whispered, her voice filled with emotion.

The cub's fur shone brightly in the sun. Its innocent eyes moved from one face to another as if fascinated.

"I've never seen such beautiful Beasts before . . . Of course, the cub is amazing, but look at its parents. The color of those wings! Lapis lazuli with fine lines of red, just like a gemstone! And their breasts of shining silver. They are more magnificent than any Beast I've ever seen. The large one is Eku, and the smaller one, Leelan, yes?"

"Yes," Esalu whispered from behind her. "Forgive my rudeness, but I must ask Your Majesty to please stop here."

The Yojeh stopped, but Damiya smiled and looked back at Esalu. "Surely a little farther won't hurt. That Beast was a gift to the Yojeh. It would never harm her."

The Yojeh hesitated for a moment, but then, as if pushed on by the thought of the long distance she had traveled, she stepped forward toward the Beasts.

With a frown, Esalu whispered to Ialu, "You must stop her. If we approach any closer, it will alarm the Beasts. Remember, they are protecting their cub . . ."

Ialu nodded and was about to call out to the Yojeh when Eku began to quiver. Letting out a shrill warning cry, he raised his wings protectively. As the startled teachers raised their Silent Whistles to their lips, a stern voice cried out. "No!"

Ialu was stunned to see the teachers release their whistles. Nocking an arrow to his bowstring, he spun in the direction of the voice. The young woman was racing toward them. "Don't use your whistles!"

The maidservants, who were crowded along the fence, screamed.

Damiya whispered fiercely, "What're you doing? Use your whistles! Hurry!"

But the young woman ran straight toward the Beasts, without even a glance at the Yojeh. She spoke to them, and then began plucking her strange instrument, which, although it sounded like a harp, had a duller tone. She played a complex melody, and the Beasts mimicked it, as if in response. Eku flapped his wings angrily two or three more times, but then reluctantly folded them in response to the soothing sounds Leelan was making in her throat.

For a moment, Ialu forgot his mission and stared at the tall girl. She was standing so close to the Beasts that she could have touched them. Gazing up at them with a worried frown, she plucked the strings of her harp, oblivious of all else. From here, her eyes looked green.

Impossible. Could she be Ahlyo?

At that moment, a shaft of sunlight shone through the thin clouds and softly lit her hair as she exchanged sounds with the Beasts.

"What is she doing?" the Yojeh whispered.

Esalu wore an anxious frown. "She's calming the Royal Beasts."

"She can do that? With a harp?"

"Yes," Esalu answered and then abruptly changed the subject. "Your Majesty, we must leave this place. Please understand that it is particularly dangerous to approach Royal Beasts when they are rearing their young."

Leaving the Beasts with the young woman and her harp, they quietly exited the meadow.

2

DAMIYA'S PROPOSAL

The Yojeh was enjoying a conversation with Esalu over tea and sweets in the dining hall, which had been specially decorated in her honor. The headmistress, whose skin was like tanned leather, appeared intimidating, but the Yojeh seemed very taken with her. She asked her many questions, not only about the Royal Beasts, but also about everything from education to the management of the school, and made no move to retire, even though the afternoon was wearing on.

Ialu, as usual, stood listening to the conversation from a slight distance with his attention focused on their surroundings, yet he noticed that every time the Yojeh tried to bring the conversation back to the young woman who had calmed the Beasts with her harp, the headmistress casually changed the topic. When the Yojeh said, "I have never seen anyone calm the Beasts with a harp before. Is that a method you often use at the Sanctuary?" Esalu was silent for a moment, as though considering her words with care. When she finally responded, she was still hesitant.

"No, Your Majesty, we do not . . . In the case of Leelan . . . She has been listening to that harp since she was a cub . . . I believe that may be why the sound of it soothes her."

Ialu was puzzled. Why did she become disturbed every time the young woman was mentioned? Did she fear that she would be reprimanded for entrusting a Royal Beast to an Ahlyo?

"I'd like to talk to her myself," the Yojeh said.

Esalu bowed, but then replied, "I am afraid that that is not possible . . . The girl is coming down with a cold, and therefore I have strictly forbidden her to approach Your Royal Highness."

Damiya drank his wine and listened to the two of them for some time without uttering a word, his eyes on Esalu's face as if he was pondering something. Presently, he put down his glass and rose from the table. With a flick of his eyes, Ialu directed the guard beside him to follow him. Even when close to half a toh had passed, Damiya had still not returned.

Noticing that the light shining through the window had turned the color of honey, the Yojeh smiled. "My, look at the time. It was so interesting talking with you that I could not stop. But we should be going soon." Yet despite her words, she appeared very reluctant to leave. She looked at Esalu. "The Royal Beasts return to the stables for the night, don't they?"

"Yes. It is almost time for their evening meal. They are most likely returning to the stables now."

The Yojeh laughed lightly. "I would love to see the Royal Beasts and their cub one last time before we leave. Please take me to see them. Surely you will let me see them feeding?"

Esalu did not respond immediately. Her face went blank for a moment, as though she were thinking, but then she nodded. "Yes, of course, Your Majesty. It would be a great honor . . . Allow me."

Esalu took the lead. Ialu directed his men to encircle them as they walked, while he himself walked at Esalu's side. The procession moved through the long shadows of the trees and the golden light of the westering sun that filtered through the leaves.

Esalu pointed out the largest of the stable buildings and said, "That is the stable that houses Leelan, her mate, and their cub." Ialu noticed that the guard he had sent with Damiya was standing idly by the door.

"What are you doing?" he asked as they approached.

The man's face went rigid. "He ordered me not to come in . . ."

Peering inside, Ialu frowned. The young woman was standing by the bars where the Royal Beasts were. Her face was stiff, and she was staring at her feet. He could hear a man's voice.

"There's no need to be so defensive. I'm a straightforward man. I like you, and I'm just letting you know that."

It was Damiya's voice. Hearing footsteps approach, Ialu looked over his shoulder. Before he could speak, the Yojeh put a finger to her lips and shook her head. Her face taut, Esalu also stopped and stood listening to the conversation inside.

"Think about it. My offer is to your advantage, too, isn't it? There's no need for you to be separated from these Beasts. All I'm asking is that you bring them with you and move to Lazalu. If you think that working with the teachers there will be a problem, I can simply replace them for you with the staff from Kazalumu."

The young woman made no response. Damiya grasped her arm, as if he had run out of patience. She raised her face with a startled expression, but her eyes went not to Damiya but to the Beasts. They had begun to growl, perhaps out of concern for her, and she seemed to be desperately trying to calm them with her eyes. She turned quickly toward Damiya and said in a low but clear voice, "I beg your pardon, but as I have already told you, I am not in the position to make such decisions. Forgive me. Please, would you let go of my arm?"

Standing by the door, Ialu suddenly smiled. Damiya's charms appeared to have no effect on this girl. He could imagine the surprised look on the man's face.

Damiya dropped her arm abruptly. Accustomed as he was to courting women, he must have recognized that pushing her would only have the opposite effect. "You're a coolheaded woman, aren't you? That was a bit of a blow to my confidence. I thought myself a little more attractive than that. Did you feel nothing? Not even when I touched you?" She did not answer, but gazed at him steadily. There was not a trace of flirtation in her face.

"What beautiful eyes. I have never seen eyes like yours so close before. Now I can see why people say the Ahlyo have magic." He reached out his hand and gently touched her cheek. Her face froze, but she said nothing, only glaring at him.

"Now don't be angry with me," he murmured. "The Ahlyo are wanderers who have not sworn fealty to the Yojeh. If it became known that such a person was caring for Royal Beasts, people would be bound to talk. The position of the headmistress might be jeopardized. But I have fallen in love with you. I will protect you."

From behind him, Ialu heard the Yojeh's sigh. She walked past him and entered the stable. The young woman turned, and Ialu saw her eyes widen in surprise. Then he heard Damiya's laughter.

"Were you listening? Well, that's embarrassing. How long were you there?"

"Long enough to know that you were pestering this girl and that she refused your advances." She sounded amused. Turning to the girl, she said, "I apologize for my nephew's behavior. It's a bad habit of his. When he sees an attractive girl, he just can't help but approach her. I hope you'll forgive him."

The young woman knelt and bowed her head. "Your Majesty, please pardon my rudeness."

The Yojeh smiled. "Rise. I was most pleased by the way you stood firm in the face of my nephew's flattery. Tell me your name."

Elin rose and bowed. "My name is Elin, Your Majesty."

"Elin . . . 'mountain apple.' I see. The fruit with a lovely fragrance that grows deep in the mountains. The name suits you."

Elin's pale face suddenly relaxed.

She looks so different when she smiles, Ialu thought. He had first guessed her to be about twenty-five, but when she smiled, she looked about twenty.

The Yojeh smiled gently and gazed at Elin. "So you are Ahlyo. Tell me, how did an Ahlyo come to be working here? You don't need to worry. I have no intention of reproaching anyone, so please speak freely."

"If it pleases Your Majesty, I am not Ahlyo." The Yojeh's brows rose, but Elin continued calmly. "When my mother met my father, she chose expulsion from her people in order to marry him. So I have never lived as an Ahlyo. I entered this school because I aspired to be a beast doctor, and I have lived here ever since."

The Yojeh's eyes shone with curiosity. "I see. Your mother must be a very determined woman. What is she doing now?"

A shadow crossed Elin's face. "She's dead. I have no parents. My father also died when he was very young."

The Yojeh frowned. "I see . . . So this is your home."

At that moment, Leelan let out a cry. She had been pushing her head against the bars for some time, as if trying to touch Elin, but now, apparently having lost patience, she began complaining loudly. The cub at her feet followed suit, beating its little wings and shoving its snout through the bars as it tried to lick Elin's hand. Only Eku stood aloof and seemingly unconcerned.

Giving Alu her fingers to lick, Elin looked pleadingly at the Yojeh. "I beg your forgiveness, Your Highness, but the Beasts wish to be fed."

The Yojeh laughed. "It is I who must apologize. I interrupted their dinner. They must be very hungry. I'm so sorry, Leelan. Go ahead and feed them, Elin. May I watch from here?"

Elin cast a quick glance at Esalu and, when she nodded, bowed to the Yojeh. "Yes, of course, Your Majesty. Please watch from there."

Elin took several chunks of meat from the corner of the room and, opening the gate, walked inside the enclosure. Ialu and Damiya watched with amazed expressions.

"She doesn't use the Silent Whistle?" Damiya whispered.

Esalu sighed and said in a low voice, "Because she has been caring for Leelan since she was a cub."

With the cub fawning at Elin's feet and the mother beast demanding her attention, the scene seemed to contradict the idea that Beasts could never become accustomed to humans. Elin did not give any meat to Alu, nor did she respond to Leelan's persistent calls. Instead, she threw a large chunk at the feet of Eku, where he stood protectively by the cub. He held the meat down with his hind foot while he tore it into smaller chunks and fed these to Alu. When the cub was breastfeeding, Leelan had never left its side, but once it was weaned, Eku had taken over its care. Now the father Beast never left its side, while Leelan spent much of her time basking in the sun as she pleased. Once Eku began feeding the cub, Leelan butted Elin's back with her belly while calling insistently, as if to let Elin know that it was her turn. The Yojeh, Damiya, and Ialu watched speechlessly.

Wiping her hands on her apron, Elin came back through the gate. As if trying to excuse her behavior, Esalu murmured, "Leelan was near death, you see . . . Elin cared for her day and night, never leaving her side. She saved

Leelan's life, so, as you can see, unlike the other Beasts, Leelan has become very attached to Elin."

"I see . . ." Damiya said. "Leelan was the cub that was hit by the arrow."

The Yojeh raised her brows. "The arrow?"

Damiya looked at her quizzically. "Why yes. You remember, don't you? This is the cub that I presented to you on your birthday, my dear aunt."

"Oh . . ."

The Yojeh's face darkened, but Damiya paid her no heed. Laughing, he said to Elin, "This Beast that you raised saved the life of that man over there."

Elin looked at Ialu questioningly, and he nodded. "The arrow grazed Leelan's shoulder," Damiya continued, "so that by the time it lodged in his stomach, it had lost much of its force. Isn't that right, Ialu?"

"Yes, but to me it was still sufficiently painful."

Damiya laughed cheerfully, but Elin frowned, as if she could feel the pain. "The arrow struck him in the stomach?" she whispered.

"Ialu served as my shield," the Yojeh said. "He threw himself between the arrow and me . . . But let us speak of this no more. I have no wish to recall that incident."

Ialu stared at Leelan as she licked the mouth of her cub. So it was you who saved me . . . He recalled how she had looked so pitifully anxious when the men had dragged her on a cart into the garden, and her terrified scream when the arrow had sliced through her shoulder. She must have been in miserable shape when she was brought here. What an amazing recovery.

"I can understand why Damiya was trying so hard to seduce you," the Yojeh said in a cheerful voice, as though attempting to lighten her mood. "I, too, wish that you would come and care for the young cubs at Lazalu. You do not use the Silent Whistle, do you? I am glad, for I, too, hate that whistle. If it were possible to raise the Beasts without it, then that would be my greatest wish."

Elin and Esalu looked like children who, expecting to be whipped, had been given a sweet. "What's wrong? Are you reluctant to leave here?"

Elin blinked, as though the Yojeh's voice had suddenly brought her back to her senses. "Oh, ah, yes . . . This is my home." She drew a deep breath to calm her nerves. "Also, Alu is still a cub, and therefore I do not wish to make it move a long distance . . . If it is possible, I would prefer to stay here."

The Yojeh looked disappointed. "I see. Well, I do not wish to force you against your will, but do think about it. I have taken a great liking to you, and would very much like you to care for the cubs at Lazalu. I am sure that Leelan was able to bear young because you raised her with so much love and without the Silent Whistle. I would so like to see the young Beasts at Lazalu raised in the same way. Wouldn't it be wonderful to see the meadow filled with Royal Beast cubs? I will be in touch again."

Elin bowed deeply. "I am honored, Your Majesty."

As the Yojeh's procession rolled out of sight, fatigue etched the faces of everyone at Kazalumu. The teachers breathed a sigh of relief that the visit had gone smoothly, but when Elin thought of what Esalu must be thinking, she could not bear to look at her.

"How could you do that when I begged you to stay out of sight?" Esalu scolded her when the teachers had gone.

"I'm sorry."

Esalu sighed. "It's not that I don't understand how you must have felt. I was so worried about Alu, my heart almost stopped."

The cub was far younger than those that were captured and brought to the Sanctuary. When the Yojeh had insisted on going closer, all the teachers had been concerned that the whistle might harm it. And that was why Elin had shouted for them to stop when they had been about to blow.

"Still, it's very odd," Esalu murmured with a frown. "I wonder if the Yojeh doesn't know the purpose of the Royal Beast Canon . . . Or did she say that even though she does know?"

Elin recalled the Yojeh's face when she had said that she hated the whistle too. "She didn't seem to know, did she?" she said.

"No, you're right. She didn't." Esalu brushed back her hair. "Perhaps we were reading too much into this. Maybe the Royal Beast Canon doesn't have the meaning we thought it did."

Although Elin thought this unlikely, it was also clear from the Yojeh's response that, unlike the Ahlyo, she did not wish to keep the Royal Beasts confined within the Law.

"At any rate," Esalu continued, "we'll have to figure out what to do if she really wants the Royal Beasts to breed and increase . . . Her nephew seemed pretty intent on having you under his thumb, too."

The thought of Damiya made Elin's flesh crawl.

After leaving Esalu and returning to her room, Elin found it difficult to sleep. Anger flared whenever she remembered how Damiya had pressed her. She had been very afraid. No man had ever touched her like that before, and fear had made her cringe. It was this that made her angry. How she missed Yuyan. Confiding in her friend would have helped to dispel the feelings that weighed like mud on her mind, leaving it free and clear.

Yuyan must be living happily in her village now, working as a beast doctor. Kashugan, as the third son in his family, had no obligation to carry on the family line, and, if they married, he would probably be adopted into Yuyan's family. Elin gazed absently out the window. A cold loneliness spread through her chest. The solitude to which she had long grown accustomed had suddenly returned.

As she gazed at her reflection in the windowpane, the faces of everyone she had met that day flitted through her mind. For some reason, the person who had left the strongest impression was neither the Yojeh nor Damiya, but rather the guard who had stood quietly in the background. Perhaps it was the air of solitude that had enveloped him, like the silence of an empty forest in midwinter. He had hardly spoken, yet he did not wear the grim expression of the other guards. Rather, he seemed to be one step removed from everyone there.

To use his body as a shield and throw himself into the path of an arrow aimed at the Yojeh . . . What kind of a life was that? Would he go on like that forever, never knowing when he would have to throw his life away?

A wind must have sprung up. Elin stood for a long time gazing out the window at the branches moving in the darkness.

3

AMBUSH

The whole school had gathered on a bluff overlooking the Kazalumu River where it wound along the edge of the highlands. From here, they could see the many streams that flowed from the wooded hills to join the river, slowing it and widening its course. The vessel that would bear the Yojeh back to the capital would leave Salano around noon and, after passing below this spot, would vanish under the broad forest canopy.

One of the teachers had complained that to look down on the Yojeh from the bluff would be disrespectful and proposed that they abandon the idea, but everyone else pretended not to hear. After all, they might never have another chance to see the lavish ship in which the Yojeh sailed.

Elin was leaning against a rock and chatting with Tomura and the others. The sun-warmed stone made her drowsy. A well-prepared student had brought a telescope and was under orders to announce the boat's appearance.

"There they are!" he shouted, and everyone jumped to their feet.

Far in the distance, three ships glided toward them on water so calm that it gleamed like molten silver. Two small ships sailed in front. Behind them, they towed a large vessel topped by a cabin adorned with glittering gold. Cheers rose from the group on the hill.

The ships had just passed the mouth of one of the tributaries when the student with the telescope said, "What's that? . . . What are . . . those . . . things?"

The boys beside him gave him a friendly shove. "What're you babbling about?"

But the lookout ignored them, keeping his eye glued to the telescope. "They're coming out of that stream. Lots of them. They look like logs . . . with men on top . . . They've got bows slung over their backs . . ."

A confused clamor erupted from the other students, and the teachers shielded their eyes with their hands, peering up the river. Although they were too far away to discern any bows, they could make out men astride what appeared to be logs, gliding from the shadow of the forest into the river. With a start, Elin realized what they were.

Toda! . . .

Toda bearing Warriors. And they were closing in on the vessel that carried the Yojeh. It was only too clear what they planned to do.

When the boy with the telescope shrieked, "They're going to shoot!" Elin set off at a run.

"Where do you think you're going?" Tomura yelled, but she did not stop to answer.

You're about to do something very foolish, Elin, she thought. She knew she shouldn't do it. If she did, something terrible would happen . . . But if she didn't, the Toda would rip the Yojeh to shreds. The vivid image of what that would look like spurred her on.

Faster! Faster!

She raced down to the meadow. "Leelan!" she yelled.

Leelan had been romping about in the grass, but she raised her head and then bounded across the field. As they met, Elin shouted, "Take me up!" Leelan turned around and dropped into a crouch.

Everything seemed surreal. Before she even realized what she was doing, Elin had shimmied up Leelan's back and grasped her neck, pressing herself against her body. There was no time to get the saddle. She would have to fly like this.

"Fly?" Leelan asked.

"Fly!" Elin answered. Leelan's muscles rippled beneath her as the Beast spread her huge wings and leapt into the sky.

"To the river. That way." Shifting her weight, she leaned to one side to indicate the direction. Leelan responded instantly, veering to the right. As they flew over the crowd of spectators on the cliff, Elin heard the faint sound of surprised voices, but she had no time to look.

The Toda Riders had already reached the stern of the Yojeh's ship. Arrows fell like rain on the deck, striking several soldiers, but the Yojeh's men put up a stiff fight. Standing near the stern, Elin saw one man in particular loosing arrow after arrow. With each shot, another rider fell from his mount into the river. But this did not slow the Toda. They rammed the lead ships, capsizing them, and the men on board were thrown into the river, where the Toda snapped them in their jaws.

As they swarmed around the lead boats, the Yojeh's ship began to tilt, pulled to one side by the ropes.

It'll capsize!

The vessel listed sharply, and the gunwale almost touched the water. Several men who had been thrown from the boat clung to the thick cables. The Se Zan in the stern threw down his bow and drew his sword as he half slid, half ran to the gunwale. He raised his sword and severed the ropes with a single stroke. They shot into the air, and the ship ponderously righted itself, rocking slowly back and forth. Before it could come to a standstill, however, Toda began slamming into it. Bursting through the rails, one beast clambered onto the deck and made straight for the cabin. The man who had cut the ropes flung himself away from the gunwale and leapt in front, blocking its path. The Toda reared its head, preparing to snap him in two, but at that instant, the man plunged his sword deep inside its gaping maw. The Toda crashed to the deck, squealing in pain, and the man, dragged by its weight, fell with it.

"There!" Elin shouted, but before the word had even left her mouth, Leelan launched into a dive, her muscles as hard as steel and her fur standing on end. Although Leelan had never seen a Toda nor been taught how to respond, the sight of this natural enemy seemed to trigger an instinctive hatred that told her exactly what to do.

A piercing sound cut through the wind roaring in Elin's ears—a long, high-pitched whistle that she had never heard from Leelan before. The Toda below paused, then rolled over and exposed their bellies to the sky. Their Riders screamed as they were flung into the river. One of them fell onto the deck, and he bravely raised his bow, aiming straight at Leelan's belly. Elin closed her eyes as the arrows flew toward them, but when the shafts met the Beast's steel-hard muscles, they bounced off and fell harmlessly into the river. The archer stared openmouthed, then dived into the water.

Leelan attacked the huge serpents in a frenzy, ripping their bodies to pieces with her sharp claws. The cloying scent of Toda and the metallic odor of blood filled Elin's nostrils. Overcome by a wave of nausea, she closed her eyes again. The sound of rending and crunching seemed to go on forever, and it was all she could do just to hold on and not fall off.

The Yojeh's men and Damiya, who was peering through a hole in the cabin wall, watched dumbfounded as the Royal Beast, with a young woman perched on its back, slaughtered the defenseless Toda.

Only when she had killed every last Toda did Leelan seem to come to her senses. She flapped her wings and flew leisurely across the river to alight on the bank. Elin was shaking so violently that she could not move. She clung to Leelan's back even when the Beast waded into the shallows to wash the blood and slime from her belly. Every time she bowed her head to lick her chest, Elin felt herself jerked forward. At the sound of Leelan's lips smacking, her stomach heaved. Sliding off, she crumpled to her knees in the shallows and vomited.

A thin film of Toda slime spread across the water's surface and drifted slowly away. Chunks of flesh fell from Leelan's fur and plopped into the water. She poked them with her snout and sniffed, then plucked them out with her pink tongue and ate them. Oblivious to the water soaking her clothes, Elin knelt in the shallows and watched her blankly. A deadly chill spread from the pit of her stomach—as if a block of ice had slid across her insides. Gripping her thighs with her hands, she tried to still her trembling, but to no avail. Shuddering uncontrollably, she stared at the blood-spattered Beast.

Elin heard shouting—someone calling a name over and over, as if trying to keep a dear friend from dying. For a long time, the sounds of people screaming in agony had only registered as distant background noise, but the sudden realization of their meaning jolted her back to reality. A horrifying sight met her eyes.

Tattered fragments of warriors, boatmen, and Toda floated down the river. Perhaps because of their weight, those Toda corpses that were still relatively intact had floated in to shore, where they caught in the shallows and bobbed against the bank. The smaller vessels, still upturned, had drifted away, but the Yojeh's boat remained in the middle of the river. Without a steersman, it would be carried precariously downstream. A voice from on board was frantically calling someone's name.

Elin rose. If there were survivors, then they would need help. And for that, they would have to bring the boat to shore. She walked slowly over to Leelan.

4

HEALING

The teachers rode straight to Salano and reported the news to the Lord of Kazalumu. Then they, and others from the manor, traveled swiftly downriver by boat. By the time they reached the scene of the attack, however, an hour had already passed.

While she waited, Elin made Leelan tow the Yojeh's boat to shore, following the direction of the current. Then she climbed aboard. She considered riding Leelan back to the school to get supplies, but decided that her first priority was to bind the wounds of those who were bleeding profusely.

She had ripped open the sleeve of a man whose arm was pierced by an arrow and had just begun staunching the blood when she heard someone call her from the cabin. One of the Yojeh's menservants was beckoning her from the cabin door.

"Come quickly! The Yojeh's hurt! Hurry!"

Elin stayed to tie off the man's wound, from which blood was gushing. The servant, however, ran over, grabbed her by the arm, and yanked her to her feet.

"I said, 'Hurry!' The Yojeh's badly hurt!"

The damage inside the cabin was pretty bad. A huge hole gaped in one wall. The Yojeh's servants lay sprawled on the floor or sat crouched over, groaning with pain. They must have been thrown against the walls when the Toda had rammed the boat. The Yojeh lay on a mat, pale-faced, with her lips slightly parted and her eyes closed. Damiya sat beside her, his face chalk white and filmed with sweat. His left arm hung awkwardly and appeared longer than his right. He must have dislocated it, Elin thought.

A maidservant knelt on the other side of the Yojeh, calling her. Elin dropped to her knees by the mat.

"She hit the wall hard when the Toda attacked," Damiya said, breathing shallowly. "I tried to catch her, but I was too late . . ."

Elin brought her face close to the Yojeh's mouth and felt a breath of air brush her cheek. Relieved, she sat up and took the Yojeh's wrist in her hand to feel for her pulse. Then she raised her eyelids to check whether the pupils were different sizes and how they responded to the light. Closing the lids gently, she glanced around the room. Seeing an armrest lying in a corner, she asked the maidservant to fetch it. She was a young woman and seemed to be still in shock, for her hands shook violently when she handed Elin the armrest.

Elin slipped it under the Yojeh's neck as a brace and then turned to the maidservant. "Fortunately, the injury is not life-threatening at the moment. But I must ask you not to move her head under any circumstances. Please keep her still." She picked up a small blanket from where it lay on the floor and carefully covered the Yojeh. Then she stood up to leave.

Damiya stared at her. "Surely you're not going to leave without treating her?"

Elin shook her head. "There is nothing more I can do for her right now. The teachers were watching from the hill, and I'm sure they're on their way with the medicines and equipment we need." She grasped the shoulder of the maidservant who was gazing up at her and said, "You must not let anything jar her. Listen to her breathing and if you notice any change, let me know."

The woman nodded, her face very pale. Concerned, Elin looked at her closely. "How about you? Are you all right? Do you feel any pain?"

The young woman looked surprised, then smiled faintly and shook her head. "Thank you. I'm fine."

Elin turned to the manservant who was standing behind them. "Damiya's shoulder is dislocated. Will you help me fix it?"

The man nodded. "He hit his shoulder against the wall when he tried to catch Her Highness."

Elin knelt beside Damiya. Leaning over him, she looked into his eyes. "Did you hit your head?" she asked.

"Yes . . . I feel a bit nauseous."

She checked his pupils to see if they responded properly to light. "You probably have a slight concussion. When the doctors come, be sure to tell them that you hit your head."

"I will."

Elin glanced at the manservant. "Do you have something stiff that we can stabilize his neck with? Even thick paper will do."

The manservant looked around the room in a fluster, but the maid-servant held up a book that had fallen on the floor. "What about this?"

"Ah! That might work." Elin placed it against Damiya's neck. The width fitted perfectly between his shoulder and his ear. She placed it against the back of his neck to support his vertebrae, then wrapped it securely with a sash that the maidservant gave her. When she was finished, she turned once again to the maidservant and said, "Resetting his shoulder may be extremely painful. Do you have a piece of cloth we can put between his teeth so that he doesn't bite his tongue?"

"Don't worry," Damiya interjected. "I can use my sleeve." He raised his right arm, bit his sleeve, and grinned.

Elin nodded. "Thank you. It may be very painful until the bone is back in the joint, but once it's in, it should feel better. Try and bear the pain until we're done."

Damiya let the sleeve fall for a moment. "I may not be a warrior, but I believe I'm strong enough. If you fail, I'm not going to blame you, so you might as well go ahead and get revenge for yesterday."

Elin smiled in spite of herself. "All right, then. Let's begin."

The manservant supported Damiya from behind while Elin grabbed his left wrist with both hands. Relocating a shoulder is hard work, and Elin, as well as the white-faced Damiya, was drenched in sweat by the time she finished. When the bone finally slipped into the socket, none of them could speak for some time.

Damiya spit out the gag and let out a long breath. "Amazing . . . The pain seems to have almost disappeared."

Elin secured his arm with a sling made of some bleached cotton recovered from a trash basket, and said, "Don't move your arm. And please remember to tell the physicians that you hit your head."

Damiya looked at her. "I understand. And thank you. We owe you our lives."

Elin bowed her head. "It was nothing." She rose and looked around the room. Even those who had been lying prostrate when she came in were now sitting up. Although some held their heads in their hands, there were none with life-threatening injuries. The wounded on deck were in need of more urgent attention.

As she bowed to Damiya and turned to leave, he said, "Is there really nothing you can do for the Yojeh? Surely you could use the secret powers of the Ahlyo."

Elin stopped and looked at him. "I have no secret powers."

He gazed at her steadily. Although he said nothing, his eyes gleamed with a strange light.

As Elin passed out the door, she almost collided with a man coming in from the deck. It was Ialu, the Yojeh's guard. He seemed to exude a savage heat along with the smell of blood, sweat, and Toda, and Elin shrank back instinctively.

"How is the Yojeh?" he asked in a low voice.

"The fall was severe, and she's still unconscious. The fact that she hit her head worries me. Right now, however, all we can do is keep her still and warm."

Ialu nodded as he gazed over at the Yojeh. His right arm was blood-soaked from the shoulder to the fingertips. Even with a tourniquet tied round his right armpit, blood still dripped from his fingers. Elin suddenly recalled the man who had plunged his sword and arm down the Toda's throat.

"Were you cut by Toda fangs?"

Ialu looked at his arm. "Ah, this? It's just a gash. It should be all right. The bleeding will stop if I put pressure on it."

Elin frowned and gently raised his blood-drenched sleeve to examine the wound. Then she looked up at him and said, "Toda fangs are poisonous. If it isn't washed with a brew of shilan leaves, you could lose that arm."

Expressionless, Ialu gazed down at his arm as if it belonged to some-one else.

"Please wait while I go and get some," Elin said, and turned to leave, but Ialu grabbed her arm.

"Help my men first. Please."

Elin stared at him intently, but his face remained unmoved. She nodded and then went out onto the deck. Many men lay bleeding and groaning in agony. A life or an arm—Ialu was right. She should stop the bleeding first.

Behind her, Damiya's voice rose in fury. "Ialu! How could you let this happen? Why weren't you aware of the Aluhan's treachery?"

She could not hear Ialu's reply.

She was busy tying a tourniquet when Ialu came out of the cabin. He immediately joined her, deftly using his good arm to help. By the time a ship bearing the Kazalumu flag drew near, first aid measures were complete.

"Did you bring stewed shilan leaves?" Elin called out as soon as the ship was close enough to make out the faces of those on board.

The teachers looked dismayed. "We brought bandages and ointments for treating most injuries, but we were in such a hurry, we didn't think of that. Have some of the injured been bitten by Toda?"

"Yes, the wounds are mostly arrow wounds or lacerations from Toda fangs and scales, with some broken bones and bruising. Her Highness, the Yojeh, was slammed against the cabin wall and hit her head. She's still unconscious."

There was a commotion as people boarded from the other ship. While the teachers could see the wounded lying on the deck, the true extent of the slaughter was not apparent, as most of the bodies had already been washed downstream.

Quietly, Elin said to Ialu, "I'm going to ask Leelan to take me to the school so that I can get some shilan potion."

Ialu nodded. "Please. But don't bring it here. Go to the lord's hall. I'm going to have this boat towed there. The Aluhan is a clever general. If he has a second unit waiting to attack, we can't possibly repulse them here." Then he added in a low voice, "When you come to the hall, come by horse, even if it takes more time."

Elin looked at him in surprise. He was warning her not to let people see her riding the Royal Beast. She nodded. "I understand."

On her way back to Leelan, Elin had to pass the corpses of the Toda where they had washed against the shore. Whether she wanted to or not, she could not avoid seeing them. At the sight of their dorsal fins, however, she frowned. There were no notches. A chill ran through her as she realized what that meant.

It can't be . . .

She glanced back to where Ialu stood on the ship. Should she tell him? But if she did, she would have to explain why she knew so much about the Toda. Still frowning, she walked over to Leelan.

The Beast was grooming her fur, but she paused and looked up. "Fly?" she asked.

Elin nodded. "Fly."

Leelan crouched down to let Elin mount as if it was the most natural thing to do, then, once Elin was on, she shot into the air.

As he watched the Royal Beast dwindle into the sky, Ialu struggled to understand his own heart. He should not have let them leave—not if he were considering the best strategy for defense. With no one left in any shape to fight, they would be slaughtered should the Aluhan send a second wave of Toda. So why had he let the girl go? Why had he been so anxious that she leave as soon as possible?

Remembering that he had told her to come to the lord's hall by horse, he closed his eyes. While he knew what he had thought and the choice that he had made, he could not understand what had moved him to do so.

I must be getting used to this, Elin thought, for she had lost her initial fear of flying. With her cheek against Leelan's neck, she could hear the sound of the Beast's breathing and her mouth moving. At times she heard a clicking noise, like nails being clipped. For a while she wondered what it was, then she recognized the source. Leelan must have Toda scales caught between her teeth, and she was nudging them out with her tongue and cracking them between her jaws.

The sound of Leelan tearing the Toda apart leaped vividly into her mind—a sound like shattering glass. Something twisted in her gut, and a shiver ran up her spine. The sensation was disturbingly pleasant. Realization dawned. When she had ridden Leelan, wild with the scent of blood, when she had felt her invincible power and heard her crush Toda hides like mere glasswork, she had experienced not just fear, but pleasure as well.

Pressing her face into Leelan's fur, she closed her eyes and did not open them again until they began to descend.

When Leelan landed in the meadow beside Eku and Alu, Eku sniffed the air. His hackles rose, and he began to growl. He quieted reluctantly when Leelan responded in a low, soothing tone, but his fur still stood on end.

Elin slipped off Leelan's back and looked up at her with a heavy heart. She seemed as calm as if her killing frenzy had never occurred. And that very calmness alarmed Elin. If Leelan had been human, she could have talked to her about what their actions meant. But Leelan was not human. No matter how much Elin might wish otherwise, she could never share with her the fear, or the elation, that violence could evoke. Nor could she consult with her about what they should do next.

Royal Beasts were beasts. They did not think like people. With a word, she had made Leelan fly and kill the Toda, and Leelan had done exactly as she had been told. Like a sword that fit perfectly in the hand, once tamed, Royal Beasts could become convenient tools to be wielded as their master pleased. And by using Leelan as a weapon, Elin had just demonstrated that fact to the world.

Alu brushed up against her and licked her hand. Elin looked down at it, then squeezed her eyes shut.

Royal Beasts must never become accustomed to people.

Intoxicated with the joy of communing with them, she had trained them to respond to her. Now she could see all too clearly where this would lead. She buried her face in her hands. Although she had washed them in the river, they still smelt of blood.

Passing through the back door of the school and into the dark hallway, she felt as though she were seeing it for the first time, despite its familiarity. All sound—the clamor of the students, the voices of people who spoke to her—seemed to come from very far away.

Someone must have told the headmistress that she was back. With swift strides, Esalu approached, her face fierce with anger, but when she saw Elin's expression, the fury in her eyes ebbed. She grasped Elin's hands in her own. "Are you all right?"

Elin looked at her in a daze. "Yes. I'm all right." Even her own voice seemed to come from a great distance.

"Well, you certainly don't look it. You look like the walking dead."

Elin shook her head. "No, I'm fine . . . But some of the wounded were bitten by the Toda. I need to brew a potion of shilan leaves and take it back."

Esalu nodded and fell in beside her as they walked to the dispensary. "I saw what happened from the hill. Is the Yojeh safe?"

Elin spoke softly. "She was thrown against the wall and hit her head. She's unconscious."

Esalu frowned. "I hope it's just a mild concussion."

"I checked the pupils of her eyes, and she didn't seem to have any internal bleeding. For now, at least . . ." She knew that even when nothing happened immediately after a hard blow to the head, bleeding could begin much later, and that could be fatal. But she could not bring herself to say something so unlucky.

"I told the Lord of Kazalumu to take physicians and sent our most experienced teachers," Esalu said. "There's nothing more we can do but leave Her Highness in their hands."

As she helped prepare the potion in the dispensary, Esalu glanced frequently at Elin, as if there was something she wanted to say, but in the end she said nothing. Elin concentrated on her work, pretending not to notice. She was all too aware of the gravity of what she had done. But she was not yet ready to confront it.

The finely chopped dried shilan danced in the boiling water. Her eyes were focused on the leaves bubbling in the pot, but her mind was racing round and round, seeking excuses for what she had done. Reasons why she had had no choice floated up one after the other.

So this is how the human brain tries to protect itself when exposed to shock, she thought. But none of the reasons her mind suggested could erase the coal-black darkness at the bottom of her heart. Quietly and coldly that blackness declared the reality. She had opened a door that must not be opened. If she acted now, she might still have time to close it with her own hands. But if she went any further, she would never be able to do so again.

She watched the leaves dye the boiling water red.

5

THE MARK OF THE TODA CLANS

The gate to the lord's hall was firmly shut and guarded by soldiers, but when Elin dismounted and told them why she had come, they let her in. Ialu must have warned them in advance. The hall and garden were surrounded by thick mud walls roofed with clay tiles. Inside, everything seemed to be chaos. Men hurried to and fro, many of them dressed in obviously makeshift armor.

The scene reminded Elin of a hive of honeybees when a hornet approached. At least three times as large as their prey, hornets were ferocious, and, if they attacked in a group, they could exterminate an entire hive. But honeybees did not give in passively. Elin had once seen them swarm over a lone hornet, wrapping it in a ball. When the bees had dispersed, she saw not only the corpse of the dead hornet but also that of a tiny honeybee, crushed by its fellows with its mandibles still sunk in the hornet's leg. In her mind's eye, the tiny corpse merged with the figure of a man, and she shook her head to dispel this gloomy association.

Someone was weeping quietly, fighting to suppress their sobs. Perhaps a loved one had been killed by the Toda. The sound made her want to plug her ears. A maid came running up as she stepped into the lord's hall and led her into a room beside the entrance. The wounded Se Zan lay on mattresses on the floor. There were already two men fewer than those she had treated on the ship. A young man whose arm had been bitten off and another whose breast had been pierced by an arrow were nowhere to be seen. They had not made it. She closed her eyes for a moment.

Only two others had been gashed by Toda . . . It was, she realized, a miracle that as many as two of those within range of the Toda's fangs had survived at all. She smeared their wounds with the shilan ointment and helped them drink the antidote she had brought, all the while wondering where Ialu was. When she finished treating them, she went out into the corridor and stopped a maid who was hurrying past.

"Excuse me, but do you know where I can find Ialu, the Se Zan?"

The maid shook her head impatiently. "I've no idea. I'm sorry, but I'm in a hurry."

Elin watched her as she rushed away, wondering what to do. She could not leave without treating his wounds. She began walking along the corridor deeper into the hall and bumped into a middle-aged man coming through a door on her right. He was speaking to someone in the room behind him.

"Be sure to follow my instructions. You can serve dinner in about an hour," he said. Turning, he noticed Elin and stopped, staring at her as if she were a ghost. His face was familiar, and she realized it was the servant who had been on the boat with the Yojeh. Judging from a blue bruise along his jawline, he must have hit his chin when they were attacked. He was a very lucky man to have come away with such a minor injury.

"How is Her Majesty, the Yojeh?" she asked quietly.

"Ah . . ." He blinked, as if recollecting himself. "Her Royal Highness has not yet regained consciousness. But according to the physicians, while we must be vigilant, her condition is not life-threatening at this moment."

Elin let out a sigh of relief. "I am very glad to hear that."

"Yes, well, Lord Damiya's injury is also not dangerous, but he has gone to bed with a fever."

"I'm sorry. Please take good care of them, and of yourself." He nodded, and Elin asked, "Forgive me, but can you tell me where I might find Ialu, the Se Zan? I have brought him some medicine."

"Ialu? He's in the middle of a meeting."

"A meeting? When he was that badly hurt?"

The manservant frowned. "He failed to save Her Royal Highness, the Yojeh. As a Se Zan, he has no right to be concerned about his own health."

Elin's temper flared at the tone of his voice, but she hid her emotions. "I am very sorry to trouble you," she said, "but may I ask you a favor? Could you please tell Ialu when the meeting is over that I am here treating the wounded Se Zan?"

The manservant nodded haughtily and stalked off down the corridor.

Ialu did not come. Even when the last rays of the sun falling through the window had faded and a blue darkness spread across the land, he still had not appeared. A servant came and lit the lanterns, but when Elin asked if the meeting was over, she just shrugged her shoulders.

The medicine administered by the physicians must have been working, because the wounded were all sleeping. While she listened to their shallow breathing, Elin noted that the tension inside her must have eased, for she was suddenly starving. Thinking back, she realized that she had not had a bite to eat since breakfast.

Annoyed, she stood up. She had just put her hand on the door when someone pulled it open from the other side. It was Ialu.

He raised his brows. "You're still here?"

"You mean you didn't come here to be treated? I asked the servant to tell you that I was here." It was obvious from his expression that no one had told him. "Well, never mind. We need to do something about your wound."

She led him to a corner of the room. Being careful not to wake the sleeping men, she brought a candlestick over and set it beside him where he sat on the floor. Someone must have dressed his wound already, for his arm was securely bandaged, but his thumb, which protruded from it, was red and puffy. Gently removing the bandage, she found that not only the area around the wound, but his entire arm had swelled.

"Why didn't you come to me sooner? You knew that I must be here."

"There was no time."

Elin frowned as she cleansed the gash with the ointment. "You could lose the use of your arm with the poison spreading like this. How could you put off taking care of yourself like that? Especially your right arm."

Staring dully at the wound, he whispered, "It wasn't much use to me when I needed it most."

Elin's eyes flew to his face. He raised his head and looked at her. "I never even thanked you, did I? Forgive me. It was you who saved all of us, yet we didn't even offer you a meal . . ."

She shook her head and turned her gaze back to his arm. "It's better that way. It would be so much easier if everyone would just forget what I did . . ."

His face darkened. "That will never be . . . Now everyone sees you as a wielder of the Ahlyo's secrets."

Pain pierced Elin's heart. Washing his wound carefully, she said, "Do you also think so?"

"There's too little evidence as yet," he said quietly. "If raising a Royal Beast from infancy can make it tame enough to lick your hand, then you wouldn't need any secret powers to get on its back and fly." He smiled faintly and added, "And besides, if it is you who wields those secret powers, then as a Se Zan, I have nothing to fear."

Elin looked up. "Why?"

"Magic is the same as martial arts—what matters most is the user. If you had attacked us, then we should worry. But as you saved our lives, there should be no need for concern, right?" Still, there was a shadow in his eyes. He started to say something, then shifted his gaze to his companions where they lay in the darkness.

"Whatever the case, these lives you saved won't last long."

Elin shook her head. "Yes, they will. They'll all get better. None of their wounds are fatal."

"I wasn't talking about their wounds." He looked at her again. "Today it became very clear that the pillar which has shored up this country for so long is too rotten to last. The Yojeh has no army. If the Aluhan has decided to dispense with reverence and awe, with faith in and loyalty to the Yojeh, and to take up arms against her, then this country will never be the same again."

Elin watched him, saying nothing. Gazing into her green eyes, he continued, voicing thoughts he normally would never have shared with a woman or a commoner. "It is not the Se Zan that have protected the Yojeh. It is the hearts of the people who love her and believe that she, as the divine ruler, brings happiness to this land. There are only forty-three Se Zan in all. While we may be able to protect her from assassination, we would be no more than a wall of straw against even the smallest of the Aluhan's Toda troops." He spoke simply, without either belittling or romanticizing the Se Zan's state.

He knows exactly what he's protecting, Elin thought. He isn't sacrificing his life from a blind belief in the Yojeh.

As she listened to him speak, it was as if the kingdom as she knew it had grown thin and transparent, exposing the structure beneath—a land held together by placing an army-less ruler at its summit, a ruler supported solely by her people's will.

She looked down at the floor. Yet someone is trying to shatter that will like brittle glass. Clearly, he believes that the Aluhan has finally revealed his intention to rebel. Because Toda were used in the attack. But he's probably wrong.

From the moment she had noticed the lack of notches on the Toda's dorsal fins, Elin had been thinking, and her thoughts always led her to the same conclusion. The Aluhan could not have ordered the attack. Rather, someone had used the Toda to implicate him. If she were to tell Ialu this, she would have to tell him about her mother. If she did not tell him . . . both the Yojeh and the Aluhan would be forced down a terrible path, dancing to someone else's tune.

She raised her eyes and watched him sip the medicinal brew she had given him. "Those Toda . . ." she said. "They weren't the Aluhan's."

He took the cup from his lips and stared at her. "How can you be so sure?"

"Their dorsal fins bore no clan marks."

"Marks?"

Elin continued. "There are twelve villages that care for the Aluhan's Toda. The Stewards of each village take great pride in the Toda they raise. In order to determine which village's Toda excel on the battlefield, each clan makes distinctive notches in their dorsal fins so that they can tell them apart . . . There were no notches on the fins of the Toda that attacked you today."

Ialu frowned. "But what if they were raised especially for the purpose of assassinating the Yojeh . . ." he began, then shook his head. "No, there would be no point. The Toda themselves are the symbol of the Aluhan. And if the Aluhan indeed attacked with the intent to kill the Yojeh, then he would have no reason to hide his intentions . . ."

He rested his chin in his good hand and stared into space. Finally, he returned his gaze to Elin. "If you speak the truth," he said in a strained voice, "then I must reexamine the meaning of what happened today. Not even I, a Se Zan, knew about the notches. It's not that I doubt your word, but can you be absolutely sure?"

Elin nodded. "The Toda marks were developed out of clan rivalry. I doubt that anyone outside those clans would know about them." She closed her eyes briefly, then looked straight at him. "There is no mistake. I know because I was raised among Toda from the time I was very small. My mother was a Steward."

His eyes widened in surprise. She told him about her upbringing, her mother and the reason she was killed, and finally about how she had ended up in Yojeh territory. She told him everything, except the fact that her mother had controlled the Toda.

Ialu listened, his face expressionless. When she had finished, he still said nothing. In the wavering light of the candle, they sat in silence while he stroked his chin thoughtfully. Suddenly, a spark of amusement kindled in his eyes. Seeing the look on her face, he explained hastily, "Don't get me wrong. I wasn't laughing at you . . . I'm not quite myself, maybe because of everything that's happened today. I feel like I've been telling you a lot of things that I shouldn't. And I just thought that perhaps the same was now true for you."

A faint smile rose to Elin's lips. He might be right. She did not know why, but telling him about her mother had been much easier than she had expected, even though she barely knew him.

Just as he opened his mouth to speak, a bell rang in the distance, heralding the coming of night. As though waking from a dream, he said, "It's so late . . . You should stay here tonight. I'll let the servants know."

Elin shook her head. "No, I have to get back to take care of Leelan."

"Ah, I see."

Standing carefully so as not to knock over the candle, Elin said quietly, "You should rest. Even if just for a little while. You'll probably have a fever tonight. I'll ask someone to bring you some water. Be sure to drink as much as you can."

"I will." Ialu paused, then said, "I won't return your kindness with disloyalty. You can rest assured that I won't tell anyone about your mother."

Elin smiled. "Thank you . . . But if necessary, don't hesitate to tell. It may still be hard for me to talk about, but it's over." She bowed and left the room.

Ialu watched her leave. Only when she had closed the door behind her did he lie down in the dimly lit room and turn his eyes toward his men. Listening to their breathing, he thought of those who breathed no longer. Like him, in return for serving as the Yojeh's shields, they had all gained a station and lifestyle far beyond that into which they had been born. Yet, even so, a life was a life. Was there not something he could do before they were caught and crushed within the schisms of this kingdom's twisting structure? He ran a hand through his sweat-damp hair.

If it was not the Aluhan who attacked us . . . The ambush now revealed a scheme completely different from the one he had been considering. Because the attackers were Toda Riders, he had simply assumed that they were the Aluhan's men. Now, however, he realized that the Aluhan would never stoop to such underhanded measures. It was completely out of character. If he ever decided that the Yojeh must be removed, he would announce his intentions openly and surround the capital with his formidable army.

What can that man be thinking?

The man he had suspected for so long . . . If the attack were his doing, then the scheme made more sense. Yet, the falsely accused Aluhan would be furious. Even if the man had connections with Toda dealers, surely he could not have amassed a force large enough to oppose the Aluhan. He could never prevent the destruction of the Yojeh's sovereignty if the enraged Aluhan should attack, and what could he possibly gain by bringing the Yojeh's reign to an end?

He sighed. As he puzzled over the meaning of the attack, an image of a woman's face distracted him. Half hidden in the shadow cast by the candle, it flickered in the back of his mind and would not let go.

She saw her mother devoured by Toda, right before her eyes . . . Maybe that's why she had a quietness that set her apart—because she carried such a cruel memory concealed within. He recalled her face as she had cared for the Royal Beasts, and closed his eyes. He did not want to drag her into this any further. But that was likely impossible.

The sight of the Royal Beast descending from the heavens and feasting on the docile Toda like sacrificial offerings had been burned into the mind of every person there. He could see all too clearly the path that she would be forced to tread.

6

RESOLUTION

Four days after the attack, Elin received an invitation to dine with the Yojeh. She found the lord's hall much calmer than when she had last visited, and the maid who greeted her at the door treated her with deference. As she followed her down the wide, shadowed corridor, Elin's agitated mind raced madly. It was highly unlikely that she had been invited here purely out of gratitude for saving the Yojeh's life. There would be no turning back once she stepped into the room at the end of the corridor. Now was her last chance to decide, yet her mind was still frantically seeking a way out.

Two guards with unsheathed swords stood on either side of the entrance. As she approached, they swung the doors open, and light spilt out of the room. Myriad candles burned in a glass chandelier, shedding a soft glow over the rich gold-threaded tapestries that covered the walls. A feast of sumptuous dishes had been spread across a low table in the center of the room, and servants knelt near the door. At the far end of the table, the Yojeh reclined on a rug bolstered with soft wadding, while Damiya sat on one side of the table holding a wineglass in his hand. His other arm was still in a sling, but he looked far better than the last time Elin had seen him.

When she entered the room, all eyes turned to her.

"Elin," Damiya said happily. "It's good to see you. Come, come. There's no need to stand on ceremony. Come and sit beside the Yojeh." He gestured with his hand.

Elin knelt where he had indicated and then bowed her head to the carpet in formal greeting. "Your Majesty, I am here in response to your summons."

The Yojeh smiled and said gently, "Raise your head, Elin."

She did as she was told. There was a bright gleam in the Yojeh's eyes, despite her neck brace, bandaged head, and sallow skin. "It is thanks to you that we are able to sit together at this table tonight," she said. "We owe you our lives."

Elin bowed her head again. "I do not deserve such praise . . . Please accept my humble felicitations on Your Majesty's speedy recovery."

"Thank you. Now raise your head and relax. There is no need to speak so formally with me." She gestured to her lady-in-waiting. Rising gracefully, the woman approached Elin and placed a large, heavy brocade bag in her hands.

"Forgive me for not giving you a greater reward at this time," the Yojeh said, "but as you know, I am traveling. Ask for anything you desire, and I will make sure it is yours."

Elin set the bag she had been given on the carpet. "I am very honored, but—"

Before she could finish her sentence, however, Damiya interrupted. "There's no need to hesitate. Your service was outstanding. When you dropped from the sky on that Royal Beast to rescue the Yojeh, I shook with awe . . . It was as if the legends of the gods were coming to life before my very eyes."

Elin kept her eyes on the floor, but he ignored her, continuing gaily. "With you and that Royal Beast on our side, we have nothing to fear. Even if the Aluhan were to send more Toda against us, you could easily repel them. How could we be any safer than that?"

Elin stared fixedly at a single point on the carpet.

In her soft voice, the Yojeh added, "It's just as Damiya says. Thanks to you, we can sleep soundly at night."

Elin bit her lip and closed her eyes. The heat seemed to ebb from her body, yet sweat beaded her brow.

"While we stay here, let Leelan sleep in the garden and watch over us," Damiya said. "Then, when the Yojeh has recovered, the two of you can guard us on our journey to the capital."

Elin took a deep breath and opened her eyes. A cool stillness spread through her, and she knew that the time had come . . . Here, right before her, was the last line. Once she had crossed it, it would no longer be in her power to close the door.

She raised her face and looked straight at the Yojeh. "While you are here, Leelan and I will protect you. However, I beg of you, please do not ask me to take Leelan to the capital."

The Yojeh's eyes opened wide. Before she could speak, however, Damiya leaned forward. "What exactly are you saying?" he asked quietly, as if trying to reason with her. "Do you realize what that means, Elin? Think carefully before you speak. What you just said could be interpreted as a refusal to protect the Yojeh."

Elin turned to him. "I beg your pardon, Lord Damiya, but I am fully aware of what it means."

His expression changed abruptly. "Then no doubt you are equally aware that it is a crime for which the punishment is beheading."

The Yojeh did not protest. Her gentle expression had turned cold, and there was a stern glint in her eyes as she gazed down at Elin. Damiya calmed his breathing, but his voice still resonated with suppressed anger. "Let us pretend that we did not hear what you just said. Elin, I hereby command you to take the Royal Beast and accompany the Yojeh to the capital."

With a face drained of color, Elin gazed at the Yojeh. "Please forgive me. I beg you."

Silence fell over the room. She heard Damiya draw a deep breath. "Did you not hear me say that you would refuse on pain of death?" The words sounded as though he were forcing them through his teeth.

Elin nodded. "Indeed, I heard you, sir." The air was so taut with tension that she felt it must snap at the slightest touch.

"So you're prepared to die for this, are you?" Damiya said quietly. "But I am afraid that your life alone can hardly atone for such a heavy crime. The fault lies also with those who allowed you, who would refuse to protect the Yojeh, to care for the Royal Beasts."

Elin could scarcely breathe. Gazing steadily at the Yojeh, she inhaled shallowly and said in a shaking voice, "To accuse the teachers who trained me of treason . . . such a punishment would be far worse than killing me . . . it would feel like being torn in two. If you wish, you can torture me like that . . . but you cannot make me obey you." Just to utter those words was like spitting blood.

Looking intently at her white face, the Yojeh frowned. "Why would you refuse to protect me, even to that extreme?"

Elin inhaled slowly. She closed her eyes for a moment, then opened them. Struggling to keep her voice steady, she said, "I would tell that reason to you alone, Your Highness."

Damiya turned pale. "Are you saying that you can't tell me?"

Elin ignored this outburst. "Your Majesty, you told me that you would grant me whatever I desired. If you will honor your word, then I beg you to grant me this wish. Please ask the others to leave this room."

The Yojeh raised her hand to silence Damiya and gazed sternly at Elin. "Are you suggesting that I remain alone with someone who has just refused to protect me?"

"If you fear that I may betray you, then please have the Se Zan here remain by your side."

The Yojeh narrowed her eyes. "You mean that you trust Ialu, is that it?"

"Yes. I can trust him because he used his body as a shield to save Your Majesty's life."

Turning to Damiya, who was demanding in a shrill voice whether Elin meant that she could not trust him, the Yojeh said quietly, "Please take the others and leave this room."

"Aunt Halumiya!" Damiya protested, but she did not bother to repeat herself.

When the door had closed behind them, quiet descended on the room, as if a thunderous wave had receded from the shore.

"Well then, let me hear what you have to say," the Yojeh said.

"It will be a long tale, Your Highness," Elin said, her voice tenuous. "May I suggest that you lie down while I speak?"

A cold smile lit the Yojeh's eyes. "After all that, you now show concern for my well-being? Do not trouble yourself. Get on with it."

Elin sat up straight and rested her hands on her knees. "Before I begin, allow me to ask one question. Was it not in fact in accordance with Your Majesty's wishes that I should refuse to use the Royal Beast to protect Your Highness?"

The Yojeh looked bewildered. "My wishes? . . ."

At that moment, Elin, who had been watching her intently so as not to miss the slightest nuance of expression, felt her last thread of hope snap. She had thought that, if the Yojeh were forbidden to speak of the Canon and its secret purpose in front of others, she might be merely feigning ignorance, but it was clear from her answer that she simply did not know.

Apparently impatient with Elin's silence, the Yojeh demanded, "What on earth are you getting at? Speak plainly so that I can understand."

Elin made up her mind. If she doesn't know, then I'll have to start by explaining what I think about the Canon.

"I was told that it was the first Yojeh who wrote the Royal Beast Canon," she began. "Therefore, I assumed that Your Majesty must already know why I refused to manipulate the Royal Beasts. It would seem, however, that I was mistaken."

The Yojeh raised her brows. "The Royal Beast Canon? Yes, it was written by the first Yojeh. Is there some connection?"

Elin nodded. "Yes. If those who tend the Royal Beasts follow the procedures written in the Canon . . . the Beasts they raise will never fly and never bear young."

The significance of this must have been lost on the Yojeh, for she merely gazed at Elin silently.

"The first thing we learn about caring for Royal Beasts is that they can never be tamed. The rules for their care make sure that they have no human contact. Their handlers are taught to place food in their cages when the Beasts are outside and to paralyze them with the Silent Whistle before treating them. Repeated use of the Silent Whistle and daily doses of tokujisui prevent the Beasts from sexually maturing. That is why, for several centuries, no Beasts in captivity have ever borne young."

The Yojeh stared at her intently, as if searching for the meaning behind

267

her words. "Are you saying that the first Yojeh purposely made the rules to prevent the Beasts from multiplying?"

"Yes."

"But why?"

"It would be presumptuous of me to guess what the first Yojeh intended, but I believe that she wished, at whatever cost, to avoid repeating the catastrophe that she had experienced in her homeland."

The Yojeh's expression suddenly changed. Although her eyes never wavered from Elin's face, they no longer saw her. After a long pause, she finally spoke. "So you know what happened on the far side of the Afon Noah?" Then, as if to herself, she added, "I, myself, do not."

Elin looked at her in surprise. This was not what she had expected to hear. The Yojeh's eyes were as still as glass.

"When the palace burned and my mother died, I was only three. My grandmother died of the aftereffects when I was just five. I ascended to the throne knowing nothing . . ." Anger twisted her face. "The filthy Sai Gamulu! They took everything. My mother, my grandmother, and the memory of my people that had been passed down for three hundred years!" She clenched her age-stained hands, as though to suppress the wave of anger that disturbed her thoughts. Shakily, she took a deep breath and opened her fists, then pressed her fingers against her mouth. After a few moments, she dropped her hands and looked once again at Elin.

"My ancestor came down from the far side of the Afon Noah. That is the only memory of my people with which I was left. I do not know what gods lived in that land far across the mountains or why she left it to come here.

"Elin, how do you know what happened on the other side? Do the Ahlyo have some kind of connection to the gods?"

Elin gazed at her and said, "I do not know if the story I was told is true. But having seen firsthand the clever way in which both Royal Beasts and Toda in captivity are prevented from breeding, I feel that it is quite likely. Will Your Majesty listen? It is a very long tale."

The Yojeh nodded. "Let me hear, no matter how long it may be."

Elin took a deep breath, then began to speak. She told the Yojeh about her mother, about how she had commanded the Toda with her finger whistle and chosen death because she believed this was an unpardonable sin. And she shared the terrible tale that had been told to her by the Ahlyo. She told her everything. When she finished, the Yojeh stared at her unblinking. Her face seemed tragically aged, as though Elin's tale had sucked all the vitality from her.

"I see . . ." she whispered. Placing a trembling hand over her eyes, she was silent for some time.

"Your Majesty . . ." Ialu said. It was the first time he had spoken.

His voice must have penetrated her mind, for she said hoarsely, "There's no need for concern." She placed her hands, still trembling, into her lap and looked at Elin. "If your tale is true . . ." Her words died away. She appeared to be struggling to grasp the reins of her mind in the maelstrom of her confused thoughts. Closing her eyes, she waved her hand. "You may leave me now . . . You shall hear from me in due course."

Uncertain, Elin glanced at Ialu. He nodded and, with his eyes, gestured for her to leave. She bowed deeply and left the room.

Ialu slid forward on his knees and sat formally before the Yojeh. She opened her eyes slowly and murmured, "Ialu, you have wasted your life by serving as my shield."

He regarded her sternly. "If you will pardon me, Your Majesty, I must beg you never to say such things. Regardless of who the first ancestor was, Your Majesty is, without doubt, the true ruler of this kingdom."

The Yojeh stared at him with a look of surprise. He continued quietly, "If what Elin said is true, then the previous Yojeh, and the Yojeh before her, knew. They knew, and yet they still fulfilled their duty as rulers of this land. I am Your Majesty's shield, but it is you who are the shield of this kingdom. Without a strong and sturdy shield, this land would still be doomed, regardless of the past."

As his words permeated her mind, she felt the familiar weight of responsibility wrap itself around her like a cloak of steel. A faint smile crossed her face. "You never lose your head, do you? Even when the pond is murky with mud and debris, you can reach in and seize the fish."

Ialu bowed his head. "Your Majesty, while there are no other ears to hear, there is one other thing of which I must speak."

As she listened to what he said, her eyes clouded with pain. When he had finished, however, there was no longer any doubt in her face. She might be old and hurt, but she was still the Yojeh.

Two days later, Elin received a message from the Yojeh. In it, she praised Elin's service and expressed her gratitude for sharing what was in her heart. And she declared that she had no need of the Royal Beast's protection. Ten Se Zan arrived from the capital and, with them as her guards, the Yojeh began her journey home to the palace.

If she had reached the capital safely, Elin's fate would have been very different. However, as the Yojeh passed through the palace gate, she complained of a severe headache and fell into a coma. Although her bruises had faded and her head injury appeared to have healed, blood must have been seeping slowly into her brain. The long journey home in a jolting carriage had aggravated the damage. Carried into the palace, she never regained consciousness. Her sudden death caught everyone by surprise.

EIGHT

THE GATHERING STORM

I

A MARRIAGE PROPOSAL

"Six, seven, eight cartloads . . ." the Aluhan murmured as he looked down from his window at the castle gate. He snorted. "She's returned everything."

Noting the vein throbbing in his father's temple, Shunan said soothingly, "It was only to be expected. If I were in her shoes, I would not accept them either."

The Aluhan turned slowly toward him but said nothing. The rumor that the Yojeh had been ambushed by Toda had reached his ears the morning after the attack. He had immediately dispatched messengers to the Yojeh in Kazalumu and to Princess Seimiya at the palace to deny any involvement, but they had been turned away, unable to fulfill their mission.

Again, as soon as he had learned of the Yojeh's passing, he had sent gold, silver, silk, and other precious goods to Seimiya as mourning gifts. But now these, too, were being returned, still packed in their horse-drawn carts. Even before the carts arrived, the messenger bearing his letter of condolence had returned to say that Seimiya had refused to even let him pass through the palace gate.

"She may be the Princess," the Aluhan said in a low voice, "but to respond like this without even attempting to verify the facts is unpardonable." Backlit by the window, his figure was sunk in shadow. "This kingdom is doomed if its ruler can be deceived by such an obvious attempt to frame an innocent man."

"Father—" Shunan interjected, but the Aluhan ignored him.

"Using Toda to brand us as the Yojeh's assassins is beyond contempt. If, by any chance, the one behind this foul scheme finds a way to manipulate the Crown, the kingdom will rot from the inside and perish. We cannot leave this ship on which we all sail in the hands of such a foolish captain."

"Father!" Nugan pushed his brother aside to stand before the Aluhan. His eyes shone with outrage and his voice lashed out like a whip. "How can you be so disrespectful? I demand that you retract your words!"

Even as Nugan spoke, the Aluhan swept his sword from its scabbard and smacked his son on the ear with the flat of the blade. Nugan fell to his knees and clutched the side of his head. Shaking with rage and astonishment, he gazed up at his father.

The Aluhan glared down at him. "It's about time you grew up," he said coldly. "If your shortsighted, obstinate stupidity ever threatens your brother's position, I will not hesitate to lop off your head." His sword whistled as he whirled it into its sheath. He turned to Shunan. "Do you have some objection too?"

"No. It would seem that the time has come," Shunan said.

At this, the Aluhan smiled. But before he could speak, Shunan added, "I believe, however, that it would be wise to allow the Princess a period of grace—to give her some time to think."

The Aluhan frowned. "At times like this, speed means everything. It's far more effective to respond immediately."

Shunan shook his head. "If we were launching into battle with a foreign country that possessed an army, yes, of course. But I think this case is different." He walked over to his younger brother, grasped him by the elbow, and helped him to his feet. "Winning this battle will be easier than snatching away a baby's blanket. The hard part will come after." He looked at the Aluhan. "Father, I have an idea. Would you be willing to leave it in my hands?"

A fishmonger selling his wares for the evening meal rattled by with his cart, accompanied by the high, trailing note of his horn.

Ialu rested his arm on his forehead and stared at the ceiling. He had woken much earlier, but had not felt like getting up. Instead, he had lain in bed, gazing absently at the pattern of the woodgrain in the ceiling where it caught the early afternoon light. For the last ten days, from the Yojeh Halumiya's funeral to the coronation of the new Yojeh, there had been almost no time for sleep. While everyone in the palace dashed to and fro in a state of anxious confusion, he had watched over the new Yojeh, just as always. This morning, when the night watch changed, he had not felt like returning to the antechamber set aside for the Se Zan. Instead, he had left Kailu in charge and returned to his house for the first time in weeks.

When he had fallen exhausted onto his bed, he had failed to notice the thin film of dust coating the floor and windowsills, but now he could see it plainly. His room seemed to belong to a stranger—empty but for a single chest of drawers and his woodworking tools, which had lain idle for far too long.

The emptiness that always lurked deep inside seeped slowly up his spine and spread through him, until his body felt thin and transparent. He had lived as an arrow to kill, and as a shield to block the arrows of others—that and nothing more. He had no life companion and never would. Before him lay endless days of empty solitude . . . At times like these, this reality, from which he could never escape, permeated his being.

The fishmonger's voice grew suddenly fainter. He must have turned the corner.

This land . . . cannot possibly survive, he thought. It won't be long before it changes forever.

Regardless of what form it took, it was no concern of his. It was not his job to ponder how the country should be. He was simply a shield to guard the Yojeh. All he needed to think about was how to protect her.

Still . . . He closed his eyes. What should I do about that man now?

In the lord's hall in Kazalumu, Ialu had told Yojeh Halumiya what he suspected, and she had promised to consider how to deal with it. But she had died suddenly, and he was back to where he had started. In his mind, he could still hear the fragile voice of the young Yojeh, Seimiya, as she conducted the funeral rites. He could not leave her ignorant of who had murdered her grandmother. Yet would she believe him if he told her?

He sighed. He could guess what the man planned to do with her. Unlike her grandmother, there was not much chance that he would take her life. In that sense, this case was already outside Ialu's line of duty. Except that now he must serve as the shield of a Yojeh who was only a puppet in that man's schemes. At this thought, a grim smile rose to his face.

Despite the nature of the life he had lived, he realized that somewhere deep inside he still yearned for a cause worth dying for. If he had to sacrifice this life, such as it was, he would still rather do it for something meaningful. But he already knew, didn't he, the value of his life? One bag stuffed with large gold pieces. His life as a person had ended the day his mother had accepted that bag of gold.

He covered his face with his hands and, for a long time, simply listened to the sound of his own breathing.

When Seimiya returned to her room and was finally alone, she thought that now, finally, she could weep. She sat on her familiar chair and stared numbly at the floor where the late afternoon sun cast shadows through the latticed window frame. But the tears would not come.

Her grandmother's death had been far too sudden. Even as she had performed the funeral and coronation rites, standing center stage throughout, Seimiya had felt strangely dull and removed, as though she were watching herself from a distance. That feeling did not leave her even when she was on her own. She felt as though she were in a dream where reality had no substance.

There was so much to do. In particular, she must decide quickly how to punish the Aluhan for his vile betrayal. Yet even this thought, despite its importance, merely floated in the forefront of her brain, stirring no emotion.

A servant at the door announced that Damiya was requesting permission to enter, and Seimiya glanced up.

"Let him in . . ."

The door opened, and Damiya walked in. His face still looked pale, although he no longer used a sling. Ever since she was a child, he had been Seimiya's father, brother, and friend. The moment she saw the gentle concern in his eyes, a sense of normalcy, of everyday life, rushed back with startling vividness, and she was hit full force with the knowledge that her grandmother was no longer a part of that life.

Seeing her lips tremble, Damiya strode across the room, opened his arms wide, and wrapped her inside them. Enveloped in his warmth, she felt tears spill from her eyes. Suppressing her sobs, she clung to him tightly and wept. Damiya buried his face in her hair and patted her on the back while tears coursed down his cheeks.

For some time, Seimiya wept. When her tears were almost spent, she whispered into his chest, "Thank you. Thanks to you, Uncle, I was able to mourn my grandmother."

Damiya said nothing, merely stroking her hair gently.

"If death can come so suddenly, I had better get around to having children soon, hadn't I?" She smiled and, with a catch in her voice, said, "I must make sure there's another heir to the Yojeh's throne."

Damiya, his eyes still closed, took a deep breath and gently shook her slight frame twice. "Don't say that." His voice was almost a sigh, and he stroked her hair yet again. "You are not a tool for passing on sovereignty, Seimiya."

She rested a hand on his chest and drew slightly away to look up into his face. "Uncle, I beg you. Please don't try to comfort me with empty words. I know too well what I am, what my duty is." Her smile turned fierce. "From the time I was old enough to understand, I have never forgotten, not even once."

Damiya shook his head. "No, Seimiya, you do not realize what you truly are. You have never seen what really matters."

Seimiya raised her brows. "What really matters?"

"That's right. The throne does not exist just to make the ruler suffer. If you must sit on it, then why not enjoy the view that can only be seen from there? Seimiya, you have never once thought of enjoying your sovereignty, have you?"

She gazed at the ground. Damiya placed a finger under her chin and gently raised it. "You are the only woman in this land who can choose any man she wishes. Choose the one you love and marry him."

"Impossible," Seimiya said with a mocking smile. Her scornful expression was just like her grandmother's. "I am the only woman in this country who truly cannot choose the man she wants. You know that."

"No, in fact, I don't know that. Why?"

She sighed. "Just think of the choices, Uncle. If we go by blood, perhaps you are thinking of my distant cousin, Oliya? That feeble boy with all the presence of a mayfly? Or, instead of the sacred bloodline, shall we opt for members of the nobility instead—all those spoiled, arrogant youths. Enough of this fruitless discussion."

Damiya's grip on her chin strengthened. "What do you mean by fruitless, my dear? This is a very important question, Seimiya. If there is anyone, say so."

"Anyone?"

"A man that you truly like."

Seimiya held her breath. Her eyes slid from his, but then she raised them defiantly, gazing straight at him. "No, there's no one."

Damiya laughed. "Come, come. Love affairs are the one thing at which I'm a veteran. Your face just spoke far more eloquently than your words." He let go of her chin and embraced her, rocking her like a little child. "Relax. At least when you are in my arms, be at peace." He buried his face in her hair again and whispered, "Remember, you are not alone. I am always by your side."

Ialu, who was standing in front of the Yojeh's room, sword and shield in hand, turned his head. Far down the hall, someone was hurrying toward him. There was an urgency in his step and his face was tense. It was Kailu, who had been on duty at the gate.

"What's wrong?"

"The Aluhan's eldest son," Kailu whispered hoarsely. "He's here and requests an audience with the Yojeh."

"How many soldiers has he brought?" Ialu asked sharply.

"Actually . . . none. They bear no arms."

"What did you say?"

"He's brought only three men, none of whom are armed, and they're all missing something—like a hand or a leg."

"Missing a hand or a leg?"

"Yes. And one of the men's faces is pitifully scarred."

Ialu was silent. He thought he could guess what Shunan, a quiet, intelligent young man, sought to tell the Yojeh. "I will announce their arrival. Wait here."

Standing before the Yojeh's room, he requested permission to enter. After a few moments, a voice from within bade him in. As he walked into the room, he could not help noticing how close Damiya and Seimiya stood. Seimiya's eyes were red, indicating that she had probably been crying, but there was color in her cheeks, and her expression was unexpectedly cheerful.

Ialu's heart sank, but he bowed and announced that Shunan was waiting at the gate.

The color drained from Seimiya's face. "What did you say?"

Damiya put his arm around her thin shoulders as if to support her and said soothingly, "There's no need to see him. You can turn him away."

She cast him an imploring glance. He tightened his hand on her shoulder. "To refuse to meet him is also an important way of expressing your will. Don't allow yourself to be swayed by your emotions. Be firm."

She turned her eyes from Damiya and looked at Ialu's rigid face. Her eyes reflected the turmoil in her heart. She took a deep breath, then said in a faint voice, "Usher him into the audience chamber."

Shunan entered the chamber alone. Seimiya's eyes widened slightly when she saw him. In the last four years, he appeared to have matured into a wise and reserved young man. In comparison, she felt that, except for losing her youth, she had not changed at all, and for an instant she regretted agreeing to see him.

He dropped to one knee and bowed his head. "I thank you for granting me an audience. I was sincerely grieved to hear of the untimely passing of Her Majesty, Yojeh Halumiya."

Her face rigid, Seimiya whispered, "You? Grieved? Why?"

Shunan raised his head, but rather than opening his mouth to speak, he seemed to be waiting to hear what she would say. Instead, Damiya, who sat beside her, spoke on her behalf. "Both we and you know very well who murdered my aunt. You have some nerve to utter such false condolences. I see you've inherited your father's shameless arrogance."

Shunan gazed back at Damiya, his expression unmoved. "I beg your pardon, but do you in fact know who attacked the Yojeh Halumiya?"

Seimiya's cheeks flamed. "How dare you! My grandmother was attacked by Toda. Who else is there who wields those filthy beasts but the Aluhan?"

Shunan frowned slightly. "Surely, my lady, you must be aware that ever since the horsemen of Lahza began attacking our eastern border, the demand for Toda has drastically increased, and there are now many among the Yojeh's people who handle them."

Seimiya's brows flew up. "And what of it? Are you saying that the Holon would scheme to assassinate their own Yojeh?"

"Your Highness, Seimiya," Shunan paused to take a deep breath and then continued, "What possible benefit could we gain by assassinating the Yojeh in such a contemptible manner?" Seimiya frowned, clearly puzzled by his question. "The foolish Sai Gamulu are one thing, but why on earth would we need to stoop to such measures? It never occurred to me that Your Majesty would fail to realize such an obvious truth."

Seimiya retorted sharply, "With the Yojeh dead, you would become the rulers, of course. What could be of more benefit than that?"

"If we killed the Yojeh, the Aluhan would be king? In that case, assassination makes no sense at all." There was an edge of steel to his voice now. "I never dreamed you would misjudge us to that extent. If we ever decided that this land could not be entrusted to the rule of the Yojeh, we would have no need whatsoever to stoop to assassination. We could seize power openly. We have at our command a hundred Toda troops and ten thousand horsemen, all of which have protected this land for centuries from external enemies, repulsing repeated invasions. We possess the power to destroy you and take over this palace tomorrow, if we so desired."

Damiya gave a bark of laughter. "Well done. Now you are showing your true colors. My Lady Seimiya, I am sure you now understand all too well the true nature of the Aluhan. He intends to seize the throne by force." Shaking his head, Damiya smiled at Shunan. "It is just as you say, Shunan. It would be so simple for you to kill us and usurp the throne. But by doing so, you will gain the throne of a country doomed to die.

"The Yojeh is a god. If you are so blind to the divine will revealed in the Yojeh that you take the throne by force, this land, bereft of its god, will perish."

Shunan fixed his eyes not on Damiya but on Seimiya. After a long silence, he finally said quietly, "Do you also believe this, my lady?"

"Of course," Seimiya responded immediately. "You mean you don't?"

Shunan shook his head curtly. "No, I don't." He rose. "I do not believe that the Yojeh are gods. How can anyone who is incapable of bringing happiness to this land possibly be a god?"

Seimiya's cheeks turned pale. Damiya leapt to his feet and opened his mouth to shout, but she silenced him with her hand. "Why do you say that I cannot bring happiness to this land?"

"Let me ask you this, my lady. How do you intend to heal the mortal illness that afflicts this land?"

"It is the greed and ambition of your people that is the cause. I will heal it by refusing to be swayed by such contamination, by retaining a pure heart. It is true that I have no warriors to protect me. But if you use your military might to destroy me, this country will lose its soul. And at that moment, it will die. It will be you, not I, who destroys this country."

279

Shunan shook his head. "No warriors to protect you? Surely you cannot be serious. Who on earth do you think has been protecting you all this time? Not you as an individual, but this entire kingdom?" The anger in his eyes was unmistakable. "I wonder if you have the courage to look upon those who have defended this land."

"I am never, ever afraid," Seimiya answered in a hard voice.

Shunan nodded. "Then let us look. Come in!" he cried.

The doors opened, and three men shuffled into the room. Seimiya caught her breath at the sight. They were young, not yet twenty. One was missing his right arm from the elbow down, another had lost his left leg at the thigh and walked instead on a wooden peg. The last one to enter was a boy who looked to be only fifteen or sixteen and had not even begun to grow a beard. A hideous burn, centered round his right eye, disfigured his otherwise smooth complexion, and there was only an empty socket where his eyeball should have been.

Shunan placed his hand on each man's shoulder in turn as he introduced them one by one.

"This is Lahalu. The year before last, he lost his arm while fighting to protect a fort when the Lahza attacked from Hosalu Pass. Yunan here fought in the same battle with the cavalry and was badly injured. The wound festered, and in the end, his leg had to be amputated from the thigh down. And this boy is Lokalu. His keen eyesight made him a great lookout, but a flaming arrow pierced his right eye while he stood on the lookout tower."

Shunan turned to face Seimiya. "Thousands of soldiers with devastating injuries like these live in this kingdom. Thousands more lie rotting beneath its cold earth. If they, and their fathers and mothers, their children and lovers, knew that you believed you have no warriors to protect you, I am sure they would rise up and demand to know what on earth their deaths, and the deaths of those they loved more dearly than life, were for."

Unable to breathe, Seimiya stared at the boy with the empty socket. He stared back at her with his one remaining eye, as if he could not believe he was really face to face with the Yojeh. His confusion was painfully evident.

Was it right to feel awe in her presence? Was it safe to voice his doubt and anger? What feelings should he show her?

Seimiya could not even begin to identify the emotions that welled up inside her. She did not even know if she should weep. All she wanted was to be alone. To be alone and think. The right words to say at this particular moment simply would not come.

"Seimiya," Shunan said, addressing her by name. "We have shed blood and tears for centuries to prevent this country from being laid waste by foreign powers. I am not seeking to romanticize our role or to demand your pity. But I simply cannot believe that it is right for one who does not know our reality to rule." His voice was like the shadow cast through the window by the late afternoon sun. While regretting the dying of the day, he calmly announced the coming of the night.

"If you insist that you are a god and that placing the Aluhan on the throne will lead to this country's destruction, then prove it. Four months from now, on the day we celebrate the dawn of this country's founding, let us determine who is right. On that day, we will wait for you on Tahai Azeh, the Plain of Advent, where our nation was born. We will wait for you with our finest Toda troops, the ones that you despise as 'filthy,' but that I believe symbolize this country's reality.

"If the god truly blesses your actions and watches over you, the Toda will, just as legend recounts, be so awed by your divine majesty that they will bow their heads before you. If this miracle should occur, then my father and I will rein in our troops and once again serve as your vassals, shedding our blood without complaint . . ."

He looked at her pale face, the one that had stayed imprinted on his heart all these years. Then he drew a deep breath and continued. "However, if such a miracle fails to occur, then, Seimiya, I ask that you, for the sake of your people, give yourself to me."

Seimiya's eyes wavered. Shunan held her gaze as she stood speechless and dazed, then bowed his head slowly. "If you decide to accept my proposal, raise a blue flag. When we see that flag, the advancing Toda will halt before you."

Without asking her leave, he turned on his heel and, urging the young soldiers ahead, quietly left the room.

2

THE NATURE OF BEASTS

Flowers dotted the meadows of Kazalumu, and a light breeze carried their sweet fragrance along with the scent of grass. While Alu and Eku bathed in a small pond, Leelan munched on yellow keema blossoms some distance away. Keema cleansed the stomach of parasites, and Royal Beasts liked to gorge themselves while they were in bloom. The fact that Leelan did so without ever having been taught by her kind made Elin pause to wonder at the innate knowledge of living things. She was watching dreamily as Leelan snapped the flowers in her jaws when the Beast suddenly reared her head and, wrinkling her nose, began to growl.

Surprised, Elin followed the direction of her gaze and saw three men on horseback swiftly ascending the gentle rise toward her. Behind them, she could see several teachers, one of whom she recognized as Esalu by her white hair. They were on foot, running after the horsemen, but the distance between them widened rapidly.

Leelan's growl turned menacing. Elin raised a hand to still her and walked toward the men. As they drew closer, she could see that they were all dressed as Beast Handlers. Although she knew none of them, one look at the crests sewn to their uniforms told her who they were.

The first, who appeared to be the elder, dismounted, and the other two followed suit. They watched her warily, fingering their Silent Whistles. The leader looked down at her haughtily. "Greetings. I am Ohooli, Head of the Lazalu Beast Sanctuary." He gave a polite bow, an act that contrasted starkly with the disdain in his eyes.

Elin bowed in return. "I am honored. How may I help you?"

There was a pause before he replied. His jaw clenched and bulged, and his neck turned red. He reminded her of a fighting dog she had once seen in a market, restrained by its master yet trembling with the urge to bite.

"I have come to escort you to Lazalu," Ohooli said, as if forcing the words from his throat. "Her Highness, Yojeh Seimiya, has graciously deigned to convey this message. In honor of your distinguished services in saving the previous Yojeh, Her Highness has commanded us to welcome you as the Head of Lazalu Beast Sanctuary. You are to move yourself and the Beasts you have raised at once to Lazalu, in order to protect the palace."

Pain shot through Elin's heart. From the moment she had heard of Yojeh Halumiya's passing, she had feared that this day must come. Breathing with difficulty, she said, "Her Highness is far too gracious. I am afraid that I must decline."

The men's faces remained unmoved. Clearly, they had been expecting this response. "We were told not to accept no for an answer," Ohooli said coldly. "If you refuse to comply with this generous offer, our orders are to bring you back to the palace by force."

Before she could even open her mouth, the two men standing behind Ohooli moved swiftly to each side of her and grasped her arms.

Ohooli's mouth lifted in a mocking smile. "Your colleagues were far more agreeable than you."

The men gripped her arms with more force than necessary, but Elin had no intention of struggling. "What did you say to them?"

"Just that we had come to carry out the Yojeh's wishes."

He's so vain, Elin thought. He must be furious with her for taking away his job. While he longed to ease the resentment smoldering in his heart by scoffing at her, he was afraid to show his feelings in case it jeopardized his future. Despite this, he could not resist making spiteful little jabs that spoiled his pretense of politeness. A cold, heavy lump sank in her stomach, and she let the tension drain out of her. She had lost any desire to even try to reason with him.

Leelan had continued to growl, the sound growing steadily louder, but now it crescendoed to a deep and ominous thunder that Elin had never heard before. The men on either side of her grabbed the Silent Whistles that hung round their necks and placed them to their lips. An icy fear gripped her. At this distance, the whistles would paralyze not only Leelan, but the cub as well.

"No! Please don't!" she cried, and twisted from their grasp.

The men, who had been focused on Leelan, were caught off guard and staggered. One of them dropped his whistle. The next moment, there was a loud snap, and the hand of the other vanished in a swirl of dark wind. Blood spurted from the stump of his wrist, while Leelan, her blood-smeared lips pulled back in a snarl, crunched his hand, bones and all, in her jaws. Her fangs had torn off not only his hand, which had held the whistle, but his lips and nose as well.

Elin and the men stood frozen in disbelief, gazing up at the Beast towering over them. Then the man who had lost his hand threw back his head, and a scream erupted from his throat. At the sound, the man on Elin's other side jerked to his feet and, turning on his heels, broke into a run. Perhaps attracted by the movement, Leelan leapt into the air.

Elin felt like she was in a nightmare. She dashed after the fleeing man. He stumbled and fell, and she flung herself over him, waving Leelan back with her hand.

"Leelan! Stop! Stop!" she pleaded.

Intoxicated by the taste of blood, Leelan followed the hand that fluttered before her face and bit reflexively. Elin heard the bones in her left hand shatter. In the next moment, sheer agony shot from her hand to every corner of her body. Leelan's frenzied, snarling face loomed over her. Spittle, frothy blood, and bits of broken bone spattered Elin's face, and she prepared to die.

Just then, her hand brushed something on her neck. Light flashed in her eyes as she realized what it was. She brought the Silent Whistle to her mouth and blew.

All sound ceased. Gasping for air, her shoulders heaving, Elin stared at Leelan's face, rigid as stone, fangs still bared. Pain throbbed in her hand and blood gushed forth, but it was as though her body were too far away for these to reach her consciousness. She watched in a daze as someone ran up, shoved her out of the way and dragged the fallen man from beneath

Leelan's wing. That was the last thing she remembered before she tumbled into darkness.

All night, she lay tormented by fever and burning pain. Nightmares disturbed her sleep. When she finally woke on the morning of the second day, her fever was gone, but she was weak and weary, and her body felt like an empty shell.

Seeing Elin's eyes open, Esalu rose from beside her bed. "Are you awake?"

Elin looked at her foggily for a moment, then nodded slightly. As consciousness returned, the pain in her left hand came rushing back, and with it, the memory of that awful nightmare. A crushing fear seized her.

"That man . . ." She could barely force out a hoarse whisper, but Esalu guessed what she wanted to know.

"He's still alive. You can thank the gods that no one died at least."

As the words penetrated her mind, a hot lump rose through the mist that wrapped her heart, and tears welled from her eyes.

The Beast Handlers who had come from Lazalu were the same men who had dragged Leelan before the Yojeh when she was a cub. She had never forgotten being paralyzed by their Silent Whistles in the palace garden, and, worse, being shot by an arrow. She was so agitated, she had had to be chained in her stable. The wounded Beast Handler was being cared for solicitously in the room next to Elin's. Three fingers on Elin's left hand from her baby finger to her middle finger had been bitten off, and although the wound had been sewn up, she might lose the use of that hand.

All these things Esalu told her. Elin heard the words, but her brain registered their meaning only dully. Something black and heavy had spread through her mind, and all she could feel was the weight of it. Over and over, she saw herself twist out of the men's grasp, saw one of them drop his whistle. Again and again, she saw Leelan swooping down like a black wind, heard the sound of the man's hand being chopped off, bones and all, felt her fingers shattering, heard the man scream . . .

Whether her eyes were open or closed, the same scene, the same sounds, the same pain were constantly replayed in her mind, like a nightmare from which she could never escape.

Around midnight on the third day after she regained consciousness, she heard the sound of falling rain. As she listened, a thought spread through her mind.

Leelan ate my hand . . .

She had snapped at Elin's hand just like that, without any hesitation. She would have eaten her, even though they had lived together for so long.

How could anyone even begin to understand how beasts thought?

She should never have projected human thoughts onto beasts and assumed that she understood them. In doing so, she had forgotten that they would always be a mystery to man and had convinced herself that she knew what they were thinking. On that fateful day, Leelan had growled in a way that Elin had never heard before, yet she had ignored her. Her own carelessness and arrogance had brought about this disaster. She could never undo what she had done. No matter how hard she might pray or plead, she could never, ever change it.

The man who had lost his hand and half his face must be in terrible pain even now. He would never be the same again. For the rest of his life, he would have to live without a hand, without a nose, without lips . . .

Elin could not breathe. She closed her eyes and gulped for air like a fish. She did not hear the sound of her own breathing or the incessant rain drumming on the roof. The only sound that rang through her brain was the man's anguished scream after Leelan bit him.

It was seven days later that Elin was finally able to rise from her bed. As soon as she could, she went next door to visit the injured Handler. She apologized and gave him all the money that the Yojeh had given her, asking him to use it to get the care he would need. The Beast Handlers from Lazalu listened without a word, their eyes cold with hatred and contempt. With bowed head, she bore their gaze.

Ohooli finally spoke. "We cannot wait for your hand to heal. We'll leave with the Beasts for the palace within the month, so be prepared."

Elin bowed wordlessly, then turned and left the room.

Esalu, who was waiting for her in the hall, came up to her. "Are you all right?" she asked.

Elin nodded. "I'd like to see how Leelan is doing."

Esalu stared at her silently, but then acquiesced. They had begun walking slowly down the corridor when Esalu suddenly put her hand into her robe and pulled out the Silent Whistle. Elin took it and hung it around her neck.

The stable was dark inside, and the stench of dung filled the air. Leelan swung her head up abruptly when Elin entered, but instead of cooing the way she usually did, she snorted and huffed loudly. The smell of Beast permeated the stable. Golden eyes stared warily through the bars. Bald patches on Leelan's chest oozed blood. She must have been gnawing her fur.

"We removed the chains but she refuses to go outside," Esalu explained. "We can't clean her stall, so we've had to leave it like this."

Elin said nothing. She did not even hear Esalu's voice. The instant those golden eyes had met her own, the sight of Leelan's snarling face close to hers had flashed through her mind, and her left hand jerked in its sling. She gasped for air and tried to stop the trembling that seized her body.

"Elin." Esalu grabbed her elbow, and she started. Beads of cold sweat ran down her body. She turned toward Esalu and waited until her face came into focus. Her brain was numb; she could not think. It was all she could do to suppress her panic.

"That's enough for today," Esalu said. "Wait until you're feeling a bit better before you try anything more." And taking Elin's hand, she urged her gently toward the door.

At that moment, Elin heard a low, questioning rumble. She stopped and looked up at Leelan. The huge Beast towered above her like a shadow, her head almost touching the ceiling. Elin feared she might break down the bars at any minute and attack. Sweat broke out on her frozen face and dripped down her temples. A thought floated into her numbed mind. I must not leave the stable like this. If I refuse to face Leelan now, I will never, ever be able to face her again.

"Please," she whispered. "Open the stall."

Esalu frowned and searched Elin's face, then nodded and went outside. Elin heard the sound of the pulley. The wall behind Leelan opened, and light poured into the stable. Leelan turned toward the door and squinted against the light.

"Leelan, out," Elin said. The Beast swung her head back toward Elin and stared at her intently.

"We need to clean, so go outside," Elin said in her usual voice, but still Leelan did not budge. Noticing that her eyes were fixed on the Silent Whistle hanging round her neck, Elin raised her hand and grasped it. Instantly, Leelan's hackles rose. She growled, showing the tips of her fangs.

"Stop it!" Elin commanded sternly, but Leelan ignored her. Baring her fangs fully, she snarled menacingly. Anger flared inside Elin as she realized that Leelan was threatening her. She glared at the Beast and raised the whistle to her lips. Leelan's growl rose in pitch, and all her fur stood on end.

"I said stop it! If you don't, I'll blow," Elin shouted. She drew a deep breath, and Leelan ceased growling abruptly. A crackling tension filled the air as they glared each other down. Then Leelan's eyes suddenly wavered and slid away. Elin did not miss this sign. "Go outside," she commanded in a low voice.

Leelan flapped her wings two or three times, as though shaking something off, then folded them and lumbered outside. Elin gasped for air as she watched Leelan's figure disappear into the white sunlight. Her eyes filled with tears. She felt Esalu's hand gently touch her elbow, and she covered her face with her right hand.

Twenty days later, the three Beasts, having been thoroughly sedated, were chained and placed on carts. Elin climbed into a carriage with Ohooli. As they passed through the school gate, she glimpsed the anxious faces of Esalu, the teachers, and the students watching her from the windows. With a crack of the whip, the carriage picked up speed, and the school vanished from view.

A blinding shaft of summer sunlight shone into the carriage. Cloud shadows dappled the vast meadow covering the highlands. The blue vault of the sky and the meadow where the Royal Beasts napped in the sun disappeared behind her. Six years had passed since Joeun had brought her here. The days she had spent with Yuyan, the happy years she had lived on this plateau, were all speeding away. She closed her eyes and lowered her head, surrendering to the swaying of the carriage.

3

DAMIYA'S COMMAND

Elin remembered almost nothing of the journey downriver to the capital. Her thoughts were so consumed by what lay before her that the scenery never even penetrated her mind.

Once in the capital, she was taken to the Lazalu Beast Sanctuary, where Leelan and the other Beasts were transferred to a stable. She herself was confined to a single room. Although she was given a sumptuous meal and a luxurious bed, her door was guarded at all times, and she was not permitted to leave, even to feed the Beasts.

The next day, it rained from early morning, and there was a chill to the air despite the season. She was led to the palace through a dark curtain of rain, but it seemed to breathe life into the forest surrounding it. Leaves fluttered like beckoning hands each time a large drop fell, and the air echoed with a ceaseless *pitter-patter* of sound. Peace filled her heart as she passed through the wood, redolent of bark, rich earth, and fresh green leaves.

An aged palace emerged abruptly before her. Wrapped in mist, it looked as if it had stood there for a thousand years. Having no idea how the buildings were arranged, Elin could not know that she had been led to Damiya's hall rather than to the Yojeh's. She only realized this fact when she was ushered through the doors of the inner chamber and saw Damiya watching her languidly from a chair set on a dais at the far end of the room. Her guide went out, leaving her alone with Damiya. The hush of the rain shrouded the room in a shimmer of sound.

Damiya frowned, startled perhaps by her haggard appearance. "How is your hand?" he asked.

Elin bowed her head slightly. "It does not hurt much now."

289

"I'm glad to hear that, although I must say, you still look ghastly. Have a seat on that chair." He waited for her to sit and then said quietly, "It was quite sudden, I heard. No matter how accustomed they are to you, it would seem that Royal Beasts are still beasts. A terrible accident, yes. But Ohooli tells me that you didn't give in to fear, even though you were bitten, and that you're still able to control the Beast very well."

Elin spoke solemnly. "We no longer have the bond we once had. I will never be able to face Leelan again without a Silent Whistle in my hand."

Damiya smiled. "Even so, the Royal Beasts still obey you. That's what matters." He leaned forward in his chair. "Did you hear that the Aluhan's son visited the palace?"

Elin shook her head, and his mouth curled in a smile. "That boy doesn't know his place. He came to demand that the Yojeh give herself to him." There was no outrage in his voice as he described to her what had happened. Rather, he sounded almost amused.

"And," he concluded, "that is why the Yojeh must face the Aluhan's Toda on Tahai Azeh two months from now. If the Toda bow their heads before the Yojeh in recognition of her divine will, just as they did when the first Yojeh descended onto that plain, the Aluhan will recognize her as a true god and surrender. However, if no such miracle occurs, the Toda will advance across the plain and devour the Yojeh. If she wishes to avert such a fate, she must marry the son of the Aluhan. Or so he said."

Smiling, he gazed at Elin. "And here you are, just at the time our country needs you. The workings of the gods are wondrous indeed." Elin did not respond, nor did Damiya expect her to. "It seems unfair to be so harsh when you are still recovering from your injury but, Elin, would you really defy divine will? Because believe me, if you choose that road, I will make your life a living hell. I know you can't be tempted by greed or ambition. However, neither are you capable of heartlessness, no matter how you may deny it. You proved that when you could not stand by and watch the Toda devour the Yojeh.

"After that incident, I used every means in my power to find out more about you. I know who you care for, and how you came to train the Beasts. I know everything." He turned his face to the window and gazed at the falling rain. "I have already seized Esalu. If that's not sufficient, I can certainly bring in the young woman who was your bosom friend. I would be most interested to see if you are capable of watching her die before your eyes . . . to see if anyone can be so true to their beliefs.

"Oh, and you will not be permitted an audience with the Yojeh either. There is no one here who will protect you."

A low ringing sounded in Elin's ears. She remained motionless, her gaze focused on the floor. She had expected this. Yet even so, it did not ease the pain spreading through her chest. When she had told Halumiya that she would not change her mind, even if the lives of her loved ones depended upon it, she had meant it. But she had been able to say so precisely because she believed Halumiya would understand.

Damiya, on the other hand, would do exactly as he had said.

She closed her eyes. Esalu's life. Or the countless lives that would undoubtedly be lost should she open the door to this calamity. In terms of numbers, Esalu was clearly a sacrifice that must be made. But there was no way that she could choose that. She opened her eyes, and her gaze collided with Damiya's.

"I do not know why you refuse to use the Royal Beasts to guard our divinely ordained ruler," he said quietly. "Because you did not tell me, you see. However, if it's because you fear using the Royal Beasts as weapons of war, your reasoning is faulty."

He rose slowly and walked over to her side "The cracks in this country are caused by a disruption in the balance of power. The equilibrium between the military force of the Aluhan and our authority to rule has been upset, and one side is about to be obliterated by the other, as if by an avalanche." His voice was calm and detached. "I simply wish to restore the balance that is being threatened by one side amassing too much power. It's the only way to prevent the people of this land from killing one another. Or do you think that there is some other way?"

Elin opened her mouth, but her lips felt stiff and clumsy. "Even if I were to fly Leelan and protect the Yojeh, would the Aluhan really be so foolish as to believe that a miracle had occurred?"

Damiya's eyes widened.

"He might be sufficiently impressed in that moment to pull back his troops," Elin continued almost in a whisper. "But once time passes and he begins to think objectively, the same problem would be sure to arise again. The root of the disease afflicting this land is certainly not going to vanish with a single, flashy miracle. As long as the cause of the imbalance remains, the seeds of division will never disappear.

"And besides, I don't believe that Leelan can restore the balance of military power. One Royal Beast is not enough for that."

Damiya stared at her intently. "Well, well, what a surprise," he murmured, then changed his tone. "You're quite a clever girl. If you've got enough insight to understand the situation that deeply, then let me speak plainly. I'm not planning to use the Royal Beast to destroy the Aluhan. As you pointed out, it's unrealistic, although I do hear that you're capable of controlling Royal Beasts that you haven't raised yourself." Her eyes wavered in surprise, and Damiya smiled. "I told you, didn't I? I found out everything. But never mind that. Even with a pack of Royal Beasts, if you are the only one who can command them, then we can never hope to destroy the Toda troops led by the Aluhan.

"But for now, one is enough. If a miracle occurs on Tahai Azeh, the Aluhan will have to keep his word. That alone will turn the tide. If we can just get through this crisis, it will give you enough time to train others and form a formidable army of Royal Beasts. Royal Beast troops to match the Toda troops—a perfect balance, don't you think?"

Elin's lips parted, and she gazed unseeingly at Damiya. The ringing in her ears had ceased.

"Of course, the purpose of the Royal Beast Corps would not be indiscriminate slaughter. In fact, we may not even need to use them at all. Think about it. Their very existence would give us the power to keep the Aluhan in check."

Elin lowered her eyes and stared blankly at his chest. Control the Toda with Royal Beasts. Just as we control the Royal Beasts with the Silent Whistle . . . I see. So this is the way people think.

With this realization, the heavy weight that had been crushing her heart crumbled like sand, and in its place, an icy chill crept through her. Now she knew what she must do, but she felt not the slightest enthusiasm for it. With her eyes still averted from his, she said, "I am afraid that that is impossible."

Damiya's face stiffened. "What?"

"I am the only one who can wield the Art that controls the Beasts." When her voice ceased, the pattering of the rain came rushing back, and, for several moments, they stood listening to the sound.

Finally, Damiya shook his head slowly. "You expect me to believe that?"

"Yes. If you doubt me, I can prove it," Elin said quietly.

Damiya raised his eyebrows. "Prove it?"

"Yes. When the rain stops, please bring your most skilled Beast Handler to Leelan's stable. I will teach him the skills I use, and he can try it for himself. If you think that Leelan is too used to me, then any other Beast will do. If anyone can acquire these skills, then any Beast should respond to the person who plays the same notes that I do."

Damiya gazed at her wordlessly. She relaxed and gazed back at him with eyes as fathomless as the sea. Finally, he shrugged. "All right, then, let's try it and see." He clapped his hands. The door opened and a servant appeared. "Take this woman to the Flower Room. See that she gets bathed, fed, and rested."

The servant bowed and waited for Elin, but she did not move.

"I have two requests," she said.

"What are they?"

"Please free Esalu immediately, and make sure that her position and her reputation have not been damaged in any way."

Damiya watched her steadily. "Does this mean that you agree to obey my command?"

Elin nodded and continued in a steady voice. "My second request is that you let me care for Leelan and the other two Beasts. They are being cared for by the Handlers of Lazalu, but I'm sure they won't have eaten any of the food that has been given to them."

Staring into the green eyes that looked up at him, Damiya nodded. "So be it. You shall care for Leelan and the others."

4

THE DEVIL-BITTEN CHILD

It rained all night, finally clearing at dawn. The Royal Beasts went out into the fields after the sun had risen higher, but even then, the grass was still damp. The three Beasts from Kazalumu at first seemed puzzled by the different smells of the land. They sniffed the air repeatedly and were wary of the other Beasts scattered about the meadow. As they bathed in the bright summer sun, however, they began to relax, and each one eventually chose a spot to doze.

Wrapped in the thick scent of grass, Elin stood and watched them. Leelan's fur shone brightly in the fresh, clear light, and the sight of her majestic figure brought back the memory of Elin's first encounter with Royal Beasts in the wild. The same awe she had experienced then welled up inside her. What beautiful, fearsome creatures.

Royal Beasts must never be tamed . . .

This thought penetrated her mind. They were meant to be gazed upon in wonder from afar. Although she had longed for coexistence without any need of the Silent Whistle, that had just been a sweet fantasy. To control beasts of such dreadful power, the whistle was indispensable. Yet Beasts raised that way became empty shells, devoid of spirit.

No matter how she might protest the cruelty of it, Leelan and the other Beasts raised in captivity could never live in the wild. Anger rose inside her . . . at the royal family for perpetuating this brutal impossibility, and at herself for meekly submitting to their will.

What on earth am I doing here, when all I wanted was to let Beasts born in the wild live as nature intended?

Fingering the thick bandage binding her left hand, she stared at Leelan.

It was almost noon when Damiya arrived at Lazalu Beast Sanctuary accompanied by a single Se Zan. By then, the clouds had parted, and the sun was beating down. Stifling grass fumes rose from the meadow as they crossed it. With a high whine, a mosquito zeroed in on Damiya's earlobe. He smacked it, and his guide, Ohooli, looked apologetic.

"My lord, you honor us by deigning to visit a place so plagued with mosquitoes," he said.

Damiya chuckled. "It's not your fault that I'm being eaten alive. Never mind."

The Royal Beasts were probably never bothered by mosquitoes, he thought. Not with their coats of fur. He could see them dotted about the field, soaking up the sun.

"There she is," Ohooli said, pointing, and Damiya squinted his eyes. The two adult Beasts stood with their cub, just as he remembered them at Kazalumu, and beside them was a small figure.

"She's an odd woman," Ohooli remarked. "She spent the entire night with them."

Damiya started walking toward her. Ohooli hurried after him, hastily grabbing the whistle hanging around his neck and holding it ready to blow at any moment. When he was close enough for his voice to reach her, Damiya stopped and called out, "Elin! Come here."

The fur rose on the necks of the Royal Beasts, and they growled threateningly, but when Elin spoke to them, they lowered their voices. She walked toward Damiya, carrying her strange harp crooked under her left arm. She looked calm, but her skin was even pastier than the day before.

"Are you all right?" Damiya asked.

Elin looked at him quizzically. "What do you mean?"

"I mean your health. You look awful."

A smile touched her eyes. "I didn't get much sleep last night . . . But it won't affect my ability to control the Beasts. If you're ready, then let's get started." She shifted her gaze to Ohooli. "Are you the one who's going to test it?"

His eyes froze.

"There's no need for you to push yourself," Damiya said mildly. "If there's anyone else who is skilled at handling the Beasts, have them do it."

Ohooli shrugged. "I'm the best Handler here. Let me try it." Then he added, "But I wonder about using these particular Beasts. They have a special bond with Elin. If we really want to test her method, it would make more sense to choose a Beast she has never handled before."

Elin nodded. "You're right. Let's pick one that you've raised yourself from infancy. The results will be more reliable that way. Which one shall we use?"

Ohooli looked surprised that she had agreed so readily, but he pointed to a large male Beast on the south side of the meadow. "How about Sawan? I raised him with my own hands. He's the largest and most magnificent of the Beasts here."

Elin looked to where he pointed. It was true that the Beast was far bigger than any of the others, but the luster of his fur came nowhere near Eku's and could not even compare to Leelan's.

Perhaps Ohooli noticed her expression, for the blue veins in his temples bulged. "Is there something wrong with the Beasts at Lazalu?"

Startled by the depth of animosity in his voice, Elin looked at him. "No, not particularly."

Damiya reached out a hand and grasped her shoulder. The tension that had suddenly sprung up between them was instantly defused. "So what are you going to do?" he said calmly.

He's very sharp, Elin thought. "Let me teach him how to feed the Beasts."

They both looked at her questioningly, as if they were having difficulty understanding her words.

"How to feed the Beasts?"

"Yes, I will show him how to feed a Beast without using a Silent Whistle."

The expression on Ohooli's face changed. "You can't be serious. You mean you're going to get close enough to that Beast to feed it without using the Silent Whistle?"

Elin nodded.

Ohooli stared at her. "You'd do that? Despite having caused such a horrific accident?"

She returned his gaze, her expression dark and sad. "Yes . . . As long as we protect one another by holding our Silent Whistles ready, we don't need to worry about any accidents. Are you willing to try it?"

Ohooli's face grew tense, and he said nothing for some moments. Finally, however, he nodded reluctantly.

Elin nodded in return. "All right. I'll go first. If I succeed, I'll show you how it's done, and then you can try it."

She began walking in the general direction of the Beast, as if she had no particular interest in him. Royal Beasts kept a certain distance from each other. This boundary had meaning, and they were wary of anyone who crossed it. Although Elin appeared to be walking casually, she was actually testing that distance. The Beast named Sawan watched her steadily as she approached. When she came within ten paces, he rose and spread his wings.

Elin stopped and took one step back, then faced him. The moment her gaze met the eyes of the huge Beast, fear rose from the pit of her stomach to her chest. She breathed deeply several times until it passed. An invisible wall seemed to have reared up between them. She began to stroke the harp, as if stroking that wall, plucking the sound that made the Beast feel contented and sleepy.

The moment he heard the harp, Sawan pulled back his head, then remained motionless. After a short time, he began to emit a much higher note. The tension flowed out of Elin's shoulders as she mimicked the same sound on her harp, like a greeting.

Ohooli gasped.

Still playing the harp, Elin walked toward the Beast. When she had come close enough to touch him, she threw him a chunk of meat. "That woman is a sorceress," Ohooli murmured.

Damiya glanced at him. "If you're scared, bring someone else. There's no point in testing this on you if you're just going to be paralyzed by fear."

Ohooli shook his head. His face was transfigured, almost feverish. "I wouldn't dream of giving up this opportunity . . . Of course I'm afraid. But I definitely want to try it."

Damiya smiled. They waited silently as Elin walked back toward them. Brushing back her windswept hair, she began methodically teaching Ohooli how to hold the harp and which strings to pluck. She made him practice until he could produce exactly the same notes as she, and then taught him the distance at which Sawan would begin to feel threatened.

"Are you ready?" she asked. Ohooli nodded, his expression intent. "Whatever you do, don't push yourself. Even if it doesn't work the first time, it may work if you try it repeatedly. If you feel yourself in any danger, run. The whole effort will have been pointless if you're injured. I'll be right behind you with my whistle ready."

"All right." He took a deep breath and began walking. Just as before, Sawan watched him approach. Following Elin's instructions, Ohooli carefully tested for the boundary beyond which Sawan felt threatened. When the Beast spread his wings, he stopped. Holding his breath, he stretched his stiff fingers gently and then plucked the harp as Elin had taught him.

Sawan listened intently to the sounds, the same way he had with Elin. But no matter how long he played, Sawan did not make the high-pitched sound he had made for Elin. Ohooli played and played, sweat beading his forehead, but still Sawan did not respond. Feeling the eyes of Elin and Damiya on his back, Ohooli lost his patience and took one step forward.

"Oh no," Elin whispered. She ran forward just as Sawan roared and charged at Ohooli. His arms flew up as he threw the harp away. Putting the whistle to her lips, Elin blew. Sawan pitched over, as though he had hit an invisible barrier, collided with Ohooli, and fell like a statue to the ground. Elin raced up and grabbed Ohooli's arm with her right hand to help him out from under the Beast.

"Are you all right?"

Pale-faced, he nodded. "Y-your harp . . . I threw it . . ."

"Don't worry. I'll get it later." She slipped her shoulders under one of his arms and helped him to rise. Unable to put weight on his right leg, he gritted his teeth and hopped on one foot, leaning on Elin the whole way back to Damiya. Just as they reached him, Sawan shook himself and got up.

"Is there any chance he'll attack?" Damiya asked, but both Elin and Ohooli shook their heads. Although Sawan gnawed at himself in agitation for a while, in the end, he settled back down on the ground. Having made sure of the Beast, Damiya returned his gaze to Elin. "Why? Why didn't he respond to Ohooli's harp playing?"

Elin shook her head. "I'm not sure. But the same thing happened at Kazalumu when both my friend and Esalu tried it. They played the harp just like me, but the Beasts did not respond."

She helped Ohooli sit down on the grass. "Would you roll up your trouser leg for me?" she said.

Nodding, he pulled it up past his knee, exposing an ugly purple bruise. As she explored it gently for broken bones, she said, "Lord Damiya, have you ever heard of Akun Meh Chai?"

Damiya's brow furrowed slightly. "Of course, but what of it?"

Her hands went still, and she looked up at him. "I am Akun Meh Chai, a devil-bitten child. When I was young, I often heard people talking about how I should never have been born. I hated the expression, but now I think there is some truth in it." She dropped her eyes back to Ohooli's knee and murmured, "I should never have been born."

Damiya sighed and shook his head slowly. "Elin, why would you think that? Do you despise using the Royal Beasts so much that you would call yourself Akun Meh Chai?"

She stared at the ground without replying.

Damiya said quietly, "I think it's strange that someone as intelligent as you can't see how performing a miracle on Tahai Azeh would actually save the Royal Beasts."

She frowned up at him, unable to grasp the meaning of his words.

"Don't you understand? The Aluhan is a Toda Rider. His power depends solely on the Toda. When he and his Riders see your Royal Beast effortlessly overpower their serpents, surely you can guess what they will think."

Elin's eyes widened. Oh . . .

Seeing her expression, he smiled. "Now do you see? The survival of you and your Royal Beast depends upon our victory." He pressed his point home. "Never forget that, Elin. The perpetuation of our rule is crucial for you and the Royal Beasts, too."

But Elin did not hear. Her blood pounded in her veins, and her mind was stunned by the possibility that had suddenly presented itself. If other nations knew that a single Beast could subdue countless Toda, it would jeopardize the future of the Aluhan's army. If the Aluhan became ruler of this land, not only would he do away with Elin and Leelan, he would surely also seek to bury all knowledge of training Royal Beasts before any other country learned of it. And that would change everything.

If a Toda Rider rules, he will seal away the Art of controlling the Beasts forever . . .

As she gazed at Ohooli's bruised and swollen knee, this thought, and this thought alone, filled her mind.

5

DISCOVERED

"You summoned me, my lord," Ialu said with a low bow.

Damiya nodded. "Take a seat. There's something I want to ask you."

The sun had long since set, and the light from a large candelabra shimmered on the gold fittings adorning the furniture. When Ialu had sat on the chair indicated, Damiya picked up a flask made of dark green glass from a round table. Removing the stopper, he poured an amber liquid into two goblets, passed one to Ialu, and then raised the other slightly. "Don't worry, it's not wine. It's halaku, an herbal infusion flavored with molasses . . . Let us drink in honor of my aunt. Even if it's just one mouthful, drink with me."

Seeing Damiya drain his glass, Ialu took a sip. A pungent herbal fragrance pierced his nostrils, and a bitter tang within the sweetness pricked his tongue.

Damiya placed his goblet on the table and sank deeply into a chair. "Did you hear what happened today?"

"Today?"

"The test Elin performed for us."

Ialu nodded. "Yes, I heard about that."

Damiya poured himself another glass and said, "Of course, we can't judge for certain just from today's results. Perhaps if we tried again after raising a Beast the same way that Elin did, it might be different. But that would take years. For the moment, Elin is the only person capable of manipulating the Beasts." He smiled slightly and looked at Ialu. "That girl is strangely attractive, but she's too serious, wouldn't you say? She's the only one in the world who wields such awesome power, yet she looks so grim."

His smile vanished. "That's why I summoned you. Tell me, what did she say to my aunt? And why did she tell her, but not me?"

Ialu responded quietly. "Please forgive me, but that is not for me to say. I am sure that if she feels it is necessary, she will tell you herself."

Damiya sighed. "You're too stiff and rigid, Ialu. Try standing in my shoes. If using the Beasts might result in some kind of trouble, I need to know. Otherwise I might make a mistake, you see."

Ialu gazed at Damiya. "Is there any possibility that you might choose not to use the Royal Beasts?" he asked.

A cynical smile touched Damiya's eyes. He leaned forward and said, "No, not a chance. How could there be?" He paused, then added, "A man will commit even the most reckless of deeds to protect his land and his spouse. Isn't that so, Ialu?"

Ialu's face froze. He felt as if he had been slammed in the chest.

Damiya looked almost bashful. "We are not able to make it public at this time because of the current circumstances, but just before you arrived, the Yojeh accepted my offer of marriage."

Ialu stared at Damiya for a few moments and then bowed his head. "Congratulations, my lord."

Damiya laughed gaily. "Yes, I must admit that I am not only happy but also relieved. The country will now be safe."

Raising his head, Ialu was startled by the look on Damiya's face. Despite his smile, a cold light shone in his eyes.

"Swift-footed Ialu," he said mockingly. "Such a sharp-witted man. You saved my aunt's life countless times. I'm sure you keep far more hidden inside than you ever show. While you offer me your congratulations, I can see that you're thinking something else. I believe, however, that you misjudge me." His eyes were fixed unwaveringly on Ialu's. "I did not seek this marriage out of personal ambition . . . Think about it. Other than Seimiya, the blood of the Yojeh runs thickest in my veins. Our union is the best thing that could happen to this country. Instead of watering down the sacred blood, we can strengthen it and purify the land.

"For three hundred years, the divine Yojeh has ruled, pure and stainless, and the Aluhan has guarded her from defilement, by accepting it in her stead. It's a perfect system of governance, one not found in any other country, wouldn't you agree?"

There was no trace of his usual bantering tone. "The fissures in this country are caused by people losing faith in the Yojeh. You heard what the Aluhan's son proposed, didn't you? What a perfect demonstration of the disease that afflicts this land. He himself is the root cause. Yet, in one sense, his very existence is fortunate for us. What could more obviously demonstrate divine will than for the source of that disease to be punished?"

Sweat trickled down Ialu's back. Chills ran in waves through his body, and he struggled to control them. Damiya's voice sounded like distant thunder. "On Tahai Azeh, the Aluhan will witness a miracle and know that the Yojeh is a god."

He stood and pointed to the door. "You may go now, Ialu. Soon you shall be released from your onerous task."

As Ialu stepped into the corridor, the Se Zan standing guard outside handed him a small envelope. "A servant brought this a short time ago. He said that he had heard you were here."

Ialu took it with a nod and began walking down the broad roofed passageway that led to the Yojeh's quarters. It was empty, and the stillness of the summer evening hung heavy in the air. He stopped and leaned against the handrail as he opened the letter, then stared at his fingers. They were trembling.

Surely not . . . He had been plagued by chills during his interview with Damiya, but now he broke into a cold sweat. There must have been something in the halaku. He closed his eyes. So he knows . . .

Opening his eyes, he tore the letter open with his teeth and spread it out with shaking fingers. It was from the man he had ordered to investigate Damiya. The message said only that he was waiting in the east stable.

Shoving the letter into his robe, Ialu stepped through an opening in the rails and entered the garden. His ears seemed to be plugged with throbbing metal. A dull ringing swelled slowly in his brain. With his left hand, he pulled off the decorative sash that hung around his shoulders while with his right, he removed the dagger from the sheath at his back. He wrapped his right fist, dagger and all, with the sash and, clamping one end between his teeth, tied it tightly. He let that arm hang loosely at his side and began cutting through the forest to the stables. Although he tried to move quietly, twigs and branches caught at his arms and legs, cracking noisily. The trembling must be making me stagger, he thought.

The moon was full. The thin shadows of the trees cast a dark net on the ground through which Ialu walked doggedly. At last he came to a break in the trees and stumbled out into a wide grassy area. He had reached the east stable. The moonlight gave the night sky a yellowish tinge and cast a pale glow over the grassy field, as if it were covered with frost. The stable roof was fringed with light, while the building beneath it sank into blackness.

The scene seemed to warp and waver in Ialu's eyes. The ringing in his head intensified, interfering with his ability to discern the presence of any enemies. All he could hear was the incessant stomping of the horses in their stalls.

Breathing shallowly, he placed his hand on the door and pulled it open, leaning his weight against it. In the light of the moon shining through the stable window, he glimpsed a man lying facedown on the floor with his hands tied behind his back.

As he stepped across the threshold, Ialu swung his right hand out suddenly. A scream erupted from a man who had been lurking beside the door. The man's blood spurted across Ialu's back as he dropped to one knee to evade a sword blow from the left. Swinging his right arm in a horizontal arc, he slashed open the thigh of the man wielding the sword. Though roaring with pain, the man swung the sword upward. Ialu could see the blow coming but could not avoid it. He barely managed to turn his head as the blade pierced his chest between his collarbone and his shoulder. There was a thud as it struck his collarbone, and the impact shuddered through him, followed seconds later by searing pain.

Still on one knee, Ialu fell forward, thrusting his dagger into the man's belly. There was a sickening sensation in his hand as his blade pierced the man's clothing and sank deep into his flesh. Without uttering a sound, the man dropped his sword and fell, grasping Ialu's sword arm in both hands. Ialu fell with him, eyes closed and nostrils filled with the stench of blood and entrails, which spilled from the twitching body.

When the man finally lay still, Ialu opened his eyes. His breath came in shallow gasps as he pulled his dagger from the man's stomach. Then he dragged himself over to his fallen comrade. He was still alive. A slit of eye glittered as he raised his swollen lids. Through cracked and bleeding lips, he croaked, "I'm . . . sorry . . ."

Breathing raggedly, Ialu sawed at the ropes, his blade sticky with blood. "No," he whispered, "I'm sorry." He pushed himself against the man to turn him faceup. "Can you get up by yourself?"

The man nodded. He raised himself and hunched over, cradling his abdomen.

"Take a minute to rest. Then get out of here . . . Find somewhere to hide, and don't move until you're sure it's safe." Ialu placed his left hand on the man's shoulder and, clenching his teeth, stood up. Using his teeth and one hand, he removed the sash wrapped around his right fist and shook the dagger from his hand. Then he untied the sash at his waist.

Perhaps because of the drug, he felt the pain of his wound only dully, as if he were numb, but blood flowed down his side and soaked his clothes. He took the letter he had received from inside his robe, folded it in half, and pressed it against the wound. Then, using the same method as before, he wound his belt around his shoulders to tie the paper securely in place. Staggering to one of the stalls, he slipped inside. The horse reared away from him, eyes wide with fright, but he spoke softly until it settled. He was shaking so badly he could not saddle it, but he managed to clamber astride, using an upturned tub retrieved from a corner of the stall to stand on.

"Where will you go?" his comrade asked hoarsely, but he did not answer. It was all he could do to wrench himself back from the brink of oblivion. He turned his horse's head north as he left the stable. There was only one place he could think of where someone might take him in, although he doubted that he would be able to make it even that far . . . It was half a toh away, but right now it seemed like it would take forever. At this time of night, if he followed the forest around the palace, he might make it without being seen. Pain jolted his body with every step. Using this to keep him conscious, he clung to his horse and vanished into the moonlit forest.

6

THE FUGITIVE

Alu's eyes glittered in the light of the lantern that hung from the post. Unlike Leelan and Eku, who were already sleeping, the cub was wide awake and appeared still ready to play. It had shot up in height and was now as tall as Leelan when Elin had first met her. It was also at the peak of its need for affection and attention. It just could not stay still, even while Elin was combing its fur with a horse brush. Being with Alu brought back the warm bond she had once shared with Leelan. Even though she told herself it was just an illusion, the cub's affectionate behavior warmed her heart.

"Be still, will you? The brush will get caught in the tangles." As she chided Alu in a hushed voice, Eku suddenly raised his head. Leelan looked up, too, and stared at the stable entrance. Turning, Elin saw someone leaning against the doorframe. In the dim light of the lantern, she recognized his face and gasped.

"Ialu?"

The sight startled her. It was as if the man who had battled the Toda on the ship had leaped through time to appear at her door. Once her confusion had passed, however, the oddness of his appearance hit her. Sweat plastered his hair to his head, and his clothes were wet with blood. His face was ghastly pale, and his eyes were glazed.

Elin dropped the brush and ran to him. His eyes were open, but she could tell that they saw nothing. As she put an arm around him, he crumpled, as though a string had been cut. His knees buckled, and his head knocked against her shoulder. She almost fell as his full weight bore down upon her. Holding him up, she staggered toward the wall, where she laid him gently down on the wool blanket she had spread out for her bed.

He did not open his eyes, even when she lowered him to the floor. He had used his belt as a tourniquet, and his robe fell open, exposing his abdomen. Elin undid the strings that held his collar closed and carefully explored for wounds. Despite his blood-drenched clothes, his only injury was the one he had bandaged himself. Elin bit her lip.

If she were at Kazalumu, she would have had everything she needed to treat him, but here, she did not yet know her way around. And she hesitated to ask anyone for help. Why had he come here if he was this badly hurt?

She sighed. It would do no good to waste time thinking. She had better treat him as best she could under the circumstances. Using her fingernails, she slowly pried loose the piece of paper, which was now as stiff as a thin board. Ialu groaned, and Elin stopped, but he did not open his eyes. She began again, gently peeling back the paper to reveal an ugly gash. He must have been stabbed with a very sharp blade, for the single stroke had penetrated deeply. It had missed any large veins, but had it struck only a fraction to the right, it would have severed the artery in his neck, and he would not have survived. He was a lucky man.

But the wound would not heal on its own. It would need stitches. She frowned. She could probably get a needle and thread, but how was she to sterilize the wound?

Leelan, probably disturbed by the smell of blood, began to growl. The sound sparked an idea in Elin's mind. Of course! Tokujisui . . .

Tokujisui contained atsune root, which acted as a disinfectant. As this was a Royal Beast sanctuary, each stable was bound to have the ingredients on hand. She rose and went to the sleeping quarters, where she asked the caretaker for a needle and thread. Then she returned to the stable and found a bottle of atsune root extract on a shelf in the shed outside. Bearing these, she hurried back to Ialu's side.

The atsune extract must have stung, because when she poured it over his wound, Ialu cried and swung out his arm, barely missing her nose. She grasped his right hand. "Ialu," she said. "Don't move!"

Pressing his arm down with her knee, she slapped his cheek. He opened his eyes slightly, but they were unfocused. "Can you hear me?" Elin asked. "Don't move! It's dangerous." His eyes slowly came into focus, and she saw a light gleam within. "Ialu, do you hear me? Answer me if you can."

He blinked as though with a great effort. She brought her face close to his ear and said slowly and clearly, "I'm going to sew up your wound. It will hurt, but please don't move . . . Do you understand? Nod your head if you do." He gave the barest of nods.

She sterilized the needle and thread, and began to sew. With only one hand, it was much harder than she had expected and seemed to take forever. Yet Ialu gritted his teeth and bore it without a whimper. Stitching up a man was very different from stitching up a Beast; the whole time she worried about how much pain she was causing him.

She must have been holding her breath, because when she finished, her forehead was beaded with sweat, and silver specks of light flickered before her eyes. Realizing that she was about to faint, she put her head between her knees and stayed still for some time. When the ringing in her ears had faded and her dizziness had passed, Ialu was lying limply with his eyes closed, unresponsive to her voice.

She took his pulse, then relaxed. His heart was beating regularly. A wave of relief washed through her, followed quickly by a rush of fatigue. Perhaps because she had slept so little the night before, it took a supreme effort just to stay sitting. It was as if her body were being sucked down into the bowels of the earth. She forced herself to reach out and cover Ialu with the blanket. Then she lay down beside him and instantly fell asleep, unaware that she had even closed her eyes.

Ialu woke abruptly, just as the night was paling to dawn. The pain, which had never left him even while he slept, became acute. For a moment, he did not know where he was or why he hurt so badly, but as he gazed up at the pale blue glow beyond the window near the ceiling, the events of the previous night came back, one by one.

He heard someone breathing gently in his ear. Turning his head slowly, he saw Elin's sleeping face next to his. Although in the dim predawn light he could make out neither eyes nor mouth, the touch of her breath upon his cheek sent a sharp sadness through his chest—a pang of the agonizing grief that he had locked away at the age of fifteen or sixteen when he had first understood the cruel meaning of the oath he had been forced to swear as a child. Before he could stop them, tears pricked his eyes and welled from the corners. For a long time, he lay staring at the vague outline of Elin's face.

Elin sat up, startled by the menacing growls of the adult Beasts. Leaping to her feet, she went and peered out the door. Several figures were moving through the morning mist, heading purposefully toward the stable.

"Have they come after me?" Ialu whispered, sitting up.

"Yes." She ran back to his side and, grabbing his arm, helped him to his feet. If he tried to escape, they would surely catch him. But there was no place for him to hide in the stable either, and the bloodstains on the blanket made it impossible to deny that he had been here. She turned and looked at Leelan, then made up her mind.

"Leelan, hide him!"

A light gleamed in Leelan's eyes, as if she were remembering something.

With her left hand useless, Elin could not support Ialu and still use her

Silent Whistle, but that was a risk she would have to take. There was no time to lose.

"Trust me," she whispered. "And don't make a sound." With one hand she opened the stall gate, then she half carried Ialu between the Beasts. Eku and Leelan raised their hackles, but moved to one side and let them through. As soon as she had lowered Ialu gently to the floor and covered his body with straw, the Beasts sat back down where they had been before.

Elin was stroking Alu, who was mewling anxiously, when she heard the sound of running feet. Several men appeared at the doorway. Behind them came Damiya. The first man through turned to him with a triumphant expression, like a hound who has caught the scent of its prey. "There's blood on this blanket!"

Damiya strolled inside, glanced at the blanket, and then looked at Elin. "Where's Ialu?"

Elin stared at him, her face bloodless. Her chest felt as stiff as a board and it was hard to breathe. "I don't know," she answered finally.

Damiya smiled. "There's no use hiding him. It's all too obvious that he was here."

Breathing shallowly, Elin kept silent, watching the men as they searched every corner of the stable. At last they said, "He's not here."

"Search outside," Damiya ordered. "He can't have gone far." The men left, but Damiya remained behind. He stared at Elin, though he gave no clue as to what he was thinking.

Unable to stand the silence any longer, she whispered, "What did he do?"

"He killed two gatekeepers," Damiya said, without moving his gaze from her face. His voice hit her like a shock of cold water.

"Why would he do that?" she murmured.

He shrugged. "That's why we're looking for him. To find out. If you would answer truthfully, you could save us a lot of trouble, you know."

Elin was not a good liar, and Damiya was very shrewd. She did not think she could lie to him and get away with it. Terrified that even this thought might show on her face, she remained silent.

Damiya continued to regard her carefully, but finally he smiled again. "Do you like him, then?"

He ignored her failure to respond and continued in a quiet voice. "It's of no consequence really. If you wish to protect him, go ahead. It just means I have one more chain with which to bind you. There's nothing more that he can do now anyway." He rested a hand on a post and sighed. "The poor man. Not even I am made privy to where each Se Zan comes from, so I don't know his origins. But I do know that all of them were sold by their parents for a bag full of gold. That's the kind of family he comes from.

"He was sworn to solitude before he was old enough to understand, and he has lived solely to shield the Yojeh ever since. That's the only life he knows. It's the kind of job no man could bear without at least seeking solace among the prostitutes, yet he's so serious, they say he never dallies with women." He raised his eyes to look outside the window. "It would not do for a man like that to look at the narrowness of his world, and especially not for someone as smart as he. Once he did, he'd no longer be able to endure the suffocating closeness."

His smile faded, and his expression turned serious. "Elin, you're an intelligent girl. If you but chose, you could see the structure of this world in its entirety, couldn't you? Then do so. So that you can judge what can and cannot be, and accept your fate accordingly."

With that, he turned and left.

7

WINDY NIGHT

Elin slipped her arm under Ialu and helped him to a sitting position.

He bowed his head. "I'm sorry to cause you so much trouble."

She shook her head and brushed the straw from his hair and clothes, then helped him over to her blanket.

Little by little, he told her what had happened the previous night. It did not surprise her to learn that Damiya was likely behind the attack on the Yojeh Halumiya; the knowledge merely increased the cold revulsion she already felt for him. But she wished that she had never heard of the plot conceived by those in power. When she thought of how it had twisted the lives of herself and so many others, she felt sick with anger.

Ialu's clothes were so stained with blood they seemed to be coated in glue. She helped him undress and wrapped him in her blanket, then placed his clothes in a tub and filled it with water.

"I'll go get some breakfast," she said. Ialu nodded, and she added suddenly, "Please don't try to leave here out of concern for me."

"I won't. Damiya is probably having the stable watched. He seems to have hired his own private army."

Elin nodded and left.

For the rest of the day, armed men patrolled the area around the stable. None of them, however, attempted to enter, perhaps under Damiya's orders. The Beast Handlers of Lazalu were somewhat wary of Elin, and they did not interfere when she chose to take her meals to the stable and even sleep there with the Beasts. Thus, Ialu was able to spend the entire day resting in the stable.

He lay alone in the muggy building from early afternoon when Leelan and the others went out to nap in the sun. Smoke from a mosquito smudge drifted lazily in the air. His sleep was disturbed by feverish dreams, but by the evening, he was feeling much better and shared Elin's supper of gravy and fahko, the unleavened bread made with mixed grains.

As soon as she had finished eating, Elin rose and began feeding the Beasts. Watching her, Ialu was struck by how much thinner and more careworn she looked than he remembered. It was not so long since they had met in Kazalumu, yet she seemed like a different person. He had heard that Leelan had bitten her left hand, which she cradled as she fed the Beasts, and the expression on her face was that of someone who had left her soul behind.

"You still feed them by going inside the cage, then, do you?" he murmured.

She turned, as if startled by the sound of his voice. "I have my Silent Whistle."

"Even so, the other Handlers never feed them like that. And the Beasts seem completely relaxed with you."

Her eyes shone, but she said nothing.

"Deep inside, they must trust you . . . I still can't believe they actually hid me."

At that, her smile deepened. "When I was a student, there was one teacher I just couldn't stand. Whenever I saw him coming, I used to get Leelan to hide me like that."

Ialu smiled. "Even so, I'm amazed that they accepted me. They didn't even growl, despite the fact that they don't know me."

"They didn't growl at you because . . ." Elin paused and glanced at the Beasts. "They could see that I trusted you. Royal Beasts are able to sense human emotions to a frightening degree."

Eku and Leelan began grooming their fur. Elin and Ialu watched them silently for some time in the dim candlelight. Finally Ialu spoke in a soft voice. "Is that why the Royal Beast didn't respond to Ohooli's harp? Did it sense his fear?"

Elin turned to him with a look of surprise. "You knew about that?"

"The Se Zan who guarded Damiya told me."

"I see . . ." She returned her gaze to the Beasts. "That may have been part of it . . . But I think the main reason was that Ohooli was the one who raised him."

Ialu looked at her questioningly. Elin picked up an empty tub and stepped out of the stall. "If Ohooli raised that Beast, he must have used the Silent Whistle on him many times. The Beasts hate what it does to them . . . Would you lower your guard if someone who had beaten you repeatedly suddenly switched to a coaxing tone? I'm sure that that's how the Beasts would feel. They would have a hard time opening their hearts to someone who had used the whistle to control them."

She took Ialu's clothes off the railing where she had draped them and pressed them against her cheek to test whether they were dry; then she sat down beside him and helped him dress. Her smile was gone. Holding his robe to make it easier for him to slip his arm into his sleeve, she said quietly, "When we use the Silent Whistle to raise Royal Beasts, we build a cold wall between them and us—cold but necessary." She uttered these last words as if speaking to herself.

Watching her face, so close to his own, Ialu suddenly said, "Are you planning to die?" He plowed on before she could answer. "Do you plan to die and take with you the knowledge of how to control the Royal Beasts, so that you can seal it away forever?"

Elin shook her head. "Until a short while ago, yes . . ." she whispered. "I planned to do that. But now, no, I don't."

The wind must have picked up. Ialu could hear the rustling of the leaves in the trees beside the stable.

"For a long time," Elin said in a low voice, "I believed I could always avert a catastrophe if I died—that I must never cross that line beyond which a disaster could no longer be prevented. I didn't want to use the Silent Whistle or tokujisui to raise Leelan or the others, and so I did as I pleased, regardless of what anyone said. In return, when the time came, I planned to take responsibility for this choice. But after hearing you describe Damiya's scheme . . . I just don't care anymore.

"If that's the way people think and the path they choose, then let them. If it's simply human nature to maintain the status quo by killing each other, then even if I sacrifice my life and bury the Art with me, someday the same thing is bound to happen all over again. If humans are just going to destroy themselves anyway, why not let them . . ."

This savage thought must have lurked deep inside her for a long time, because when she voiced it, she knew it came from the core of her being. Yet even voicing it did not ease the fury she felt in her heart. A warm breeze blew through the open window, making the lantern flicker.

"But I don't want to make the Royal Beasts fight the Toda," she said. "Not ever." The thought that her dream, everything she had aimed for, should be twisted and exploited in such a despicable way made her burn inside. She gazed at Ialu. "There's something I wanted to ask you, if we ever met again."

Ialu blinked. "Me?"

"Yes. I want to know your thoughts. If I performed this so-called miracle, do you think it could actually right the imbalance in this country?"

Ialu hesitated for a moment. Gazing up through the window at the indigo sky, he said in a low voice, "To be honest, until now I have avoided thinking about what would be best for this country. Having taken an oath as a Se Zan, my paramount duty was to protect the Yojeh. If I thought about the consequences of protecting her, it would cause me to doubt my actions. In that sense, Damiya hit the mark. I have deliberately avoided looking at the narrowness of the world in which I live."

Thoughts unexpectedly thrust themselves into his mind and fell from his mouth. "He spoke of my family with scorn, but my father was a skilled carpenter. If he had not been crushed beneath a building in an earthquake, my mother would never have sold me. If my father had lived, I would have become a carpenter like him. My hand would have held a chisel, not a weapon meant for killing."

His mouth crooked in a smile, and he looked at Elin. "I enjoy working with wood. When I'm off duty, I like to make furniture. I find it much more relaxing to throw myself into a project like that than to spend time with prostitutes, who hide their brutal sorrow behind a mask."

His face glowed indistinctly in the wavering light. In her mind, Elin could see his hands caressing the results of his handiwork. She was suddenly reminded of the Toda. Captured as hatchlings, they had their ear flaps removed and were kept only to fight. Now she could understand why her mother had watched them with such sorrow in her eyes.

"Still, I have seen the workings of government close at hand," he continued, "which is something I would never have done if I were a carpenter. And I'm human. No matter how hard I may try to control my mind, I can't help thinking about the meaning of what I see and hear.

"When Shunan, the Aluhan's eldest son, visited the Yojeh the other day, his words moved me. I thought that what he said made sense. And when the Yojeh said that she had no warriors to protect her, I confess, my heart went cold. I could not help wondering what my existence meant to her."

He told her briefly what Shunan had said and done. As she listened to him describe Shunan's character, a light kindled in her eyes. "I see," she murmured when he was done. "So the Aluhan's eldest son is someone who cares."

Ialu nodded. "If he had wanted, he could have forced her to yield. The fact that he chose a different method suggests he has compassion. He also has resolve. If he marries Seimiya, he will certainly try to show her the reality of this land, something she has never confronted before."

He took a deep breath. "I have killed many men. I slew my first assassin the year I turned eighteen. All winter, whether waking or sleeping, his death throes flashed before my eyes. Even now, the men I have killed come to me in my dreams. The smell of their blood still clings to my nostrils. I expect that I'll be haunted by such apparitions for the rest of my life, but I have no intention of trying to escape that fate. That's what it means to kill. Those soldiers who have defended this country for generations through bloody wars must have experienced the same thing."

He wiped his face with one large hand and said, "I can't believe that it is right for the ruler not to know this truth."

The wind must have died down a little, for the sound of the branches scraping against the wall grew fainter. "It would be presumptuous of me to assume that I understood her mind, but I feel Lady Seimiya would not want to remain ignorant. While the facts about Damiya and about her own bloodline seem very cruel, I think that she should be told . . . I do not think it should be allowed to go on like this."

Quiet filled the stable when he finished speaking. Elin sat for some moments thinking, her face down. Finally, she raised her head and looked at him. "Is there any way of speaking to Her Highness without Damiya intruding?"

Ialu's eyes widened.

She gazed back at him, unblinking. "I want to tell her . . . all of it. I don't know if that will change anything, but I must try."

Ialu stroked his chin and thought. After what seemed a very long time, he returned his gaze to Elin. "There is a way . . . For you, it might work."

8

ORIGINS

The natural rock cavern was always filled with steam from a hot spring deep inside. Unglazed clay pipes carried hot water from the spring to a large bathing pool built of smooth stones.

The bathing hour was the one time of day when Seimiya could truly relax. Garbed in a single light robe, she sank into the hot pool and gazed at the glistening rock surface, which reflected the hazy glow of the light through the mist. Soaking in the hot water like this always brought back the peace she had once felt in her mother's arms.

During winter, powdery flakes of snow would stray through the hole in the ceiling where it widened, but thanks to the hot steam, she never felt cold. Her favorite times were those evenings when she could see the full moon through the hole, which she liked to call the "skylight," and when it was covered on rainy days, she felt like something was missing.

The steam gathering above the pool rose like a shimmering white pillar through the opening. She was gazing at it, mesmerized, when suddenly it broke and scattered, as if blown by a strong wind. Seeking the cause, she lifted her eyes and saw a huge dark shape swoop down from the skylight. With each beat of its great wings, the mist rolled back and waves rippled across the milky water of the pool, far back into the cave.

A Royal Beast landed and folded its wings. As a small figure slipped from its back, the cave echoed with the frightened screams of the maidservants.

A woman's voice rang through the mist. "Your Highness, Yojeh Seimiya! Forgive me this impertinence. I mean you no harm. I had no choice but to come like this in order to speak with you."

Seimiya heard the voices of the Se Zan at the entrance to the cave asking what was wrong. They must have heard her servants' cries. With her eyes still on the Royal Beast, she said sternly, "Cease your noise. Tell the Se Zan to remain outside."

Then she sat up straight and called out to the figure who knelt on the other side of the mist. "Are you the beast doctor they call Elin?"

"Yes, I am Elin. I beg you to pardon my rudeness."

"You may approach."

The shadowy figure touched her forehead to the floor and then stood up. Turning to the Beast, she said something in a quiet voice, and then walked around the bathing pool toward Seimiya. The light of a lantern set in the rock wall fell upon her face, and Seimiya stared at her with open curiosity.

"So your eyes really are green." The words must have fallen from her mouth involuntarily, for she spoke like a little girl, without formality.

Elin knelt down before her and bowed low once again. "I had to speak with Your Highness. That is why I came."

Having recovered from her initial surprise, Seimiya softened her expression. "I hear that you have been blessed by the Afon with a rare gift. Damiya told me that the Afon sent you to rescue me from this crisis. I intended to summon you very soon to meet me. You would have been granted an audience easily. There was no need to go to such lengths as this."

Elin raised her head. "I beg your pardon, Your Majesty, but I was forbidden explicitly by Lord Damiya to seek an audience with you. That is why I had no other way of meeting you."

Seimiya's eyes widened slightly. "By my uncle? But why?"

Elin gazed at her. "I believe he did so because he feared that I would share with you the wishes of the late Yojeh Halumiya."

Seimiya's eyes froze. Hard as stone, they were fixed on Elin, but they did not see her. After a long silence, she said, "You wish to convey to me the words of my grandmother, is that it?"

"Yes, but that is not all. Forgive me, Your Highness, but are you aware of the promise that Her Majesty Halumiya made to me?"

"No, I do not know. What is it that she promised you?"

Elin answered quietly. "She told me that I need not use the Royal Beast to protect her. Even though she knew she might be attacked again by Toda Riders."

It was clear from Seimiya's expression that this statement had caught her completely off guard. Elin guessed that she must have been expecting a very different answer. "She refused the protection of the Royal Beast?"

"Yes."

"Why?"

"I believe because she judged my tale to be true."

"What tale?"

"The tale engraved on the hearts of my mother's people and passed down from one generation to the next. Her Highness Halumiya accepted it as the history of her ancestor that was lost in the fire." Taking a deep breath, Elin continued. "It is a tale that took place far beyond the Afon Noah and that must cause one to despair of the human race. It is the story of your ancestor, too, Your Highness. Are you willing to listen?"

Seimiya stared at Elin with a frown before she finally spoke. "Tell me," she said.

Elin nodded, and began the tale told to her in that winter forest by the man who had come from her mother's people, a story from long, long ago.

Once, there were many ancient kingdoms that flourished far beyond the white peaks of the Afon Noah. One of these was the land called Ofahlon. Although small, it was blessed with a good port and prospered as a strategic trading post between the surrounding kingdoms and the lands that lay beyond the sea. Its people never went hungry.

One day, however, rumors reached the king's ears that the ruler of a neighboring kingdom was planning to invade, to gain control over this profitable trade. While Ofahlon was prosperous, it was small. It might not survive even three months in the face of such an invasion. As the king pondered what to do to save his land, Sakolu, a senior advisor responsible for the diverse ethnic groups in the kingdom, suggested that he ask the Toga mi Lyo for help.

The Toga mi Lyo, the Green-Eyed Ones, had originally come from across the sea. Driven from their own land after losing a struggle for power, they had found their way to Ofahlon with only three ships. As they excelled at handling and healing beasts, the kings of previous generations had showered their favors upon them, granting them land within the capital to build their own community. Sakolu informed the king that they had been taming wild Toda and training them for battle. While the king doubted that Toda could be of much help, he was desperate, and so he asked the Toga mi Lyo to protect the country's borders.

The results far surpassed even the expectations of the Toga mi Lyo. Although they rode only a few score Toda to battle against thousands of horsemen, they decimated the enemy troops and slew their general. The king was overjoyed at this victory. He awarded the Toga mi Lyo a large tract of land and ample gold. He commanded them to increase the number of Toda and appointed Sakolu general of the Toda troops. This was the beginning of the tragedy to come.

Tens of thousands of Toda were trained, and with this overpowering force, the king soon conquered the surrounding lands. His power had reached its zenith, but the discontent of the conquered who now lived within this expanded kingdom grew. The king, who had never ruled such a large territory, had no idea how to govern it. He tried to suppress his subjects by force alone, which was like trying to seal a seething bog of rot and decay under a thick metal plate.

When they saw the miserable condition of the people, Sakolu and the Toga mi Lyo were overcome with remorse. They had used the Toda to save the king, but the country that had once welcomed people of all races had vanished, replaced by an empire founded on tyranny and oppression. Sakolu, with the Toga mi Lyo, lit the beacon of rebellion.

The king did not stand a chance against an army that could bend the Toda to its will. Protected by a few vassals, he fled with his family and close kin, deep into the rugged ravines of the Afon Noah, narrowly escaping the pursuing Toda. The fugitives, who were only about two hundred strong, spent the next decade hiding in the mountains. Having amassed the world's wealth and become accustomed to the height of luxury, this sudden fall to a life of destitution and exile, where not even their next meal was certain, sowed a bitterness in their hearts. Resentment served as the bread that sustained them through ten long years of cruel cold and hunger.

When they first ventured into the mountains, they came upon a race of hunters—tall, stately people who lived in the mountain ravines and hunted with huge winged beasts. Their leader was a man, but their spiritual guide was a young woman. One day, the son of the exiled king witnessed an incredible sight. Winged beasts fell upon a pack of Toda, ripped them apart with their claws, and devoured them as if they were no more than sacrificial offerings. When he heard this tale, the king visited the head of the hunters with a proposal.

"If you raise an army of winged beasts and help us regain our country, I will make you rulers over that land." His hatred ran so deep that he was willing to trade his sovereignty to avenge the loss of his kingdom.

The head of the hunters rejected this offer. "We are content with what we have," he said. "We do not need a kingdom."

The priestess, however, thought differently. She was still very young. Here was the chance to be freed from spending half the year snowbound in the mountains, a chance to live in Ofahlon, a great and shining land of which they had only heard stories . . . Perhaps it was not greed but a dream that drove her. Still, the choice she made set the stage for a great catastrophe.

The king's offer, she claimed, was a sign from the gods. She gathered the young people around her to train the Royal Beasts, so named by the king of Ofahlon. Within a decade, they had created an army two thousand strong.

In the deep midwinter, when snow clouds darkened the heavens, two thousand Royal Beasts flew concealed within the clouds, each bearing a golden-eyed warrior dreaming of a kingdom in the sun, or a member of the royal family with hatred carved in his bones. Over the mountains they flew and fell upon Ofahlon.

The battle between Toda and Royal Beast was indeed a massacre. Once the slaughter began, the Toda and the Royal Beasts, natural foes, became so crazed with blood that they ignored the commands of their riders and, in a frenzy of tooth and claw, trampled over field, shore, and hill, through the villages and towns, until nothing was left but a blood-soaked wasteland. The slaughter did not end until the capital had been engulfed in a sea of flame, and everything had been utterly destroyed.

When the battle ended, all that lay before the young woman, who had dreamed of a kingdom filled with glorious sunshine, was the sight of the torn limbs and members of countless corpses stretching as far as the eye could see, and the burning, crumbling city belching black smoke into the air. No trace of the kingdom remained. If it had been an ordinary battle, only soldiers would have died. But with the addition of two thousand Royal Beasts and tens of thousands of Toda, an entire empire had been reduced to ashes.

Thus was the kingdom that flourished far beyond the Afon Noah destroyed. The land, contaminated by the blood and gore of countless dead, was cursed. No country ever prospered there again, and it remained covered by a thick forest where no man dared to venture.

Elin finished speaking. For a long while after, Seimiya and her maids sat as if in a daze. Seimiya had come out of the water to sit on a stone at the edge of the pool. Now she shivered suddenly, as if with a chill, and slipped back into the hot water. Elin shifted her knees, trying to ease her body, and said, "The few who survived scattered in all directions. The Toga Mi Lyo sealed away their knowledge of how to control the beasts, believing that it would only bring disaster. They chose to wander in exile to the end of time, living by a strict set of laws so that this tragedy would never be repeated. These are my mother's people, the Ao-Loh, the People of the Law, who are known as the Ahlyo."

Hugging her thin shoulders, Seimiya whispered, "And my ancestor? . . ."

Looking straight into her eyes, Elin said quietly, "The tall hunters with the golden eyes, tamers of the Royal Beasts, refused to let the young woman who had led her people to such terrible destruction return to her homeland in the ravines . . . Her name was Jeh. She was your ancestor, the one who crossed the Afon Noah to become the divine ancestor of this land."

The maidservants paled at the implication of what they had just heard, but Seimiya did not appear to be surprised. In fact, she was gazing at Elin with a puzzled look. "Do you expect me to believe that?" she asked quietly.

"You don't?"

Seimiya burst out laughing. "Of course not. I think it rather incredible that my grandmother would believe it either."

Elin remained silent, staring at her. Her skin, which was as smooth as porcelain, had a delicate flush, perhaps from the warmth of the bath. She's so young, Elin thought. She had heard that Seimiya was two years older than her, but she did not look anywhere near older than twenty. She could understand Damiya's desire to protect the kingdom's sovereignty by keeping her ignorant, as if wrapping her in silk floss.

But I think he's underestimating her . . . Elin was almost sure that she was not as fragile as she appeared. Deep within her round, childlike eyes, Elin could see a mature and objective gaze.

"Why would I need to make up such a story?" Elin asked.

Seimiya smiled coldly. "That is exactly what I have been trying to decide. If, for example, you were in league with Ialu, and if he, in turn, were in league with the Aluhan, then it would make sense."

Elin was startled. That was, she realized, one possible interpretation.

Seimiya's smile deepened. She had not missed the slight quiver in Elin's eyes. "Who told you that you could meet me if you came when I was having my bath? . . . Who else could have but Ialu?"

Angered by her accusing tone and cold smile, Elin opened her mouth to protest, but at that moment, she heard the hard sound of claws scraping against stone. Seimiya and her maids looked past her with startled expressions and half rose to their feet. Turning, Elin saw Leelan poised to enter the pool.

"Leelan! No!" she said sharply. Leelan stopped with one paw hovering over the water. "It's hot, not cold." She said it again. Leelan brought her snout close to the edge of the pool and then gave up trying to get in.

Seimiya shook her head and laughed. "Amazing. She responds to you just like a child."

Still looking at Leelan, Elin said, "Sometimes her behavior does appear childlike, but Royal Beasts are fearsome creatures with much deeper intelligence than a child."

Seimiya looked at her. "She understands what you say, doesn't she? How much can you understand one another?"

"We can tell each other what we want," Elin said, her fathomless gaze still on the Beast. "But . . . even if we can communicate what we want, there is still a gap between us that we can never, ever bridge. The world we see, what we feel, are completely different. For Leelan, there is only the present. I was never able to convey to her the concept of 'tomorrow.' In addition . . ." Leelan must have sensed that Elin was talking about her, for she was watching her intently. "Leelan thinks nothing of slaughtering Toda. For her, it is merely a natural impulse to kill those creatures that try to steal her young."

Slowly, she turned her eyes to Seimiya. "But I do not want to use Leelan as a tool to kill Toda. I did not spend all these years raising her and nurturing this bond by which we communicate in order for her to become a convenient tool.

"I hate seeing the Royal Beasts bound by the Silent Whistle and living as if their souls have been snatched away. A Beast that is given to the Yojeh can never return to the wild. Even so, I hoped at least to set them free from the invisible chains that bind them. Yet instead . . ."

Rage surged inside her, and she gripped her knees tightly, staring at Seimiya. "If I make Leelan perform a miracle on Tahai Azeh, far from freeing the Beasts, I will be binding them with even thicker chains. If my teacher had not been taken hostage, I would never have consented to this farce, even on pain of death."

Shock ran through Seimiya's eyes. "What did you say? Your teacher?"

"Lord Damiya told me that if I refused to play the part of a divine miracle, he would kill my teacher." Elin's voice was rough with anger. "I was not sent to you by the Afon. I am forced to be here by a dirty threat."

The blood drained from Seimiya's face. An emotion akin to sorrow stirred in Elin's breast at the sight, and her face twisted, but still she plowed on. "Even if I use her as a weapon to slaughter the Toda, I doubt that Leelan will feel any pain at all. It is I, not Leelan, who will suffer."

The light from the candles in the rock wall wavered in a puff of warm air. "The reason I hate using the Royal Beasts in this way has nothing to do with the tale I told you. It is not for the sake of my mother's people, nor for the sake of this country. It is just that I can see, as plain as day, the net woven by the actions of men, a net that Leelan can neither see nor feel . . . And being forced to play a role within this treacherous plot makes me sick."

Something fierce crossed Seimiya's pale face. Wordlessly, she stared at Elin, who returned her gaze steadily.

Seimiya felt something within her fade to ashes and begin to crumble. Something that must not crumble, something that, should it disintegrate, could never be retrieved and would vanish forever. Yet, despite the hollow emptiness within, she was still the ruler. Feeling a deep lethargy sink into her bones, she gazed blankly into space.

"I, too . . ." she whispered. "I, too, can see the mesh of that net woven by the actions of men. Yet I will never, ever be permitted to say that being forced to play a role within it is so repulsive it makes me ill." Elin stared at her, as if stunned. "If what you say is true, Jeh was a foolish woman." Seimiya smiled thinly. "Even though she was expelled from her homeland, she couldn't give up her ambition to rule the world."

Her lips trembled, and Elin averted her gaze. "It was a long time ago," Elin said. "Who can guess what it was like to arrive in this strange land after leaving her home far behind? But, personally, I think that she was sincerely searching, walking a tightrope through her pain and doubt, to build a nation where neither men nor beasts would suffer."

"Why do you think so?"

"Because, while on the one hand she used the Royal Beasts as a symbol of sovereignty, on the other, she wrote the Royal Beast Canon." Elin shifted her gaze to Leelan. "My Lady Seimiya, is not Leelan very different from the other Beasts?"

Seimiya's eyes narrowed as she looked at Leelan. The Beast's wings, damp with steam, sparkled in the glow of the lantern.

"Well, yes. In fact, I have never seen a Royal Beast as beautiful. And isn't she the one that bore a cub? A miracle in itself."

"Yes." Elin nodded. "The Royal Beasts raised in the sanctuary never fly, never mate, and never bear young."

Seimiya frowned and looked at her. She knew this, yet hearing it said like that, she suddenly realized just how unnatural it was. "Why?"

"Because they were raised in accordance with the Beast Canon. Surely you know that it was your ancestor who wrote the Canon. Those who raise the Beasts are strictly required to follow its tenets. But Leelan here . . ."

A memory from long ago, of Leelan as a cub, her eyes gleaming in the darkness as she gnawed at her fur, came rushing back. "She was wounded, both physically and emotionally, by the arrow loosed at Her Majesty Halumiya's birthday celebration. She was taken to the Kazalumu Sanctuary, and by chance, I met her and came to raise her. At the time, I was only fourteen. I knew nothing of the Beast Canon, so I decided to raise her without the Silent Whistle or tokujisui, just like Royal Beasts in the wild."

A light dawned in Seimiya's eyes. "I see . . . So the Beast that was raised without following the Canon became this beautiful creature who could fly and bear young."

"Yes."

Seimiya looked at Leelan anew. "Why, then, would my ancestor make such rules?"

"I believe that she did not want the Royal Beasts to multiply." Seimiya glanced at her. It was clear from her eyes that she understood.

"If she was driven by selfish motives to secure her power, she would never have made those rules. I believe that although she accepted the role of ruler to help the people on this side of the Afon Noah, this ironic turn of fate caused her much grief. She didn't want to repeat the terrible tragedy she had caused, so instead of brute force, she used the Beasts—the appearance of which people considered a miracle—as a symbol of her divine authority to govern . . ." Elin sighed. "I believe she developed the Canon as a way of raising Royal Beasts without making them into weapons. To prevent them from multiplying, she used tokujisui, which inhibits them from mating, and by having their keepers use the Silent Whistle, she erected an invisible, yet impenetrable, wall between man and Beast . . . So that people and Beasts, which are highly communicative by nature, would never be able to share their thoughts."

For a moment, emotion gripped her throat, and she could not speak. "If I, a fourteen-year-old girl, who knew nothing of the Canon, had not met

Leelan by chance—and it really was just by chance—the wishes of your ancestor would still have been followed. And Leelan and I would never have learned to communicate, would never have flown through the sky . . ."

". . . and would never have come here," Seimiya said, finishing her sentence.

They said nothing for a while. Finally, Seimiya dragged herself out of the pool and sat on the edge, gazing at Leelan.

"Perhaps this, too, is the work of the gods. Don't you think so?"

Elin bit her lip as she looked at Seimiya's delicate, doll-like figure. She wished that she could say, "Yes, perhaps you're right." She closed her eyes. She did not want to torture her anymore, but she just could not bring herself to lie.

"No, I don't," she whispered. "I do not want to believe that our meeting today, which was precipitated by the death of Yojeh Halumiya, is the work of the gods." Taking a deep breath, she opened her eyes and said, "To me, it looks like I am here today because of a man who tried to lay the death of Yojeh Halumiya at the Aluhan's door, a man who has manipulated events all along to create this situation."

The blood receded from Seimiya's cheeks. "What are you saying?"

Keeping her eyes fixed steadily on Seimiya's face, Elin explained why the Toda that attacked Halumiya could not have belonged to the Aluhan. She shared the plot that Ialu had recognized once it was clear the attack could not be the Aluhan's doing, the facts he had uncovered through years of investigation, and the price he had paid for it. When Elin named the one person to whom all these facts led, Seimiya's snow-white face did not move. In a low voice, she asked, "Why would he need to kill my grandmother?"

"If Lady Halumiya had lived, would she have allowed you to marry him?"

Seimiya did not even blink at this response . . . It was clear that this had already occurred to her long before. Her eyes, which glittered like shards of metal, suddenly blazed fiercely. "It's true, my grandmother didn't like him—but for me, he was my father, my brother, the kindest person in the world, one of the most beloved of my kin." She closed her eyes and hugged herself. The hands with which she gripped her shoulders trembled.

"Your Highness," one of the maidservants said hesitantly, but she did not respond. For a long time she remained hugging her body. Then, taking a deep breath, she looked up. Rising, she gazed down on Elin with cold eyes.

"When I stand on Tahai Azeh, stand with me, Elin . . . You need do nothing but watch. Let me give you that freedom—the freedom that is not mine to choose."

9

EMPTINESS

Though the moon had long since set, a faint glow still lingered in the heavens. This appeared to be enough light for Leelan, whose pupils were dilated like a cat's; she showed no sign of searching through the darkness as she flew.

They had flown over the dark forest that encircled the palace, and the Lazalu Beast Sanctuary was about to come into view when a rumbling growl began deep in Leelan's throat. Elin looked up and saw what looked like fireflies whirling beside the Beast's head. She heard a low buzzing, like bees' wings vibrating, a disturbing sound that made her uneasy. The lights gathered together and dropped below. Following their descent, she saw several black shapes standing at the edge of the wood. One of them waved a small light.

The phosphorescent glow faded. For a moment, Elin hesitated, but the people below were obviously summoning her, and she did not feel that she could ignore them. She touched Leelan's cheek and pointed to the light below. Leelan began to descend. Before she had reached the ground, Elin knew who waited for her. Hooded and silent, like forest shadows, her mother's people watched her come.

Leelan growled menacingly as a hooded man raised a Silent Whistle to his lips, but Elin did not try to stop him from blowing. When Leelan did not freeze, he looked surprised.

"I plugged her ears," Elin said. "It would be a disaster if someone blew a Silent Whistle while we were in the air." She removed Leelan's ear flaps and slid to the ground. "Please keep your whistle at the ready, though," she said quietly, and then looked around at the gray-cloaked figures. "What do you want with me?"

One of them stepped toward her, an elder judging by her curved spine. She pushed back her hood, revealing a shock of white hair. Even in the faint light, Elin could see the woman's startling resemblance to her mother.

"Elin, daughter of Sohyon, granddaughter," she said. "We have come to take you home. Come with us."

Elin's skin prickled from her forehead to the nape of her neck. "Where?" she asked hoarsely.

"To where your people are . . . If you stay here and go on like this, you'll end up making a terrible mistake. Come and live with us."

A quiet chill spread through Elin's chest, as if the night air were soaking into her skin. Ah . . . so that's it . . . she thought. They had come to take her away, away from the circle of people with whom she had spent her entire life, to wander for the rest of her days with them. If she went, she could close the door before she caused a catastrophe. Yet even at that thought, her heart remained cold and unmoved.

She shook her head. "I do not wish to go with you."

Sorrow and hurt flickered across her grandmother's face, and Elin felt a stab of pain in her chest. The silent disapproval and fierce disappointment radiating from the gray hoods, the grief of countless ancestral ghosts milling in the darkness, rolled over her in a heavy, aching wave that pulled her skin tight.

"Will you choose the path of sin? Will you open the door to calamity?" her grandmother demanded in a shaking voice. "Is that how you were raised?" Her eyes probed Elin's, but when it became clear that Elin had no intention of responding, her shoulders fell, and she sighed. "I see . . . Sohyon's spirit must surely regret having saved your life."

Her words shot through Elin like a lightning bolt. Fixing her eyes on her grandmother's face, she took a deep breath. "My mother gave her life to save mine. If she were really the type to regret that act, then I would hate you for having raised her that way." She had to force the words through clenched teeth. Her grandmother cringed, as if she had been slapped. "I know what my mother, and what you, too, call a 'sin' . . . I can understand that you have made tremendous sacrifices and adhered to the Law to avert disaster. But I despise the way you use the word 'sin' to manipulate others."

Feelings locked deep inside her suddenly rushed from her mouth as if a dam had been broken. "You use that word to paralyze the mind, just like we use the Silent Whistle to freeze the Beasts and Toda. I can't bear to see people bind others like that."

A gray-hooded man stepped forward and placed a hand on her grandmother's shoulder. "Let us go," he said in a low voice. "There is no saving her. She believes that what she feels is more important. She will not listen, no matter what you say."

Elin felt her grandmother's eyes questioning her. Pain stung her heart, but she kept her face expressionless as a deep despair spread across her grandmother's features. Silently, she watched as her mother's people turned away from her with anger and loathing.

The night breeze, warm and humid, blew across the empty field. Elin looked up at the sky. Stars were strewn across it like grains of silver sand. She wept, unable to dislodge the heaviness that stuck like a thick plank in her chest.

Mother . . . Do you regret raising me this way? Is the path I am taking so wrong? Unlike Seimiya, I can choose which path to take.

Since the day she had decided not to use the Silent Whistle to control Leelan, she had simply chosen the path that felt right. She had longed to raise these creatures, who were born in the wild, the same way they would have been raised if they had been left in the wild. But she had loved Leelan. She had been thrilled by the bond that grew between them as they crossed the wall that separated beast from man. She knew that she was here, now, as a result of that choice, but she just could not believe that what she had done was a sin worthy of death. Even so, the emptiness that gnawed at her chest did not fade away.

Where would her love for Leelan, the tentative, step-by-step efforts she had made to get closer to her, lead her now? Had it all been for nothing, just self-gratification?

Perhaps.

Esalu had probably been right—the one emotion all living creatures shared was not love, but fear. This, most likely, was the hard truth. Men, beasts, all sentient beings that inhabited the planet, were incapable of trust. Somewhere in their hearts, they would always harbor the fear of others. To ensure their own survival, they would continue to devise ways to dominate and control.

Only by binding each other with force, with laws, with religious precepts . . . and with the Silent Whistle, do we finally feel safe . . .

No matter how hard I study the nature of living things, in the end, that's all I will find—just this empty futility.

Even if she returned to Kazalumu safely, how could she ever stand in front of a class to teach? What could she possibly say to her students if the nature of living creatures only made her feel hopeless?

Humans, beasts, bugs—all are but tiny pricks gleaming in the night—a herd of countless points of light, bound in the darkness of distrust.

She gazed up at the star-spangled sky as she listened to Leelan purr contentedly behind her.

NINE

THE BEAST PLAYER

I

DAWN

The wind, which had picked up in the middle of the night, did not abate even at dawn, rattling the tent cloth incessantly. Shunan had woken long ago, but he lay in bed listening to the groaning of the wind. His father, who lay in the tent beside his, must be listening to it, too. It sounded like someone choking back tears.

Flowing as it did between heaven and earth, did the wind voice the wailing of the ghosts scattered on Tahai Azeh so long ago? Or was it the bitter resentment that must lie in the breast of that willowy maiden who would bring to a close the history begun on this field three centuries past?

Shunan took a deep breath and sat up. He had dressed without summoning his servants and stood up to leave when he noticed a slip of paper on the tent floor. Picking it up, he ran his eyes over the three lines.

We have been waiting long for this day to come. We convey our joy and swear once again our steadfast allegiance. Though we stand in the shadows, we will guard you.

It bore a seal in the shape of a Toda scale—the seal of the Sai Gamulu. He crumpled it in his fist.

A shadow moved outside the tent, and he heard the voice of a loyal retainer. "Are you awake, my lord?"

He went outside to find the retainer standing there with a worried frown. "What is it?"

"As I reported earlier, my lord, last night the Yojeh's men erected tents on the hill. I have come to inform you that just before dawn, under cover of darkness, a huge cart was drawn up the hill and taken into one of them."

Holding back his hair, which was whipped by the wind, Shunan looked up at the hill. The contours of the earth, pregnant with the sun, glowed faintly, and the gentle slope rose black against the sky. On top of the hillock he could see the small shadows of tents.

"Rumor claims," the servant continued, "that when Her Highness Halumiya was attacked by Toda, a Royal Beast swooped down from the sky to protect her."

Shunan stood silent, his gaze fathomless as he looked at the hill.

"If they have brought a Royal Beast here—"

At these words a smile rose to his lips. "Soldiers' corpses filled the plain and a cry of sorrow rose to the heavens," he recited in a low voice. "Behold! The golden-eyed goddess descends from far across the Afon Noah. Toda bow their heads to make her path, Royal Beasts soar in the heavens, protecting her . . ." He looked at his servant.

"We have not come here to do battle. We have come to confirm the will of the gods. Let us stand and witness whether the Royal Beast has indeed come to perform a miracle and save the Yojeh."

Watching his father emerge from the tent beside his, he said calmly, "The time has come. Prepare the troops."

While Shunan gazed up at the hill, Ialu woke from a light doze. He was perched in an old tree in the wood that covered the southern slope. It was a sturdy tree, with thick roots, but the wind had rocked it all night long, so that slapping branches kept him awake.

If this wind doesn't die down . . .

It would severely impair his aim with bow and arrow. Although it was risky, he would have to get closer. As promised, Shunan had gathered his troops at the foot of the hill. He had brought about a third of the entire army, leaving the rest under his younger brother Nugan's command, but it was still an imposing force. That sobering sight should distract the Yojeh's men enough to let one man disguised as a Se Zan pass unnoticed.

Kailu had been worried about Ialu as he knew he had been investigating Damiya for some time. A sense of impending doom hung over the palace, and everything that had once seemed solid now seemed precarious. Walking on shaky ground, where even the meaning of loyalty was no longer clear, Kailu had begun to fear that he would die as the Yojeh's shield on Tahai Azeh. Although he was troubled by his own wavering doubts at this time when loyalty was most in question, he had still brought Ialu a Se Zan uniform, just as he had asked.

"I don't know what you're intending to do," he had said, "but just knowing that you'll be there with us gives me a little courage."

Ialu glanced at the bundle of clothes as he spoke. "In this situation, I'm about as useless as a piece of straw caught in a gigantic wave . . ." His face sobering, he had added quietly, "But I was picked up and thrown onto this path without any choice. I'd like to at least see how it ends."

That was true. Although he had no idea of what he could do, he wished to see with his own eyes what unfolded today on Tahai Azeh, and to choose his own actions.

The image of the late Halumiya, tall and regal, floated into his mind. When he had first met her, he had been surprised at how tall she was. She had favored him with a gentle smile, but he had remained motionless, head bowed. Something about her had inspired awe and discouraged familiarity.

His sole purpose in life had been to protect her, but he had failed, and she had died. She must have felt such regret. How bitter it must have been to leave this world so abruptly, foisting such a heavy burden on her granddaughter, who is still so young.

While he knew that affairs of state are never governed by compassion, Ialu found that he could not forgive Damiya for the heartless murder of his own kin.

The sky through the branches above his head slowly turned from ultramarine to pale purple. No matter how this day ended, tomorrow, the dawn would come again. He closed his eyes. Elin must be in the tent on the hillock by now. He wondered how she felt. He stayed there a long time, his eyes closed, listening to the wind.

2

UNEXPECTED MUSIC

"The sun has risen," said a voice from outside the tent. The cloth covering the entrance was raised and propped up on both sides. As Seimiya stepped through the opening, a swirling gust of wind, fragrant with grass, set her robe fluttering. She gasped at the sight in front of her.

Countless shafts of light burst through the clouds to fall on a plain that stretched as far as the eye could see. Although the clouds were gray and sullen, they glowed dull silver where the sun lay behind them, and trailed across the sky in the wind. She felt as if her soul would ride that wind and be carried across that great expanse.

"There's no need to weep, Seimiya," a gentle voice said. Unnoticed, Damiya had come up beside her, where he stood protectively. It was only at his words that she realized tears were streaming down her cheeks. "I admit it's rather overwhelming to see so many Toda gathered in one spot, but remember, that is your army, Seimiya. You have no need to fear."

She shook her head. "I was not looking at the Toda."

It seemed strange that she could have missed them, but until that moment, she had not even noticed the massive army. Row upon row of black-scaled beasts with Warriors astride them, resplendent in their armor, and thousands of banners flapping in the wind—all these had been nothing more than part of the scenery. It was the glory of heaven and earth itself that had moved her heart. The land which she was seeing for the first time in her life, the land in which she had been born, was majestic, beautiful, and, most of all, incredibly vast.

Tears rolled down her cheeks, one by one. How pitiful that she had never been allowed to see the land she ruled. How pathetic the rank of ruler. This knowledge struck her forcibly, and she could not stop the tears from falling.

The wind must have changed direction. The scent of Toda thickened, and Leelan's hackles rose.

"Calm down," Elin said. "The Toda are far away." She frowned as she watched her. Leelan was already saddled, and they were just waiting for the signal to fly, but it might become hard to control her if the Toda came too close.

At that moment, she heard a commotion outside. Quietly, she approached the doorway, where she could hear the guards' voices.

"What's going on? Are those reinforcements?"

"That's Nugan's flag. I guess he couldn't stand to stay home and miss this."

Elin stepped outside, but the guards only glanced at her and made no attempt to stop her. The sight before her was chilling. Toda packed the skirts of the hillock. Unlike in the drills she had watched many times as a child, they were assembled in full battle formation—men and beasts fused together in a single black mass. The guards had stopped talking, and the only sound was the wind. Even the summer birds and insects were silent. Frightened by the sudden appearance of the Toda, they must be hiding.

The Toda troops made so little sound, it was hard to believe how many were there. They massed at the bottom of the hill, shrouded in a heavy silence and brimming with the tension of something about to happen.

A memory came vividly to her mind—the bee swarm long ago, when the whole hive had left their nest and followed the queen bee . . . a single black mass. So, she thought, men abandon their old queen in the same way. Except that bees only split the hive, whereas men could not keep themselves from crushing their former ruler.

Elin took a deep breath. The feeling that rose in her chest was akin to sorrow, yet somehow emptier.

Something peculiar was indeed happening on what from her vantage point was the right wing of the assembled troops. New Toda regiments were drawing up alongside, one after the other. She wondered if a flag with the Toda scale pattern was the one the guard had said belonged to Nugan. The newly arrived troops far outnumbered those that had come first.

A messenger on horseback bearing the scale-patterned banner was sent from the newly arrived ranks to two figures in the center front line who wore particularly bright and splendid helmets. They must be the Aluhan and his son Shunan, Elin thought. They sat regally astride their Kiba with a standard-bearer behind them holding aloft the Aluhan's flag.

The messenger passed back and forth between the Aluhan and his younger son several times, but in the end, the new troops did not pull back. Elin looked around her tent, and her eyes fell upon Seimiya and Damiya. They were gazing down at the scene below and conversing quietly when Damiya, perhaps feeling her eyes upon him, glanced her way.

"Elin," he called. "How's Leelan?"

Elin pushed back windswept strands of hair from her eyes. "She's fine."

Damiya smiled. "Good. When it's time, we'll pull the tent down on either side. As soon as you see the sky, hop on Leelan and fly."

Elin turned her eyes to Seimiya without answering. But Seimiya did not look at her. She stood staring at the Toda army as if lost in thought.

The clouds flowed by, and the sun suddenly appeared, illuminating earth and sky. In that light, the Aluhan raised his right hand, and hundreds of war horns blew. Their high peal seemed to erupt from the earth like the cry of a newborn babe, and, riding the wind, it shook the plain and caused the skin of all those who heard to shiver.

With it came the rumble of scraping earth. The Toda were on the move.

As Seimiya watched the Toda climb the hill like a slow, black wave, a strange thought occurred to her. Does Damiya realize that he let his true intentions show? "That is your army," he had said. Her lips twitched in a faint smile. The moment I accept it as my army, the Yojeh will vanish from this world. What would vanish was an invisible something that wrapped the hearts of her people. And once broken, it would never be recovered.

She did not want to give up that pure something, guarded for three centuries by generations of Yojeh . . . But she could not protect it, even if she were to marry Damiya. She was certain of that now. Watching the approaching army and seeing that it was close enough for her to make out the faces of Shunan and his father, she turned to her maidservant. "Bring me the blue flag."

Damiya turned to her with a startled expression. "What?"

Seimiya looked up at him and said quietly, "I cannot marry you, Uncle Damiya. Not you who seek to rule this land with a heart that could murder my grandmother."

All expression was wiped from his face. After a slight pause, he sighed. "Do you remember the craftwork I gave you once?" Seimiya frowned, unable to follow his train of thought. "That miniature palace, it was exquisite, wasn't it? Seimiya, what counts is the form. If you can make a perfect, unshakeable form, people can settle down comfortably within it and live contentedly."

She turned her face from Damiya and looked at Shunan as he climbed the hill. "No matter how perfect and beautiful," she whispered, "I do not want to live in a box that never changes." With her eyes still on Shunan astride his detestable Toda, she continued, "The children born to Shunan and me will bear not only that which is sacred, but also the defilement of this land . . . My children will not be gods but human. And they will see this land with their own eyes, right from the start."

If she had been looking at Damiya, she would have seen the sorrow that rose in his eyes at that moment. But by the time she noticed anything, he had already moved. Hearing a cry of surprise from her maidservant, she turned to see Damiya grasping the blue flag.

"I won't let you do this, Seimiya." He smiled the way he often had when she was little and had done something naughty.

"Give it back!" She held out her hand, but he continued smiling and made no move.

"Se Zan!" she cried. "Seize that flag!"

But not a single Se Zan responded to her call. Half of them had whipped out their daggers and placed them against the throats of the others.

"At times like this, it is foresight that determines one's fate," Damiya said calmly. He turned his eyes to Elin. "Come now, Elin. It's time. Go back to your tent and get on Leelan. You're a clever girl. I'm sure I don't need to tell you which Toda to attack first . . . Off you go now."

Elin stared at him and gritted her teeth. Shining with a light as hard as stone, her eyes never wavered. On feet that did not seem to be hers, she moved slowly toward the tent, but as she approached the entrance, she noticed that the Se Zan who had been standing there an instant before was gone. She glanced at the space where he had stood and, at that moment, a black shadow moved by her. Just as it passed, something bright flew from its hand. Turning, she saw a trail of light, and then something sank into Damiya's right hand. It had taken less than a second, and happened in complete silence. Before blood even began spurting from Damiya's hand, the running shadow had slipped behind him and wrapped an arm around his neck.

"Elin!" With his voice, sound returned to Elin's ears. "Grab the flag and give it to Seimiya."

For a moment, Elin stood frozen, too stunned to move. Even though she understood that it was Ialu holding Damiya, she seemed to have gone numb.

"Hurry!"

At his urging, her body came to life, as if her soul had returned. She ran toward them and snatched the flag from the ground at Damiya's feet. The grass was red and wet with the blood dripping from his arm. She shook the flag to remove the dirt and then handed it to Seimiya. With a bloodless face, Seimiya took the flag. As if fearing that she would hesitate, she thrust it high above her and waved it at the men surging up the hill.

At that moment, the young man beside the Aluhan stopped his Kiba and removed his helmet. He looked as though he could not believe what he saw. In the next instant, a cheer rose from the front line and spread like a wave through the ranks behind. The sound shook the earth. However, it was not

338

taken up by the army's left wing. Oblivious to their silence, the Aluhan and Shunan removed their armor and dismounted. Leaving their Kiba with the standard-bearers, they began walking up the hill.

When they were just twenty or thirty paces from the top, the earth suddenly began to rumble, and the Toda forces broke into disarray. The Toda at the head of the left wing charged after the Aluhan and Shunan with ferocious speed, and the rest followed suit. In no time, the two men were cut off from their troops.

One Toda rider, his banner flying in the wind, raised his sword to the heavens and charged straight at the Aluhan. Fleeter than a horse, his mount charged up the hill as if flying through space and whistled past the Aluhan, who barely had time to draw his sword. When the Toda stopped, blood was spurting from the Aluhan's neck. His knees buckled, and he crumpled face-down on the grass.

"Father!" Shunan cried. He raised him in his arms, but the Aluhan had breathed his last. Covered in his father's blood, Shunan looked up. The Warrior raised his helm, and his face leapt into Shunan's eyes—his own brother, eyes wild and face strangely contorted.

"Nugan . . ."

"The Aluhan's proper station is that of a faithful vassal!" Nugan shrieked. "I will not let it be sullied by rebellion." Again, he raised his sword, dripping with his father's blood, and pointed it at the heavens.

Troops rushing to the Aluhan's aid collided with Toda Riders who sought to stop them. Cries of "Sai Gamulu! Sai Gamulu!" could be heard among those loyal to the Aluhan. Thus began a fearsome battle of Toda against Toda.

Seimiya and the others stared aghast at the melee of Toda troops. When the Aluhan fell and Nugan turned his blade toward Shunan, Seimiya cried out, "Somebody! Please, please save him!" Her voice shook, and she looked around desperately for help, but there was nothing anyone could do. Finally, she turned, white-faced, to Elin.

"Elin . . ." Pressing her hands together as if in prayer, she begged. "Elin!"

Her plea washed like a wave through Elin's heart. Should Shunan die, Seimiya would have no choice but to marry Damiya and appoint Nugan as the next Aluhan, even though he had murdered his own father. The calm composure on Damiya's face when she glanced his way was in stark contrast to the distraught Seimiya. Suddenly, she knew. This is exactly how he planned it. In that instant, she made her choice.

Turning to Seimiya, she nodded. "I will save him."

Tears rolled from Seimiya's eyes. "Please! I promise you. If you save Shunan, I will free the Royal Beasts and make sure that the ruler never again uses them as weapons of war."

Elin held her eyes. Then she nodded once more and dashed toward the tent.

If she flew on Leelan in front of this many people, then Seimiya's vow would probably be meaningless. But she no longer hesitated. If a Toda Rider ruled, everything must change. To see that change, she would have to rescue Shunan.

She knew that Leelan could never understand what she felt, even if she tried to share it. She knew her thoughts would only spin around in her own brain, yet she could not help speaking to her in her mind.

So, Leelan, I am using you as a weapon after all.

With each stride, the Silent Whistle bounced, and each time it struck her chest, she felt a pang in her heart and clenched her jaw. When she reached the tent, she stepped across a body that lay upon the ground and pulled the ropes. With a dull sound, the canvas split in two and fell away. Leelan blinked in the sudden brightness. The scent of Toda carried by the wind was so thick it made Elin feel ill. Leelan's nostrils flared, and her fur stood on end with the anticipation of falling upon her natural foe.

Elin quickly unwound the bandage binding her left hand, on which only two fingers remained. Waving it, she looked into Leelan's eyes. "Let me up!" Leelan obediently bent down so that she could climb on. Swiftly, she wound the reins around her left fist and shouted, "Fly!"

She felt the movement of Leelan's wing muscles against her stomach. Leelan dropped into a crouch and then sprang into the sky. "Take me there," she shouted, pointing at Shunan, then, spreading her arms wide, she placed the plugs in Leelan's ears.

A tumult arose from below when people saw the Royal Beast glide through the air, straight for Shunan. A long, high-pitched whistle issued from Leelan's mouth. At the sound, the Toda surrounding Shunan flipped over en masse, exposing their bellies to the sky. Warriors who failed to leap in time from their rolling mounts were crushed beneath them, or sent flying through the air to lie sprawled on the ground, staring up at the sky in bewilderment.

Leelan's claws sank first into Nugan's mount, ripping it to shreds in moments. Splattered with Toda blood and chunks of flesh, Nugan was thrown to the ground. He stared at Leelan with a look of blank astonishment.

Leelan did not stop there. One after another, she ripped the prostrate Toda with her claws. Snarling with rage and crazed with blood, she butchered them until she was covered from head to foot in gore.

As the Warriors regained their senses, they grabbed their bows and shot at Leelan, but she was impervious to their arrows. Before their eyes, the lone Royal Beast slaughtered Toda by the dozens.

"Leelan . . . Leelan!" Elin pounded on her back with all her might. Reaching out one arm, she removed an earplug and yelled into her ear, "Stop! That's enough! Enough! Put me down over there!"

But the Beast showed no sign of halting the carnage.

"Leelan! Stop! Now! Or I'll blow the whistle!" Elin shouted. Only then did Leelan reluctantly drop the Toda corpse in her claws and glide a short distance away. Dismembered Toda radiated in a broad circle around her. Beyond them massed those Toda that had remained unaffected by her whistle. Their Riders had, at first, been so overwhelmed, they had failed to grasp what was happening. Now, however, they began to tighten the circle around Elin and the Royal Beast. They raised their bows, and a hail of arrows whistled toward them.

Elin ducked her head. Sliding off Leelan's back, she ran over to Shunan. "Hurry! Come with me!" She grabbed his arm and half dragged him toward Leelan. "Take him!" she shouted. "Take him over there!" As she shoved him onto the Beast, she felt something thud violently into her back and pitched forward. She choked, unable to breathe, then realized that she had been struck by an arrow.

"You . . ." Shunan began, but she pushed his chest.

"Get on," she gasped. "Hold on to the reins."

"You, too," he said, grabbing her hand, but she yanked her arm away.

"She can't carry two. Go!" She shoved the plugs into Leelan's ears. "Go!" she yelled again. While Leelan probably could not hear her, she understood Elin's gesture. She flew up into the air and sped off without looking back. Her figure blurred in Elin's eyes. Falling to her knees on the grass, she gazed up at the sky. Leelan's figure, shining in the sun, grew hazy.

Pain coursed through her with every breath, and tears trickled down her cheeks. The Toda drew closer, and their scent overwhelmed her. The thought occurred to her that everything until this moment had been nothing but a dream.

She was with her mother now, about to be eaten by Toda.

In those few moments before the Kiba reached her, she dreamed her whole life.

Faces floated into her mind and out again, like clouds blown by the wind. Joeun, Esalu, Yuyan, Tomura, and Ialu.

Images rose in her mind's eye: Leelan when she had first responded to Elin's harp, her first flight, her shining figure as she mated in the sky.

What a rich dream it was.

She smiled. With shallow gasps, her body crumpled slowly to the ground.

Mother.

She felt the grass caress her cheek, and awareness returned. Ruthlessly, the knowledge that she was about to be devoured by Toda pierced her mind, and an indescribable despair spread through her. Is this how her mother had felt? When she had known that her life, which she had lived so hard, was to end like this, had she, too, felt a desolation that gnawed her very bones?

I don't want to die yet . . . This thought hit her with sudden force. I don't want my life to end this way.

Sobbing, she struggled to move. The ground shook as the Toda drew ever nearer. Pressing her left elbow against the earth, she turned to look up at the sky. Tears blurred her vision, and everything seemed very far away.

As her consciousness began to fade, in a corner of her mind, she thought she heard her mother's finger flute. And with that high note came the sound of beating wings. Something huge was gliding toward her.

Leelan! Her eyes widened. But why . . .

Breathing like a bellows, her fangs bared in a snarl, and her fur stiff and straight as needles, Leelan dropped from the sky. The shouts and screams of the Toda Riders echoed all around her, and arrows began to fall like rain. Elin could only screw her eyes shut and cover her head with her arms. Something blocked the light of day, plunging her into darkness. The sounds of arrows whistling and people shouting grew distant, and her body was wrapped in stillness, as if she were in the sudden lull of a storm.

Opening her eyes, she saw Leelan's face right before her, fangs bared. She had covered her with her wings. Elin froze, staring at that snarling face.

Suddenly, Leelan shoved her muzzle at her, and butted her in the chest before she could grab the Silent Whistle. Pain seared her back where the arrow had pierced her. Groaning, she uncurled from the protective ball in which she had been huddled. As if waiting for that moment, Leelan snatched her up in her jaws.

Elin screamed, and her muscles went rigid, but for some reason she felt no pain. Instead of the agony of rending fangs, she felt only a dull pressure, as if she were being pressed by thick fingers. Leelan, she realized, must be holding her in the back of her mouth where there were no teeth. She was caught between her gums. At that moment, she felt something warm and soft move beneath her.

Leelan's tongue. Deftly, she used it to roll Elin's body so that she lay on her side, with nothing touching her wound. Then she kicked the ground with her feet and flew up into the air.

Elin felt her body lift. Wind roared in her ears and whipped at her hair. Her arms were stretched above her, and she rested them against Leelan's muzzle, gazing at her shining fur. Leelan's saliva, still smelling of Toda blood, soaked into her clothes. She closed her eyes.

A hot lump rose from the pit of her chest into her throat. Why? . . . Why would she do this for me? When I'm not her child, or her parent, or her mate. When I used the Silent Whistle like a whip to make her obey me. Why?

Her feelings for Leelan, which she had locked away deep inside for fear of that sweet delusion, burst forth and shook something awake inside her.

Leelan, I just wanted to know. That's all I ever wanted . . . I stood on the edge of that abyss between man and beast and played my harp for you, checking each note, one by one, to see if it would reach you. Because I wanted to know. I wanted to know what you thought.

And you—you spoke to me, one note at a time. We explored each other's incomprehensible minds from across that yawning chasm.

Sometimes we hit the wrong notes like clashing echoes.

Yet sometimes, just by chance, the notes we played for one another made unexpected music, like this.

Her eyes filled with tears.

As long as the life you have given me continues, let me stand on the shore of that great abyss and play. Let me pluck my harp, note by note, and speak to the creatures of earth and sky, so that I may hear music as yet unknown.

Opening her eyes, she turned her head and saw Tahai Azeh stretching far into the distance. The Toda and their Riders were now so far away that she could no longer distinguish one from the other. They dwindled to tiny black dots, like a swarm of bees, while the earth and sky went on forever, brimming with light.

Elin listened to Leelan purr in encouragement from deep in her chest and gazed, transfixed, at the land below.

ELIN MUST CONFRONT HER DESTINY
AND HEED THE DIRE WARNINGS OF HISTORY
IN THIS THRILLING SEQUEL TO

THE BEAST PLAYER.

KEEP READING
FOR AN EXCERPT.

FROM IALU'S DIARY

I still ponder the meaning of what happened on Tahai Azeh. And its effect on your future, Elin.

Where will the path you have chosen lead you?

And where will the path I have chosen lead me?

When the rebel army clashed with the Aluhan's forces on Tahai Azeh, I was driven by a longing for change, but now I wonder if I made the right choice.

Generations of Yojeh had protected this kingdom's purity by renouncing the corruption of war. Their unwavering integrity and sanctity were the soul of this land, the very heart of its people, making Lyoza rare among nations. But it was wrong to maintain that purity through the sacrifice of others' blood.

Even though each successive Aluhan chose defilement willingly to protect this realm on the Yojeh's behalf, only those who lived in Aluhan territory were forced to kill and be killed. The Yojeh and her people should have considered more carefully what that meant.

Like the Toda, those ferocious beasts whose blood-drenched fangs decimate enemy troops and rout their cavalry, the Aluhan and his people were feared, despised, and carelessly discarded, even though they had protected this country for centuries. It was only natural that they should long for change.

So many choices were made that day on the plain of Tahai Azeh. Uncertain of the answer, yet guided by their own convictions, each person made what seemed the only possible choice. And now those choices have generated a relentless surge of change.

I doubt you can escape that wave unscathed, Elin.

On the plain of Tahai Azeh, the Aluhan witnessed how easily a Royal Beast could slaughter his 'invincible' Toda troops. We all knew that those majestic creatures, the symbol of the Yojeh, could kill Toda. But we believed they could not be tamed or controlled, and so the Aluhan had never thought to fear their existence. On that day, however, he saw you command Leelan to vanquish the Toda.

If Royal Beasts can be controlled by man, that changes everything.

The Yojeh vowed never to use them as weapons again. As her promise is sacred, I am sure she will try to keep it. But that does not change the fact that you and the Royal Beasts are in a precarious position. If people in other countries learn what you have done, someone is bound to try to capture and use the Beasts. Although the skills required to handle them cannot be acquired overnight, the day will come when a rival country develops its own Royal Beast corps. And when it does, this kingdom will be threatened with extinction.

The young Aluhan will never overlook such a risk. He will arise to protect his army of Toda, the symbol of his power and the key to this country's safety. And whatever steps he may take, they will most certainly impact you, Elin. The only person in the world who can control the Royal Beasts.

ONE

VOICE FROM THE PAST

I

THE KIBA CHAMBER

For a split second, the sky lit up like it was midday, followed moments later by a deafening crack of thunder. Before the last stomach-wrenching rumble had faded, the rain began to fall—a torrential downpour, as though the bottom had dropped from the heavens.

The officer sitting in the carriage reached out and closed the window with a crooked smile. "Well, that's inconvenient," he said. "We'll have to pull up at the entrance to the Stone Chambers unless we want to get soaking wet."

The woman sitting across from him, however, stared vacantly out the closed window without responding. Running a hand through his salt-and-pepper hair, the officer regarded her silently for a moment before trying again. "Lady Elin. You told the driver to stop before we reached the entrance, but it's pouring. Shall I tell him to drive us to the entrance after all?"

Elin started as though waking from some reverie and turned her eyes toward him. "Pardon me? What did you say, Yohalu?"

A faint smile rose to the man's lips, but he repeated what he had just said. Elin cast him an apologetic look. "You're right," she said. "We will get sopping wet. But it's forbidden to bring horses too close because it could excite the Toda."

Yohalu blinked. "Yes, I know, but surely the horses' scent wouldn't reach inside in such a downpour."

"You are probably right," Elin said. "But Toda Stewards hate to break the rules."

At this, Yohalu nodded. "True. I suppose we must get wet, then." He reached down, picked up two conical hats of braided sedge that lay on top of a bag between his feet, and handed one to Elin. "Although I suppose these won't do us much good in this rain," he said.

Elin took the hat but did not put it on even when the carriage stopped. Instead, she placed it gently on the seat. Seeing the frown on Yohalu's face, she said, "I appreciate your concern, but the Stewards don't like people to enter the caves with their faces concealed. You are wearing a uniform, so in your case, I'm sure it won't matter. But I had better enter with my face bare."

She bowed and then reached out to open the door. Yohalu gently moved her hand aside and raised the handle himself, pushing the door open. "After you," he said.

Elin bowed once more and then stepped into the onslaught. Although she was drenched in seconds, she silently thanked the chill rain that soaked her body, dripped from her hair, and ran down her forehead. This way, no one would know if the drops that poured down her cheeks were water or tears.

The smell of wet trees and grass enveloped her. The huge rock face was split by a black fissure, the entrance to the caves where the Toda were kept. It loomed ominously through the haze of rain, and the figures hurrying in and out of that crack reminded her of ants scurrying to and from their nest.

Yohalu stepped down from the carriage to stand beside her. Catching sight of him, the guards outside the entrance snapped to attention. The sweet scent of Toda slime, which not even the rain could erase, wafted toward Elin, and she gripped the collar of her robe tightly. As she made a dash for the entrance, taking care not to slip in the mud and conscious of the curious stares directed toward her, she fought to shield her mind and keep herself from being swept into the maelstrom of memories that surged inside her. Even so, she heard once again the mourning wail of the Toda, a shrill keening sound like wind whistling through a broken pipe. With it came the memory of a dawn more than twenty years ago that had changed her life forever. She shuddered.

Although this was not the Toda village where she had been raised, the caves were built just like the ones she remembered from her childhood: A large cavern inside the entrance, known as the Hall, branched off into multiple caves called the Stone Chambers. Torches in wall brackets burned vigorously, sending shadows dancing across the damp stone.

The Toda Stewards, who were gathered in the Hall, stared at Elin, wariness evident in their faces. Enormous Toda carcasses lay on straw mats spread across the floor. Five days had already passed since their deaths, and the mucous membrane that cloaked their bodies had dried, making them appear like wooden carvings coated in glue rather than the bodies of once-living creatures.

All Toda were fearsome beasts that could bear warriors swiftly across the battlefield, scattering cavalry before them, but the largest and strongest were the Kiba or "fangs." These formed the vanguard, and they could massacre enemy troops.

Five days ago, every single Kiba in the village of Tokala had been found dead, a disaster for the Toda Stewards that managed the Stone Chambers. It was the chief inspector's job to investigate the cause of death and punish those responsible. Soon after the news had reached him, he arrived in the village and seized the man responsible for their care. But for some reason, the man's punishment had been deferred by order of the Aluhan, and a new inspector had been summoned. It now dawned on the Stewards that the new inspector was a woman, and their consternation deepened.

Shifting her eyes from the Kiba carcasses, Elin walked over to where the Stewards stood along the wall. "Who is your chief?" she asked.

A white-haired man jerked, then inclined his head timidly. When she drew near enough for him to see the color of her eyes, surprise suffused his face.

"I am not an Ahlyo," Elin said quietly before he could speak. "My mother was, but she was expelled by her people when she chose to wed my father. My father was a Toda Steward."

The man's eyes flickered, and he frowned as though trying to dredge up some distant memory. Suddenly, his eyebrows shot up. "So you . . . You're the one? From Akeh Village?"

Elin nodded. A murmur rose behind him. The younger Stewards looked puzzled, but the elders could not conceal their shock. Tokala was close to Akeh, and many of them had kin there. Despite the strict ban on even mentioning that incident, they had all heard about the Ahlyo woman from Akeh who had been blamed for the death of the Kiba and executed by being thrown into the Toda swamp.

Hearing a commotion at the entrance, Elin turned to see the guards move aside. A man robed in red with a wide ornate sash stepped into the cavern. The chief inspector. She drew in a sharp breath and felt her scalp tighten. A wave of fierce loathing rolled through her.

He must have heard that she had arrived. There was a suspicious look on his arrogant face as he marched boldly toward them. Even though he could not possibly be the same man who had executed her mother to protect himself, just the sight of his robe set her pulse racing.

Returning her gaze to the Chief Steward, she said quickly and quietly, "I didn't come to punish any of you. I came to prove that you weren't responsible for the deaths of the Kiba. Please lend me your aid." The man's eyes widened slightly.

"I heard that the Aluhan's envoy has arrived," the inspector called out in a booming voice. "Where is he? In the Stone Chambers?"

Elin turned to face him. "Chief Inspector, I am his envoy."

The man halted and gaped at her. "You?"

"Yes."

A frown twisted his features, and he took a step forward, as if to intimidate her. Elin stood her ground, returning his gaze calmly. At that moment, Yohalu ambled over to stand beside her. He nodded at the inspector and said, "So you're the son of Yalaku? You look just like your father. It must be two years now since he passed away."

The inspector looked puzzled, but when his gaze fell upon Yohalu's sash, his eyes widened. "Sir! You . . . You're a member of the Black Armor?"

"No, no," Yohalu said, waving his hand. "I no longer wear the black armor. Too old for that now. I just serve as a companion for the Aluhan when he needs someone to talk to." He placed a hand on Elin's shoulder. "And sometimes I serve as an escort. I suppose it must be hard to believe that a woman could be an inspector, but I can assure you that she was indeed sent by the Aluhan."

The inspector blinked rapidly. "I beg your pardon, sir, but the fact that a new inspector was sent . . . Was there some aspect of my work with which the Aluhan was displeased?"

Before Elin could respond, Yohalu shook his head. "No, not at all. There's no need for you to worry. Your task is to manage and inspect the Toda Stewards. In other words, your job is to investigate the mistakes made by men. But she has been sent here to investigate the Toda, not men at all."

As she listened to Yohalu smoothly allay the man's fears, Elin reflected once again that he was no ordinary bodyguard. The Black Armor was an elite band of warriors that protected the Aluhan, and she had heard that they were chosen from his own kin for their exceptional intelligence and military prowess. If Yohalu had been a member of the Black Armor, then he must be Shunan's blood kin.

She gazed at his calm, friendly features. Maybe he was sent to keep an eye on me, she thought. Shunan would have chosen someone of such high rank because he trusted Yohalu. Although she had already guessed that the Aluhan felt she needed not just protection but also supervision, her heart sank every time she confirmed this suspicion.

She took a breath and pushed these thoughts away. There's no point in dwelling on it. You chose this path yourself. Thanks to that, there are still things you can do.

She turned toward the row of carcasses.

Elin had reached the Aluhan's castle, Aluhan Ula, in the morning three days earlier. With little time to prepare for the journey, she had been thrust on a horse almost as soon as she had received the Aluhan's summons. Although she did not know why she had been summoned, the sight of his castle, surrounded by formidable walls of enormous stone and watchtowers that pierced the sky, had filled her with a strange, crushing dread that made her feel very small.

A fortress for men who wage war, she had thought. It was a far cry from the Yojeh's palace, which was surrounded not by walls, but by a forest in which birds warbled.

She passed under the magnificent gate built by master craftsmen, walked along a colonnade that stretched far into the distance with a ceiling so high it caught her breath, turned down a passageway, and climbed a flight of stairs. By the time she reached the Aluhan's sitting room, she felt almost dizzy. The room into which her escort ushered her, however, was surprisingly small.

Through the wide-open windows she glimpsed the tops of slender tohk trees. Their small white blossoms were bathed in the soft light of early spring, and when they swayed in the breeze, the light danced across the floor. The room was empty, and once her guide had left, the only sound to be heard was the rustling of leaves. As she stood gazing absently out the window, she heard the door open. Shunan strode into the room followed by a tall, middle-aged man.

"Hello, Elin. Sorry to have kept you waiting when it was I who summoned you here." At the sound of his voice, Elin hastily knelt on the floor and placed both palms to her forehead in a proper salute.

Shunan acknowledged her greeting with a smile and gestured for her to sit in a chair by the fireplace. Examining her face closely, he said, "You haven't changed a bit."

Elin's cheeks dimpled. "I wish that were true, but I'm already past thirty and feel sure that I must have changed a great deal."

"Well, you haven't. Although I hear that you're a mother now. How's your son?"

"Too well, I'm afraid. Sometimes I don't know what to do with him."

A father of two himself, Shunan grinned appreciatively. "I can imagine. If he's anything like you, we can expect great things in the future."

Elin looked away at this, but Shunan's keen eyes must have caught the shadow that crossed her face, because he changed the subject smoothly. "And how about you? Do you have any stiffness in your back from that old arrow wound?"

Elin shook her head. "Thank you for your concern, but fortunately, no, I have not had any problems with it."

The arrow that had struck her when she had shielded Shunan had penetrated deeply into the muscle, but a bone had stopped the point before it could damage any organs. Even so, it took a long time for her to move her arm without pain. Both the Yojeh Seimiya and the Aluhan Shunan had granted her request to return to the Kazalumu Beast Sanctuary to heal. Eleven years had passed since then, and during that time, Elin had fallen in love, wed, and borne a child. Back then, she could never have imagined that such changes would happen in her life.

During the last ten years, the kingdom had also changed. Yet there were times, such as on a quiet summer's afternoon, when she could almost imagine her life would go on like this forever. The grim-faced guards stationed at the Beast Sanctuary, however, always reminded her that this was merely a transient peace. When the Aluhan's messenger had arrived unannounced, her first thought was that the time had finally come.

The morning light etched shadows on Shunan's face. His expression was gentle, but the muscles around his eyes were tense. He probably wasn't getting enough sleep, she thought. His sallow skin exposed an underlying fatigue.

On Tahai Azeh, Shunan's younger brother had murdered his father. When he realized that he had been used, he had hung himself by his belt in his cell without waiting for judgment. Shunan's mother had lost her mind, unable to bear the tragic deaths of her husband and younger son. Alone, without any parent to bless him, Shunan had succeeded to the position of Aluhan and married Seimiya. Having wed the woman he loved and launched a new era with his own hands, he should have been a happy young man, but he had lost so much to achieve that union. Although he had willingly accepted all this suffering to gain a brighter future for the kingdom, the fruits of his efforts had been far from satisfactory.

The Aluhan's union with the Yojeh had taken a great weight from the hearts of those who lived in Aluhan territory. Many were deeply moved that the Yojeh had chosen to wed him. They rejoiced at the new opportunity to qualify for posts in the central government, a path formerly denied to them, and longed for this marriage to erase the resentment and sense of misfortune that had smoldered in their breasts for generations.

But the revulsion with which the people of the Yojeh's territory had greeted the marriage was far greater than Shunan had anticipated. Viewing the increase in the Aluhan's authority as a threat, the nobles took issue with his policies at every turn and sought to restore the Yojeh's control over him. People whispered that the Aluhan had angered the god by defiling the Yojeh. They claimed that this was the cause of successive crop failures and the epidemic that had spread from Aluhan territory throughout the kingdom, taking many lives. It was the threat of foreign invasion, however, that shook the kingdom most. The horse riders of Lahza had stepped up their attacks on the caravan cities that were governed by Lyoza, and Elin had heard that the lives of many warriors had been lost in these skirmishes. Shunan and Seimiya shouldered the burden of all these things.

The silence in the room was so profound that Elin could hear the wings of the birds that flitted in the treetops. Shunan's voice barely disturbed the quiet. "If I had asked you to come when I was still at the palace, it would have been a little closer for you, but I needed to talk about this here. You stayed at the Silver Branch last night. Did you sleep well?"

Elin had barely slept at all, but it wouldn't do to say so. "Yes," she replied. "Thank you for arranging such luxurious accommodation."

Shunan smiled reassuringly, as if he sensed the uneasiness beneath her words. "You must be thinking that I summoned you about the Royal Beasts, but I didn't. To tell you the truth, I still don't know what we should do about them, although I do know we'll have to address that issue soon."

Elin blinked. He didn't call me here about the Royal Beasts? The rod of tension inside her loosened, and her shoulders relaxed. Although she knew the decision was merely being deferred to a later date, she was glad that at least for a little longer, things would stay the same for Leelan and the others.

But if this isn't about the Royal Beasts, why would he wish to speak with me when he's so busy?

As if he could read her thoughts, Shunan said quietly, "I summoned you because I received a report that all the Kiba in the village of Tokala were wiped out."

As the meaning of his words penetrated her mind, Elin froze. She felt as if a hand had reached out from the past to seize her heart. Her face paled, and Shunan looked at her with pity in his eyes. "Your mother was blamed for the loss of the Kiba and sentenced to death, wasn't she?"

Elin opened her mouth, but couldn't find her voice. Swallowing to moisten her throat, she answered hoarsely, "Yes, that is correct."

Shunan gave a short nod. "The records show that the Kiba were wiped out in a single night, which is exactly what happened this time. They were quite healthy the day before, swimming around as usual, but by dawn, every single one was dead."

Elin's eyebrows drew together. She remembered that after her grandfather had cursed Sohyon for letting all the Kiba die, her mother had told her not to worry—because it had happened before.

Elin looked up. "Does this kind of thing occur very often?" she asked.

Shunan's mouth crooked. "If it did, our army would be rendered impotent in no time."

Elin blushed. "I see. Pardon me for asking such a foolish question."

Shunan shook his head. "No, it's not foolish. That's actually an important point." He turned to the tall man who had accompanied him into the room. "Yohalu, please give me those."

The man handed him a sheaf of papers.

"Here, Elin," said Shunan. "Read these."

There were holes along the right edge of the pages as if they had been taken from a book. They were all written in the same format, and most were yellowed and brittle with age. Elin stiffened when she saw the title on the first sheet.

"Those are from the records preserved by Toda villages in every district," Shunan continued. "We took only those pages that recorded mass Kiba fatalities."

Although Elin heard him, her eyes remained glued to the page. The title read "Concerning Sohyon's Improper Management of the Kiba in Akeh Village and Her Punishment." She read the words beneath, then her eyes blurred, and she could no longer see the page. The content was so blunt and simple.

Despite having been entrusted with the care of the Kiba, the female Toda Steward, Sohyon, failed to maintain water quality in the Pond. As a result, the Kiba died of poisoning. She was strictly punished to prevent this from happening again.

That was all. Nothing in those words conveyed the brutality of her punishment, the way she had been thrown into a swamp to be devoured by wild Toda, or her grief at orphaning her young daughter.

Closing her eyes, Elin bowed her head and took a slow breath.

"The inspector who sentenced your mother died long ago." Elin raised her head at the sound of Shunan's voice. "But what he did was inhumane. The maximum sentence for someone who lets the Kiba die is the loss of their right arm. To feed her to the Toda was a gross injustice. We've never monitored the judgments of inspectors in each district, so in some ways perhaps I am responsible for your mother's death. I intend to review whether inspectors should be allowed to pass a death sentence."

Shunan's red-rimmed eyes and tightly pressed lips revealed his anger at the ignorant cruelty of the officer and his remorse for having let men like him do as they pleased. His expression made him appear so unbearably young that Elin averted her eyes.

"But I didn't summon you here to apologize," he said. He pointed at the documents. "Take a look through the rest. There's not much time so just skim them. You can read them more thoroughly later."

Elin flipped through the papers. There were nineteen pages, all reporting mass Kiba deaths. As she focused on the dates, locations, and numbers, she felt a growing excitement. She sensed that there was some kind of regularity to their deaths. Although the intervals between the incidents varied, making it hard to pin down the correlation, the deaths had occurred in several villages at once. The year Elin's mother had been killed, all the Kiba in the neighboring village of Yoson had also died.

She raised her head and looked at Shunan. He nodded. "That's right," he said. "These mass fatalities were not the fault of the Toda Stewards. It would be unthinkable for Stewards in multiple villages to make the same mistake at the same time. There must be another cause."

Something hot gushed from a point deep in Elin's chest, and she bit her lip.

"I want you to find out what it is," Shunan concluded.

There was a dull ringing in Elin's ears.

Did Mother know?

The disturbing doubt she had carried in her heart ever since she was a child reared its head again. In her mind's eye, she saw her mother in the dimly lit Stone Chamber, standing up to her chest in icy water as she gently stroked the dead Kiba. In her face, there was no trace of surprise or bewilderment, while in her eyes, there was only a profound sorrow.

Another scene floated into view as though pulled by a string, and Elin's heart began to race—the last time she had seen her mother, when she had played her finger flute to command the Toda and save Elin's life.

Her mother's words came back to her as clearly as if she had just spoken them. "Elin," she had said. "You must never do what I am going to do now. To do so is to commit a mortal sin."

Elin gripped her knees. Mother could control the Toda. She knew things that not even the Stewards knew.

Of course she did. Because she was an Ahlyo, one of the People of the Mist. As a descendent of the Toga mi Lyo, the Green-Eyed Ones, she had inherited the knowledge they had brought with them from the other side of the Afon Noah, the Mountains of the Gods, where they had once raised Toda as weapons.

If so, then why? If she knew that the Kiba deaths were not her fault, why didn't she tell the inspector?

Elin closed her eyes. She could think of only one reason: because it was taboo. Whatever had killed the Toda must be related to the knowledge the Ahlyo had been forbidden to share, even if it meant death. Although Sohyon had been banished by her people, the rigid laws of the Ahlyo, designed to prevent another tragedy, had remained firmly rooted in her heart. If the cause of the mass deaths had touched upon those laws, that would have silenced her. Just as the Royal Beast Canon had been designed to conceal the true nature of the Royal Beasts, there must have been some reason for concealing the nature of the Toda.

Elin stared at her hands, which lay clasped in her lap. This was a turning point. If she continued in this direction, she would open yet another door that should remain shut. Even though she knew this, however, she could not suppress the burning urge that flared inside her. She longed to unravel the mystery of the Kiba deaths, to find out what her mother had given her life for.

Raising her face, Elin looked at Shunan. "Please send me to Tokala. I will try to determine the cause of the Kiba deaths."